Not Your Crush's Cauldron

Also by APRIL ASHER

Supernatural Singles

Not the Witch You Wed

Not Your Ex's Hexes

Written as APRIL HUNT

Steele Ops

Deadly Obsession

Lethal Redemption

Fatal Deception

Alpha Security

Heated Pursuit

Holding Fire

Hard Justice

Hot Target

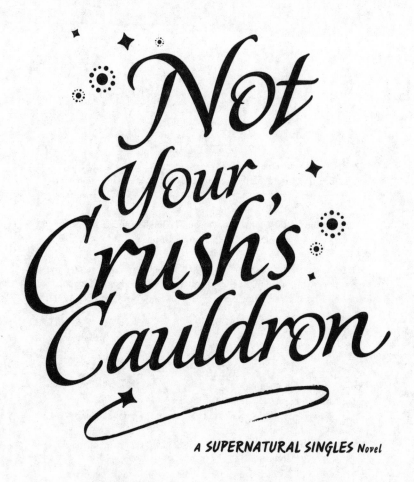

Not Your Crush's Cauldron

A SUPERNATURAL SINGLES Novel

APRIL ASHER

ST. MARTIN'S GRIFFIN
NEW YORK

This is a work of fiction. All of the characters, organizations, and events portrayed in this novel are either products of the author's imagination or are used fictitiously.

First published in the United States by St. Martin's Griffin, an imprint of St. Martin's Publishing Group

www.stmartins.com

Library of Congress Cataloging-in-Publication Data

Names: Asher, April, author.
Title: Not your crush's cauldron / April Asher.
Description: First edition. | New York : St. Martin's Griffin, 2024. | Series: Supernatural singles ; 3
Identifiers: LCCN 2023036057 | ISBN 9781250808035 (trade paperback) | ISBN 9781250808042 (ebook)
Subjects: LCGFT: Witch fiction. | Romance fiction. | Humorous fiction. | Novels.
Classification: LCC PS3608.U5713 N686 2024 | DDC 813/.6—c23/eng/20230825
LC record available at https://lccn.loc.gov/2023036057

Our books may be purchased in bulk for promotional, educational, or business use. Please contact your local bookseller or the Macmillan Corporate and Premium Sales Department at 1-800-221-7945, extension 5442, or by email at MacmillanSpecialMarkets@macmillan.com.

First Edition: 2024

10 9 8 7 6 5 4 3 2 1

To *you*—flip those witch switches, fire up the cauldrons & let's ride

Not Your Crush's Cauldron

1

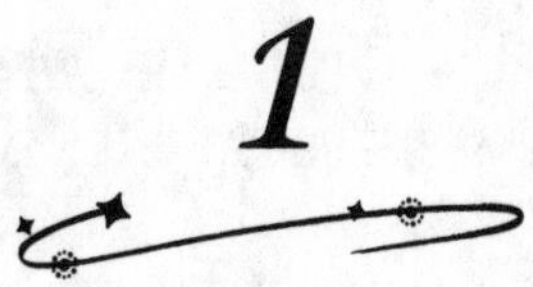

Super Soakers & Nipple Piercings

Committing a felony had never looked so appealing to Olive Maxwell. It wouldn't take much. With a little hustle in her bustle and a flick of the ignition, her witchy behind could be on the Sunrise Highway before anyone questioned "What happened to Olly?"

Hell, if luck was on her side, that wouldn't happen until she nabbed the ferry to Block Island, changed her name to Petunia, and embraced beach-hermit living with a bonfire burning every single high-heeled shoe shoved in the back corner of her cramped closet.

People teleworked all the time, and if the college didn't support the transition, she'd gladly sacrifice her job as NYU's Supernatural Studies department head to ensure this day never happened.

Okay, so not really. Giving up a position at a prestigious law firm to become the youngest department head at the well-known university hadn't happened without a hell of a lot of hard work and sacrifice—specifically to her social life. No way could she let it go that easily . . . but a witch could fantasize.

Olive slowly relinquished her hold on the driver's side handle and sighed, her shoulders dropping along with her chances of escape.

"I have the keys, so unless you've taken up pickpocketing in your spare time, this is happening." Rose, walking to the rear of the rental moving truck, flashed her triplet a knowing smirk.

"No keys or pickpocketing required." With a quick call on her Magic, Olive snapped her fingers. An immediate golden-green flame flickered just above her pointer. "This is my ticket to ride."

And hide . . .

"Uh-huh. Sure. Then why are you standing in the middle of the road, glaring at the driver's side door, instead of riding your way into the sunset?" Rose reached out, snuffing Olive's Magic with a gentle, supportive hand squeeze. "Because buried deep in your gorgeously gifted brain, you know this is for the best."

"Then it must be buried earth's core kind of deep because I'm still not convinced this isn't an impending apocalyptic-grade catastrophe."

"A catastrophe is sleeping in your office for another night. It's not a sustainable life choice, Olly."

"I didn't always sleep there," she muttered defensively, pushing her glasses up higher onto the bridge of her nose.

"You sure as hell didn't *sleep* at your old place, either." Rose gifted her a Grandma Edie–worthy look.

Point made.

Ever since Olive's old roommate combined her love of herbal-remedy entrepreneurship with a twenty-four-hour pickup option, Olive had ceased getting a solid eight hours. Anything more than three was cause to set off fireworks and quite possibly notify the Guinness World Records. Sheer Maxwell determination—and Red Bull—were the only two reasons she'd lasted this long.

"Think of it this way," Rose prodded into her internal mope-fest. "If the zombie apocalypse *does* happen, you'll have your very own Guardian Angel able to literally fly around the city scavenging for water and other supplies. You won't succumb to the horde right away like Vi. You'll probably last, I don't know, an entire week."

Rose chuckled at her own joke and the mention of last week's zombie apocalypse survival conversation.

While Olive didn't put Baxter Donovan at the exact same danger level as a zombie horde, it was a hell of a close race. Much closer than Rose and Vi, her trip-witch sisters, believed.

Nothing about the tatted-up Guardian Angel screamed rest and relaxation. Panty-melting bad-witch fantasies? Absolutely. R&R? Not in the least.

Her law school education evaporated the second his impressive biceps twitched while in close proximity. Now she'd *live* with those colorful, vein-bulging arms.

And with the abs.

And with the double nipple piercings she was 75 percent certain he had thanks to a summer BBQ and Vi's game of Shoot the Guys with Super Soakers.

Olive pulled her knit cap off her head and fanned her suddenly warm face. Where was a good zombie horde when you needed one?

"Olly." Rose tucked a box into her hands. "This is happening. Enjoy it, and this adorable Astoria, Queens, neighborhood, and get your ass moving. These boxes won't move themselves."

Rose's half-demon veterinarian hottie, Damian Adams, stepped out of the building and headed their way. Her sister's eyes instantly lit up as she soaked in the sight of her soul mate.

Olive smiled. Of all the rampant changes for the Maxwell triplets over the last few months, the most satisfying one was Rose and Vi both finding their perfect matches. Vi, after thinking Magic had abandoned her for her entire life, now stood center stage in the magical community, preparing to take over as the Prima—witch leader—from their grandma Edie.

And Rose, who'd been groomed for the role since she lost her first tooth, had stepped down to find her own thing. A few failed jobs and a run-in with the law later, she'd found that thing in Supernatural bounty hunting . . . and Damian.

Everything had changed. Everyone evolved.

Except her.

Her fine dirty-blond hair still refused to hold a curl—or hair dye—and her astigmatism made going without her thick glasses a high-risk life choice. She had the same job, which she loved, and was still convinced olives were the byproduct of an evil mastermind. And despite the occasional attempt in masking her five-foot-three-inch stature with heels, she was still vertically challenged and had inherited what her grandma called *extra cushion for the pushin'*.

Packing up her meager belongings and switching New York City boroughs was the most exciting thing to happen to her in years.

"She didn't make a run for Jersey yet? Easiest twenty bucks I've ever made. I should've doubled my bet," Damian murmured against Rose's lips as he pulled her in for a quick kiss.

"Bet? What bet?" Olive's gaze shot back and forth between the two lovebirds.

Rose grinned sheepishly. "That would be—"

"The one on whether or not you'd steal the truck if we left you out here alone long enough," Bax supplied. The Guardian Angel—and her new roomie—stepped out from the building with a smirk on his face, as he'd obviously overheard part of their discussion.

Loose basketball shorts and a sleeveless T-shirt showcased his full-sleeve tattoos, and his caramel-colored hair, bunched in a low, messy man-bun, made an on-a-dry-spell witch such as herself wonder what those long tresses felt like between the legs.

The man was the visual definition of *sex* and *sin* . . . the kind that would be oh so bad in a really, really good way.

As if sensing her detour into Naughtyville, Bax lifted his scar-sliced left eyebrow and threw her a sexily suggestive wink. Muscles, tattoos, and motorcycle aside, the real threat to libidos everywhere? Those eyes.

Born with heterochromia, Bax possessed one gorgeously gray

iris and one hazel that leaned heavily into blue, and they possessed the ability to stare straight into a witch's soul and caress it as if it were a purring kitty cat.

And damn it if she didn't want to purr right then and there.

"Just so you know, Damian and I had faith you'd stick around." Bax reached for another of her boxes. His arm brushed hers, the touch sending an immediate zap to all her bits.

She dragged her attention away from Bax to shoot her sister a gentle glare. "So much for sisterly solidarity."

Rose shrugged unapologetically. "You know me. I always hope for the best, but I'm a pragmatist. Flight had the best odds . . . but I'm super proud you stuck around. Vi will be, too, when I tell her we lost the pool."

Bax chuckled, tucking a large box underneath his arm. "Damn, angel. *More* books? Not that I couldn't embrace a nudist lifestyle under the right conditions, but did you bring any clothes?"

She tugged a large duffel from the back and slung it over her shoulder, nearly hitting him in the head. "Here. Clothes. Happy?"

"More like disappointed," Bax quipped with a wink.

Ignoring Rose's and Damian's chuckles, Olive tucked another smaller box beneath her chin and headed to her new second-floor apartment. Bax's inclination to keep his angel domain private meant she'd only been there a handful of times. That's why his offering her his second room had come as a shock.

Their friend group had multiple hangout spots. Potion's Up, their version of Central Perk but with alcohol, provided late-night meet-ups of the fruity-drink variety. Vi's cozy studio apartment had been used for movie marathons, but now that she and Linc—her True Mate and the Alpha of the North American Pack—had moved into Linc's adorable brownstone, they not only hosted movie nights, but barbeques and game nights as well. Basically anything that required elbow room and privacy.

The group had even given Damian and Rose's place at the animal sanctuary a trial run, but Olive's allergies and her eyes' tendency to swell shut with the slightest speck of pollen and dander ensured that had been a onetime event.

But Bax's place? *Nope.* Not even a single debut. It was basically the Eighth Wonder of New York City, if not the world.

Not long ago updated, the cozy two-bedroom apartment sported a modern, clean white theme, its only other color coming from the gray hardwood flooring and stark black fixtures. But despite its lack of color—or personality—it was a huge upgrade from her previously microscopic dwelling with its faulty heating, sucky water pressure, and crapshoot cell signal.

The kitchen opened into the small living room area, and Bax, a huge movie buff, had hung a big-screen TV above a massive fireplace she couldn't wait to light up. The protective glass screen was so clean she doubted it had ever been used.

Bax headed into the wrong bedroom with her third box of books.

She quickly followed him, freezing in the doorway. Surrounded by brown boxes, the full bed already sported her familiar patchwork quilt made of old band T-shirts and her pale beachy-green sheets. "Wasn't this your room?"

He stacked the box he carried onto the others. "It was, but now it's yours."

She opened and closed her mouth a few times. "But . . . why? I thought I was just sliding right into the spare room?"

"But then I thought about it more. This one has the balcony, which I never use and thought that you would. There's enough space out there for a chair and maybe one of those little tables. You could use it to read . . . or people-watch . . . or whatever."

She blinked behind her thick glasses. "I can't take your room, Bax."

"It's not my room anymore. It's yours." He turned toward her, crossing his tattooed arms over his chest, and walloped her with his soul-searing gaze until she was forced to put down her own boxes or risk dropping them on her toes. "Are we about to have our first roomie fight, angel?"

"Are you going to keep insisting this is my room when we both know that we already agreed to me taking the spare?" She met him stare for stare, locking her knees so they wouldn't knock together like she was a freaking cartoon character.

The longer the silence continued, the more Olive resigned herself to the fact she wasn't winning this argument.

His small smirk indicated he'd realized the same. "It's not a big deal. I'm not here much, and when I am, I'm usually sleeping. For all I know, the sliding door is nailed shut and doesn't even open."

"But . . ."

Bax slowly ate up the distance between them, each step not only shrinking the gap but sending her heart rate into a frenzy. He stopped a scant few inches away, close enough that one deep breath would push her chest against his . . . well, abs, considering their massive height difference.

"Don't make it a thing, angel." His deep voice and close proximity tilted her head up reflexively. "Take the room. Please."

She gulped, wincing at its loudness, and nodded.

A bump, followed by a sisterly giggle, floated in from the dining room and broke the tense moment. "Damian . . . be careful."

Olive thanked the Goddess for a reason to excuse herself from Bax's close proximity, but quickly changed her mind at the scene in the other room. "Gah!"

Slapping a hand over her eyes and nearly smacking her glasses off her face, she turned away from the image now burned into her retinas and walked nose-first into Bax's chest. "Don't look! Save your eyes. *Save your eyes!*"

His arms caught her before she bounced off him like he was a trampoline.

"Isn't it the new tenant who's supposed to break in the new digs, not the visitors?" Bax's chest rumbled with laughter.

"Please don't paint the picture," she pleaded, burrowing herself further into his shirt with a groan.

As a large hand skated through her hair to cup the back of her head, she nearly groaned for another reason.

Not only did his fingers feel damn good gently caressing her scalp, but pushing against her cheek was a definite telltale bump. Call her Nancy Drew because she had just solved a mystery.

Bax definitely sported some cool metallic hardware right around the nipple level.

Olive pried open the eye not smushed against the massive Guardian Angel chest and slid a tentative glance to her unapologetic sister. "Can you not do that where I'll eat my breakfast tomorrow?"

Giggling, Rose placed a quick kiss on Damian's lips and gently eased the half-demon back from where he'd pushed her ass against the small table. "Sorry. We started debating the sturdiness of tables and things got a little out of hand and . . . well, good news! Yours is pretty darn durable."

Bax snorted. "Out of hand? Looked like things were *in* hands, if you ask me."

Olive shook her head with a groan and grumbled, "Never getting that image out of my head now. Not even all the Ian Somerhalder binge-watching in the world . . ."

Rose sent a regretful look her way. "About that *Vampire Diaries* binge . . . Charlie called and asked me to meet her downtown at Supernatural HQ. We picked up another bounty assignment."

"I can drop you off on my way back to the sanctuary," Damian added.

Olive cocked a blond eyebrow. "Since when does Char *ask* you to meet her anywhere?"

Her sister's Hunting partner and trainer—Charlotte "Charlie" Deveraux—wasn't the type of wolf shifter who asked for anything. Demanded? Yes. Barked? Loudly. But *asked*? Nope.

"Point taken," Rose chuckled. "But she's finally warming up to me, so I don't want to rock the boat, but you'll be okay, right? All your things have been brought up. Now it's just a matter of putting them in their correct spaces, and I know organization is foreplay for you, so I don't want to get in your way."

She wanted to disagree, but couldn't. Even if her sorting method looked chaotic to some, it made sense to her. She was a one-woman *Home Edit* show.

"I'm proud of you for taking this leap, sis." Rose pulled her into a tight hug. "And to commemorate the moment, I left a housewarming gift in your left bedside drawer. Use it well."

"Do you think you'll make it to Potion's Up later?" She reluctantly released her hold, asking about their plans to meet up with Vi, Linc, and the others tonight.

"Barring entrapment in six feet of sewer sludge and looking for an escaped Tactor demon, I'll be there." Rose hiked her purse onto her shoulder and headed to the door, Damian's arm in a protective position around her waist. "Have fun organizing . . . and doing roommate-bonding exercises!"

"Be safe!"

"Always! Love you!" Rose left with a wave and an air-kiss.

And then there were two . . .

Olive glanced around the room, prolonging the intensifying awkwardness. It was so quiet she could hear her heartbeat thumping loudly in her ears, and the harder she tried not to focus on it, the more she did.

Bax watched her, his attention conjuring a tingling heat to her cheeks. "Organizational foreplay, huh? Sounds like it could be a fun roommate-bonding exercise."

Her mind blanked. All thoughts washed away. At least all non-horny thoughts . . . but foreplay and bonding exercises trampolined inside her head, jumping right to the forefront.

"It's not foreplay. I just like it when things have their own spot,"

Olive admitted, forcing herself to meet his twinkling eyes. "It makes things easier to find in a pinch."

He smirked. "Everything having a home is fine by me."

"I'll try not to invade your space."

"It's really not a problem."

"Just let me know if something's in your way and I'll find another spot for it. And speaking of places, do you have a preference where I put my toiletries and things?" She picked up the bag that held new soap and shampoo and turned toward his confused look. "What?"

"Wouldn't toiletries go wherever toiletries and things usually go?" Bax asked, his brow furrowed.

"I didn't know if you'd prefer me keeping them in my room and using a shower caddy, or if it was okay to leave it all in the bathroom." Her cheeks warmed in embarrassment. "My old roommate always complained about my things taking up too much space. I don't want to crowd you out or anything."

One second, Bax was three feet away, and in a blink, he was right in front of her, finger hooked beneath her chin as he dragged her gaze to his.

"Let's set one thing straight right now, angel. I'm not that roommate." His eyes glittered fiercely as he paused, making sure he had her full attention. "I won't put you in dangerous situations by inviting strangers into this apartment, and I won't complain about your things hanging around. Hell, air-dry your lingerie on the shower curtain rod for all I care."

Her cheeks heated as she imagined him coming face-to-lace with her newest bralette. "You say that now, but—"

"No buts. If I didn't want you to *crowd* me, I wouldn't have asked you to move in." He gently pushed his thumb against her lips the second she opened her mouth to speak. "This is officially your space, too. You don't need my permission to put your things wherever the hell you want. Throw your mail on the kitchen table. Walk around barefoot. Toss your dirty dishes in the sink. It's all good."

She scrunched her nose.

Bax smirked. "Which one of those things put a bee under your broomstick? The mail, walking sockless, or dirty dishes?"

"Leaving dishes in the sink only makes them more difficult to clean later, and if you throw mail into an ever-growing stack, you might miss something important. Like a bill."

"Do you forget about the books on your to-be-read pile?"

"I don't forget about books," Olive scoffed in mock outrage.

He chuckled, the sound sending a fluttering wave through her lower abdomen. Too soon, he released her chin and gifted her a warm smile. "I'm jumping into the shower and leaving you to your organizational foreplay. When it's time to meet the others at Potion's, we can take my bike, okay?"

She cleared her dry throat. "Yeah. Sure. That makes sense . . . roomie."

When the bathroom door clicked shut, she banged her head on the wall. "Way to go, Olly. Could you be any more awkward?"

Honestly? She could, and if Bax hadn't escaped when he did, they both would've found out exactly how much more.

She traced her fingers over her chin and lip, feeling the warm tingles his touch had left behind. The water in the bathroom kicked on, and then it wasn't just her lips that tingled as she pictured the soon-to-be naked angel a short distance away.

Organizational foreplay, she reminded herself, and set to work on her most important task: making a home for all her books. Soon enough, she lost herself in her cataloguing system and got through one box before reaching for a second. But then her bedside table, its drawer slightly open, caught her attention.

What kind of housewarming gift would Rose have left for her?

Curious, she opened the drawer and picked up its only contents, a sparkling silk-lined pouch that looked as if it would hold fairy dust. She pulled out the only thing inside . . . and it definitely wasn't fairy dust, although it did sparkle a bit.

Hot pink and rubbery, and sporting what could only be described as a swirling tenacle, the contraption sported a thick end and a little suction cup tip. She pushed the large button and the damn thing jumped to life.

Almost literally.

She dropped the vibrating sex toy with a squeal and watched it dance its way across her bedspread, sounding like a buzzsaw in the middle of a quiet museum. She dove on top of it, hands fumbling to turn it off, but it vibrated faster—and louder—hitting a new cycle.

Blowing a loose strand of hair away from her eyes, she tried again, playing with the buttons until she was finally met with blessed silence. "Ha! You're no match for me, Tentacle Teaser 2000. Olive Maxwell—one. You—the big zip."

"Oh, hey, before I forget . . ." Bax appeared in her open door and froze. His gaze dropped to the toy in her hand and then slowly lifted . . . along with a crooked smirk. "Glad to see you're taking what I said about making yourself at home to heart, angel. And here I thought I'd have to remind you a few more times until you got the message."

"What? No. No, no," Olive said adamantly. "That wasn't what . . . This is a housewarming present."

His dual-colored eyes twinkled with mischief. "And here I thought most people gave plants or candles or, hell, even small appliances."

"Most people don't have a Rose. I swear Vi and Harper are rubbing off on her more and more." She threw the toy back into her nightstand and closed the drawer a bit harder than necessary. "What didn't you want to forget?"

"Right now, I'm trying not to forget the sight of you with that toy in your hand."

With the tease, her face burned and she closed her eyes, praying the floor swallowed her whole, or at least sucked her into their downstairs neighbor's apartment. Except when she convinced herself to finally look the Guardian Angel in the eye, he didn't look all that humor-filled.

Hands fisted at his sides, Bax tensed, his body frozen in position except for the wildly ticking muscle in his square jaw, the one that twitched when someone was barely holding their shit together. She'd seen her father do it more than a few times, and Damian and Linc, her sisters' mates, practically had the broody look down to an art form.

Holy hexes . . . could he have been serious?

She quickly dismissed the idea, passing it off as shock. "Sorry to traumatize you with all . . . that."

"Definitely not what I'd call it," he murmured, his words almost inaudible as he shifted a little awkwardly on his feet.

"You were saying when you . . . ?" She flailed her hands toward her nightstand.

"Oh. Yeah. The hot water . . . I wanted to warn you there's a very fine line on the dial between Warm & Comfortable and Melting Skin Off Bone."

She nodded. "Warm Comfort and Melting Skin. Got it. Anything else?"

His eyes flickered to her bedside drawer. "Nope. I think that's it. Oh, and I have to head out for a bit, but I should be back in plenty of time to head over to Potion's together. If not, I'll call."

"No worries. I'll be here unpacking." *And contemplating ways to kill my sister that don't involve jail time or getting a disapproving look from Gran Edie.*

She waited until the front door clicked open and closed before falling face-first onto her bed.

What the hell did she let everyone talk her into?

2

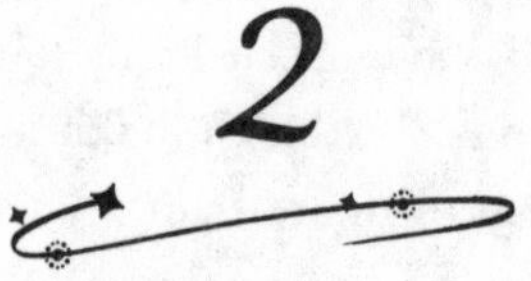

Wings & Limbs

Bax second-guessed his intelligence along with his ability to keep his junior guardian—aka his dick—undercover. Or under covers. However the hell you looked at it because both ways fit the situation.

He'd moved his things into what he'd once used as an office and repository for odds and ends and shit, knowing Olive would enjoy the balcony in his room, but seeing her standing in his space—holding a damned sex toy of all things?

It was a miracle she hadn't noticed the hard-on pushing against his zipper, and he'd needed to skip out before that changed.

Even though he now questioned his genius idea, the move-in offer made sense. Working for Guardian Angel Affairs, he wasn't home much, and when he was, he was usually unconscious, exhausted after a long shift, or watching TV in the hope of expunging the memories of it. He'd thought the limited contact would help curb his reaction—and attraction—to the fair-haired Maxwell, but apparently he'd thought wrong.

So, so fucking wrong.

This living arrangement was about to become a complication he didn't need, but he wouldn't take it back for anything. Hell, if given an opportunity for a redo, he'd repeat the same decision all over again, because as a Guardian, it was in his nature to protect, and her ex-roommate had put her in far too many dangerous situations with strangers coming and going at all hours of the day and night. It had been a ticking bomb prepped to blow.

But the second motive for offering his spare room wasn't nearly as altruistic, or very Guardian-like.

He *liked* being near her . . . as evidenced by the dick in his pants that was still at half-mast. Her smarts continuously impressed him, and her big, open heart made him strive to be the same. When she wasn't working or with her family, she volunteered at the Kids' Community Center or at the children's hospital.

It was obvious the witch didn't see herself the way others did . . . the way *he* did . . . and it made her all the more irresistible.

A combination of sweet torture and salty goodness, Olive's presence even got his mind off the suck-fest that was the GAA and the summons he expected any day now. To date, he'd now broken two of the three central—and most important—GAA Rules of Conduct.

The first: Don't tell your Assignment that you're their designated Guardian.

The second: Don't get your Assignment killed.

The third, which he'd yet to break and had no intention of doing so: Don't fall in love with your Assignment.

The third Rule of Conduct had been an easy one to keep intact with his previous long-term Assignment, but the first two? Not so much.

His normal Guardianship mode meant flying under the radar. See things, but do not *be* seen, even during an intervention. But when his forty-something-year-old biker Assignment, Hogan, decided to lead a raid on a rival club, Bax had been too intent on not breaking GAA rule number two that he hadn't been as careful with the first.

After Hogan realized he had a Guardian, the man used the information to justify taking more and more risks, relying on Bax to bail him out. More raids. Higher stakes. More and more enemies accrued, and considering he was the leader of one of the most notorious East Coast biker clubs, Hogan already didn't win any popularity contests.

Throw it all together, and it led to Bax inadvertently breaking that damn second rule.

He'd always stretched a few protocols here and there. Every Guardian did to suit the situation, but that one fuck-up led to another, and another, which eventually cost his Assignment his life. The GAA didn't handle their Guardians' failures well, and it was why he was waiting for yet another black mark in his file, evidence to fuel his father's belief that Bax really was the disappointment he'd always believed him to be.

To the great Mikael Donovan—one of the Archangels' right-hand Warriors of Peace—a Guardian was a mere half step above human status. Toss in Bax's dislike of flying and his lack of fucks given regarding angel hierarchy, and he was the all-around gold-place winner of the Screwup Award.

Bax walked the streets without having a destination or a plan, just knowing he needed open space and fresh air to shake off all the uncertainty of the last few days. Before he realized it, he found himself in downtown's Dark Side neighborhood, home to a line of dance clubs and bars notorious for break-out fights and the flouting of Supernatural laws.

He'd barely passed the entrance to Glow, the first in the line of clubs, when his phone vibrated his ass and a message came through from the GAA.

Assignment Safety Check Needed
Glow
Downtown Manhattan
Please Respond

Bax pulled up the Assignment's file and studied the kid's picture. A student at NYU, the guy looked barely twenty, and that was pushing it. The smug smile stretched across his face indicated he didn't often worry about pesky questions like "Should I?" "Would I?" "Could I?"

He was a trouble magnet, but not nearly as much as the trouble that would come Bax's way if the GAA found out he literally stood at Glow's door and didn't respond.

He glanced at his watch and cursed at the time, thinking about Olive waiting back at the apartment. The second he did, a secondary image nudged its way to the forefront, her standing in the middle of his old room, hot pink vibrator in hand.

Hell . . . maybe he needed a few more minutes to drag his mind from the gutter.

If he made this quick, he'd still get home in enough time to pick her up and head out to Potion's.

Bax typed a quick on it. Bypassing the long line of waiting clubgoers, he slipped inside with a faint nod to the bouncer, a hulked-out vampire who looked seconds away from sinking his fangs into anyone who annoyed him.

After half an hour of earsplitting club "music," Bax started counting down the minutes until he could make tracks and do something that didn't make his ears bleed.

Pulsing lights lit up the inside of the converted firehouse, flickering over the bodies jumping up and down in time to the heavy musical thumping, in movements that very loosely resembled dancing. He didn't need the gift of premonition to tell this night wouldn't end well.

Leaning against the wall, he watched Riley West down his sixth Neon Numb-Maker, to the repetitive chanting of his college buddies. If they continued with this rate of alcohol consumption, they were all headed toward a stomach-pumping at the ER.

Good fucking times, but nothing that warranted a GAA intervention.

Still, he hadn't gotten an all-clear from HQ, which meant someone from the higher-ups still detected a lingering threat. He couldn't leave until it either appeared for him to kick its ass, or it evaporated into oblivion.

He secretly hoped it was the first option. After all this standing around, his muscles could use a bit of exercise.

Cho, a fellow Guardian, took the wall spot next to him, a drink in their hand. "Look what the cat dragged in. Glad to see news of your demise was greatly fabricated. What brings you to the Dark Side?"

Bax smirked, nodding to their left. "Dude-bro with the palm tree board shorts and neon green shirt. Not sure where he's surfing in New York in the middle of winter, but who am I to be fashion judge, jury, and executioner?"

"Feel your pain. Two nights ago, my Assignment snuck onto the airfield at JFK and played chicken with a 747. I counted my lucky stars when tonight's activities revolved around getting shit-faced and laid."

Bax chuckled. "Aren't those the dream details?"

Dude-bro Riley laughed with his friends, and then, as a group, they hightailed it toward the back of the club, their eyes practically lit up with excitement.

"Looks like I'm on the move." Bax pushed off the wall. "Hope your guy's night ends on a happy note. I'll see you later."

"Same, friend." Cho laughed, giving him a head nod.

Keeping his Assignment's neon shirt in his sights, Bax swerved through the crowd, all his Guardian alarm bells ringing as the friends slid their gazes around. They played the part of looking for no good well.

Two dancing shifters stepped into Bax's path, temporarily blocking his view. He slid left, they moved left. He went right, they glided right, oblivious as they ground against one another to the sultry tempo.

"Do you fucking mind?" he growled, throwing them a glare.

They chuckled and danced off, but it was too late. He'd lost sight of Riley and his frat brothers. He followed his gut toward the back hall, where there was nothing but bathrooms and the exit leading to the back alley.

"Can people not do their shady business in cute mom-and-pop diners once in a while? Why is it always freaking dark alleys?" asked a familiar voice.

Bax paused as he reached the back door at the same time as an equally shocked witch.

"Bax?" Rose's eyes went wide. "What the hell are you doing here?"

"I could ask the same of you."

The middle Maxwell triplet glanced around. "Please tell me Olly isn't here, too. And if she is, tell me what kind of magic you performed on her to get her to agree to it."

"She's back at the apartment, safe and sound. What are *you* doing here?"

"Oh, for fuck's sake. You two talk like grannies in a quilting circle." A low snarl had them both turning to the leather-clad wolf shifter who pushed her way through the emergency exit. "While you two are gabbing, our Target is making another play. Get with the program, Maxwell, or you're cleaning the traps we used to collect the rabid demonic sewer rats."

Rose snorted. "She says that like she won't have me cleaning them regardless."

"You're here collecting a bounty?" Bax's alarms blared, slowly registering both her and Charlie's presence.

"And you're . . . Guarding?" Rose asked.

He nodded. "A human kid looking for trouble. You?"

"A Tartan demon who loves helping human kids get into trouble with tainted gargoyle dust."

"Fuck," they said in unison, quickly rushing through the exit after Rose's Hunter mentor.

Bax and Rose stepped out from the club and into pure chaos. Charlie was already pounding the face of a shadowlike creature, its eel-like physique squirming in an attempt to slip away. Its red eyes glowed in the dim alley, locked on the three human college students—Riley included—who were doubled over, howling in distress.

The tallest of the group hit the asphalt just as dark gargoyle-esque wings tore through his shirt. Another, his pupils dilated like those of a cat high on catnip, spun in circles as he tried catching his own offending growth.

But it was Riley who sent Bax into a cursing streak. The kid kicked off from the ground and, flapping his newly acquired stone wings as hard as he could, reached takeoff.

The sound of stone rubbing against stone was worse than nails on a chalkboard, but the human didn't let it stop him, getting a few feet off the ground, and higher by the second.

Bax cursed.

"I take it that one's your Assignment?" Rose smirked.

He grunted in reluctant agreement.

"Good luck." Rose jumped to help her instructor wrangle the demonic drug dealer, summoning a pink swell of Magic and conjuring a pair of thick magical restraints. "And you complain about me playing around all the time. Do you want to finish the job, or should I give you a little more time alone with your new friend?"

"About damn time you show your face, Maxwell," Charlie grumbled, her breath heaving.

"Good things come to those who wait, Charlotte," Rose quipped.

Bax almost laughed at the duo's banter . . . until Riley's loud howl ripped through the night.

"I'm flying!" Riley giggled louder the higher he rose into the sky.

"Look! I'm flying! Holy shit! I'm actually flying! Quick! Someone record this shit! I'm going to go fucking viral, man."

Remaining on the ground, his friends urged him higher and higher, still testing their own new appendages.

"Get the hell down here, kid," Bax growled testily. "Now!"

"No way, dude! Look at me! I'm Batman!" Riley pumped his wings harder, until he was nearly eight stories up. "This is unreal. I wonder if I can make it up to the Empire State Building."

"You'll end up plastered on the sidewalk in front of the ESB when that gargoyle dust wears off."

"Do it, Riley," the kids' friends goaded.

With a determined look on his face, Riley flapped his wings faster.

"You want a little help?" Rose stepped up next to him, Magic sparking around her fingers.

"Probably not the best idea." Bax hated to admit it, but if the GAA got wind of magical interference instead of direct Guardian action, he'd be peppered with a whole host of questions he didn't want to answer. "I got this."

With a grunt, he ejected his wings. They erupted from his back, ripping through his favorite shirt and stretching to their nearly eight-foot width. He gave them a test flap, working out the joint cramps that came with infrequent use.

Ignoring the unease curdling in the pit of his stomach, he pushed off the ground an inch and hovered for a few strangling heartbeats before rising another. Sweat broke out across his forehead as he convinced himself into a slow and steady air-climb.

Above him, Riley's stone-like appendages shrank to half their size in the blink of an eye. The kid screamed as he dropped nearly two flights before stalling his descent.

"The gargoyle dust is leaving his system," Rose shouted in warning. "He's got another minute—tops—before he's crashing to the ground, and from that height, it won't feel like a tickle."

Bax mentally cursed himself out for not just hiding in his room and dealing with his Olly-boner the normal way. The heavy pound of his heartbeat echoed in his ears as he pushed himself another foot higher.

He hated flying with every fiber of his angelic being and had ever since his father "tossed him into the deep end" angel edition—aka pushed him off the roof of their house. Some angels relished the sensation of the air rustling their feathers or the scent of the clean, unpolluted air.

Not Bax. He experienced the same thing if he stood in front of an overzealous AC unit and held a car freshener over the vent. Feet firmly on the ground was and always would be his preferred method of travel.

Well, his own feet or his motorcycle.

He forced himself up another inch, but for every inch he gained, Riley dropped another foot.

Eyes wide and legs flailing, the kid finally looked rightfully freaked out. "Dude! I think I'm falling! You gotta catch me!"

"Working on it," Bax grumbled. Another inch to go and another stream of sweat rolling down his back.

Riley's hands stretched and latched onto Bax's shirt. If he'd kept his hold to the clothes or, hell, the arms, it would've been fine . . . but the kid went for the wings.

"Get me down, man! This shit isn't fun anymore." He yanked out a fistful of feathers in an attempt to shimmy onto Bax's back.

"Can't fly if you're on the wings . . . or plucking me," Bax warned with a growl. *Fuck, that stung.*

They dropped another foot as Riley effectively strangled his arms, wings, and legs in a death grip . . . and then they plummeted to the alley below.

Bax flipped them at the last minute, catching the brunt of the fall, but a distinct snap and an animalistic howl indicated Riley's landing hadn't been without injury.

"My leg!" the kid screamed. "Holy fuck! You broke my leg, man! Not cool, dude. Not cool!"

Rose shot Bax an apologetic look as she eased a screaming Riley off his back and offered him a hand up. "You okay? That was quite the fall."

"I'm fine. Just fucking hate heights." He brushed the alleyway remnants off his jeans and practically heard the new ding added to his record. At this rate, the damn thing would be longer than a family of twelve's Costco receipt.

3

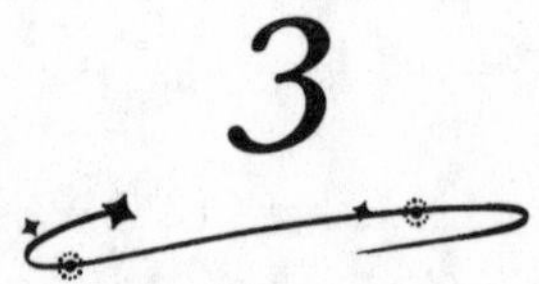

Angeling . . . and Things

The low thrum of voices and familiar scents of leather and spice struck Olive the second she stepped into Potion's Up. On any normal day, both would've given her comfort, the Supernatural-themed bar being a home away from home for her and her friends.

Instead, she was accosted by a strong desire to walk right out. Not the type to ignore a gut instinct, she turned and collided with a knowing green-eyed succubus.

"Shit," Olive cursed, startling. "When the hell did you learn Gran's *poof* Magic?"

"I didn't Magick my way over here. I glided, like a proper demon." Harper Jacobs stood between her and the door, a pitcher of fruity margarita in one hand and a golden ale in the other. She cocked up a single auburn eyebrow. "Tell me you weren't trying to leave. You literally walked through the door three seconds ago."

"Would you believe me if I did?"

Harper's eyebrow lifted higher, indicating a big fat no.

"What would it take for you to pretend you didn't see me?" she pleaded. "An agreement to let you dress me for our next Girls' Night? Because if that's what it'll take, you got yourself a deal."

"No restrictions?" Interest twinkled from the sex demon's eyes.

Olive faltered, hit with a mental image of a red leather catsuit. Or worse . . . something with more holes than fabric. "No . . . ?"

"Is that a question or an answer?" Her friend's bright pink lips twitched. "It doesn't matter. As tempted as I am by your offer—and just know, I am *so* tempted—you wouldn't make it unless you were seriously desperate to get out of tonight, and while my curiosity is piqued, so is my worry. Turn around and march your sweet ass to the back table, cupcake."

"Har-per," she whined.

"Oll-y," the redhead mimicked back. "First Rose shows up looking like she went ten rounds with a slimy Quall demon, then Bax no-shows, and now you're attempting to unshow. Our Friends' Night Out is at serious risk of turning into Boring Night Out, and I will not have it on my watch."

"Bax texted that he'd be late, but that he'll be here." Olive nearly winced at the obvious disappointment in her tone.

It wasn't as if she'd contemplated her outfit choices for an hour knowing he'd mentioned going together on his bike, or that she'd fidgeted on the couch while nibbling her lower lip raw for a good thirty minutes before his text came through.

Oh, wait . . . she did. All of it.

"It was probably a Guardian thing," Olive added.

"If I orgasmed as many times as he's used that excuse, I'd never drink a horny person's pheromones ever again," Harper quipped. "But my point is, now that you're here, you're not leaving my sight. About-face and march, bwitch. Back corner table."

The demon depleted all hope of escape with a single look, and Olive turned, following instructions and telling herself ten minutes. Fifteen, max. She'd stay long enough for Vi and Rose to take her pulse and get distracted by the walking masses of muscle that were their significant others, and then she'd go home and get reacquainted with her PJs.

As she approached the table, Vi pulled her dreamy-eyed gaze

from Linc, her True Mate. "Well, well, well. Look what the succubus dragged in."

"Almost literally," Harper joked, sliding the drink pitchers across the table.

"I walked. There was no dragging involved." Olive commandeered one of the empty seats and searched for a new topic. Any topic. And found it in Rose's torn shirt and dirtied jeans. Her triplet didn't look like the well-put-together Prima Apparent of a few months ago. "Rose is sporting the 'dragged-in' look more than I am. You got a little something sticking to your hair, sis."

Rose ran her fingers through her dark locks, cursing when she pulled away something that looked suspiciously like part of a greasy fast-food wrapper. "I knew I should've showered before coming."

"Probably twice," Vi teased, wrinkling her nose. "Although they say third time's a charm, right?"

Rose subtly sniffed her shirt and grimaced. "I can't say I wasn't aware of the questionable hygienics of Hunting, but theory and reality are two vastly different beasts. At least tonight involved club-hopping and alleys and not dumpsters or sewers. There's no saving *those* outfits . . . not even with Magic. Trust me, I've tried."

"So you and Charlie are getting along?" Vi smirked knowingly.

"Oh yeah. We're besties. She just hasn't fully accepted it yet."

Olive studied each of her sisters as the entire table chuckled. In six months, their lives had flipped upside down. Vi now stood at Edie's side, well on her way to becoming the next Prima, and Rose, who'd trained for the role since before they'd all sported training bras, now wore leather pants and hunted Supernatural nasties hell-bent on disturbing the peace.

Not to mention they'd both found their soul mates.

And then there was Olive . . .

In the same job—which she loved. Owned the same wardrobe—

which she dubbed "comfy chic" and really didn't want to change. And her seat at the singles' table—which she didn't intend on giving up for just anyone—practically left an imprint of her ass.

Not that there weren't a few fleeting moments when she didn't contemplate going out on more than a low-risk coffee date, but the attention a relationship would pull away from work had her shelving it for later.

But seeing her sisters happy and in love tempted her more and more to the idea of it.

"How did the move-in go?" Vi sipped her refreshed margarita. "I wanted to be there, but the visit with the Alphas went longer than expected, and considering Linc and I proposed the summit, it wouldn't look good if we'd bailed early."

"It went fine," Olive said a little too fast, and attempted recovery with, "Boxes were carried, unpacked . . . and housewarming gifts unwrapped."

Rose smirked. "You liked it?"

"Could've done without it wriggling across my bed when Bax knocked on the door, but . . . sure. It was a choice."

Someone pulled out the chair next to her, and the roommate in question sat, his broad shoulders brushing against hers as he reached for the beer pitcher. "Houseplants are overrated anyway. What can you really do with them besides water and serenade them?"

Rose choked on her drink as he laughed and threw Olive a wink that instantly heated her cheeks.

"Glad you could join us, angel cakes," Vi welcomed him. "Tough day in the office?"

"You could say that."

Seeing Bax, Damian nudged Linc and his Second-in-Command, Adrian Collins, and the trio paused their dart tournament and returned to the table. Chairs shifted, squeezing everyone closer together, and Linc pulled Vi onto his lap.

Adrian took the newly vacated seat and, with a mischievous smirk, glanced at Harper and patted his lap. "Want to share a seat?"

"About as much as I want a root canal without anesthesia." Harper dragged a chair from a nearby table and crammed it on the other side of Olive, forcing everyone to shift again.

The fit was so tight Olive couldn't even shrug her shoulders. "Oh, yes, this is so much more comfortable."

"I got you." Bax draped his arm along the back of her chair a split second before he tugged her seat closer to him. "Better?"

It freed up an inch or so and yet somehow felt even more intimate than before, the right side of her body effectively cocooned against his left. Butterflies swirled in her stomach as she hyperfocused on the drink in front of her instead of his enticing scent of cinnamon and heat.

Oh, who was she kidding? She couldn't help but be focused on that, too, and it spun her head until she was glad she was sitting.

Everyone around them broke into individual conversations, and Bax leaned closer, his mouth close to her ear. "Sorry I couldn't get home in time to pick you up. Something popped up."

"No worries," she assured him, fixing a smile on her face. "It's not like I didn't know how to get here."

"Right. I know. I just felt bad . . . and a bit disappointed."

"Disappointed?" She turned to meet his gaze, temporarily forgetting how close they sat. The shift brought their noses less than an inch apart. "Why would you be disappointed?"

Something akin to a blush rose high to his cheeks. "I was looking forward to giving you your first ride."

Her mind immediately tanked to the maturity of a thirteen-year-old, and she wasn't the only one.

Harper ceased her banter with Adrian to shoot them a volleying mischievous smirk. "I know Olly exudes that sweet-little-librarian vibe with the put-together outfits and cute little glasses, but I hardly think you'd be her first."

"I wouldn't?" Bax, obviously not cluing in on the sex demon's train of thought, shot a confused glance to Olive. "I didn't realize you've already ridden with someone."

"I haven't." Olive's cheeks heated as Harper cackled.

"So you're still up for that ride sometime . . ."

Harper snickered, murmuring, "Judging by the pheromones oozing off her at the moment, she'd be up for that ride right about now."

Olive subtly kicked her friend, shaking the table.

The succubus winced at the direct hit, but her smile never wavered. "Tell me I'm lying. I dare you."

Bax's gaze bounced from Olive to Harper and back. "Do I even want to know?"

"This is Harper we're talking about," Olive pointed out. "The chances are pretty high that you don't."

Harp chuckled. "But I know you have it in you to figure it out, angel cakes. Just think about it."

"Please don't," Olive pleaded.

It was too late. Realization hit, and Bax, his eyes widening, coughed until he wheezed. "Sorry. Choking on my . . . beer."

"You haven't taken a sip yet."

"Then choking on my spit." He coughed until his eyes watered, earning concerned looks from their friends.

With the seed of mischief firmly planted, Harper returned to her table banter with the hunky lion shifter.

Where's a good sinkhole when you need one?

"You know I didn't mean *that*, right?" Bax shot her a wary look, his breathing still a bit labored.

"Trust me. I know," Olive mumbled.

"Not that I wouldn't be up for it." He froze, quickly backtracking. "I didn't mean . . . just that anyone would be lucky to . . . not just me. Fuck. This isn't coming out right. You understand what I'm saying, right?"

"Honestly? I had difficulty following the conversation after you said you were disappointed."

They glanced at each other and both broke into laughter.

"So we know Bax is serially behind schedule," Vi announced from her perch on Linc's lap, "but we never found out what had you walking through the door late, Olly. You're practically allergic to tardiness, and yet you tried pulling a no-show. What's up?"

Olive sighed. Evidently, she wasn't getting out of talking about it. "My initial presentation with the college's grant board is tomorrow, and it's just a lot."

"This is to get funding for your Supernatural exchange project?" Bax asked.

She shot him a stunned look. "Uh, yeah."

He chuckled. "Your surprise that I remembered is almost a little insulting, angel. I pay attention when you talk. It's a college study-abroad program, but within Supernatural communities."

"That's the one."

"You'll have them practically throwing that money at you."

"Wish I could be that positive."

"It's an incredible idea, Olly," Vi added, agreeing with Bax.

"I know, but college boards are notorious for wanting instant results, and that's not the SupeEx Project. It'll take months, if not longer, before we can identify any true benefits from it, and that's if I get routine funding." She crossed her fingers. "But tomorrow is only the project introduction. I'll have until the end of term to convince them that it's worth the institution's backing."

Rose said supportively, "And we all know your ability to convince a room of anything."

"Hear, hear!" Vi lifted her fruity margarita. "That magnificent magical brain of yours is the reason I'm not mated to a badger shifter from Alaska right now. You'll rock the presentation. I have absolutely no doubt."

Olive wished for that degree of certainty.

"You know what this calls for?" Harper drained the last of her drink and slammed her empty glass onto the table. Cupping her hands around her mouth, she bellowed toward Gage, the bar's cantankerous vampire owner—and her boss. "DJ! Play our jam and turn it up until the floor shakes!"

Gage glowered from behind the counter. "Do I look like your damn DJ, Harper?"

"No, you look like a vampire in serious need of—" Gage shot her a warning growl. She smiled way too sweetly. "—a pint of O positive. Although the other thing would probably help, too."

Vi snickered as she dragged Olive from her seat. Rose had already headed to the jukebox in the corner, and after the press of a few buttons, T-Swift's "Shake It Off" played through the bar speakers.

"Now that's what I'm talking about." Grabbing Olive's spare hand, Harper led the way to the middle of the dance floor.

It was impossible to hold on to her funk, and not just because belting out T-Swift lyrics did magical things to soothe the soul. Olive loved these people more than she loved those butterscotch candies her grandma always had stashed in her pocket, and if they believed in her this much, she'd try doing the same.

One beat turned to another, and after a few more, she bounced along with the tempo, her foul mood entirely forgotten. With everyone's lives splintering in different directions, it felt like a million years since they'd hung out this way.

She let herself enjoy the silliness, throwing her head back and laughing, getting lost in the moment and the music. On the next song, Damian eased in behind Rose, and Linc latched onto Vi's hand, spinning her directly into his arms.

Poor Adrian . . .

One step toward Harper and the succubus shot him a glare that would've turned him to stone if she'd been a Medusa. With a grin, he kept his distance and settled into a side-to-side shimmy.

Distracted by the unfolding scene, Olive didn't sense Bax's

approach until two large, warm hands settled on her hips, and the angel's muscled body brushed against her back.

Goose bumps erupted over her skin, and by the time the song changed to a slow, seductive pulse, her face felt as if she'd given herself a molten lava facial. Prehistoric-sized butterflies attacked her stomach as Bax gently steered her toward him, putting them face-to-chest.

She willed her cheeks to cool as she forced her gaze to his. "Hi."

His multicolored eyes twinkled in the bar's flickering lights as he grinned down at her. "Hi to you, too."

"You don't normally dance unless under duress."

He shrugged his broad shoulders. "This is more like a shuffling hug. And with the right gorgeous woman, I can handle it."

Her heart skipped a beat. "You mean with your new roommate?"

His crooked grin twitched. "You could say that."

It was on the tip of her tongue to ask him what else you could say.

"Olive Maxwell. I thought that was you over here." A familiar voice yanked her from her dreamlike state. "What are the chances of running into one another?"

Bax tensed against her as he swiveled his head toward their newly acquired audience, both the mood and the moment broken.

Olive disguised her disappointed sigh with a forced friendly smile. "Hey, Mason."

✦ ✦ ✦

Bax's day had seesawed from good to bad to decent, and after the scene with Riley and his friends, it had plummeted straight to what-the-fuck status with little to no hope of climbing any higher. And then he'd stepped into Potion's and laid eyes on Olive.

His mood improved instantly, so much so he couldn't help but sit a little closer and, despite a lack of rhythm, join her on the dance floor. The phantom touch of her body swaying against his would probably haunt him for the rest of the week, if not longer.

But the real highlight of the day had been when she'd turned in his arms and gifted him with a look into those deep blue eyes.

Talk about drowning on dry land. Time had stood still as she bespelled him without a single spark of Magic, melting away the world around them and depositing them onto their own private island.

And then a dark-haired stranger blew that island solitude to smithereens, and with it, seesawed his day straight back to the depths of *Is this day over yet?*

Sitting at the bar, he clenched his untouched mug and glared across the room to where Olive sat with Mason Carlisle, a "colleague," her head tilted back as she laughed at something the guy said.

Again.

No one was that fucking funny, and they'd been smiling and chuckling for the past fifteen minutes. Not that he'd counted.

He was a Guardian, so reading people was second nature. Moods. Intentions. Hell, in the Guardian Academy, an entire class revolved around it because learning a person's motives increased the likelihood your Assignment remained breathing. Something the higher-ups usually recommended.

But this Mason? He radiated something other than an overload of Axe body spray.

Insincerity with a heavy splash of deceit.

With an inhuman amount of effort, Bax battled against his internal alert system and pulled his focus away from the scene on the other side of the room.

"And here I thought Harper was top dog in stare-downs," Adrian quipped, taking the stool next to him. "She'll be unhappy to know she's got competition."

"I don't know what you're talking about," Bax lied.

"Sure you don't. You glare at everyone like you're trying to liquefy their insides." Linc leaned against the bar top, his smirk widening. "Shifters get a bad rap for marking their territories, but they evidently have nothing on angels."

"Again, no clue what you're—"

"Talking about," Damian finished, snorting. "I'm a vet. I can smell loads of shit from a mile away, and you, my friend, reek of it. What gives? You have a run-in with Olive's friend from angeling or something?"

Friend. Bax scoffed. Judging by the occasional hand touch and leaning body position, friendship was the last thing on Carlisle's mind. He couldn't completely blame the guy—Olive Maxwell was temptation personified—but it didn't mean he had to like it.

"No run-ins with him personally," Bax admitted reluctantly. "But I've dealt with a lot who give off his same vibes, and it almost never leads to anything good."

"Ah, *vibes* . . ." Linc shared glances with Adrian and Damian. "Then we should put a stop to this before it goes any further. What are you thinking? A burial under a bridge in Brooklyn or a dunk in the Hudson?"

"The Hudson is always my go-to," Adrian played along. "If the water itself doesn't get him, the toxins in the water will."

"Good thinking."

Bax glowered at his friends. "You think Olive's safety is funny?"

"Absolutely not." Damian failed to suppress a grin. "What's funny is you thinking she'd need you intervening on her behalf, or that she'd let you. Hey, we've all been guilty of the same mistaken belief. So I get it. I do. But unless you're prepped to deal with the wrath of a Maxwell witch, it's best letting sleeping dogs get their flirt on . . . or maybe that's the actual problem."

"What?"

"It's not about Olly's safety as much as it is the flirting happening."

He lifted a single eyebrow. "Are you implying I'm jealous or something?"

Adrian chuckled. "Don't think it's the *or something*, dude. And now that Damian mentions it, you do look a little green around the gills."

"I'm not jealous."

His three friends stared at him, their silence bristling his patience.

"I'm not," he repeated. "Olly's my friend, and now she's my roommate. I don't want some guys with . . . vibes . . . taking advantage of her big heart."

The others didn't say a word, and in their prolonged silence, he heard it . . .

He wouldn't call it a *blatant* lie, but there was a definite ring of something other than truth. Other than the protectiveness engrained into his DNA—literally. But jealousy? He couldn't remember a time he'd ever experienced the emotion other than in elementary school when a classmate had his favorite chocolate chip cookies packed in his lunch and he'd been relegated to a red apple.

Yet the second he glanced toward Olive and her friend, his stomach contents soured, leaving a bad taste in the back of his throat. He sipped his warm beer to chase away the foul taste, but grimaced when it remained, growing stronger than before.

He didn't like any of this one damn bit, or what it could mean for things down the line. Jealousy was a gateway emotion, paving the way for more feelings to worm their way into the fold, and before a Guardian Angel knew it, they were surrounded.

Outnumbered and outwitted by something that didn't have an ass to kick.

Guardian Angels worked alone, and largely undercover, to prevent that very scenario. He was already a peculiarity thanks to his friendship with the Maxwell triplets and the rest of the group. No way could he afford to make his situation even worse.

In front of him, his cell phone vibrated against the bar's countertop in two long pulses, announcing an incoming text. The caller

ID flashed *HQ*. Not surprising. What shocked him was not receiving a summons immediately after delivering his Assignment to the emergency room.

> Meeting with Commissioner Wright
> Tomorrow. 8pm.
> Don't make me find you.
> —P

Bax snorted at the not-so-thinly veiled threat from the Commissioner's assistant. On the outside, Patrick looked the part of a mousy pencil pusher, but word in the agency whispered that he'd kicked many asses to secure his spot just outside the Commissioner's office door.

He teased the man, but he wasn't stupid enough to fuck around with a Patrick edict.

"You okay, man?" Linc watched him carefully.

"Never been better." Bax stuffed his phone in his back pocket. Out of sight, out of mind . . . at least for now.

"You know what you need? A vacation. A chance to turn off that Guardian switch for a long weekend," the wolf shifter suggested. "Vi and I talked about heading up to the mountains sometime before her Exchange Ceremony. Enjoy the solitude. Play in the fresh air and even fresher snow. Just unwind. Fuck knows when we'll get another chance after she becomes Prima. We should make it a group trip."

"Wouldn't you want that time to yourselves?"

Linc flashed a roguish grin. "Oh, we'd claim a room in the cabin to ourselves, that's for sure, but she'd love for everyone to come. She hates that she's missed out on so much over the last few months, and the potential for missing more is one of the things she's dreading about taking over from Edie."

"Fresh powder, skiing, and hot tubs? You know I'm in," Adrian agreed.

Damian grinned. "Rose would probably jump at the chance for a little time away from Charlie and the New York sewer systems. I'll run it by her, but I have a feeling it'll be a fuck-yes."

Linc glanced at him expectantly. "What do you say, angel man? You in if you can get the time off?"

"I could probably be convinced . . . but I'm not strapping death gliders to my feet. Speeding balls-first down the side of a mountain isn't exactly my type of good time. I'll leave that for you thrill-seeking shifters."

Bax didn't mention that the oopsie tonight with his temp Assignment probably meant he'd have time to go on multiple vacations without conflict. He'd lost count of how many black marks he had on his record, but it had to resemble a damn Scantron test by now.

A low, sexy laugh from the across the room dragged his attention back to the small corner table where Olive propped her chin on her open palm and listened intently to something the human said.

He ignored that swirling lump in his stomach and instead focused on the fact that she no longer looked nervous about what she faced tomorrow.

Now he just needed to channel that exact energy himself and do the same.

4

Biker Bwitch

Some days a witch bounded out of bed, ready to take on the world . . . and some days they just wanted to climb back beneath the covers, turn on a streaming service, and only emerge from their blanket cavern when their bladder reached DEFCON-1 status.

Olive definitely wished for the latter.

After staying out way too late with her sisters, she slept through two alarms, dissolving any extra time she'd cushioned in for going over her presentation for the grant board. Hell, it evaporated the ability to do anything but break out the bath wipes and perform a quick wipe-down of all the important bits. Then, as if lack of hygienics wasn't bad enough, at some point during the big move her comfy commuting shoes had gone AWOL.

Vanished . . . either left in the back of the U-Haul or at her old place, never to be seen again.

But what pushed her over that burrowing-beneath-the-blankets edge was the realization, halfway into her walk to the subway station, that she'd left the thumb drive with her SupeEx presentation on her dresser.

She would've attempted her Grandma Edie's *poof* Magic, but with her level of exhaustion and misfortune, she'd probably end up in Times Square. No New Yorker went there unless under extreme duress or with visiting relatives.

She cursed the forming blister on the back of her left heel as she keyed herself back into the apartment.

Running water echoed from the bathroom, indicating Bax was up.

After the whole dancing thing the previous night, he'd been atypically quiet, even for him. Not that she'd done a whole lot to encourage additional conversation, especially not after thinking—for a few heart-rate-escalating seconds—that he'd been flirting with her right there among their friends.

At the time, she'd sucked down a groan hearing Mason Carlisle's voice interrupting what she'd thought of as *a moment*, but now? No longer under the influence of Bax's soul-stirring eyes and intoxicating leather scent?

She reluctantly admitted the interruption had been for the best. She'd obviously needed an intervention before she did something embarrassing like . . . flirt back.

She could count the times she'd openly flirted with someone on one hand, and it never went well. One guy thought she was blinking through the pain of a stye when she winked, and another assumed she needed to use the bathroom—don't ask. And those were mild embarrassment levels, unlike the other two stories, which she'd take to her grave.

Bax's quiet brood on the train ride home last night had been one angel-sized bullet dodged. Unlike her last roommate, Gina, who never stopped talking, Bax was a man of very few words. Lots of looks, but few words.

Once upon a time, she'd thought that an ideal quality in a roomie, but she now realized that looks left room for a lot of interpretation, and her imagination was just too damn wild not to need some reality-sized boundaries.

"At least something is wild about me . . ." Olive muttered.

She dove into her room and, grabbing the USB drive, gave a quick, longing look to her closet and wished she had time to swap out her top for one that wasn't suctioned to her chest with stress sweat, but rushing against the clock—and her blister—meant there wasn't time for a wardrobe change.

Preoccupied with making the next D train, she didn't register the opening bathroom door until she crashed into the wall of damp man muscle stepping through it.

It wasn't a graceful crash.

On impact, her teeth clamped down on her tongue and her body teetered backward, her ass leading the charge to the floor. "Shit on a broomstick!"

"Whoa." A corded, tattooed arm banded around her waist and pulled her solidly back onto her own two feet.

Nose pushed against a solid wall of yum, Olive felt her heart stumble into a slow restart.

"You okay?" Bax's words ruffled her hair. "You scared the hell out of me, angel. I thought you left twenty minutes ago."

"I came back because I forgot my presentation." With their bodies still pressed together, she slowly registered every inch of the man to whom she was still plastered.

Every. Warm. Inch.

Only her thin linen pantsuit prevented a skin-on-skin rubdown.

"I don't think I'm the only one who forgot something." Eyes rounding behind her glasses, she slowly lifted her gaze to meet his. "Your towel seems to be MIA."

Amusement hooked his lips into a crooked smirk. "It's actually not so MIA. It's puddled around your feet."

"*Oh.*"

"Oh."

"I can get it for you." She shifted, but his grip tightened, keeping her from retrieving the lost towel. "What's wrong?"

He groaned softly, briefly closing his eyes. "Can you not squirm . . . or move? Just . . . give me a minute? Or ten."

"I don't under . . ." The words died on her lips.

An erection the size of a baseball bat, a phenomenon that would've been inches away from her face if she'd bent to get his towel, pressed against her soft abdomen. "Oh."

"Not that I couldn't stay in this exact position forever because I'm obviously enjoying the hell out of our new closeness, but if memory serves me right, you have someplace to be later today."

She gulped audibly. "Uh . . . I do."

His fingers flexed on her back, temporarily pulling her closer before slowly sliding away, leaving a warm tingle in their place. "Fair warning, I'll be stepping back and retrieving my towel."

"You're warning me so I can close my eyes?"

A wave of heat darkened his gaze, turning his two different irises a stormy blue and green. Not wanting to be outdone, her mouth moisture evacuated straight to her panties.

Bax's lips twitched into a mischievous smirk as if scenting her sudden arousal like a freaking shifter. "I'll leave that decision up to you, angel. Although don't avert your eyes for my sake."

Talk about torn between two hard decisions.

Olive's cheeks heated and her survival instincts kicked in. She smacked a hand over her eyes, nearly knocking her glasses off her face in the process. Bax's low chuckle did funny things to her insides.

His damp hair brushed her arm as he retrieved the towel. "All is safe and decent-ish."

She fixed her glasses, her eyes reflexively dipping to his waist, where he had just finished knotting the low-hanging towel. Something distinctly metallic flickered into view before it was abruptly concealed.

Safe? She nearly snortled. That was a matter of opinion, and not one she shared.

A fully clothed Bax endangered dry undies everywhere—

her own case in point. A half-naked Bax with double bar nipple piercings and a loosely knotted towel—which might or might not be shielding her view of additional piercings—needed a flood warning.

Curiosity forced her mouth open. "Did your nipple piercings hurt?"

He glanced at his chest before hitting her with a naughty grin. "Not as much as you'd think, and definitely not as much as it did in other places."

Stick her in a cauldron and turn it on high . . . Did it just get a billion degrees in a single witch-blink?

"You said you forgot something?" he asked, blessedly changing the topic.

She held up the thumb drive still clutched in her palm. "My presentation would've gone up in flames before it began if I didn't have this . . . although I missed the early D train by now, so I guess I didn't avoid the fire entirely."

He glanced at the time. "Yeah, the next one will be a sardine can with everyone heading into Manhattan. Give me five minutes to throw on pants and a shirt and I'll give you a ride to campus. I'm heading that way for a work thing anyway."

"Are you sure?"

"Absolutely. Why deal with stuffy train air when you can have exhaust-fume air in your face? I'll be ready in five."

He was ready in three.

She didn't fully compute his ride offer until he stepped up to his black-and-silver motorcycle a few minutes later and threw her an expectant look.

She hesitated. "So I should probably warn you that the last time I rode astride anything it had three wheels and rainbow tassels."

That damn sexy eyebrow lifted. "I'm sorry to hear that, angel."

She busted out a laugh. "Get your mind out of the gutter, Donovan."

"We'll hoist ours out together since they're evidently keeping each other company." Smirking, he pulled a spare helmet from the bike's back compartment and handed it to her, grin still firmly in place. "If it makes you more comfortable, I could check with a few neighbors to see if anyone has tassels lying around."

"Just get me to work." She rolled her eyes and, looping her bag over her chest, accepted the helmet. It wasn't until Bax easily got onto the bike and waited for her to do the same that she identified a second problem. "How the hex am I supposed to get on this thing?"

Even if she'd opted for the platform shoes in the back of her closet, her short leg span wouldn't give her enough height to clear the seat.

"Do you need a boost?" His lips twitched from behind his helmet's half visor.

She threw him a glare. "Ease it closer to the curb and I'll be just fine."

Maybe.

With a chuckle, he rolled the bike up three feet, the curb giving her a few more inches with which to work. With a prayer to the Goddess and a small boost of Magic for extra flexibility, she anchored a hand on Bax's broad shoulder and hoped for the best. One left-leg swing later and she sat on the back of a motorcycle.

Give her a patched-up leather jacket and call her Biker Bwitch.

Bax wrapped his hands around her outer thighs, above her knees, and tugged her flush against his back. "There we go. We wouldn't want you flying off at the first turn. Hold on tight and lean into the movements like I do. Don't fight it."

She nodded, even though he couldn't see her, and wrapped her arms tight around his waist, her cheek pillowed against his back.

Being molded against the Guardian Angel beat being plastered to sweaty strangers on the subway, but it also meant an entire commute debating if she'd really seen—and felt—a cock piercing, or if Harper's imagination was simply contagious.

After the first few turns, she forgot about personal jewelry and lost herself in the sights of the surrounding city and the rumbling sway of the bike. She didn't know why Rose hated riding behind Damian. If anything, she felt freer than she had since she could remember. So much so that when they hit a short expanse of straight road, she unleashed her grip around Bax's waist and did a short spell of no-hands.

She giggled, wiggling her fingers through the breeze, until the angel's attention pulled away from the road, and one of his hands recaptured one of hers and returned it to his waist.

"Let's make sure you actually live to make your presentation, okay, angel?"

A few minutes later, they pulled up to the curb in front of the R. H. Kline Humanities Building.

Bax's hand glided over hers in a gentle caress, and her Magic sparked, shocking them both. "Sorry . . . my Magic seems a little out of sorts. Guess it liked the ride, too."

"Then we can do it again anytime. But for now, the special package is delivered safe and sound."

Olive climbed off the back as limberly as she could, fully aware of both students and teachers stopping to give them second and third looks. She had no delusions about who they were staring at.

Bax Donovan commanded the attention of anyone in his proximity whether he meant to or not. Unfortunately, that meant her go-under-the-radar modus operandi had gone up in a puff of six-foot-plus Harley-riding Guardian Angel smoke.

"Thanks for the ride. You're officially my Guardian Angel." She handed him back the helmet, a jolt of awareness sparking as his fingers brushed over the back of her hands. If he felt it again, he didn't say.

"Not a problem. Call me if you need a ride back." He pushed a wayward lock of hair off her cheek. "And knock 'em dead with your presentation."

"Thanks."

With a head nod and a roar of his engine, he pulled back into traffic, gifting her a little wave.

Olive ignored the continued stares and, after flattening the wrinkles in her pantsuit, headed toward the building. She'd barely reached the front doors when Mason fell into step beside her.

"Long time no see, stranger." The history department head flashed her a megawatt smile that could've starred in a toothpaste commercial. "I enjoyed spending some time together last night. I'm glad I listened to that little voice telling me to step into that kitschy little dump."

Olive kept a polite smile on her face. "I wouldn't call Potion's kitschy . . . or a dump. Gage has done a lot with the place over the years."

"Oh, I don't mean that in a bad way," Mason quickly redirected.

"You think calling something a dump is good?"

He laughed, the noise grating on her nerves a bit. When he'd interrupted her dance with Bax, she'd been more than a little annoyed, and then he hadn't gotten the hint when she told him she was there with her sisters and friends.

Being the youngest department head in the history of the college didn't come without those who thought she didn't deserve the title, but when most faculty had snubbed her, Mason had been one of the first professors to befriend her.

They'd met while on a committee designated to help freshman undergrads fit into college life, and while they'd gone out a few times, the dates had been simply *okay*. She hadn't felt *it*.

That spark that connected two people.

Like the one between Vi and Linc, and Rose and Damian. The one with the ability to scorch your entire being just by standing near the other person. With Mason, there hadn't even been a risk of a minor sunburn.

"You're later this morning than I thought you'd be, with the grant board and everything," Mason pointed out casually. "I thought you'd be here early running through things."

"I missed my usual train, so I had to improvise."

"With someone on a motorcycle? I walked up when it pulled to the curb. The driver looked like that guy from the bar last night." Mason's tone seemed deceptively light.

She shot him a side-eye and kept walking. "*That guy* happens to be my roommate, and he was nice enough to give me a ride this morning because taking the train would've been a disaster."

Mason chuckled. "Ah. That makes more sense, and sounds like the Olive we all know and love. I heard a few people whisper tall tales about you going all biker chic."

She bristled at his words but stayed focused as she reached her classroom and unlocked the door for the few students already waiting in the hall. She nodded her hellos to each person as they entered.

"So are you ready for the big presentation?" Mason asked.

"As ready as I'll ever be."

"There's no way they won't award you the grant money. It's a great idea."

"Yeah, but I'm sure mine isn't the only good idea, and I know I'm definitely not the only one vying for it." Olive said hello to a few more students as they passed by her. "Celeste Fitz literally salivated when she informed me she was throwing her hat in the ring, too, and let me tell you, it's eerie watching a vampire foam at the mouth."

Mason waved a dismissive hand, the move sloshing his cup of coffee. "What the hell does the math department need with that kind of money? It's not like they can discover new ways to teach one plus one equals two."

"Actually, math linked to NASA and the space program is always—"

Mason shot her a look.

"You're right," she agreed. "I just hope the board sees the same need for a program like SupeEx as I do."

"They will," Mason said supportively. "You've done the research. You've supplied all the supporting facts. It has a hell of a lot of merit."

It did, and there was a drastic need for something like it, but SupeEx wouldn't produce immediate, measurable results. It was a long-haul project, her version of study abroad, except instead of students studying in other countries, they'd experience other Supernatural societies.

The common factor in every Supernatural war throughout history? No one understood one another, feeding off hearsay and stereotypes manufactured from Hollywood movies. People feared what they didn't understand, and when fear guided people's actions, bad things happened.

Edie had told Olive and her sisters some pre-Reveal stories that made *The Shining* seem like a preschool fairy tale, and she was determined to make sure history didn't repeat itself.

To give SupeEx a fighting chance, she needed ammunition to plead her case, and today's class lecture was the first step to procurement.

"Thanks for the escort to class, but . . ." She gestured to the waiting students.

"Oh yeah. Sure. Well . . . if I don't see you before your meeting, good luck. But I'm sure you won't need it," Mason added.

She thanked him and closed the door. Dropping her things on the lectern, she turned to the tired faces of her waiting class. "I was about to say I have a dose of Monday blues, but you lot appear to have it worse than me."

"Are you canceling class so we can get caught up on our very important Z's?" A junior, one of her more outspoken students, spoke up, a charming smirk plastered on his face.

"Oh, Omar Khan . . . your love of fantasy is as refreshing today as it was the first day you stepped into my class."

Students chuckled as she brought the day's lecture up on the smart screen behind her.

"The Supernatural Reveal . . . and the impact that stepping out of the shadows had on the world. Who can tell me about it?"

Hands immediately lifted into the air.

"And more than 'It was the beginning of Supernaturals coming out to human society'?"

A few hands dropped, making her chuckle.

She loved higher education . . . young people with views and ideals, prepped to debate hot-button topics. As always, her students didn't let her down, a few engaging in a wholehearted back-and-forth on whether the Reveal should've been handled differently, and how.

A sophomore witch from the back row glared at Omar, sitting in a front-row aisle seat. "The very definition of change is to do something different. Stepping outside of usual norms is how people evolve, and it's closed-minded thinking the Reveal would've happened regardless."

"I'm just saying that all secrets eventually come out . . . at least mine do," Omar joked.

A few students chuckled, but not the petite witch. "Prior to the Reveal, Supernaturals stayed safely within the confines of their own shadows—a secret—for hundreds and thousands of years. It wouldn't have just *leaked*."

"Social media and freaking security cameras weren't on every block a hundred years ago. Look, I'm not saying that the Reveal shouldn't have happened. But maybe instead of some great big *True Blood*–esque sideshow, an organic approach would've worked better."

The sophomore girl snortled. "Know when an organic approach last happened?"

"Uh, never?"

"The Salem witch trials," she corrected. "Maybe you've heard of it. Throughout history, humans have shown over and over that they're resistant to change regardless of whether it's planned or organic, so why not control the narrative? Or at least attempt it?"

He shrugged. "That makes a small bit of sense, I'll give you that."

"Oh, you will? Gee. Thank you."

"You're welcome." Omar flashed the young student a wink from across the room.

Smiling at the antics, Olive raised her hand, regaining control of the class. "Iliana and Omar may have slightly different views, but those views have one underlying commonality. People—in general—resist change. Humans. Supernaturals. Animals. Creatures of habit come in all shapes, sizes, and pairings. It's why shifters build packs and witches create covens. There's comfort in remaining within a boundary you presume safe . . . but what happens when we step out from that safe space and enter someone else's?"

She flicked her smart screen to the next image. "Which brings me to your term project."

The Dare I Docket.

"What is the Dare I Docket, you ask? I'm about to tell you. In short-answer form, it's your life over the next few weeks. In a slightly longer answer, it's a self-exploration trip meant to show you exactly what happens when you step out of your comfort zone."

She signaled to her teaching assistant, and the grad student immediately passed out the packets.

"On the very first page, you'll find a pre-assessment tool that's designed to help you identify your experiences, strengths, and weaknesses."

Omar snorted. "So our term project is a *Cosmo* quiz?"

A few students chuckled.

Olive smirked. "You're part of Zeta Psi, correct?"

"Go ZP!" he shouted in response.

"You're a junior. You've been involved with the same fraternity, I'm assuming, since your freshman year. The house on Greek Row is almost as familiar to you as the one in which you grew up. It's *home*. Right?"

"Damn straight. ZP is my family for life."

She nodded. "What if I told you to pack up your room and move into the Kappa Sigma house down the street?"

"Uh . . ." The student shifted awkwardly in his seat.

"Would you be as comfortable there as you were at ZP?"

"No, because it's not my . . ." His voice trailed off. "Ah. I see where you're going with this. Point made, Professor Maxwell. Point made."

"I'm so glad." Olive chuckled. "After taking the pre-assessment, you'll do a write-up of your findings and use them to create your *individual* Dare I Docket, a list of no more than ten ways you plan on broadening your comfort zones. If it's something you'd do without hesitation, it doesn't belong on your list. I'd like for all of you to dig deep on this, okay? But remember, deep doesn't mean *big*."

Iliana's hand rose. "What if we can't think of ten things?"

"List as many as you comfortably can, and don't feel as though you need a completed Docket before beginning to stretch your boundaries. Life is spontaneous, and if you're out and about and doing your thing, and find yourself staring into something that would be a great fit for your list, then great! Add it." She slid her gaze slowly over her class, making certain she had everyone's attention. "This project isn't meant to induce stress. I meant it when I said deep doesn't mean big. And if anyone feels they can't comfortably complete this assignment, see me. We'll come up with an alternative."

Omar lifted his hand. "So if we put streaking through Times Square on our list . . . ?"

She fought to withhold a chuckle. "Read and memorize the rules page, Omar. No breaking of laws . . . human or Supernatural."

"Well, damn . . ."

The class laughed.

Olive tried catching more than a few gazes. "Keep in mind that the Supernatural Reveal was a huge leap into the unknown. The Dare I Docket is meant to guide you into a more personal hop. Complete as many items as you comfortably can and perform the attached post-assessment. I look forward to reading your thoughts and your conclusions regarding comfort zones."

She pushed a smile onto her face, hoping like hell it looked more confident than she felt. "And for full transparency, results will be shared with the school's grant board, but kept confidential and turned from qualitative data into quantitative. Does anyone have any questions?"

Met with silence, she dismissed the class, and as with any assignment, the Docket inspired a few grumbles among the class as they packed up. Not everyone embraced change—or could, especially when the "normal" way of doing things has served them so well. She just hoped everyone came out from the other side realizing that expanding horizons weren't always a bad thing . . . or scary.

With her first class out of her way, Olive packed up her things and pulled her flash drive from the computer. A hearty clap from the back of the lecture hall snapped her head up. It didn't take good eyesight to see Harper.

"Well done, Professor." Harp grinned. "You almost make me want to go back to school."

"That would require actually showing up for classes and stuff."

The sex demon wrinkled her nose, meeting her by the door. "Which is exactly why I said *almost*. Where you off to now? Wanna grab a coffee before your big presentation?"

"I'm a little too keyed up for coffee, but I could go for a chamomile tea."

"Then let's do it." Harper threaded her arm through hers, and they hung a left toward the student coffee shop.

"So what brings you all the way out here?" Olive asked.

"I knew you were stressed out about your big presentation, and since Vi and Rose are stuck doing badass witch things, I figured I'd act the part of backup sister."

Olive hugged her friend's arm a little tighter. "You're not a backup anything, Harp. You may not have been in the womb with us, but you're our sister all the same."

"Aww, make a demon blush, why don't you." A coy look slid onto her face, her red lips twitching. "So if I'm the fourth Maxwell sister, does that make Bax a brother?"

"No," Olive said too quickly, playing right into the succubus's hands.

"No?" Mischief twinkled in her eyes.

"With Bax, it's . . . different. I mean, he's definitely part of the group, but he's too . . ."

"Aloof? Closed-off?" Harper asked, finishing her sentence. "Broodingly distant?"

"Let's go for that one."

And stay far, far away from any mention of Bax being like a brother or any kind of family member . . . especially after this morning.

They rounded the last corner before the coffee shop, and standing just outside the café with a small group of professors—Mason included—was Celeste Fitz.

The math head's unmistakable laugh sounded above the low thrum of college background noise. "Tell me someone else finds it ironic that someone who clearly has a Monday-Wednesday-Friday outfit, and continually wears the same brand of shoes, gives students a project revolving around new experiences."

The group chuckled, but it was Mason who added, "Maybe Olive should make her own Dare I Docket and do the project with her students."

Her colleagues all laughed again.

Winston, one of the American government professors, bumped into his shoulder, a teasing smirk on his face. "How do you spend as much time with Maxwell as you do without falling asleep?"

Mason's smile grew. "A guy can only take so much heart-pounding action before craving the mundane and expected."

Mundane . . . expected . . . aka *boring*.

Harper hurled javelin-sharp glares the group's way as Olive, giving them a wide berth, dragged her through the coffee shop's side door. "It's okay. It's fine."

Harper shot her a disbelieving look. "I'm usually one hundred percent happy with being a succubus, but right now I really wish I could witch up some warts and pigs' tails. The ringleader was a vampire, right? How about a tooth abscess right under her canines?"

"They're entitled to their opinions, which I'm likely unable to change even if I wanted to . . . which I don't. Plus, they're coworkers. I see these people every day. Sometimes it's best not to rock the boat."

Harper's frown deepened. "Well, I don't work with these people, which means I can not only rock the damn boat but attach weighted shoes to their feet and push them overboard."

The succubus's protectiveness had her squeezing her friend's hand. "Love the enthusiasm, Harp, but not worth the jail time. Witch's honor."

"Guess we'll have to agree to disagree."

Despite insisting it was no big deal, Mason's and Celeste's words played on an echoing loop in Olive's head. It wasn't even that they'd hurt, although Mason jumping on the wagon did sting a little.

What annoyed her the most was that in an hour, she'd be pleading her case for the SupeEx Project to a group of people notorious for keeping the university's money under literal lock and key, and now they'd put doubt in her head about the project's viability.

She couldn't afford distractions, and she sure as hell couldn't afford to second-guess herself. It fueled her determination to get it done and show Mason and the others exactly what a teacher with a Monday-Wednesday-Friday outfit could do.

5

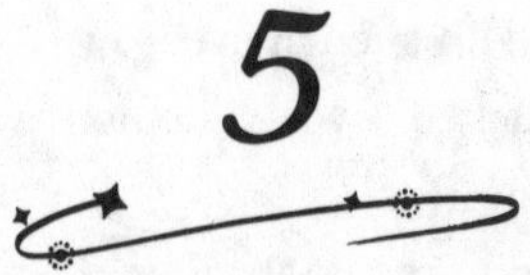

She with the Sweaty-Demon-Ass Day

Olive glanced up at the building that had at one time housed the Magical Massage and Health Clinic, her mother's go-to full-body massage destination, and hesitated. There wasn't a sign of the former business—*literally*.

A window once adorned with oversized images of people in white fluffy robes and cucumber glasses was now dubbed the SMASH-N-CRASH: WHERE YOU CAN SMASH AWAY YOUR FRUSTRATIONS.

"I'm not sure about this, Harp." Olive peered into the window, the lobby inside looking much like any other business with a welcome desk and a small waiting room tucked to the left. "Maybe we could get some ice cream or start happy hour a bit early. Not . . . this."

Harper propped her hands on her hips. "*This* is exactly what you need."

"To smash-n-crash things?"

"To destroy shit in a safe environment where you don't worry about the cleanup. Honestly, I can't believe we haven't dragged you to a rage room before now."

If Vi knew about them, she probably would have because this without a doubt screamed Violet.

"Look," Harper said, taking her hands. "Today sucked sweaty demon ass, right?"

Olive tried not thinking about her grant presentation and the board's total lack of enthusiasm for the SupeEx Project. "It definitely could've been better."

The redhead cocked an auburn eyebrow.

"Okay. Yeah, it sucked sweaty demon ass . . . complete with persistent fungal rash."

"This"—she pointed to the door to Smash-n-Crash—"is a way to go *ahhhhh* without destroying your own stuff, or getting arrested for destroying things owned by other people. Let's try it. If you're still not feeling it after the first few swings, we'll leave and get ice cream."

She glanced to the building and back. "A few swings?"

Harper held up three fingers. "Scout's honor."

She snortled. "I distinctly remember you telling me your parents wouldn't let you join the Scouts for fear all that community and togetherness would rub off on you." The succubus's mischievous grin told Olive her friend wasn't about to give up. "Fine. Three swings and then we're getting some soft serve . . . with extra rainbow sprinkles."

"Hells yeah." Harper pumped her fist and dragged her through the front door.

Fifteen minutes and a forest's worth of signed waivers later, it was almost time to smash-n-crash. Decked out in fashionable overalls, protective hard hats, and goggles, Olive followed Harper and their instructor to the designated smash room, a rubber mallet the size of her arm clenched in her hands.

"This is it." The Smash-n-Crash worker opened the door and ushered them into the room.

It was set up like any office in the city, with computers and printers on two desks, and a cluttered array of small objects, some glass. Pictures decorated the walls, and fake potted plants tucked into the corner brought an outside look indoors.

"So what do we do?" Olive looked around, still unsure.

The instructor grinned at her hesitancy. "You let it all out. Once I close the door, you'll have fifteen minutes to destroy anything and everything in sight . . . except each other. The boss frowns on that."

"The computers . . ."

"Smash 'em."

"And chairs? The desk?"

"Pulverize them into wood chips. Your crash time starts the second I close the door. Happy smashing!" He walked out, leaving her and Harper alone in the room.

Loud rock music blared from one of the high-mounted speakers, and the digital clock in the corner immediately lit up and began its countdown.

"Let's smash-n-crash some shit, babe." Harper tugged her protective goggles over her eyes and grinned wide. "First-swing honors goes to She with the Sweaty-Demon-Ass Day. That computer monitor is screaming to be pulverized, Maxwell. Do your worst."

Olive approached the desk hesitantly, not believing she was about to do this, and nudged the monitor with the end of the mallet until it toppled.

"Seriously? You have more in you than that." Stepping up to the second desk, Harper assumed a batter's position and swung—hard. Her mallet connected with a printer and it flew off the desk, smashing against the wall before raining to the floor in multiple parts. "Damn, that felt good."

"I can't believe you did that!" Olive glanced at the door, half expecting the worker to come in and start yelling at them.

Harper chuckled. "Don't make me have all the fun alone, Olly. Smash. Shit."

It really did look like she'd enjoyed it . . .

Olive glanced back to the computer in front of her and, assuming her own batter's stance, tightened her grip on her mallet. "Here goes nothing . . ."

She swung. On contact, the screen spiderwebbed into hundreds of pieces. Harper hooted in encouragement and Olive laughed, getting into position to do it again. More bits flew. Glass. Wood. Tech. All of it.

With each swing, her frustrations melted away a little more. Snooty Celeste. Backstabbing Mason. The board. Whiny students. She pounded it all into smithereens, and after fifteen minutes, she was sweaty, breathless, and grinning ear to ear, dropping to the floor in a fit of giggles.

"Admit that was epic." Harper bumped her shoulder, wiping a drop of sweat off her chin. "Go on. I'll wait for the *Harper, you're a fucking genius. I will never again question your brilliant ideas.*"

Looking around at the mess they made, she chuckled. "That was pretty damn cool . . . and definitely *not* boring."

"Definitely not." Harper smiled wanly, a hint of seriousness slipping onto her face. "You know they're all assholes, right? The entire lot of them. They're *jealous* assholes . . . because you're smarter and have accomplished more in your thirty-four years than they could have ever dreamed."

"Maybe, but they're not entirely wrong." She leaned back against the wall with a heavy sigh. "I have a Monday-Wednesday-Friday outfit and an insatiable love of Vans. Not only that, but on Mondays I wear blue. Wednesdays are green. And Fridays are typically my pink or red day. I'm predictable."

"So what? I'm addicted to bullet vibrators, and every morning before I climb out of bed, I start my day with a vibrator-induced smile. Does that make me predictable?"

"Actually, yes. If it happens *every* morning, that's pretty much the definition of predictable." She grinned. "I don't expect someone like you to get it, Harp. You're so open. You thrive on uncertainty and experiencing new things. Like this rage room. This kind of place would've never popped onto my radar if it weren't for you."

"Olly . . ."

She shook her head, silencing her friend's brewing denials. "I love you for sticking up for me, but they weren't entirely wrong.

I shouldn't expect my students to step out of their comfort zones while I remain firmly planted within mine."

Harper fell silent, a rare phenomenon for the succubus. The quiet brought a swirl of thoughts racing through Olive's mind, but one familiar one kept sneaking its way back, over and over.

"I need to do the project with them," she admitted aloud.

"The Docket thing?" The redhead studied her carefully.

She nodded. "I need to perform my own pre-assessment, build my own list. I need to step outside my safety bubble."

"Is that something you really want to do? I mean, it's not exactly something you—"

"Would normally be up for? Yeah. I think that's kind of the point." She thought about riding on the back of Bax's motorcycle, about her hesitancy slipping easily into *look, no hands* after a few blocks. "I think this is something that needs to happen. I think I need to do it."

Harper got to her feet with a groan before sticking her hand out and helping Olive do the same. "Then do it. Take a walk on the wild side and see where it takes you. Shake things up until they fall around you."

She chuckled, Harper's excitement fueling her own. "I'm not sure about shaking them . . . but tilting them is a definite possibility."

And if not able to send them into a full tilt, she'd settle for a little quiver that jolted them off their dust ring.

✦ ✦ ✦

Hollywood got practically everything wrong about the Supernatural community. Vampires didn't sparkle unless they'd recently rolled around in a vat of pixie dust. Full moons only provided shifters an excuse for stupidity. And water splashed on a witch didn't turn them into a pile of slimy green goo.

One thing they'd gotten correct?

Angels fucking loved the color white. At the GAA, there was no escaping it. It was everywhere. Walls? White granite. Floors? White marble, with a speck of swirled pearl gray. Artwork? You guessed it. White stone.

Within two minutes of stepping into the HQ offices, Bax contemplated clawing out his eyes or, at the very least, breaking into the building after hours and taking a can of red spray paint to everything.

As if sensing his deviant thoughts, Patrick, the Guardian Commissioner's assistant, glanced up from his computer screen, his deep frown elongating his already narrow face.

"What?" Bax feigned innocence. "How could I possibly deserve that look? I've literally done nothing but sit here like a good Guardian Angel for the last hour and a half."

The fifty-something British angel rolled his eyes. "Guardians who frequent this office as often as you, Baxter Donovan, haven't done *nothing*."

"Maybe the Commissioner likes me. Ever think of that?"

"Commissioner Wright doesn't like anyone."

There was probably no truer statement ever spoken.

A buzz sounded from Pat's desk.

"Is he here?" The Commissioner's abrupt voice cut through the waiting room.

Patrick's eyes flicked up to Bax. "Yes, Commissioner Wright. Would you like me to send him in?"

"Yes. I haven't got all day. Let's get this over with."

"You heard the boss." Patrick nudged his chin to the white door. "She's ready for you . . . and may the odds be ever in your favor."

Getting up from his seat, he cocked an eyebrow. "Quoting popular fiction now? The depth of your pop culture knowledge never ceases to amaze me. Next you'll knock me over by admitting that you're a *Housewives* addict."

"I have many layers," the other man joked dryly. "But *The Bachelor* is more my thing."

Bax stood outside the Commissioner's closed door and prepped himself for the upcoming tongue-lashing. He'd run through all his normal excuses earlier that morning and used the time in the waiting room to drum up a few more. But he wouldn't put any of them into rotation because he didn't give a damn, tired of constantly defending himself and his actions.

"Get in here, Donovan!" Commissioner Wright bellowed through the door. "I have things to do and messes to clean up."

With a straightening of his spine, he stepped into the office. "Good morning, Commissioner. Did you miss me as much as I missed you?"

His joke fell flat, run over by the Mack Truck that was the third person in the room.

Standing next to the Commissioner's desk, his thick arms folded across his chest, stood Mikael Donovan. *His father.*

His Royal Badass dragging himself off the front lines of the war against rogue hellions didn't give Bax baby-kitten feels. The Warrior Angel lived and breathed solely to perform his job to the best of his ability. He didn't do family. Or vacations. And definitely not family vacations.

His father being present meant that more than an additional smudge on Bax's record was on the line.

"Baxter." His face void of any emotion, Mikael gifted him the slightest acknowledgment. "Call your mother sooner rather than later. It's her opinion that your last one was too long ago."

In *her* opinion. In his father's, it probably hadn't been long enough.

"I'll do that later today." Bax shifted his attention to Commissioner Wright. "I was notified that you wanted to see me, ma'am?"

"Have a seat, Guardian Donovan."

His gaze flickered to his still-standing father and the two empty seats. "I'm partial to standing, but thank you."

"Very well. I won't waste either of our time by sugarcoating things. Your last two Assignments ended in less-than-ideal circumstances, and the one prior was successful only by an extremely thin margin." Her golden-eyed gaze lasered into him, watching him for any reaction. "Do you have an explanation for your sudden affliction? You previously had no issues, and for quite a while were considered one of our top Guardians. What's changed?"

He shrugged. "I'm not aware that anything has."

Except his threshold for dealing with people's bullshit had lowered drastically. If someone wanted to do something stupid, who was he to stop them?

The Commissioner's lips pursed, obviously not thrilled with his answer. "My initial intention during today's meeting was to put you on administrative leave and possibly send you back to the academy for some obviously needed refresher courses."

Oh, fuck no. "Ma'am, I don't think—"

"Particularly, Guardian Basics 101." She drilled him with a hard look. "However, staffing shortages and increased workloads make that plan unfeasible. If you can believe it, having a Guardian with your colorful track record in the field is more beneficial than not having one at all."

He blinked, fighting to contain his shock as he attempted to catch up. No demotion. No firing. "So that means . . . ?"

Wright sighed unhappily. "That means, Guardian Donovan, you can consider yourself under heavily monitored probation. But one misstep . . . one slight bend of a rule . . . and you'll be stripped of your Guardian status and disaffiliated with the GAA."

"I'm not sure what to say."

"I suggest you say thank you to your father for convincing me your skills are better served in the field during our time of crisis."

Bax barely suppressed a snort. The day he thanked his father for anything would be the day hell froze over and Lucifer himself started giving ski lessons. Remaining employed by the GAA wasn't necessarily a good thing.

"*And* consider this your last dance." Commissioner Wright pushed a manila Assignment file across her desk, indicating with a chin-nod for him to take it.

"What's this?" He pulled the file closer.

"A new Assignment that popped onto the Angel Risk Surveyor's radar not even a few hours ago."

His brow lifted. "And you're already assigning them a Guardian detail? Doesn't the ARS usually keep an eye on them for a while before utilizing Guardian resources? If we're as short-staffed as you say, I'm not certain this makes sense."

Mikael growled, "It's not your place to question the Commissioner's reasons. What you should do is thank her for not kicking your sorry ass onto the streets."

Bax clenched his jaw, not taking his father's bait. "I was curious, not questioning."

"And you're right," Wright admitted. "Under normal circumstances, we'd keep an eye on things from afar until intervention was clearly needed, but this case is a little too high-profile for us to sit on and see what happens. It requires a hands-on approach, not to mention a discreet one."

He disliked the sound of this more with every word out of the Commissioner's mouth.

"I can't stress this enough, Donovan. No rule-bending. If you screw this Assignment up, the GAA won't be the only one who kicks you out onto your ass."

"May I?" He gestured to the file he'd yet to open.

"By all means."

Both the Commissioner's and Mikael's eyes remained fixed on him as he opened the dossier to the first page and froze. A wedding ice sculpture had more movement than he did in that moment.

One class in which he'd excelled at the Angel Academy had been schooling emotions. It was the only reason he didn't fling out a string of volatile curses.

Dead center. Page one. Smiling shyly at the camera, her pink lips pulled up into a sweet smile with which he'd become all too familiar . . . was Olive.

Fuck me with a case of angel mange.

Mikael's eyes narrowed at Olly's picture. "Nothing to say? Maybe the slightest bit of thanks for Commissioner Wright trusting that you'll do good by the Prima's granddaughter?"

Bax finally reined in his emotions. "Are you sure the ARS got this right?"

Wright shot him a curious smirk. "Would you like to question them yourself? I can call them into the office right now."

"No, ma'am . . ." Those were some scary-ass angels. "But full disclosure: I already have a relationship with the Assignment."

"A romantic one?"

He paused, and hell if he knew why. Yeah, there'd been more than a few times when he envisioned himself kissing her—and more. And he sure as hell didn't like the idea of her flirting with Professor Smarmy.

But did they have a romantic relationship?

No. At least not anywhere that wasn't in his wildest fantasies.

"She's a friend," he reluctantly answered, "and, as of two days ago, my roommate."

Wright stood, her tone of voice indicating the matter closed. "I would think that makes your job of keeping her out of harm's way a lot easier. No reason to question your sudden increased presence."

Unease twisted his gut as he glanced at Olive's file.

"There's no official rule saying an Assignment can't know you're a Guardian, Donovan," she said pointedly. "They just can't be aware you're *their* Guardian. Keep Olive Maxwell alive, make sure no one catches feelings, and you're good to go. Any questions? Concerns? No? Then you're free to leave."

"Yes, ma'am." Bax turned toward the door.

"Donovan!" Wright called out.

He paused. "Commissioner?"

"Don't drop the ball this time, or you'll face a lot more than loss of income. The Prima isn't someone on whose bad side you want to find yourself."

"Trust me, I'm aware." He'd seen firsthand the lengths the Prima went to protect those she cared about.

Determined to get out of HQ before Mikael caught up to him, Bax took the emergency stairs and hustled toward the lobby exit. Three feet from freedom, his father's familiar growl roared his name.

Passing angels shot curious looks their way, but Bax ignored them, turning toward the Warrior storming in his direction.

"Another botched Assignment, Baxter?" Disappointment lined every inch of Mikael's face. "And what meaningless distraction hijacked your attention this time?"

"No distractions. The Guardian Rules of Conduct emphasize an Assignment's free will . . . or was that little footnote amended without me realizing it?" He didn't bother curbing his smart-assedness. If anything, his father's holier-than-thou demeaner threw fuel onto his smart-ass fire. "That Riley kid and his friends were hell-bent on taking that trip to the wild side. No one could've anticipated the tainted gargoyle dust."

"*You* should have," Mikael snapped.

"That's not how Guardianship works. I'm not gifted in premonition. There's no telling what will end in injury and what will lead to one hell of a bragging right."

"This is not a joking matter. You have no idea the strings I had to pull to get you one more chance. *This* chance."

Bax stepped closer, refusing to back down. "I didn't ask for special treatment. This time or any other."

"Are you really so content failing that this doesn't bother you?"

"Let's face it, Mikael. In your eyes, I failed the moment I left Warrior Academy. Short of entering an alternate dimension, there *is* no way to earn your favor. Not that I'd want it here, there, or anywhere. Ever."

"Feelings aside, you can't shirk this responsibility, or take Wright's warning lightly. Not even to spite me."

He scoffed. "News flash. I don't think about you—or care enough—to spite you. And as much of a screwup as you think I am, I wouldn't fuck with someone's life just to make you look bad. Not my worst enemy's . . . and sure as hell not someone I care about. We done here? Good."

Not waiting for a response, Bax pushed his way through the exit. The second he hit the sidewalk, the vast city colors assaulted his eyes. "Well, that fucking happened."

He'd expected a lecture and a reprimand from the Commissioner. Maybe even a suspension in which to "think on his actions." But being appointed the Guardian of a petite blond witch with whom he shared a bedroom wall definitely hadn't been on today's agenda.

He'd already been having difficulty convincing himself to keep his hands—and his dirty, very un-roommate-like thoughts—to himself. Now that she was his Assignment, it became even more imperative he keep things platonic.

No naked apartment collisions.

No sexy shuffle-dancing.

And definitely no jealous sulking over warm, untouched beers . . . even if it involved Professor Smarmy himself.

Bax snorted before he mentally tacked on the last NO item. He could add as many as he wanted, but it didn't make it any more likely that he'd follow them. As a matter of fact, he knew he wouldn't.

He was well and truly fucked, and not in a good way.

6

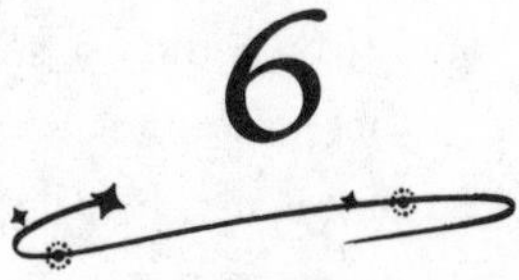

Rabid Raccoons

Edie's cozy cottage in Athens, New York, always provided Olive comfort. It was where she and her sisters had learned Magic basics, including conjuring their first hex on an unsuspecting—but totally deserving—teenage Lincoln. It was where she developed a fondness for stove-top hot chocolate and a pure love for books.

She arrived at her gran's hoping that sitting on the patio and listening to the steady flow of the river would bring her enough clarity to figure out her Docket list. Tallying ten things that weren't in her safety bubble should be easy-peasy for someone whose bubble could've been created from a child's bubble-wand. A bubble that small couldn't fit a whole hell of a lot, which meant everything else was fair game.

In three hours, all she'd accomplished was shifting from her left ass cheek to her right and decorating the page with doodles of toothless puppies. They weren't even good doodles . . . or very puppy-like, the sketched creatures resembling something Rose could encounter in the New York sewer system rather than at Mari's Animal Sanctuary.

With a weary sigh, she drew her thick thermal blanket tighter around her shoulders and snuggled deeper into the Adirondack chair. At this rate, she'd give herself a failing grade on her own project, and wouldn't Celeste and Mason's entourage have a field day with that?

Edie stepped out onto the porch, two mugs of steaming beverages in her hands. "I thought you could use a little pick-me-up, and I put some elderberries in there for a little stress relief."

Olive accepted the tea with a small smile. "Is that a subtle way of asking if something is bothering me?"

Edie's lips twitched. "You know I don't like prying, but now that you mention it, you do seem rather glum. I have it on good authority that I'm a fairly decent problem solver. I attribute it to all the strategy board games I played with my siblings growing up."

As far as grannies went, Olive and her sisters had hit the jackpot. Fiercely badass and more protective than a mated shifter, the octogenarian would do anything for her family. She meddled, but respected boundaries, and never pushed her granddaughters to follow anyone's path but their own.

Her favorite axiom—*Let your Magic guide you*—suited pretty much every occasion or dilemma. Except this one. All Olive's Magic was guiding her toward was expanding her doodling portfolio.

"Let me follow a wild hunch . . . It has something to do with that blank page you've been staring at for the last few hours." Edie slowly sipped her tea.

"My students' term project is about stepping out of comfort zones," she admitted.

"Great things can happen when someone steps into the unknown, but that doesn't mean it's not a scary inch . . . or a horrifying couple of feet."

"Exactly. And if it weren't for the Supernaturals that came before us and their decision to step out from the safety of the shadows, no one could live openly as they do today." She let out a sigh of frustration. "The Docket list was meant to bring home the importance of continuous change."

"Ah . . . the Reveal. Now those were a few million frightening inches of forward movement."

"What made you and the others decide that *then* was the right time? Why not five years earlier? Or ten years later?"

Edie paused, looking deep in thought. "There wasn't one inciting incident that made us go, *Ah, yes . . . now.* A buildup of events and of personal situations were more instigating factors. At the time, the Supernatural community had what I refer to as a fragile alliance. Violence temporarily ceased. Groups that had never gotten along struck truces and signed treaties. I still don't know if it all happened from sheer exhaustion or a true desire for change, but there was a widespread quiet that had never before been achieved and, as irony would have it, at a time when the world beyond was drowning in chaos and fear. Easing those fires, too, felt like the only right thing to do."

"Did you worry about it blowing up in your faces?" Olive asked, curious.

"Absolutely . . . but change always comes with a certain degree of risk because it's never before been experienced. You must decide if the benefits outweigh the possible downfall." Edie studied her carefully, grinning teasingly. "Are you planning to stage another Reveal for this term project? Because I have a few things I probably would've done differently if given the chance."

Chuckling, she flashed her grandma her non-puppy-infested page. "Only an Olive Maxwell Reveal, and you can tell how well that's going. I knew this assignment wouldn't be easy, but I didn't anticipate *this* level of difficulty. I'm thirty minutes away from jotting *Run away to the circus* just so that I have something written."

Edie laughed, her eyes glinting in the dimming sunset. "Now wouldn't that be a fun experience. Perhaps you should write that down."

She snorted. "Oh yeah. I'm sure NYU would have absolutely nothing to say about me taking a leave of absence so I can attend clown college."

"With how much you and your sisters loved swinging on the monkey bars when you were little, I'd think something in the aerial arts would be more your speed." Edie grinned.

"I did always enjoy the trapeze . . . and have you seen more recent acts with the silk ribbons and hoops?"

Her grandma nodded toward her notebook. "There you go. Item number one."

Olive glanced at her empty Docket. "I can't seriously write that down."

"Why not? Is it something you've thought about doing? Would you consider it out of your comfort zone?"

"Becoming a circus performer would be out of a lot of people's comfort zones." She chuckled.

"Then you answered your own question, my dear." Leaning closer, Edie picked up the pen hooked on her notebook and tucked it into her hand. "One thing I hope you and your sisters will remember long after I'm no longer meddling in your affairs is that you create your own destiny. Fate sometimes thinks she's got it all in the bag, but she's got nothing on an individual's internal Magic. Witch or not. When the Magic stirs, what made it do so is within your reach. You only ought to follow it."

Olive set her pen to the empty page, a small smile flirting on her lips. "You really should cross-stitch these words of wisdom, Gran. But let's not talk about when you're no longer meddling. That won't be happening for a long, long time."

Her gran planted a kiss on the top of her head. "I'll leave you to your list-making, but there's a storm brewing from the north, so don't be long. While you're more than welcome to spend the night, I'm sure you'd prefer getting home to that gorgeous roommate of yours. I know I would."

"Gran!" Her mouth gaped. "*No.* It's not like that with Bax. He's . . ."

Sinful. Pierced. And has visited my dreams every night since move-in day to give me a personal tour of those piercings.

To hell with Around the World in Eighty Days, and hello, Around Bax's Body in Eight-Plus Hours.

"No one would blame you if it were." Edie grinned mischievously, a devious twinkle in her eyes.

"It's not. Honestly." But boy, did she wish . . .

"But Bax has that—"

"Nope! I can't hear this right now." Olive slapped her hands over her ears. "Don't you have Prima things to do?"

"Actually, I do owe your eldest sister a *poof*-in, especially before the lot of you disappear into the woods. And speaking of the woods . . . did I ever tell you girls about the time your grandfather and I—"

"Gran, go see Vi. She loves it when you *poof* in." She grinned wickedly, knowing her sister hated it with the burning depths of hell. But desperate times called for desperate measures.

"Love you, sweetheart." After an air-kiss and a wave, Edie *poof*'d right off her back porch, leaving her alone with herself and her notebook.

She glanced at the page and the very sad-looking number one.

If it makes your Magic stir, it's within reach . . .

"I can't believe I'm about to do this." Right below one of the largest sewer-rat doodles, she scrawled her first Docket entry, and then, with renewed bravery, a second. By the time thunder rumbled in the far distance, she'd added three things.

Three things that would stretch her comfort zone.

She felt good.

She felt exhilarated.

She also felt like she should've used an erasable pen.

✦ ✦ ✦

Bax dragged his pencil across the no-longer-blank page of his sketchbook, still not sure what the image would be when finished. That was what usually happened when he got the itch to draw. His imagination gifted him bits and pieces, only on rare occasions evolving into a fully formed idea.

This one wasn't even half formed. Or a quarter. Basically, he'd been given a grain-sized snippet, and in an attempt to get his mind off the bomb the GAA had dropped into his hand earlier that day, he'd run with it.

The snippet, not the bomb.

Unable to wrap his mind around Olive being labeled a high-risk Assignment, he'd spent the better part of the day trying to pinpoint what got her on the ARS's radar and still couldn't figure it out. The youngest Maxwell triplet was as low-risk as it got, and had been since the day they'd met.

Violet, on the other hand? Given her ability to not give two fucks what people thought and her magnetism toward trouble, she was the more likely candidate to require Guardian intervention. The witch was a live wire through and through.

Even Rose made more sense with her new passion for Hunting, but *Olive*?

Olly was a damn safety manual, a walking encyclopedia with knowledge on how to handle every situation and act in a safe and orderly manner. Nothing about her actions, demeanor, or personality screamed *Assignment*, and yet her bolded name jumped out on the top of that damn dossier, fucking with his head.

It wasn't like he could come out and ask her, "Hey, angel, make any potentially life-altering decisions lately?"

With her smarts, she'd put two and two together or, at the very least, rightfully assume something was wrong with him. Neither option sat well with him.

Keys jangled in the front door and a petite someone resembling Olive dripped into the small foyer, her hair—and every inch of her clothes—plastered to her body. The thin fabric of her light sweater was practically see-through, revealing the sexy black lace bra beneath. The entire sight, combined with the curve-hugging jeans molded to her body, had him strategically shifting in his seat to fix the erection growing behind his zipper.

"What's wrong?" Her concern traveled in the direction of her see-through ensemble, and noticing what he had, she quickly draped her bag over her chest. "Crap. Sorry. I didn't realize that happened."

"No, *I'm* sorry." He cleared his suddenly dry throat. "I just acted like every body-obsessed dude-bro jerk in a rom-com movie."

Her grin returned and it brought along a chuckle. "Watch many rom-coms?"

"Lately? No."

"Ever?" Her lips twitched.

"Also no." Bax jumped up from the couch, his sketchbook falling onto the coffee table as he hustled to the linen closet and grabbed a clean white towel. "Here. Let me help you out of your things."

She cocked up a dark blond eyebrow.

His face heated. "I mean *with* your things."

He took her purse and a blue plastic container whose contents smelled suspiciously like Grandma Edie's Magical Lasagna.

His mouth salivated. "Is that . . . ?"

She chuckled. "Yes, it's for you. Gran saved you a corner slice and gave me explicit directions to make sure it gets to you."

Bax grinned, practically tasting the garlic sauce on his tongue already. "I'll make sure to give that woman a big kiss when I see her next."

"Pretty sure that's what she's angling for," Olive chuckled.

Wracked with shivers, the petite witch looked at the growing puddle around her feet and laughed. "If I don't do something to curb the drippage soon, I'll be flooding our downstairs neighbors."

"Shit. Yeah. Here." He handed her the towel and yanked his eyes off her body, desperately searching for something to do that didn't involve stripping her out of those wet clothes like he'd basically first offered. "I'll make you a hot chocolate while you dry yourself out, and then maybe I'll let you take my rom-com virginity."

"You want to watch a rom-com with me?"

Her surprised tone had him turning toward her just as she dried her glasses and returned them to her nose. It didn't go beyond his notice that she kept the towel in front of her body, probably to keep his horny self from objectifying it.

"Unless you have something else planned tonight," he said, to give her a way out.

She nibbled her lower lip as if considering her options. "*Any* rom-com?"

"Sure."

"If you make it any *movie*, you got yourself a deal."

"Then I guess we just made a deal, angel."

With a bright smile on her face, she practically skipped across the apartment, giving him a spectacular view of her wet denim-clad ass, and disappeared into her room.

Bax groaned, shifting the semi-erection in his pants to a more comfortable—and less noticeable—position. "You're so fucking screwed, Donovan."

He pretended the damn thing didn't exist and got busy warming milk for her hot chocolate. While it heated on the stove, he moved her wet things to the kitchen table so they weren't sitting in a puddle on the floor.

Her bag toppled, spilling a few items. He knew better than to handle someone else's personal belongings, so he left them alone, but couldn't help noticing the rainbow notebook that spilled open.

Olive's Dare I Docket

1. Run away to join the circus
2. Do something spontaneous

3. Do something socially frightening
4. Get a tattoo
5. Something...
6. Something else...
7. Something in addition to...
8. ?
9. ??
10. ???

What the hell was he looking at? A list of some kind, that much was for certain . . . but run away to the fucking circus?

The *circus*?

His Guardian radar blared. Was this Docket the reason she'd been flagged by the ARS? What the hell did she consider *socially frightening*? And *something spontaneous* left a bad taste in his mouth. *Spontaneous*, by definition, meant not thought out. Things not thought out had huge risk potential and . . . *fuck*.

This list was why he'd been assigned as her Guardian.

Her bedroom door opened, and she stepped out, her damp hair hanging below her shoulders and no longer wearing a see-through shirt but an oversized hooded sweatshirt and flannel PJ pants.

Her eyes dropped to the open notebook.

"Your purse fell," he explained awkwardly. "It looks like your notebook took a hard hit from the rain. You may have to rewrite your . . . list."

"I'll let it dry and see what happens. Thanks." She took the notebook with her to the couch and tucked it at her side.

It was on the tip of his tongue to ask about the Docket thing, but she'd picked up his fallen sketchbook, which remained open to his current piece. "Whoa. This is amazing! What is it?"

Embarrassment heated his cheeks as he poured the hot chocolate into two mugs. He handed hers over and took the seat on her right. "When I figure it out, I'll let you know."

Her eyes rounded behind her glasses as her attention snapped to him. "You *drew* this? How did I not know you're an artist?"

"I wouldn't call myself an artist. I doodle."

"Yeah. No." Flipping open her soggy notebook to her smudged Docket thing, she pointed to an army of hairy creatures framing the page. "*Those* are doodles . . . or prehistoric sewer rats. This?" She gestured to his sketch. "Is art. I can't believe Vi didn't tell me."

"She doesn't know. You're actually the first person to lay hands on my sketchbook—literally. Eyes, too."

She quickly handed it back to him. "Then I probably shouldn't be ogling it."

"No, it's okay. You can look through it if you'd like."

Fuck. Did those words leave his mouth?

No one but he had ever laid eyes on the images in that book, but for some reason, he wanted her to see them. The thought of her flipping page to page sent a flurry of something to the center of his chest. And, yeah, sent a slight roll of nausea to his stomach, too.

"Are you sure?" Olive asked, concerned. "It's probably like reading someone's diary."

"I'm sure. Go ahead and peek."

A slow, eager smile spread over her face. "Good . . . because I really want to see what else is in here."

Watching her reaction to each drawing was almost as entertaining as watching a movie. She nibbled the corner of her lip, her big blue eyes fastened on one page for what felt like hours before she gently turned the page to the next one. Somewhere around the sixth picture, something sparked and her gaze slid to his arms.

Her gaze did another bounce back and forth, and then she trailed one slender finger from the inside of his elbow to the pulse point of his wrist. His skin heated along the path of her touch, breathing fire into the brightly scaled dragon tattoo he'd had placed a few years back.

"You designed all your tattoos, didn't you?"

"Not all of them, but most. The dragon reminds me to be fierce and loyal, and fiercely loyal to those I care about."

She flipped the page and then looked back to his arms as if seeking out Where's Waldo. Grinning, he took her hand and lifted it to his right bicep, just under the hem of the sleeve, where the elaborate compass pointed north . . . or, more accurately, to his heart.

"This one reminds me to follow my heart." Unable to tear his eyes away from her, he watched a vast range of emotions flicker across her gorgeous face.

Olive pushed her glasses higher on her nose and smacked him right in the compass. "Bax! You could have your own gallery showing!"

"Nah. They're just for me. They're not something other people would find enjoyable. You're sweet to say otherwise, but—"

"Are you shitting me right now?" She glanced through the rest of the book until she came to the one he'd worked on before she walked through the door. "People pay ridiculous amounts of money on things that aren't even a quarter this good. For Goddess's sake, think of Campbell's Soup cans! Soup cans, Bax! Cans. Of soup."

He laughed. "It's just a hobby . . . nothing special."

"You're wrong there." She nibbled on her bottom lip, her blue eyes flickering up to meet his gaze. "You saw my Docket, right?"

He paused, debating on how to play this. "I'm not sure what I saw."

"It's this term's student project . . . to help me collect information I need for the SupeEx Project."

"The one about comfort zones. But why is your name on it if it's a project for your students?"

Scrunching her nose, she admitted, "Because I shouldn't ask of them something I'm not willing to do myself. So that means I'll be taking the leap into the unknown, too."

He smirked. "And that leap is toward the circus, something, and something else?"

She smacked him playfully with her notebook, and they both laughed. "It's a work in progress, okay? When you spend your entire life standing in the middle of your comfort zone, it's hard to figure out what lies outside of it."

"Okay. I get that." She understood a bit more why she might have gotten flagged by the ARS. He gently turned her right arm and brushed his thumb over the small flower-themed infinity tattoo on the inside of her wrist. She shivered, but didn't pull away. "But you already have a tattoo. Why would you put another on your list?"

Her gaze dropped to where he touched her ink, her cheeks pinking. "Because this one was a sister thing. We got it to show our love and support for each other. I want something just for me. It probably doesn't make sense, but—"

"It absolutely does."

"Yeah?" she asked, her face hopeful. "I wasn't sure about putting it on the Docket, but it's something I've always thought about doing and just never did. Because *comfort zone*."

She went back to nibbling her bottom lip. "So now that I know you're practically Michelangelo incarnate . . . would you design a tattoo for *me*?"

Unsure he'd heard correctly, his fingers stilled. "You want me to design your tattoo?"

"Yeah. Would you?"

"A permanent one? One that will go somewhere on your body?"

She gave him a WTF look and held up his latest sketch. "Yeah . . . and I want this one. Turn this into a design. For me. And yes, a permanent one."

He slowly released his hold on her and took his sketchbook, staring at the unfinished doodle. "I don't even know what *that* is yet, angel. For all I know, it'll be a rabid raccoon. You want a raccoon on your . . . Where do you want this to go?"

"My torso." She pulled up her sweatshirt, revealing the gap between the top of her pants and the bottom swell of her breast. "Right here."

His mouth dried at the sight of creamy exposed skin. "Centered in the middle?"

"No . . . over the whole thing. Bow to stern. Hip to under-boob."

His brows shot toward his hairline. "That's a big piece, angel."

Her smile dimmed. "You think it's too big?"

Fuck. Shit. He cursed himself for taking away that gorgeous smile. "No. I happen to fucking love large tattoos, but a piece that big needs a hell of a lot of intricate details, otherwise it's basically a paint-by-numbers canvas."

"Is that something you could do?" She reached out, her hand absently caressing the length of his full sleeve . . . and damn if it didn't feel like she was stroking other parts of him. "Yours have so much detail work. That dragon looks as if it could literally leap off of your skin. That's what I want . . . something that looks like it could come alive."

He fought the urge to purr at her touch and cleared his throat. *Should* he do it? Probably not. Did he want to? *Fuck yes.* The idea of designing something just for her, and seeing his work permanently displayed across her soft skin, gave him freaking goose bumps.

"I'd be honored to work on something for you," he heard himself agree. "Give me a few ideas of what you're looking for and—"

She tapped the open sketchbook. "*This.*"

He looked at the misshapen, unknown image. "I wasn't kidding when I said I have no idea what this will end up being."

"I have complete faith that you'll turn this into the perfect piece."

That made one of them. "Don't sic Vi and Rose on me when you end up with a rabid raccoon climbing up your ribs like a ladder."

She crossed her heart and blew a wisp of green Magic from her fingertips. "Witch's honor."

It swirled around him like a swarm of gentle fireflies, tickling his skin before melting away. He smiled, not quite sure how they'd gotten to this point. "You're something else, Olive Maxwell."

"Hopefully something good." She threw him a smile as she picked up the remote.

"Definitely something good," he murmured.

Definitely something a hell of a lot more than good . . . so much more that it was actually bad. For him.

"Now about that movie . . ." Olive began flicking through the streaming services and shot him a hopeful look. "I was thinking *The Conjuring*. You up for it?"

He kicked up an eyebrow. "*The Conjuring*? Isn't that a—"

"Horror flick about witches? Yep. I'll hold your hand if it gets too scary for you."

He chuckled as she got comfortable, pulling her feet up beneath her. The smart thing would've been sliding to the far-right cushion and keeping an empty one between them. Instead, he remained planted where he was, his shoulder brushing hers as he grabbed the throw blanket from behind him and draped it over their legs.

She shot him a warm smile and scooted closer. The smell of her fresh flowery shampoo invaded all his senses, wrapping around his own like a comforting hug as she nestled into his side.

And he was all too willing to embrace it—and her.

7

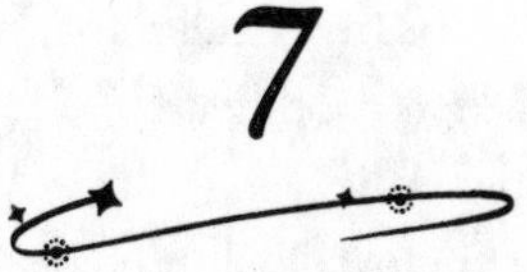

Death Luge

How many Supernaturals does it take to fill a Suburban?

Answer: Eight. And not comfortably, either.

Damian's elbow wedged into Olive's rib cage for the sixth time in as many minutes despite her protective puffer jacket, and the longer it took to reach Whispering Pines Ski Resort—the vacation resort Linc owned that helped fund wildlife conservation—the possibility of permanent left-lower-rib indentation increased exponentially.

Their four-day winter wonderland vacation officially commenced the instant they'd put the city in the rearview mirror, and it was off to a fantastic start.

Well . . . *a* start.

Linc, driving the rented Suburban, proved with a handful of near-miss collisions that driving safely while simultaneously goo-goo-eyeing Vi in the passenger seat was a statistical impossibility. If it hadn't been for her sister's quick thinking and magical intervention, those near-misses wouldn't have been so *near*.

In the second-row lineup, Rose, sandwiched between Harper and Adrian, threatened to Billy Butcherson both the lion shifter and the sex demon's lips at the hurl of one more insult.

That left the third row . . .

Bax, Olive, and Damian.

Being the filling in a hot-man sandwich definitely played out differently in her head. Not only did it not involve rib injury caused by her sister's mate, but it sure as hell didn't include improper sexual thoughts about her new roommate.

Okay, so the last one? A lie.

Every time Bax's arm moved behind her shoulders and brushed against the back of her neck, she quietly sucked in a breath and let her imagination go AWOL. So much so that at one point, she could've sworn he'd played with a loose strand of her hair, but when she glanced his way, his face had been a stoic blank slate.

It turned a long car ride into an even longer torture session, and if she asked Linc to turn down the heat one more time, snow wouldn't fall only on the mountain but inside the SUV as well.

Harper sighed from the second row. "How much longer until we're there? Because if it's not within the next ten minutes, our first order of business is a Target run for a SpotBot."

"No peeing in the rental car, Jacobs." Linc glanced in the rearview mirror. "Didn't I tell everyone to go before we left Olive and Bax's place?"

"I didn't have to go then, but I do now. *Vi*," Harper half whined.

The eldest triplet chuckled at the GPS. "Less than five minutes. Think you can manage not to pee until then? Perk of hanging with the owner is not having to check in at registration. We can drive right up to our cabin."

Adrian slid a sly look toward the sex demon. "So what's the roommate situation again?"

"Don't worry, kitty cat." Harper shot him a glare. "There's a litter box with your name on it. Just for you."

Adrian chuckled. "Litter boxes are for doing the dailies, not sleeping."

"Don't some cats treat it as a one-stop shop?"

"I don't fuck where I shit, sweetheart."

"Call me *sweetheart* again, Whiskers, and Linc will be explaining to the rental car company why the back seat looks like a crime scene." Harper fluttered her eyes way too demurely.

Rose massaged her temples. "If we don't get to the cabin in thirty seconds, I'm jumping out the moonroof and taking my chances with the wildlife."

Everyone chuckled except for Adrian and Harper, who folded her arms across her chest and mumbled grumpily about *horny cats*.

"It's a four-bedroom cabin," Vi explained, turning slightly around in her seat. "We figured the couples would each take one, and then Bax and Adrian can have the one with bunk beds, and Olive and Harper can share the one with the two queens. Unless the new roomies want to share a room . . ."

Multiple pairs of eyes, from varying positions around the SUV, shifted their way. Next to Olive, Bax stilled, a strand of her hair pinched between his fingers. She fought the instinct to glance his way, unsure she wanted to see whatever look was on his face. His silence was telling enough.

Harper snorted. "Fuck-and-no. I'm not sharing a room with someone who sheds. Olive and I will do fine with the two queen beds." She spun in her seat and hit Olive with a pleading look. "Right, Olly?"

"Right." She released a breath she hadn't realized she'd been holding. "Sounds good to me . . . roomie."

Harper turned back around, and Olive nearly sent a thanks to Goddess when the SUV slowed to a stop in front of a sprawling, one-level cabin that couldn't have looked more perfect if it had graced the cover of *Mountain Cabin Weekly*.

"Home sweet home for the next few days," Linc announced.

Nestled in a thick outcropping of trees, the cabin's inviting porch wrapped around the entire perimeter and a copper roof was dusted finely with fresh, powdery snow. The lone building was surrounded only by nature, without another cabin in sight, and yet anything they wanted to do—tubing, the ski slopes—was nearby. A brisk half-mile walk away, the main resort was far enough from them for blessed quiet, but close enough for a brief return to civilization, or an escape from Adrian and Harper's bickering, if anyone needed it.

They poured out of the SUV, the guys immediately unhooking the oversized cargo box on the roof while Olive and the others unloaded supplies from the trunk.

As Olive pulled out Harper's third suitcase, she shot the demon a look. "Three? Really?"

Harper threw the strap of one over her shoulder and grabbed the other two in each hand. "A demon needs to be prepared for anything."

"We're not even here for four full days."

The redhead stopped at the bottom of the cabin steps, a look of horror on her face. "Fuck. You're right. I should've brought another bag."

Vi chuckled and hoisted her single duffel over her shoulder. "Sometimes I can't tell if she's joking or not."

"She's not," Bax and Olive answered simultaneously.

He jumped from the roof, his shoulder brushing hers as he sat her own bag by her feet. "If there's not enough space in your room for you, Harper, and all her bags, I'm sure Adrian and I can make room for you in ours."

Grinning, he winked, dual-colored eyes twinkling.

What was it about the man's wink? From anyone else, the sight of it would've sent her into a massive eyeroll fit for the Guinness World Records, but from Bax, the rise in her body temperature had her searching for the nearest snowdrift.

Harper appeared at her side and threw the Guardian Angel a mock scowl. "Keep your soft little feathers off my witch, angel cakes. She's mine for the next seventy-two hours. You can't have her back until then."

Bax folded his arms across his chest, lip twitching. "Yeah? And if I don't want to wait three days?"

His words sent Olive's stomach into a flutter.

"Oh, you'll wait," Harper warned. "Or you'll find out why I was named Retaliation Royalty of Adventure Lagoon Summer Camp three years in a row. Like keeping your feathers intact?"

Bax chuckled, raising his hands in mock surrender as he shifted his attention—and his panty-melting grin—to Olive. "Sorry, angel, but you're on your own. Growing feathers back is no picnic."

"Traitor," she teased.

A tingling heat tickled the back of her neck as Harper ushered her toward the awaiting cabin. As she climbed the porch steps, the sensation encompassed her ass as well, making that snowdrift idea look better and better.

She glanced back toward the SUV—and the angel still standing by it—and stumbled in her newly acquired snow boots.

Either she needed a new glasses prescription, or there was a rare glimpse of stormy desire etched in every hard line of Baxter Donovan's body as he looked directly at her.

The forecast for their winter wonderland getaway was blue skies, brooding angels, and rubber snow tubes.

✦ ✦ ✦

Some people called snow-tubing a thrill ride designed to bring out even a curmudgeon's inner child. To Bax, it was hurtling down a dark mountain at the velocity of a luge sled, with no safety gear or brakes, and with no regard for life or limb. Aka, a Death Luge.

Despite his passionate attempts to convince the others that stargazing was a suitable—and equally heart-pounding—substitute, Glow-Tube's boasts about their sixteen 1,000-foot runways with 150-foot vertical drops, which at night glowed with stunning displays of neon lights, had won over the group.

Death luging was officially on tonight's agenda.

On arrival, they'd each been handed glow sticks, some to click onto their jackets and others to wear. Olive snapped hers into circles and meticulously wove her scarf through the hoops, creating a gorgeous glowing necklace that was both striking and functional.

His gaze transfixed by the pretty pink luminescence radiating off her smiling face, he didn't realize she'd said something until her blue eyes dipped into his line of sight. "I'm sorry. What?"

She held up two glow sticks. "You didn't pick up your sticks, so I grabbed them for you. We wouldn't want you getting lost on the mountain, would we?"

"No, we wouldn't want that," Bax heard himself murmur.

"So? Where do you want them?" She ran her gaze over him, frowning the longer she assessed his outfit. "How the hell are you not freezing right now?"

He glanced down at his leather jacket and gloveless hands, and shrugged. "Shifters aren't the only Supernaturals that run hot. Angels have a built-in heater system to keep us warm while flying."

She crinkled her nose, distrust in her eyes. "This is the first I've heard of it."

"Don't believe me?" Grinning, he unzipped his jacket and beckoned her closer with a crook of his finger. "Come over here and check it out for yourself. Angels make superior cuddle-bugs . . . and we don't shed."

He'd extended the dare before he thought it through to the end, but when she stepped close, hesitancy evident in the way she gently bit her bottom lip, there was no way he'd rescind it now. Meeting her halfway, he hooked an arm around her waist and securely cocooned her against his chest.

She sighed softly a second before she melted in his hold, her cheek pillowed against his sternum. "Damn. You're right. This feels nice."

"It feels really, really nice." He propped his chin on the top of her head, thawing not just his body, but every reason he'd ever made to keep his distance.

Why? Distance didn't feel so damn toasty. Or smell this good, like warm sugar and endless possibilities.

He could easily stay in this same position for hours and be happy . . . so of course the Glow-Tube attendant motioned for them to step onto the conveyor belt, the next two people to hitch their way up the side of a mountain.

The second Olive stepped onto the moving walkway, he missed her warmth. He stayed close, telling himself it was more for her benefit than his, and clenched his fingers around the handrail.

Olive's soft smile slowly dimmed as she glanced at his white-knuckled grip. "Are you okay? I can't tell if the strobe lights are turning your face green or if it's because you're about to retch."

"Not a big fan of heights," he admitted truthfully, keeping his gaze locked on her face instead of their steady incline.

"Then why did you get on the conveyor? You could've stayed at the bottom!"

"And give Adrian the ammunition to taunt me over breakfast tomorrow? Not if I can help it. That damn lion is like a cat with a catnip toy."

A few jokes made at his expense, he could handle. Growing up a Donovan, he'd developed a skin thicker than rawhide. But one thing he couldn't accept was his Assignment hurling herself off the side of a mountain—alone. If they broke a few bones, they'd break them together.

On their left, snow-tubers zipped past them in a blur of squeals and laughter, one rider hitting an unseen bump that sent them slightly airborne.

Bax swallowed a groan. He almost preferred dealing with Hogan's gun-happy biker club friends to this.

"Hey. Look at me," Olive ordered gently.

He obeyed instantly, unable to tear his gaze away from hers.

Her gloved hand settled over his thundering heart. "Our asses will most likely be dragging over the ground the entire way. We're never actually leaving land. We're just—"

"Hurtling down it at a ridiculously fast clip without any safety restraints in place? Tell me, Professor, how many injuries a year are from sledding incidents?"

"This isn't sledding in Grandma and Grandpop's backyard. This hill has been cultivated for this very purpose, the slope formulated for safety, the pathways smoothed . . . and to be technical, this isn't sledding at all. It's *tubing*. You're sitting in a rubber enclosure and not on top of a slick sheet of plastic."

Lips twitching slightly, he slid his palm over her hand and wrapped his fingers around hers. "We never leave land, huh?"

"Nope."

"Mountain burn on my ass. Sounds pleasant . . . and like I'll be sitting on a pillow tomorrow."

She chuckled, her smile twinkling nearly as much as her eyes. "Maybe you'll feel better if you go down with me? It looks like they allow duos."

She looked nearly as surprised at her offer as he was, but he wasn't second-guessing his luck. It served both his purposes: keeping her close enough to ensure nothing bad happened to her *and* keeping her close enough to ensure nothing bad happened to him.

A win-win situation. The only thing better would be not going down at all.

"You got yourself a tube partner." He squeezed her hand and made the mistake of glancing at another set of racing snow-tubers.

Shit. This mountain was really damn high.

He swallowed the forming lump in his throat. "What number is this on Olive's Dare I Docket list? Below joining the circus? Right above *Something* or between *Something* and *Something else*?"

"My Docket? Nah. This isn't on the list."

"Why the fuck not?" His voice went high-pitched. He cleared

his throat, ignoring her obvious amusement. "This would be a damn good addition."

She chuckled as they reached the top, where an attendant directed them toward a front lane. "For you, judging by the sweaty sheen to your forehead, but I'd do this a million times with my eyes closed. Headfirst. Feetfirst. Doesn't matter."

Damn . . . was the mountain spinning or just him?

"One rider or two?" the lane assistant asked.

"Two, please. Thank you," Olive answered.

He hoisted an elongated tube onto the lane. "Big guy in back. No standing. No attempting to skip lanes. Keep hands on the finger grips."

Bax groaned a low chuckle. "Yeah, that won't be an issue."

He got into the snow-coaster first and was barely in position when Olive followed, her body fitting snugly between his outspread legs.

His thighs cocooned her like bumpers as she leaned back against his chest, a smile on her face. "You okay back there, big guy?"

"Define *okay.*" Sweat suctioned hair to his neck and dripped into an eye.

"Scoot closer and don't be afraid to squeeze your arms around me." She chuckled, obviously realizing she'd loosely repeated the speech he'd given her about his motorcycle.

Brushing his mouth against the shell of her ear, he whispered, "Be careful what you ask for, angel. If I put my arms around you, I may not let you go."

She stilled, and this time *he* chuckled, his impending doom temporarily forgotten as he wrapped one arm around her waist and kept his other clenched around the snow-coaster's oh-shit handle.

"We're ready." Olive nodded to the attendant.

With a nod, he raised his hand in a signal to workers below, and pulled a lever. The little ledge that held the tube in place dropped.

So did they.

His arm buckled tight around Olive's waist as he readied himself to eject his wings from his back at the first sign of trouble. Cold air clobbered them on the way down the mountain, the thousand-foot plunge feeling like millions as they zoomed past riders in neighboring lanes.

Her hand braced on his, Olive threw her head back in a delighted squeal while his heart lodged itself in his throat, barely back in place by the time they came to a slow stop.

"Ready to go again?" Grinning wildly, the witch limberly climbed out from the tube and held out her hands to help him up. "We can ask them to turn us backward."

Damn if his legs didn't wobble. He just didn't know if it was from the downhill ride or the pure pleasure being aimed his way, but her radiant smile ensured he didn't regain that knee strength anytime soon.

"Funny." He reached out and freed a lock of golden hair from the corner of her glasses. "You're a comedian now, huh?"

"That's me. The comedic Maxwell."

As his gaze flickered to her mouth, hers did the same to his.

A needy ache stirred deep, pulling their bodies closer and tilting her mouth up toward his. One slight lean . . . just a few scant inches . . . and he'd claim his first taste of Olive Maxwell and maybe screw his head on straight again well enough to get through this latest Assignment.

But that all came to a screeching halt with a snowball to the back of his head.

Snow exploded to the chorus of laughter.

"Son of a bitch," Bax growled, whirling around.

"Hey, feather boy! That's snow tube talk for *get out of the lane*!" Vi stood with a hand on her hip, a second snowball prepped for hurling in the other. "And for your information, I'm the daughter of a *reformed*-bitch. If you can believe it, Christina's bitch level has severely dropped the closer I get to the Exchange Ceremony."

He glanced to the top of the mountain, where, sure enough, an arm-flailing attendant was indicating they needed to move. He grabbed the tube and, taking Olive's hand, guided the way back to the footpath.

"So . . ." Vi's smirk took up her entire face. "We were thinking about making a few more runs before hitting the clubhouse for some hot chocolate and spirits. Does that sound good to the two of you? Or would you prefer staying here and stargazing into each other's eyes and we'll pick you up on our way back to the cabin?"

Olive rolled her eyes at her sister before turning to him. "I can hang here with you if you're not up for another run."

"No, I'm good for one or two more," Bax heard himself say. Why, he had no freaking idea.

"Are you sure?" She didn't seem to think so.

"Absolutely. Let's go." He lifted the double tube over his head and led the way to the conveyor belt.

Three steps in, a second snowball hit the back of his head.

"Seriously, Vi?" He tossed an annoyed look over his shoulder, but was met with the witch's wide, innocent eyes.

Vi nondiscreetly pointed to her sister, and his gaze shifted to Olive, who looked in every direction except his, paying special attention to a spot on her left snow boot.

"Yeah?" Bax asked Vi.

She nodded. "It's the quiet ones you really have to watch out for . . . or so I'm told."

Olive's mouth twitched in the faintest movement as she fought to withhold a grin. Vi's warning held more meaning than even he realized. Something in his Guardian gut told him this Assignment wouldn't be as easy as he'd hoped.

It was game on.

8

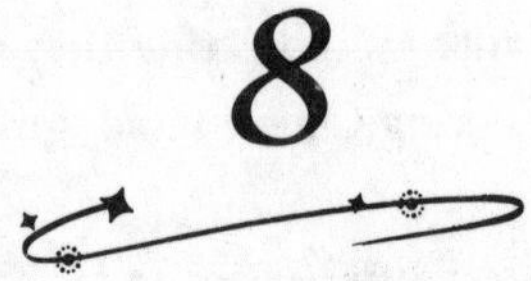

The Full Moon

Harper's soft snores filled the bedroom, pausing when she restlessly shifted from side to side. More than once, the redhead suspiciously mumbled Adrian's name and not in the annoyed tone she usually did while awake.

If Vi had been there, she'd have recorded it for blackmail purposes.

Blaming her sleeplessness on her temporary roomie would've been easy for Olive, but untrue. The fault didn't even lie with the mattress's mystery lump pushing on the base of her spine, or the unnatural quiet that came in nature.

Mental playbacks of the day whirred through her head, always freeze-framing on the snow tube runway where she swore she and Bax had shared a moment. *He'd cupped her cheek.* Probably so her glasses didn't rip out a hair chunk when she turned her head, but still.

For a brief moment in time, their bodies practically magnetized and he'd leaned closer as he contemplated . . . going in for a kiss?

She could've sworn she caught him glancing at her lips at the exact moment she did the same to his. A more superstitious person would've crossed everything—fingers, toes, and any other bendable appendage—in the hopes those scant few inches disappeared.

Of course someone more courageous would've taken the situation into their own hands.

Literally.

Her current state of sleeplessness lay entirely with her regret for not locking her fingers into the angel's gorgeous hair and dragging his mouth to hers for a kiss that would've melted every single flake of snow on the damn mountain. Hell, it would've ticked off the *do something spontaneous* item on her Dare I Docket, too. There was nothing she loved much more than efficiency.

But it was always easy to mentally play back scenes and pick apart the exact things you wished you'd handled differently when in the privacy of a dark bedroom. Being in the moment was when things got dicey.

Confronted with spontaneity, Olive froze. She'd hesitated. And then she got witch-blocked by her own sister via a snowball, both the mood and the opportunity shattered in a spray of white snow.

Finally giving up on the fantasy of sleep, Olive grabbed her notebook and, careful not to disturb Harper, tiptoed across the room and into the main living space. In truth, she probably could've marched like a herd of elephants through the cabin and not disturbed anyone. Exhausted from their night of tubing followed by warm drinks at the clubhouse, everyone had hit their mattresses hard.

Everyone except her, whose mattress—and overactive brain—fought back.

Hoping the fully stocked cabin included hot chocolate, she went on a quest through the kitchen cabinets, only to come up empty-handed.

"Sleep-deprived *and* chocolate-denied. I'm not sure how much worse this night could get," she murmured grumpily.

Shadows shifted, and a large beam of moonlight pierced through the patio window, lighting up the entire backyard in a beautiful dewy glow. While the city definitely had its ethereal moments, it had nothing on *this*.

A magical mix of darks and lights, the clear night sky twinkled with stars. To the left and indented into the freshly fallen snow, small animal footprints created artistic swirls and loops. Trees, blanketed in snow and ice, sparkled as if encrusted in diamonds. It reminded her of the beautiful landscape paintings in art galleries.

Or something in Bax's sketchbook.

Though a core member of their friend group, he'd always been a bit of an enigma, the one who'd rather listen than talk and who set clear conversational boundaries on Friendship Day One. His job with the GAA, the root cause of his hatred for ketchup on eggs, and his family were three topics far outside the safety perimeter.

More no doubt existed. The man was nothing if not a walking wall of surprise. Then there was her, open, by-the-book Olive.

Professional spread-sheeter. Reliable schedule-maker. Owner of the Monday-Wednesday-Friday color-coded outfits and massive Vans collection. Spontaneity had her chugging Pepto Bismol like one of Violet's energy drinks, which was one of the reasons why she'd included it on her Dare I Docket.

Standing in front of the patio door, she cracked open her notebook and glanced at her sad excuse for a list. She'd stared at the damn thing for days, no closer to stepping out of her comfort zone. No additional items added. No existing things checked off. At this rate of progress, she'd be forced to give herself credit for wearing her weekend underwear on a Thursday.

Dragging her attention back to the picturesque outdoor scene, her gaze landed on the hot tub nestled on the far end of the patio. She couldn't remember the last time she'd been in one. Definitely not in a private wooded wonderland surrounded by the scents of nature.

Hmm . . . privacy. Solitude. Hot, bubbling water. Soothed muscles.

Hot damn, that sounded like a sleepless person's ultimate dream.

Her gaze fixed on the second untouched Docket item: *Do something spontaneous.*

Those hives threatened to break through the surface of her skin at the mere formulation of an idea, but she fought the itch, glancing from the quiet cabin to the hot tub. She was alone, everyone passed out in their beds.

"Should I, or shouldn't I?" Olive contemplated. Another glimpse at her sad excuse for a list solidified the decision.

Tucking her notebook under her arm, she grabbed a fluffy towel from the linen closet and, five minutes later, stood next to the steaming pool of heaven wearing nothing but the aforementioned towel.

How was this for spontaneity?

She dipped a toe into the water and sighed, her muscles already relaxing. "Nice. Why didn't I think about doing this before? Bubbling cauldron, here I come."

She dropped her towel, her entire body immediately attacked by a violent shiver. As she took her first step into the hot tub, the patio door opened. Startled, she spun, boobs out and nipples proud.

Bax stood less than three feet away, mouth slightly agape as his gaze dropped along her naked body before quickly snapping back up to her face.

She was like a deer in the headlights, frozen and unable to move, except she wasn't frozen from the dropping temperatures. Her entire body felt rather warm, growing hotter as the brewing desire emanating from the Guardian Angel's eyes escalated.

Or maybe that was wishful thinking.

She reached for her towel, but her left foot slipped, the abrupt shift throwing her balance off-kilter and her arms flailing in the air. Olive cursed as she teetered backward and fell ass-first into her *something spontaneous.*

Water assaulted her airway as she struggled to get her feet

beneath her, a single second feeling like a million until her heels finally touched bottom. Two thick arms wrapped around her torso, just under her boobs, and yanked her upper body above water.

She emerged with a gasp, coughing up buckets of water while struggling to suck in fresh oxygen.

"Slow and easy, angel," Bax instructed.

"It hurts to br—" she wheezed.

"Guess you forgot you're a witch, not a mermaid," he quipped.

"I . . ."

"Shh. Slow and easy." His mouth brushed over the shell of her ear, eliciting a string of shivers that had nothing to do with the cold. "Stop trying to talk until you can do so without your chest feeling like it's about to explode."

She did as he said, the pain from inhaling a gallon of hot tub water ebbing way too slowly for her liking.

"Good girl." His large, calloused hand slowly slid from her abdomen to her hip. "You better?"

Better was an entirely subjective concept at the moment. The easier it became to breathe, the more hyperaware she became of her surroundings, of her nakedness, and of Bax's thick, hard body blanketing her back.

"I can't see." She blinked against the water dripping over her face. "Why can't I see?"

"Fixing that in two seconds." In less than one, he placed her glasses on her nose, lenses spotted but otherwise unharmed. "Good?"

She nodded, slowly catching her breath, and turned in his arms, only to lose it all over again.

Bax's multicolored gaze roamed her face as his lips pulled up into a sexily coy crooked smirk. "Sorry for startling you. The door was slightly ajar, and when I came outside to check it out, I saw . . ."

"My full moon?" She dropped her forehead to his wet T-shirt

with a groan. "Is there any chance you can wipe that mental picture from your mind? Any chance at all?"

"Not even a microscopic one, angel."

✦ ✦ ✦

Not in this reality or any other. Not after he'd fantasized about the sight for longer than he cared to admit. Hell, when he'd stepped onto the patio and laid eyes on her in all her splendid naked glory, her skin glowing under the moonlight like the Moon Goddess, he thought himself once again caught up in a dream. One from which he didn't want to wake.

Now they stood in the hot tub, his palms splayed across her lower back as he struggled to get his body under control, but the second she shifted, his cock went straight to half-mast, making control seem less likely.

"It feels like we've been in this position before," he teased.

A gorgeous pink hue flushed along her cheeks. "Except this time the roles are reversed and I'm the one who's wet and naked."

Lips twitching, he gently pushed a wet strand of hair off her cheek. "If it's any consolation, the second you slipped, I was less mesmerized by your nakedness and more concerned with your impending drowning."

She cocked up a sexy eyebrow. "You thought I'd drown in three feet of water?"

"I wasn't quite fully awake when I first stepped outside, but I am now. And since the drowning threat has been resolved . . ."

Her eyes widened, realizing his meaning: now he couldn't help but dwell on her lack of clothes. "Maybe next time we're in this situation, we'll both be naked."

And his cock went from half-mast to full throttle . . .

Seconds after the words left her lips, she backtracked. "I didn't mean . . . please forget I said that and never remember."

"Not sure that's possible," Bax murmured.

"Do you mind . . . ?" She gestured to his eyes.

He closed his eyes and mourned the loss of her body the instant she moved. He stayed still, listening to the sound of water dripping as she stepped out of the tub.

"It's all safe. Nakedness officially put away," she announced.

He snorted. *Olive Maxwell* and *safe* didn't belong in the same sentence—even when back in her flannel PJs.

As he climbed from the hot tub, she held out her towel. "You look like you need this more than me now."

Teeth chattering, he accepted it and quickly ushered her into the cabin, locking the door behind them. "Fuck. It's cold. One slight bump into anything and my nipples will drop right off."

"Then you'll have to get pierced all over again." As soon as the words left her mouth, she sighed and turned away from him to pull two mugs from a cabinet, but not before her look of self-exasperation had him chuckling. "My filter's been on the fritz the last few days. Sorry."

"Don't be. It's entertaining as hell."

"That's what I strive for . . . to be a one-witch show." Keeping her eyes away from his, she busied herself with warming water and procuring tea bags from the little side pantry.

Her slight shivers sent him dripping his way to the hall closet for a second towel, and ignoring the voice in his head telling him to simply hand it to her, he slid up behind her just as she turned with two steaming mugs of tea.

She jolted and hissed, her face distorting with a flash of pain as one of the hot beverages dripped over the rim. "Son of a witch's ti—"

Cursing, he instantly grabbed the two mugs, set them aside, and reached for the hand she cradled to her chest. "Let me look at it."

"It's okay." She grimaced at her already pink skin. "I've had worse. You don't have an Easy-Brew Cauldron as a kid and not come out with a few minor burns."

"Humor me." He extended his hand and cocked an eyebrow at her daringly.

She sighed but placed her hand in his. "It's really not that bad, Bax."

"Let me be the judge of it." He gently caressed his thumb over the back of her hand as he inspected the redness. She'd been his Assignment for a mere few days and already experienced an injury. "We should run this under some cool water."

"It's not—"

He shot her a stern glare.

"Fine, Nurse Donovan. Water away." She rolled her pretty blue eyes, telling him without words what she thought of his bossiness.

He ran the tap and tested the temperature before guiding her hand beneath. Compared to his massive one, her hand looked delicate. Everything about the woman screamed *fragile* at first glance, but looks were definitely deceiving. Armed not only with wicked smarts, the witch could send his ass into orbit with a twitch of her pinky.

All the Maxwell sisters could, and yet *Olive* was the one whose GAA file was crammed in his bedside table back home.

He tore his gaze from where her hand rested in his and transferred it to her face. As if sensing his attention shift, her eyes flickered to his and held. Neither of them looked away. Or said a word. Dripping hair and wet clothes be damned, it was getting awfully stuffy in the cozy kitchen.

Olive's breath hitched ever so slightly. "How's my hand, Nurse Donovan?"

"Huh?" His gaze dipped to her mouth and back. "Oh." He withdrew it from the water and took another look. "I think you were right. It's not that bad . . . but it was better to be safe than sorry."

"Spoken like a true Guardian, huh? Are you ever off the clock?" She smirked, teasing.

He couldn't bring himself to return it because there wasn't

a single Guardian thought floating through his head at the moment, at least not one that wouldn't get him fired seven ways from Sunday.

Like kissing her until they both forgot their names.

As Olive gently dried her hands, he saw his opportunity to actually *do* something Guardian-like.

Leaning his ass on the counter, he asked as casually as he could, "So was this near drowning your *something spontaneous*?"

"It was." She chuckled, carefully picking up her tea. "But considering I was only in the hot tub for thirty seconds, I'm not sure I can count it. I may give it a second attempt with floaties."

"And what's next on the agenda? *Something else* or *something in addition to*?"

"I'm not sure. Guess I'll have to see what kind of opportunities pop up."

"Maybe we should compare schedules and make sure I'm free to play lifeguard." He grinned, but as the reality of his taunt sank in, he no longer laughed.

That tightness he'd felt in his chest when he'd been handed her file returned full force. If Olive sensed his inner turmoil, she didn't show it, her grin lighting up her eyes as she tucked her glasses higher onto her nose.

"I'll let you know." She anchored a small palm on his chest and, lifting onto her toes, deposited a soft kiss on his cheek. "Thank you, Bax."

Taken off guard, he stilled. "What was that for?"

"For jumping into the hot tub to save me." She gifted him a shy smile that he felt straight to his damn gut. "I'll see you in the morning."

"I'll be here." He forced himself to stay perched against the counter.

"Don't forget that you and the guys are on breakfast duty tomorrow. No one wants to deal with three hangry witches and a bacon-deprived succubus. And Rose without coffee flowing in her veins?" She shivered in mock terror. "Scarier than those witches in *The Conjuring*."

"Duly noted."

"Good night, Bax."

"Night, angel." He counted to ten, telling himself to let her go.

She made it down the hall and to the door of her room before he lost his battle and followed after her. "Olive?"

"Yeah?" She turned, her hand on the doorknob.

"You know you're fucking amazing without stepping out of your comfort zone, right?" Bax asked, dead serious. "Performing dangerous feats isn't necessary."

"I know," she said a little too adamantly.

"Do you?" He kept his gaze locked on hers as he stepped close and cupped her cheek, gently searching for the truth.

"Of course." Her soft smile didn't quite reach her eyes. "But even if you know something to be true, sometimes it's nice to have reminders every once in a while. Good night, Bax."

"G'night, angel." He waited until she slipped silently into her bedroom and turned toward his own across the hall, stopping when he heard Harper's distinct giggle through their bedroom door.

"Did you seriously say 'You saw my full moon'?" Harper dissolved into laughter. "Oh, Olly, Olly, Olly. Your man-game needs a serious upgrade."

There was a muffled scuffle, and something was thrown, making the succubus laugh harder.

"I don't need a man-game," Olive protested. "And what were you doing listening?"

"Don't bend your broomstick all out of shape. I got up to pee and couldn't help overhearing because demonic ears. And you're wrong . . . everybody needs some kind of game. Lucky for you, you have me to help you."

"I'm not sure I want your kind of help."

Good girl, Bax thought, grinning proudly. *Because that would go nowhere good.*

On the other side of the door, the succubus chuckled. "Oh, honey. Everyone wants my kind of help. Even if they don't quite realize it yet. Please don't say no. You won't regret it. I promise."

Olive sighed.

"That's not a no," Harper pointed out, sounding eager.

Bax, standing in the hall like a creeper, nearly shouted no for her. Anything in which the succubus was involved definitely wouldn't make his job as Olive's Guardian any easier.

9

All Witches on Deck

Only ten minutes into her workday, Olive longed to be back at the Whispering Pines cabin. Snow-tubing. Cocoa drinking. She would've even taken a replay of her hot tub near drowning and subsequent death-by-naked-embarrassment over having to deal with *this*.

This nightmare couldn't be solved by a wake-up pinch . . . because she tried, only succeeding in giving herself yet another black-and-blue.

Held captive in her office, Olive contemplated her next course of action while Mason stood in her doorway, waiting for an answer. A flurry of responses whipped through her head. *Fuck no. Hell no. Not even if you were the last oxygen-consuming lifeform in the galaxy.*

It took a ridiculous amount of effort not to bust out with the last one, most likely Harper's influence. Instead, she considered rewinding time and leaving an hour early despite the monetary fine and community service hours the Supernatural Council would slap on her.

Hell, if she'd known *this* would be the outcome of opening her office door, she would've pulled a Violet and ducked beneath her desk to pretend no one was around.

She took a fortifying breath, prolonging the inevitable. "I'm sorry, but I think I heard incorrectly. Could you say that again?"

He stepped inside and leaned his shoulder against her favorite bookcase, his smile making her Magic itch below her skin with the need to conjure a swift breeze and knock him away from her books lest he taint them with his smarminess.

They'd only seen each other in passing since the day she'd overheard him with Celeste and the others, and now he had the nerve to ask . . .

"The NYU Alumni Gala," Mason repeated. "I'll pick you up around six thirty and we can stop for something to eat before the event. They say food will be served at these things, but you remember last year. Nothing but finger sandwiches and liquor turned Winston into an idiot."

Olive mumbled, "Pretty sure *Winston* turned Winston into an idiot."

But yeah, that's exactly what she thought she'd heard. "I must have missed you asking me to the gala . . . and me accepting."

His grin widened. "I just assumed—"

"That I'd say yes because I had no other plans? Or that I'd have no other options?"

He dismissed her questioning with an eyeroll. "That's not it at all. I thought—"

"That I'd be oh so grateful you were offering to save me from my boring existence?" She was on a roll now, not really wanting to stop.

"Olly . . . I think there's been a bit of a misunderstanding."

"It's Olive. And the misunderstanding was me thinking you were a decent guy. Now if you'll please leave, that would be great. I have a million things I should be doing."

Dropping his palms onto her desk, he invaded her personal space. "Did you forget I was one of the only faculty members who tried making you feel accepted when you first arrived? I could have easily jumped on the unwelcome wagon along with everyone else."

She snortled. "And you want what? A thank-you? Or *repayment* for all those fake platitudes?"

His haughty expression told her that's exactly what he wanted—and had expected.

"You need to leave. Now," she snapped, her patience dwindling more with each word out of his mouth.

"This isn't how I expected a Maxwell to act."

"If you don't leave my office in two seconds or less, I'll show you exactly how a Maxwell acts." Her signature green Magic crackled around her hands, brewing along with her annoyance.

Finally looking a bit apprehensive, Mason stepped back and bumped into the huge figure she hadn't seen there until now.

Bax shot her a concerned look from over the other teacher's head. "Hey there, angel. Is everything okay?"

"Everything's just fine," Mason snapped before catching sight of the broad-shouldered angel and changing his tone. "Miss Maxwell and I apparently got our signals crossed."

Bax dropped his voice to a near growl. "Would you like for me to uncross them for you, or did you manage to do it yourself?"

"Mason was just leaving," Olive added firmly.

Her colleague's mouth gaped like a fish. "You're seriously just going to—"

"Turn down the oh-so-generous offer of your company?" She weighed her ample sarcasm and decided on throwing out a bit more. "Yeah, I definitely am. Maybe Celeste is free. You two can pick up your Olive Maxwell conversation. Now leave so I can spend time with someone whom I actually like."

Mason gave Bax a wide berth as he beelined for the door. The sight of it pulled her lips into a grin . . . until Bax stepped farther into the room, eyeing her expectantly.

"Wasn't that your *friend* from Potion's?" he asked, crossing his arms over his broad chest.

She scoffed. "Yeah. Not a friend. Mason's an—"

"Asswipe. And not the gentle, aloe-soaked kind. He's fucking serrated sandpaper."

"You won't get a disagreement from me."

Hair in a half-hearted, low-lying man bun and wearing distressed jeans he'd probably owned forever, Bax looked every bit a cover model for *Trouble Weekly*. And that was before adding the battered leather jacket and the two days' worth of scruff covering his angular jaw.

A few long seconds into her Bax-admiring, she caught his knowing smirk and tried her best to ignore the sudden flush to her cheeks. "What brings you here?"

"Do I need a reason to visit my favorite roomie?" He leaned his ass casually against her desk and played with her collection of *Buffy* bobbleheads.

"Unless you count the furry creature that visits my balcony every night, I'm your only roomie."

He smirked knowingly. "Ah . . . George. He's probably looking for some roasted pumpkin seeds. Put a cup on the table outside and he'll be your best friend."

"You named the squirrel that frequents your balcony?"

"No, I named the squirrel that frequents *your* balcony, and the little dude gets grumpy if you forget his seeds too many days in a row. There's a small Ziploc for him in the left corner kitchen cabinet."

She chuckled. "Now that I know why he keeps tapping on the window, are you going to tell me why you're here?"

"The building super needs to come into the apartment for smoke alarm checks, and I wanted to make sure it was okay with you before telling him to stop by tomorrow afternoon."

She shot him a curious look. "You could've texted me. It would've saved you the trip downtown."

He shrugged. "I was in the area and knew your workday was about to end. Figured I'd offer you a ride home."

A ride home. Snuggled up against his back and inhaling his signature leather and spice . . .

Mentally willing the rising heat in her cheeks to disappear, she resumed packing her things. "You're spoiling me with all these rides to and from work. Keep it up and I'll throw temper tantrums whenever I'm forced to use public transport."

"Like you've ever thrown a tantrum over anything," Bax quipped.

"Spoken by someone who wasn't around to see what happened when my birthday Puppy Surprise pooch only had twins instead of triplets."

Bax's sweet answer aside, her inner bullshit meter twitched. No one fought to find Manhattan parking at *any* time—much less rush hour—to tell someone something that could be told later that night.

"Another question." Bax casually folded his arms over his chest. "What were you and the sandpaper asswipe talking about when I showed up?"

"Oh. Um . . ." She reached for the stack of Docket pre-assessments, but he beat her to it, handing them to her with a pointed look.

He wouldn't forget his question.

"He assumed that I'd forget about his asswipey behavior and attend the Alumni Gala with him this weekend," she admitted.

"The Alumni Gala? Sounds fancy."

"And pretentious. And pure pomp and circumstance." She tucked her remaining files into her drawer and locked them up. "It's also the one night a year that the university pulls out all the stops and tries wooing alumni into handing over more money than they did while they walked through these halls as students."

"And you're required to attend because you're head of Supernatural Studies," Bax guessed correctly.

"It definitely wouldn't look good if I don't, and I can't afford bad publicity with the fate of the SupeEx Project on the line because you bet your bubbling cauldron that everyone else hoping to get their hands on that grant money will be in attendance." She cringed remembering the pure misery that had been last year's event. "This is the side of higher education that I can really do without."

As a Maxwell, she'd done galas before, so many she could list it as a skill on her résumé. But she'd always had sister backup and, in worst-case scenarios, her phone, a reading app, and a keen ability to find a secluded corner where no one would bother her. Hiding from potential donors as a department head was frowned upon, and potentially career-ending.

The Alumni Gala was her introverted self's worse nightmare, worse than her childhood fear of coming face-to-scissorhand with Freddy Krueger.

Her gaze skittered over to her open Docket notebook and the few items she'd added.

Olive's Dare I Docket

1. Run away to join the circus
2. Do something spontaneous: hot tub skinny-dipping
3. Do something socially frightening
4. Get a tattoo
5. Something else...
6. Something in addition to...
7. Have hot, multiorgasmic sex
8. Go on a date that ENDS in hot, multiorgasmic sex
9. ?
10. ??

Her gaze snapped back to entries seven and eight, most definitely not written in her own handwriting. "*Harper.*"

The sex demon must have added them at some point over the

winter weekend, which could explain the wicked gleam in her eye as they'd traveled back into the city.

She shook off the surprise and slid her attention back to the third entry: *Do something socially frightening.*

Technically, the gala *was* a social event. Not one at which she'd have fun, but there'd be decent food, alcohol, and a high chance of someone getting caught in the coatroom doing something scandalous that would be talked about for years afterward.

"You okay, angel?" Bax scooted closer, his concerned gaze shifting from where she nervously bit her bottom lip to the notebook in her hand.

She snapped it shut before he could glimpse Harper's additions. "Yeah. Just thinking . . ."

If it would count if I magically cloned myself and sent the faux Olive to deal with all the pretentiousness.

He didn't look as if he quite believed her. "Not to be as presumptuous as the sandpaper asswipe, but if the gala isn't something you want to brave alone, I'd go with you."

Her eyes snapped to his. "Go with me."

"If you'd like."

"If I'd like?"

He shot her a small, shy smile and shifted awkwardly on his feet as he tucked a stray lock of hair behind his ear. "Or not."

She looped her briefcase bag over her shoulder before breaking into a giggle fit, and once started, she couldn't stop . . . not even when tears streaked her cheeks.

Bax's jaw muscle ticked wildly as he waited for her to finish. "Was it something I said?"

She bit her lip to keep from smiling. "Do you even own anything besides jeans and T-shirts? Because if so, I haven't seen them."

He huffed, looking cutely affronted. "I wore a suit to Vi and Linc's Bonding Ceremony."

"True, but affairs like this aren't exactly your thing. Over the years, Vi has tried guilting you into attending dozens of events, and for each one, you used work as an excuse why you couldn't go." She cocked up an eyebrow. "If you tell me that you actually worked them all, I'll part with all my books."

"That's a pretty steep bet for you."

"Is it really?" She mentally dared him to tell her she was wrong. "Somehow I'm at peace with my odds."

A few heartbeats passed before he smirked. "Good. Because you should be . . . but maybe my responses to those invites would've been different if *you'd* asked me."

Olive's smug smile slowly simmered as she digested his words, his tone, and the improbability that he meant that how it sounded.

Mistaking her abrupt silence for concern, he added, "You don't have to worry about me showing up to the gala in my gym clothes and embarrassing you. I'll be the perfect arm candy. I'll even shake hands and keep the growling to a minimum."

"I'm not worried about you embarrassing me, but the reverse," she admitted.

"I'm pretty difficult to embarrass." He pushed off the desk and, stepping closer, cupped her chin in a gentle upward tilt that made a horde of butterflies take flight in her stomach. "Maybe you're afraid I'll see another side to Olive Maxwell, or learn all your deep, dark secrets. If that's the case, I assure you, whatever shade of gray yours may be, mine are a hell of a lot darker."

She fell deep into his eyes, her breath stinted as she searched for any sign of joking. There was none.

Was Bax the silent and broody type? Absolutely. Did he keep secrets? No doubt. But until that moment, she had never considered the possibility of them being dark . . . or even charcoal gray.

"So do we have a date?" Bax's voice dropped to a husky rumble.

A *date*.

Harper's list addition threw an entire movie reel of images into her head, each one putting her more at risk for spontaneous combustion than the previous.

He didn't mean a *real* date. Just a roommate helping another roommate. A purely platonic favor, but with formalwear.

A muffled rendition of Salt-N-Pepa's "Let's Talk About Sex" blared from inside Olive's messenger bag. "Sorry. I should probably . . ." She dug through her things before pulling out her cell. "Hey, Harper. What's up?"

Bax failed to smother his laughter at the chosen ringtone.

"She's gone," Vi screeched from the other end of the line.

"Vi? Why are you calling from—"

"She's disappeared, Olly! The witch has gone freaking AWOL! She's *poof*'d! *Poof*'d!"

"Who's—"

"Why haven't you said anything?! Do you not get how serious this is? This will bring on Armageddon! Literal hell on earth! Am I talking to myself here?"

"You haven't let me get in a word. Are you done now?" Olive asked, keeping her voice calm. Vi seemed panicked enough for them both.

Her triplet's breath shook as she let out a heavy sigh. "Not hardly."

Bax, reading the room—or hearing Violet's shouts from over the line—stood upright, his attention laser-focused on the call.

"Do you want to tell me *who poof*'d?" Olive asked. "Is it Rose? Did something happen on a Hunt?"

"It's *Edie*. She's . . . gone."

Her heart stalled in her chest. In a blink, Bax stood next to her, his arms pulling her into a supportive embrace. "What do you mean she's *gone*?"

"She left us letters, Olly. Gran escaped the city and she's on the run."

Pinching the bridge of her nose, she resumed breathing and shot Bax a silent thank-you before attempting to rein in her sister. "So what you're saying is that Gran went on a vacation?"

"A vacation? *No.* No, this is some sort of elaborate ruse to . . . I don't know. The witch spelled herself so we couldn't track her, Olly. This was premeditated and well-thought-out. I'm calling an AWOD. Right now."

AWOD.

All. Witches. On. Deck.

"I'm not sure that will help. If Gran doesn't want to be found, she won't be," Olive pointed out. "Remember the lengths she went to when she played hide-and-seek with us when we were little?"

"You're right. This calls for All Supernaturals on Deck. Not just witches. I'll tell Rose to bring Damian, and Harper will have to suck up Adrian's existence. I'll just need to get hold of the Elusive One."

Her gaze flickered up to meet Bax's, his eyes twinkling as he nodded. "If by *Elusive One* you mean Bax, I got that covered."

"That's right. I keep forgetting the two of you are playing house."

"And the fact he's standing in front of me and can hear everything you say."

"Yeah?" Vi spoke louder. "Spread those sexy angel wings, suck up the height thing, and fly my sister to our brownstone ASAP, angel cakes, or the next time we have a BBQ, I'll make sure to put extra jalapeño in your burger. You get me?"

He chuckled. "You didn't say *please*, Vi."

"Baxter Bartholomew Donovan, I will curse you with a severe case of angel mange if you and my baby sister are not crash-landing into my backyard within ten minutes! I'm setting the timer on my phone!"

Vi hung up, leaving them both listening to dead air.

"I'm guessing you need an airlift, huh?" Bax joked dryly.

"I'll take the subway. I know you don't like heights."

"But I don't like angel mange more, and that's exactly what she threatened me with if I don't have you there in ten minutes or less. Take the subway and you're looking at an hour *at best*." He was already heading toward the door. "Collect whatever you need and I'll meet you up on the roof."

"Where are you going?"

"To get you a helmet. My flying might be a little . . . rusty."

She felt the color drain from her face. "Please tell me you're joking."

Chuckling, he turned and shot her a wink. "Liftoff in five minutes, angel."

✦ ✦ ✦

Four minutes later, she stepped onto the roof to find Bax, a motorcycle helmet in hand, looking somberly out over the New York City skyline. If he didn't look seconds away from throwing up, it would've been a picturesque scene, his broad shoulders framed by the gorgeous oranges and pinks of the setting sun.

"Are you sure about this? I can fire up my Ryde app in less than ten seconds. It's not a big deal." She felt bad, knowing he'd rather do *anything* else than fly.

"But angel mange is, as well as a bitch to get rid of. Hold this a sec." He handed her the helmet and plucked the clip from her hair.

Before she could ask him what he was doing, his large fingers combed through her fallen locks in an unexpected—and way too good—head massage. She sucked down a groan it felt so damn incredible.

He chuckled.

"Sorry." She blushed. "I didn't mean to . . . moan. It's just been a really long day, and that feels really good on my headache."

"I'm pretty fond of head massages myself, although I have an ulterior motive." He guided her hair over the front of her left shoulder and gently—and expertly—twined her hair into a loose braid before securing it with his backup hair tie.

"Did you seriously braid my hair?" At her inquisitive look, he smirked.

"Flight tangles are a bitch to comb out." He gave her a thoughtful once-over that left her nearly sweating despite the chill, and shrugged out of his leather jacket. "In you go."

She snorted. "I'm not wearing your jacket."

He cocked up an eyebrow at the obvious challenge. "It's cold, and with the wind while flying, it'll be even colder."

"All the more reason not to steal the warmth source of my personal angel-plane. What if your muscles freeze up or something and we end up plummeting toward the city sidewalk?"

"I'm my own personal heater, remember? But fine. You want to use logic, Professor? This is my favorite jacket—as you probably already know—and there's no way in hell I'm ripping it to shreds when I bring out the wings."

She narrowed her eyes at him as she tried to find something to counter with, but she didn't. Logic won. "Fine. Jacket me."

He smugly helped her slip it on.

Nearly three times too big, and too long for her hands to pop through, the jacket made her feel like a child playing dress-up. To complete the look, she tugged on the helmet—careful of her glasses—and struck a ridiculous pose. "How do I look?"

He drew the zipper to just below her chin. "Too fucking gorgeous for both our own good, angel."

Her eyes snapped to his and holy baby kittens . . .

Maybe it was her nearsightedness. Or being on the roof with a diminished oxygen supply. Hell, maybe it was wishful thinking. But the way he looked at her was the same way Harper looked at a sale announcement for Pleasure Palace Toys & Treasures.

Bax cleared his throat, breaking the spell. "Keep clear a second. I don't want to take you out with a wing or anything."

A rush of excitement went through her as she stepped back, giving him ample space. She'd seen angels in flight and walking about doing their thing. All her studies told her that, if plucked, an angel's feather only had a fifty percent chance of growing back, and that stroking an angel's wing was akin to foreplay.

But at thirty-four years of age, she'd never seen an angel sprout their wings.

"Do you need me to turn around?" She laughed at her own awkward eagerness. "I don't really know the etiquette for wing ejection."

He smirked mischievously, the sight sending her Magic into a warm bodily tingle. "Since when do roomies worry about etiquette? I dodged about a half dozen bra-and-panty sets on my way to take a shower this morning . . . and as an aside, it looks like we have the same favorite colors."

Her heated face was about to be the root cause of her spontaneous combustion. "I meant to take them down before I left, but—"

"No worries." He winked. "I'm definitely not complaining. Now . . . watch and learn, Professor. And no, you don't need to turn around."

One second, a hot, tatted-up, yummy specimen of a man stood in front of her, and a quick blink and T-shirt tug later, a shirtless angel.

Despite the tattoos and nipple piercings on display, it was the two huge wings in various shades of white, gray, and silver from which Olive couldn't tear her eyes. They stretched nearly eight feet across, the city's lights reflecting off their metallic hue and making them appear as if inlaid with diamonds.

Olive had no words. She barely had any knee strength as she devoured the entire visual vacation that was Baxter Donovan.

"You're gorgeous," she heard herself blurt out. "I mean . . . your *wings* are gorgeous. They're beautiful."

His lips twitched in enjoyment of the moment. "Just my wings?"

"Please. You know you could grace the cover of any angel romance book and light imaginations across the globe."

"Do I light up your imagination?"

That was a loaded question if she'd ever heard one. Every single self-preservation skill told her to abort the direction of this conversation or risk the dryness of her Friday granny panties.

"Sorry. I'm acting like this is my first time seeing wings," she rambled. "I just can't remember seeing *yours* before, which I suppose is probably a good thing, right? If I had, that would probably mean you're my Guardian and my life is in jeopardy."

As she chuckled nervously, Bax's smile slowly melted.

"Yeah. That would be unfortunate." He cleared his throat, the moment shifting. "You ready to go? The longer we stand here, the more likely I get hexed with angel mange. Feather-shedding and ointment-applying is not a pretty scenario for either of us."

She stepped closer, unsure what to do. "So how do we do this?"

"Like this." Large hands gripping her hips, he lifted her off her feet.

Olive released an unexpected squeal as his palms slid from her hips to her thighs, guiding her legs around his waist until he held her in a straddle-carry. A little shift. A tiny shimmy.

With faces less than an inch away, her gaze locked on his. "I guess this is one way to do it."

"You good?" His breath tickled her cheeks.

She nodded, not trusting herself to form words that wouldn't embarrass her all over again.

One muscled arm banded tighter around her waist while the other strayed dangerously close to giving her left ass cheek a VIP seat. "Hold on . . . and this probably goes without saying, but don't let go."

Ignoring Bax's low chuckle, she burrowed her face into the curve of his neck as much as the helmet allowed and held on for dear life as he stepped straight off the roof. They free dived for a terrifying few seconds before his large wings caught a breeze and propelled them upward.

After three solid minutes of flight time, she finally opened her eyes.

Bax remained relatively low, nowhere near high enough to brave a run-in with a 747 or a flock of seagulls, but it meant a lot of weaving in order to avoid hitting buildings. Soon enough, she found her body leaning into the turns along with him.

"This is a lot like riding the motorcycle . . . except with wings instead of wheels," she shouted loud enough to be heard over the whipping wind. "And with a lot less traffic."

Bax chuckled as he navigated them from Manhattan into Brooklyn in record time . . . easily within Vi's demanded arrival window.

Her sister's block came into view, and as they rounded the last string of brownstones, Bax pulled his wings down and let gravity do its thing. "Landing in three . . . two . . . one."

He dropped them gently into Vi and Linc's cozy backyard. "Thank you for choosing Angel Air. Before your departure from your pilot's waist, please see your steward for your complimentary bag of peanuts."

She chuckled. "You may not like flying, but you're good at it. I felt totally safe the entire time."

"Well, I had precious cargo on board, so I had reason to be extra careful." He winked and gently patted her ass. "You can depart now, angel. Unless you want me to take you on another ride."

The back door to the Brooklyn brownstone flung open, immediately halting her brewing naughty thoughts.

Vi, her hair blowing around her shoulders as if in a hurricane, stood in the doorway. Except this wasn't hurricane season, and there wasn't a single breeze. The witch's purple Magic swirled around her in a scary-ass version of a magical hamster ball.

Bax gently dragged Olive behind him, effectively putting himself between her and her triplet.

"What are you doing?" She skirted around his broad shoulders.

"Vi looks a little combustible right now." He watched Vi warily.

"You're going all Guardian because of my sister?" She snortled, shooting her sister a glare. "Vi, put away the light show. You're freaking out the big bad Guardian Angel. Seriously. I thought you've been meditating and working on your control?"

Vi let her hands—and her Magic—drop. "Evidently not enough . . . or maybe my control escaped to wherever the hex our wayward grandmother disappeared to. Tahiti. Tahoe. Toronto? Could be anywhere . . . because she basically said, *Don't waste your time looking for me. Have fun.*"

"*Basically* said?" Olive asked, curious, as she stepped into the house, Bax following.

"No, she said it. Well, *wrote* it." Vi waved something that looked like the letter in question. "At this point, I'm not sure which would be worse."

"Maybe no notice at all?" She hoped putting a bright spin on the situation would improve her sister's mood, but judging by the glare she got back, it didn't work.

Vi hadn't lied when she said she was calling an All Supernaturals on Deck, because she and Bax were the last to arrive. Even Adrian, commandeering a segment of the living room wall, nodded a hello, his unsmiling face devoid of emotion.

Olive went on instant alert.

Sitting next to Damian on the couch and looking a bare amount calmer than Vi, Rose handed Olive an unopened letter. "I saved this from Violet before she opened it herself and read it."

"Won't it basically say the same thing that's in yours?"

She shook her head. "The underlying message is the same, but—"

"She's skipped town," Vi blurted. "Performed a shake-and-break. Snuck away like a thief in the night."

"Did she take a vacation or rob a bank?" Bax joked.

All three sisters shot him irritated scowls.

"Sorry." He cleared his throat. "Too soon. Just trying to keep things in perspective."

"Don't," all three Maxwells said simultaneously.

"I don't get it." Olive looked at her unopened letter as if it might bite her. "Why would she leave without telling us? And why now, with Vi only weeks from stepping in as the next Prima? This isn't exactly the time to go off on a jolly jaunt to—"

"Tahoe . . . or Tahiti," Vi interjected. "And that is exactly what I've been saying, but no one will listen to me. There's no other excuse for her disappearance except that she's been witch-napped."

Rose hit her with a skeptical lift of her eyebrows. "She was witch-napped but was given the time to write three heartfelt goodbye letters?"

"They could've been written under duress."

"I think we should come to grips with there being another reason."

"And what reason would that be?" she asked.

"Hell if I know." Rose sighed. "I just said we had to accept she had her reasons, not that I knew what they were. Read your letter. Maybe she'll put a clue in yours that she didn't in either of ours."

Talk about a box of snakes. All eyes laid heavily on her as she slipped a finger beneath the envelope flap and pulled out what she recognized as her grandmother's ivory stationery. The good stuff, which she kept at her cottage in Athens.

My Dearest Olive,

By now, I'm sure your sisters have called an AWOD and informed you of my absence. I first want to assure you that I am well, and contrary to what Violet may believe, I wasn't witch-napped.

Second in only the written word, I am so very, very proud of you. I'm proud of all three of you . . . of the women you've become . . . of the witches that you are . . . and of the incredible forces of nature you are yet to be.

Great things lie in your future—in all of your futures—but in order for you to seek them out, to latch on to them and hold them dear, I'm gifting you with my never-ending love instead of my presence.

When others change around you, it's all too easy for a witch to be plagued with feelings of stagnancy. These are feelings I am quite familiar with, as it feels like yesterday that I was faced with the same self-questioning doubts. But rest assured, the world is always moving . . . and moving us along with it. There are simply those of us who have a greater distance to travel.

I'm sure you're probably more confused now than you were prior to your sisters' calls, but I want to assure you, my sweet Olive, that this is not goodbye. This is a loving pat on the ass and a go get 'em.

PS. This letter is yours to do with—and share with whom you please. Share with your sisters. Keep it close to your heart. The only thing I ask is that you don't let your sister call the National Guard (you know which sister I mean because she's probably staring you down right now). I. Am. Fine.

Let your Magic guide you,

Gran

Olive glanced up, and sure enough, Vi's lavender eyes narrowed on her as if attempting to pluck the letter straight from her mind.

"Okay." She tucked the letter back in the envelope.

Vi blinked. "Okay? Okay?! That's all you can say about our grandmother—the Prima of the entire hexing witch community—going AWOL!"

"She seems fine, Vi. I don't know what to say except there's no reason to call the National Guard. When she wants to be found is when she'll stroll into the room."

On reflex, all eyes drifted to the back door.

"Guess that isn't now," she cracked dryly.

Vi dropped into a corner chair with a heavy sigh, Linc right at her side, massaging the back of her neck. "This is a disaster. This really is the start of Armageddon."

"Is it really *that* bad? I mean, I know it's far from ideal, but you've been filling in for Gran here and there with the Council. She even had you take that trip to the Alaskan coven solo."

"Because she had food poisoning. I had no other choice. We couldn't exactly have her retching on the Head Warlock's lap during dinner." Her sister's eyes slowly widened. "Hex me. Do you think she faked an illness so I'd be forced go alone? She wouldn't do that, would she?"

Rose chuckled. "She totally would. Has she 'erroneously' double-booked meetings? Showed up late to others?"

"Yes, but . . ." Realization hit the Prima Apparent like an anvil. "That bwitch!"

"I'm not saying it wasn't all coincidental, but after reading my letter and thinking back to my last few interactions with Edie, I think she may have been subtly preparing us for this."

"For abandonment?"

"It's a fly-or-fall moment," Bax added.

"What do you mean?" Olive shifted her attention to where he leaned sexily against the wall.

At some point he'd put his shirt back on, and she couldn't help but be a bit sad about it. But he hadn't asked for his jacket back, so she counted that as a small win in her favor.

"It happens all the time in angel society," Bax clarified. "Hell, even birds do it. The parental figure leaves the nest and lets the next generation figure their shit out on their own. It can be scary as hell, but the result is almost always flight."

Vi scowled. "But some fall flat on their asses and end up breaking tailbones and wings and other important body parts. Stick to angeling, angel cakes, because you're a long way from being a public motivational speaker."

"He has a point." Olive stood up for him. "How many times did Rose turn down your wing-witch proposal for the exact same reason?"

"Because she was secretly in love with Damian and all the cute, furry fluffiness that surrounds him on a daily basis at the sanctuary," Vi answered with a smirk.

Everyone chuckled.

"Well, yeah." Olive grinned. "But there was also wanting you to do your own thing without having a safety net."

Rose nodded. "She's not wrong. That's exactly why I did it."

With a heavy groan, Vi flung her head back on the chair. "I hate it when everyone makes sense and I have no other option than to go along with it. Hex me. I may actually be forced into doing this Prima shit by myself."

Linc dropped a sweet kiss on her forehead. "Not by yourself. I got your backside, princess."

"Thanks, wolf-man." She grinned and pulled him down for another kiss. "I knew I kept you around for a reason other than the amazing orgasms."

Olive slammed her hands over her ears. "Nope. No. Stop right there. We've gone over how it's only slightly less creepy hearing about my sisters' multiple Os than it is Mom's or Edie's."

The room erupted into laughter, the earlier tension not gone but diminished and hanging over their heads like an ever-present cloud.

Olive hoped to Goddess she didn't convince her sisters that everything would be fine right before Armageddon really did come to claim that all . . . although experiencing the End of Days would definitely be considered out of her comfort zone and, therefore, a good addition to her Docket.

Plus sides.

10

My Little Pony Vs. Care Bears

Harper stood behind Olive as they stared at her reflection in the standing mirror. "Fucking perfection. You outdid yourself, Harp. Really."

Olive slid her friend an amused smirk. "You're also talking about yourself in the third person."

"Someone has to give me a *job well done* because you've been woefully quiet, but you're forgiven. These things happen when you're excited about an upcoming date . . . and the things that could happen afterward." The succubus smirked suggestively.

"This isn't a *date* date. This is a friend helping another friend avoid potential social awkwardness. The only thing happening afterward is three ibuprofen and my flannel PJs . . . and maybe take-out from a carton."

"I think the witch doth protest too much. I mean, did Bax *say* it wasn't a date? What were his exact words when he suggested he go with you to this peacock fest?"

She did a mental rewind of the conversation in her office, moments before Salt-N-Pepa broke into song when he said . . .

"So do we have a date . . . ?"

Her mouth opened and closed while Harper's grin broadened knowingly. "That's what I thought."

"He didn't mean it like *that*," she protested.

"Until he confirms otherwise, I wouldn't bet my sex toys on it."

"You wouldn't bet your toys on anything. They're your most prized possessions."

"Yeah, you're right." Harper tossed her head of full red curls back in laughter. "But even if they weren't, I still wouldn't bet them."

With a slight eyeroll, Olive gave herself a second glance in the mirror and blinked at the woman looking back at her. Minimal mascara coated her long eyelashes, and her familiar dark blue eyes had been made to pop behind her thick-framed glasses. Even her usually stick-straight hair had been given life via a modern take on a '40s-pinup swoop that left her shoulders and neck bare.

But the real star of the show? The dress.

The black vintage-style swing dress—*with pockets*—stopped just below her knees, its full skirt falling like ebony waves and a perfect complement to her red leather peep-toe pumps. But it was the top half from which she couldn't tear her eyes.

The fabric hugged every curve, cinching in at her waist and molding to her breasts in a sexy straight-line bodice showcasing her impressive cleavage. And for an extra touch, two finger-wide straps crisscrossed over her exposed collarbone and linked together at her nape.

Feeling both sexy and stylish, she contemplated never taking the thing off. "You really did outdo yourself, Harp. I want to scrub toilets in this dress, if you know what I mean."

"I do." Her friend chuckled, waving off her compliment. "But I only brought the dress. The rest is all you, babe. But now it's time for Cinderella to move her gorgeous witchy ass, or she'll be late for the ball."

She groaned, remembering why she'd slathered rose blossom lotion into all her nooks and crannies for the better part of the last hour. "Maybe I should stay home. It would be a shame if anything happened to this dress."

"Absolutely not. This dress—on you—was made to be seen and admired, and what better way for that to happen than hanging off the arm of the angelic eye candy waiting in the other room?" Harper steered her through the open bedroom door and, once clear, not-so-gently nudged her closer to her maybe-not-a-date.

Bax's gaze caressed her from her stocking-clad legs and up the sexy line of her bodice, leaving a trail of goose bumps over every inch he visually devoured.

In strict survival mode, she avoided meeting his eyes directly for as long as possible—which ended up being ten, maybe fifteen seconds. The second his gaze fixed firmly on hers, the heat rushing through her body wasn't confined solely to her cheeks.

"You're fucking breathtaking," he complimented, his voice a low, husky rumble. Clearing his throat, he quickly added, "You're always gorgeous, but . . . *yeah*. Daggers will definitely be hurled at my back all night."

Her lips pulled up into a small smile. "Why and from who will there be hurled daggers?"

"From everyone wishing you were on their arm instead of mine."

Movement from the corner of her eye had her turning her head just in time to see Harper flashing him an approving thumbs-up. She stopped immediately, feigning wide-eyed innocence. "What? That was good. He deserved positive reinforcement . . . like a puppy."

A bit overwhelmed by Bax's sincerity, Olive unnecessarily tucked her glasses higher onto her nose and joked, "I'll watch your back. It's the least I can do considering you're doing me a favor. Plus, we can't have anyone damaging your one and only suit."

With her attention temporarily focused on her shoes, she didn't see Bax move until he cupped her chin, gently tilting her face toward his. "Let's get one thing straight before we head out that door, angel."

"Okay . . ." she whispered, mesmerized by the fierce glint in his eyes.

"There are no favors happening here. I'm doing this for the purely selfish reason of getting to spend the evening with a gorgeous witch who possesses the ability to enchant me without casting a flicker of Magic."

All thought processes ended. "Oh."

"Oh," he parroted, his lips tilting into a crooked smirk. "Are we clear now?"

She nodded, unable to form words just yet.

"And that's my cue to make myself disappear." Harper shot her an *I told you so* look before donning her coat and grabbing her bag. "You two gorgeous people have fun, take chances, and Olive babe?"

She tore her attention away from Bax. "Hm?"

"Item eight. Within your grasp. Just reach out and touch it." She waved and left them alone.

"Item eight?" Bax asked, lips twitching.

"Just Harper being Harper," Olive explained, her cheeks flaming as she reached for her wrap. "We should probably go if we want to be considered fashionably late. I'll request a Ryde when we get downstairs and—"

"No need." Bax twirled a set of familiar car keys. "We already have a ride courtesy of Alpha Thorne."

Her eyes widened. "Linc gave you the keys to his *baby*? He barely lets Vi drive it. Of course, that could have something to do with her parking-ticket-accrual rate. She has a rare talent of finding every single traffic camera in the tristate area."

"Oh, he didn't hand over the keys before performing a very thorough background check and doling out a serious threat to my testicles if it should come out of the night with so much as a scratch."

"So, in other words, he's lightening up?"

"Practically light as a feather." Bax chuckled.

They headed downstairs, and by the time they reached the sidewalk, she'd almost convinced herself this was any typical night between two friends. Then Bax's hand fell to the small of her back and he led the way to Linc's parked Jeep.

Normally, being *guided* sent her into an eyeroll. In books. In movies. It didn't matter. The gesture always annoyed her. But Bax's large palm on *her* back not only elicited a warm, fuzzy tingle in her lower stomach, but one that intensified the longer his hand remained.

She damn near pouted when he opened the passenger's side door and the connection came to an end.

"Your ride, Professor Maxwell." He gestured to the empty seat.

"Thank you, Guardian Donovan." With a coy grin, she plucked the keys from his other hand and, leaving him by the open door, stepped around to the driver's side and slid behind the wheel herself.

Some guys would've balked or grumbled at the move, but Bax chuckled as he got into the passenger seat and buckled up. She'd barely pulled away from the curb when the angel began sabotaging Linc's radio stations, programming channels the wolf shifter would never in a million years listen to except under extreme duress—or gunpoint.

Like opera.

The second he finished reprogramming every button, he looked around for anything else with which to mess around.

She shook her head, amused.

"Don't look at me like that. This is payback for putting a Care Bears sticker on my Harley." Bax flipped open the glove compartment, looking contemplative as he shifted around its contents.

"You have a problem with the Care Bears?"

"No, but anyone with a speck of good taste knows that it was really My Little Pony that ruled Saturday morning cartoons."

"So, you wouldn't be messing with Linc's things if he'd put a Blue Belle sticker on your bike's gas tank instead of Grumpy Bear?"

Bax paused his search through the middle console and drilled her with a pensive look. "How did you know he put a Grumpy Bear sticker on my gas tank? I didn't tell a soul and I scraped that shit off before anyone saw it . . . or I thought I did."

Shit. Olive yanked her attention back to the road. "He must have told Vi, who must have told me."

Actually, Linc *did* tell her sister, who *did* inform her . . . except Olive had already known because it hadn't been the wolf shifter who'd tagged the bike.

It had been her.

Bax studied her carefully, every second feeling like an hour. By the time they hit four ridiculously long hour-seconds, she caved, slipping him a glance. "You know it was me, don't you?"

Bax laughed, the sound easing her nerves. "You're gifted with many things, angel, but a poker face isn't one of them. So yeah, I figured it out."

"It had an easy-peel adhesive. It shouldn't have damaged the paint."

"It didn't."

"And in my defense, after snapping at practically everyone that week, you'd more than earned the Grump title and the sticker."

"I know." His lips twitched.

"Vi wanted to TP the bike and hang unflattering signs from the handles, but Rose Rose-talked her out of it. You really are lucky you only got a Grumpy Bear."

"It was a really cute sticker—holographic and everything."

She shot him a glance and they broke into laughter, Olive hard enough a tear welled at the corner of her eye.

"So how's your Docket list coming along? Fill in any more spots? Cross anything off?" Bax asked casually as she maneuvered the SUV around a slow-moving Ryde car.

She thought about Harper's additions, which she hadn't yet erased for reasons she didn't understand.

Despite Bax's insistence he wasn't coming with her tonight because of a friendship favor, she couldn't shrug off the insecure voice in her head telling her he'd said it to be nice. If she couldn't quite get herself to believe it was a *date* date, she sure as hell couldn't imagine ticking off either added item.

"Like I said before, I'm not sure I should really cross off *do something spontaneous* after the hot tub fiasco, but tonight definitely fulfills *do something socially frightening*." She remembered her earlier internet search and exclaimed excitedly, "But I registered for classes at Cirque du Surnaturel, so I'll be able to cross that one off soon."

His head whipped toward her, the sight almost comical. "Circus of the Supernatural?"

"Have you heard of them? I can't wait. I only signed up for two introductory aerial classes, but if I end up liking it, they have an amateur performers club where you train weekly under one of the pros and the group puts on semiannual shows and everything."

"That's something you'd be interested in doing routinely?"

Slipping him a look, she tried—and failed—to decipher his odd tone and sudden stiffness. "Guess I won't know until I have my first class, but it's possible. My original plan was to convince Vi to do my entire Docket with me, but with Gran MIA and the upcoming Exchange Ceremony looming in the distance, she's already dealing with enough stress. Throwing in the potential for unexpected injury would definitely push her over the edge."

Bax cursed under his breath as he dragged a hand through his hair, accidently ripping out his hair tie. His long locks tumbled over his shoulders in a sexily messy contrast to the stylish, clean-cut suit.

It was a good thing she was already sitting.

"You should leave it down," she blurted.

He shot her a questioning look.

"Your hair's nice when pulled back, too, but when it's down, it's like a soft, sexy curtain framing the rougher angles of your jaw. It's . . . attractive."

He kicked up a single eyebrow.

She groaned internally. Harper's hair and makeup intervention really should've included tape over her mouth.

But he tucked the hair tie into his suit pocket, leaving his hair loose around his shoulders. "So if Vi isn't doing the Docket with you, does that mean you're—"

"A one-woman show? Yep." She let the *p* pop off her lips.

"Seems kind of dangerous, don't you think? Especially this circus thing."

"No more dangerous than riding the subway, and yet millions of people in the city do it every day."

Bax's mouth slid into a tight line for some reason, looking unimpressed and not particularly thrilled. She didn't get it, and seeing the Soho Grand's valet entrance ahead, she didn't have time to dwell on it.

She veered into the lineup of cars and waited, tapping her fingers on the steering wheel as she waited for their turn. When they reached the front of the line, Bax quickly jumped from the Jeep and beat the valet attendant in opening her door.

He helped her step onto the sidewalk and, once she had her feet firmly planted, slipped one thickly corded arm around her waist. Everywhere they touched, her skin heated, electrifying her already frazzled nerves as they stepped into the hotel's foyer.

In the lobby, swarms of people made it difficult to maneuver easily, but somehow Bax managed, guiding her to a gentle stop.

She shot him a questioning look, wondering why they'd come to a halt. "Did you forget something in the car?" she asked. "Or did you change your mind? We can leave. They probably haven't even parked the car yet."

He chuckled at her hopeful tone. "Sorry, angel. I'm not leaving until I get at least one dance with you."

"Then . . ."

"I'll do it with you."

She blinked, then blinked again. "I'm sorry, but you'll have to clear that up for me a bit more. You'll do what with me?"

"The circus thing."

Her brows shot up. "*You?*"

He smirked sexily. "Should I be offended that you look so surprised?"

"You heard me say it's a circus *aerial* class, right? That means most—if not all—the tricks learned will require being off the ground."

"After snow-tubing and being your Angel Air pilot, it'll be nothing. Besides, I have a built-in harness if it comes down to it. The pretty wings aren't all for show. Unless there's a reason why you don't want me to go . . ."

"No." *Yes—if no one witnesses you fall on your ass, did it really happen?* "I know the GAA keeps you busy . . . although it doesn't feel as though that's been the case lately, but maybe that's because I'm living with you now, and so I see you more."

"It's not a problem. Besides, it sounds like it could be fun." He glanced away, avoiding her eyes. "Maybe I can do the entire Docket with you in Vi's place."

"Why in Goddess's name would you want to do that?"

He shrugged. "It got me thinking about my own comfort zones and how I don't often step out of them. Like you said, I have my Guardian duties, too, so I don't know that creating my own list makes sense, but I'm good with experiencing yours. Unless you don't want me hanging around and in your way. If that's the case, tell me and I'll mind my own damn business."

"You wouldn't be in the way. It's just . . . I *can* do this on my own. I don't need a babysitter, or someone to hold my hand." A burly older man bumped into her from the back, sending her careening into his arms. "Okay, so maybe literal hand-holding wouldn't be such a bad idea for tonight."

Grinning softly, he brushed a loose lock of hair off her cheek, his fingers trailing gently over her skin. "Trust me. I know you're extremely capable. And I'm up for literal hand-holding whenever you'd like, but I'm not talking about babysitting. I'm talking about a . . . partnership."

He wanted to hold her hand? Wait. What were they talking about?

Doing the Docket with her . . .

"Dockets are very individualized. I don't want you to feel forced into going through with anything you're not comfortable doing."

"I won't."

She clobbered him with her best stern glare. "I mean it. This project is meant to be eye-opening, not horror-inducing."

"Says the woman who put *do something socially frightening* on her list."

She shrugged. "I'm practically a professional at not following my own advice. But if this is something you seriously want to do, I'm good with it. It might be nice to have a . . . partner."

✦ ✦ ✦

Did he *want* to hang upside down on a trapeze while the entire thing swung back and forth—or whatever else they learned at the supernatural circus? Fuck no. *Would* he if it meant spending quality time with Olive without interference from their friend circle?

Hell yes. It also made his Assignment as her Guardian a lot easier by giving him a reason for always being underfoot. Two checks in the pro column right there . . . if he survived the aerial classes.

Needing to keep her close, he slipped an arm back around her waist. "Now that that's settled, let's go show the grant board why they'd be idiots not throwing that project money your way."

They checked in at a small welcome table where Olive gave their names and was handed two small ribbon pins. Gold signified

NYU alumni, silver for administration and university faculty, and metallic bronze for everyone else.

Curious stares turned their way as they navigated the ballroom, each one making the gorgeous woman next him a little stiffer until she felt like a mobile plank in his arms.

He dipped his head close to her ear. "You okay?"

"Yeah. No. Maybe." Her delicate fingers nervously smoothed her already immaculate dress skirt. "I just really hate these things. They make me feel like a bug under a microscope."

"If it's any consolation, you're a fucking gorgeous bug."

She gifted him a small smile that flipped his insides on end. That smile could light the entire world. "Thank you . . . but no. It doesn't help."

They chuckled.

"I'm by no means a professional at these things, but when I do go, do you know what helps me get through the night? Other than having stellar company?"

Her lips twitched. "What?"

"Not giving a shit. You're the best damn thing to happen to the university's Supernatural Studies program, and I'd bet my Harley that the administration—and that grant board—know it, too."

Olive scrunched her freckle-dusted nose. "I wouldn't."

Easing her to a stop, he cupped her cheek and gently guided her gaze to his. "You have *no one* to impress here, Olive Maxwell. That means there's no pressure, nor any reason to give two fucks. Eat the food. Drink the drinks. And dance with your rhythm-challenged date."

"Hear, hear," a voice cheered nearby.

Two twenty-somethings approached, the petite brunette smacking her much taller friend in the stomach . . . the source of the cheer, Bax realized.

"Hey, Professor Maxwell." The young student stopped with an apologetic smile.

Olive's face brightened. "If it isn't two of my favorite students! It's great to see you both here." Her gaze flickered to him. "Iliana and Omar are in my Supernatural Studies class. They were also both selected by the university president to represent the student body tonight."

Bax nodded with a polite smile. "That seems like a pretty big honor."

"It is," Olive stated proudly. "They're two of the brightest critical thinkers I've ever had in my classroom."

"You're the big dude with the ass-kicking motorcycle, aren't you?" Omar asked bluntly.

Iliana gifted him an irritated look and an elbow in the rib.

"What? I swear it's him!" He shot his attention toward Bax. "It was, right? You gave Professor Max a ride to school a while back."

"Bax Donovan." He held out his hand, and both kids accepted with a smile. "And yes, that was me."

"I'd die to get a bike like yours. It's fucking sick," Omar gushed. "But—"

"He'd crash it the way he crashes his regular two-wheeled bicycle . . . on a regular basis," Iliana interjected.

"I would not," Omar grumbled.

"He would, but then, instead of eating the occasional faceful of pavement, the pavement would eat him."

Bax swallowed a chuckle, and a glance toward Olive told him she was fighting to do the same. They chatted another few minutes before Iliana dragged Omar away, and soon enough, the two students were replaced with another couple, and when *they* left, with another.

As much as Olive hated the social aspect of the gala, she handled it with apparent ease, talking about the addition of Supernatural Studies to the university's curriculum, and the importance it would play in the future. The witch really was a force of nature.

After an hour of steady questions and answers, he noted the

slight droop to her shoulders. Once she finished talking to an older alumni couple, he cupped her arm and gently steered her to a slightly less populated area of the room, procuring a glass of water from a tray along the way.

"Drink," he demanded gently.

"You read my mind." She took it eagerly and downed it in the longest, un-gala-like gulps imaginable before flashing him a grateful smile. "Thank you."

"It's my duty as your date to ensure you're happy and hydrated."

The curve of her lips slowly wilted. "I'll be happiest when I can get into my slippers and out of these shoes. They're definitely cute, but not too comfortable."

"Educating is damn hard work."

"Educating is easy compared to all this schmoozing, but hopefully all the talking impressed enough people to part with their hard-earned money." She drained the last contents of her glass and placed it on a nearby tray.

"If I had any spare money to part with, I would've already handed all of it over to you."

"You, Bax Donovan, are so much sweeter than you let everyone know. Thank you for playing my backup tonight. It means a lot." She ran her fingers over the edge of his jacket and rested her hand on his chest.

He couldn't help it. Sliding his hand over hers, he held her touch hostage, his pounding heart prepped to burst through his suit at any moment. If she felt it, she didn't say anything, and damned if he could form any words.

Her blue eyes were two oceanic pools of gorgeous in which he would gladly drown any day, anytime. He pulled his attention away from them only long enough to drop his gaze to her mouth and caught her doing the same to him. It upped his heart rate from a steady thump to a thundering gallop.

An overwhelming ache to taste her lips rushed through him,

and with her inches away, accomplishing it would be easy, but something told him that stopping at one quick sample would be an entirely different ball game.

If—or when—they kissed, he wanted no limitations except for the ones they created for themselves. And he definitely didn't want an audience.

To prevent himself from starting something they couldn't finish, he gestured to the crowd of swaying bodies. "Didn't we say something about a dance? It'll give your voice a rest and you time to decide if you're done schmoozing for the night."

She smiled softly. "Sounds like a plan."

His hand swallowed hers as he led her to an unoccupied spot. Finding it on the edge of the dance floor, he twirled her into his waiting arms and was rewarded with the musical sound of her giggles.

This was definitely not Glow-type dancing. With his one hand encompassing Olive's, and his other resting low on her hip, he drew her close, the act somehow a hell of a lot more intimate than the body-grinding sway found in NYC clubs.

Olive trailed her gaze from his chest to his face, and he forgot he didn't know how to dance. With her in his arms, agility came easy. It had been the same with their angel-flight into Brooklyn. Not even the slightest palpitation. Not a single cold sweat—at least not one caused by his fear of heights.

But when she'd nestled her nose into the curve of his neck?

He'd been a heartbeat-skipping, cold-sweaty mess . . . and wanted nothing more than to pull her a little bit closer and experience the side effects—and the soft warmth of her body—all over again.

As if reading his mind, Olive closed the small distance between them, bringing their bodies into perfect alignment. He rested his cheek against her forehead and enjoyed the moment, realizing he wasn't sure if he'd ever experienced one this perfect in his lifetime.

Movement from just off the dance floor caught his attention and immediately shattered that perfection.

Mikael Donovan stood across the room wearing a black tux that looked as if it had been tailor-made, his dark eyes drilled on him and Olive. A subtle chin lift gifted Bax his nonverbal directive.

A word . . .

With a huge dose of heavy regret, he eased away from Olive. Her confused look morphed into one of disappointment as he dropped his hands.

"Sorry, angel, but it looks like someone is attempting to grab your attention." He gestured to a tall, gangly man with a faculty ribbon pinned to the front of his jacket who was indeed attempting to gain her attention.

She followed her gaze and groaned. "That would be the university president. Do you think I can pretend I didn't see him?"

"Maybe before you made eye contact just now." He smirked.

"Do you want to join me?" She peered up at him with wide, hopeful eyes. "Maybe dazzle him with stories of Guardian life so he forgets to drill me on how the night's going?"

"Sorry, angel. Guardian life is—"

"More secretive than the CIA. I know. Well, wish me luck . . . and maybe keep those pretty wings at the ready because I might need a hasty getaway."

"You don't need luck. You *are* luck." She rolled her eyes, making him laugh.

He watched her walk across the room with confidence, only taking his eyes off her when she reached the president's side. With her safely distracted, he followed Mikael at a distance and stepped onto an empty balcony.

"What the hell do you think you're doing?" Mikael growled the second the door closed behind him.

"Working." Bax clenched his jaw. "Which is more than I can say for you. Did you manage to corral all the rogue nasties hell-bent on making this plane their next demonic playground? Because I can't explain your suddenly frequent appearances by anything else."

The older angel flung a blunt-tipped finger back toward the ballroom. "*That* is what you call work? No wonder your last few Assignments have fallen through the cracks—one of them almost literally."

"I disclosed I had a relationship with Olly, so don't you dare act like I'm doing something morally wrong here."

Mikael's brow rose. "You mean with your *Assignment* . . . and you said you were friends. *Roommates.* You said nothing of the fact that you were *fucking* roommates."

A rush of anger brought him within an inch of his father's snarling face. "Do *not* speak of her that way. Ever again. As a matter of fact, don't speak of her *ever.*"

"Do you have *no* self-preservation? You're playing a game that will not only get your wings clipped, but will ruin your future, and why? For some witch?"

"Like you give a damn about my future . . . at least not since you realized I'll never be your spitting image. Hell, I'll never come close, and that makes me fucking ecstatic."

Neck veins bulging, Mikael's face reddened to an unhealthy shade of crimson. "You'll bring disgrace to the Donovan line with your actions, and I won't have it. I forbid it."

Bax snorted. "In your eyes, that happened the moment the Warrior Academy sent me packing, so let's not pretend otherwise."

His gaze locked with his father's in a stare-down so epic, he didn't hear the balcony door open or sense Olive's presence until her hand cautiously touched his arm.

"Sorry to interrupt," she apologized.

"You aren't interrupting, angel." He gentled his voice, ripping his attention away from the man in front of him and focusing on a wary Olive. "Congratulations. You survived your conversation with the president."

Her gaze volleyed between him and Mikael. "Yeah, but it definitely drained me of any residual peopling energy. I'm ready for ibuprofen and PJs anytime you are."

"Ibuprofen and PJs it is then." Wrapping an arm around her waist, he steered her back toward the hotel.

They'd made it to the balcony door when his father's voice slithered down his spine. "Miss Maxwell, if I may be so bold—"

"No, you may not." Bax whirled around, his abruptness widening Olive's eyes. "As a matter of fact, you may not be anything except *gone*. You sure as hell can't talk—"

"To your *roommate*," Mikael finished snarkily. "You once possessed such promise, Baxter."

He held the door open for Olive and ushered her through. "Yeah . . . and then I turned five."

Despite the million questions floating around in her eyes, Olive didn't pepper him with a single one, instead walking silently by his side as they left the gala. Then she waited patiently next to him as the valet brought Linc's SUV around front. And when he drove them home, his white-knuckled grip adhered to the gearshift, she loosened his clenched fist one finger at a time and gently tugged their interlocked hands onto her lap.

Maybe he held on to her.

Or maybe they held on to each other.

Either way, they both held on. Tightly.

11

Numbers Seven & Eight

Bax slowly guided his pencil down the page, his eyes tracking the graphite left behind. He'd already worked on Olive's art piece for two hours this morning and was no closer to figuring out what the hell was forming.

It seemed attempting to figure shit out and coming up blank was his current modus operandi.

The GAA—*blank*. Olive—*blank*, but with an underlying physical ache. Mikael—*blank*, but with a not-so-hidden desperation to punch something. Then there was why the hell he was currently hiding in the back office of his second home instead of at his real home—*blank*, but with a huge suspicion it had a lot to do with the accumulation of the first three.

The unknowns fucked with his head so much that he keyed himself into Inklings before the tattoo shop had even opened and hadn't moved much since.

A throat-clear alerted him that he was no longer alone, and when he ignored it, a second—louder—clearing sounded. "Am I getting to use my office at any point today, or should I plan on balancing the books on the toilet?"

The sarcasm pulled his attention to the older man standing in the doorway.

His tatted arms folded over his broad chest, Inklings' owner didn't look a day over fifty, but as Isaiah Thomas reminded him frequently, his opportune retirement age was quickly approaching.

Honestly, the former Warrior Angel could probably still kick ass better than those half his age, but he'd become one of the very rare few who'd said goodbye to the Warrior life before life said goodbye to him.

He also still maintained an uncanny ability to call Bax out on his shit, which was why he'd hoped the angel's mammoth client list would keep him occupied a bit longer.

Bax pulled his attention back to the sketchbook in front of him, his lips twitching. "We both know you only pretend to balance the books so you can watch that Supernatural dating show. You give the actual work to Al, the accountant at the firm down the block."

Isaiah drilled him with a warning glare. "Tell Ruby and they'll never find your body. That blissful hour once a week is the only time I get a damn break."

"From her or in general?" he asked, always teasing the older man about his spunky—and driven—receptionist.

"Both."

They chuckled, and Isaiah made himself comfortable in the chair across from him before kicking his boots up on the desk. "So . . ."

"No."

Isaiah's hairline rose. "No? I didn't even say anything yet."

"But I know what you're about to say, and the answer is still no."

"You do know that the more you fight this, the more determined it makes me to get a yes out of you."

"And you know that no matter how much you hound me about it, my answer won't change, right?" he countered.

"Do I know that? I'm not sure that I do. Actually, I'm pretty certain that all I need to do is hit you at the right moment and you'll flip like a deck of cards. It's in your blood, Donovan."

"So are red blood cells . . . but the answer is still no."

Isaiah sighed, lounging back in the chair. "Fine. We'll talk about you buying me out of Inklings another time. Maybe when you're in a better mood and not using my office as a safe room."

"I don't know what you're talking about." He avoided meeting his eyes.

"Do not bullshit a bullshitter, kid. You parked your ass in that chair when the sun was barely up and you haven't taken your eyes off that sketchbook since. Start talking."

"Wouldn't you rather watch your dating show?"

"I'd rather kick your ass until you start spilling, but my back just stopped hurting from the last time I did that."

Realizing the man wouldn't quit until he gave him something, Bax dropped his pencil to the page. "It's not one thing."

Isaiah waited expectantly.

"You seriously expect me to just start spewing?" Met with irritating silence, Bax gave up. "Fine. Long stories short. I've been put on probation—again—and my last-chance Assignment happens to be my new roommate and the woman I'm pretty sure I have a thing for. Add in Mikael popping up like a bad rash, the aforementioned roomie wanting to literally walk a tightwire or some shit, and yeah . . . I need a few minutes to myself."

The older angel leaned forward in his seat, elbows resting on his knees as he digested Bax's verbal diarrhea. "Let me get this straight—you have two Assignments? A new roommate and the woman you're—"

An abrupt realization sent Isaiah's bushy eyebrows hitting his hairline. "Your Assignment, the roommate, and the crush are one and the same."

"Ding-ding. Give the man a steak."

"Fuck."

"I've pretty much replayed that same word in my head on a rotating basis for the last few weeks now."

"Let me make sure I'm clear about the sequence of events. Did you know you had a thing for this woman before or after she became your roommate?"

No. Maybe. Damn it, yes . . .

Bax scowled at the other man. "Why does that matter? She's a good friend and she was in an unsafe situation. I had the means to help her out. I didn't think it would be an issue."

"Yeah? And what about now?"

"I didn't ask for them to assign me as her Guardian."

"Then why did they? The second you disclosed your connection to her, they should've reassigned her to someone else. I know Wright can be a hard-ass, but even she wouldn't knowingly set you up for failure."

Bax glanced away.

"Oh, kid. You didn't tell them."

"There was nothing to tell . . . at the time," he defended himself. "It was a crush and, from what I could see, very one-sided. We're not exactly what others would label compatible."

Isaiah snorted. "Some people said the same thing about Jacob and I—angel and demon—and we just celebrated our thirtieth anniversary."

"Congrats, man. That's awesome! You guys do anything special to celebrate?"

"It is, and we did." Isaiah smiled, thinking of his husband. "And stop trying to shift the topic off this new crush-worthy Assignment."

"I wasn't," Bax denied.

"Liar," Isaiah scoffed. "Now that this woman is your Assignment, you realize that—"

"She's fucking incredible, okay? And I'd been kidding myself believing I could keep my distance . . . and sometimes I get the feeling she doesn't want to, either."

"You're playing a dangerous game if your long-term plan is to keep your Guardian wings."

"So Mikael has told me," Bax muttered.

"I don't envy you, kid."

"For having Mikael Donovan as a sperm donor?"

Isaiah snorted. "For that, too." To say the two Warrior Angels had not gotten along during their service together was putting it mildly. "But the way I see it, you have less than a handful of choices."

"And those are?"

"You can either keep playing the game and hope you pass the finish line without anyone getting hurt in the process. Or you call an end to it now, hope for the same . . . and then buy me out of Inklings and actually do something you enjoy." Isaiah grinned.

"You're no fucking help, old man." He threw his pencil at him, and the former Warrior dodged it easily, laughing as he headed for the office door.

"Never claimed to be, kid. Either go deal with your shit or pay me rent because I'm kicking your ass out in thirty minutes. I need to find out who Imani sent home before Ruby spoils it for me like last week.

Deal with your shit. That was usually the advice Bax dished out, yet he didn't like it aimed at him. He packed his things up anyway, tucking his sketchbook with Olive's mystery tattoo into his bag.

His head told him that every word Isaiah said rang true . . . but his gut told him that it wouldn't be as easy in reality as it was in theory.

Or maybe that was just indigestion.

✦ ✦ ✦

Olive's stomach growled loud enough to register on the Richter scale, and each minute that went by without food, the sound only intensified. At this rate, it would be five minutes or less until the upstairs tenants stomped on the ceiling, demanding she keep down the noise.

One thing she'd learned about her new roommate was to never let him go to the grocery store alone if she planned on eating that week. Everything on the shelves was disappointingly healthy—ingredients for spinach smoothies, a container of flaxseeds large enough she could've stuck her head inside, and something that looked suspiciously like human hearts but claimed to be pickled beets.

No mac and cheese. No sugarcoated cereal. Finding a jar of popcorn kernels and an air popper, she'd gotten ridiculously excited, only to discover there wasn't a single pat of butter around.

What evil creature doesn't put butter on their popcorn?

Hoping something edible had magically appeared since the last time she checked, she opened the fridge. Nope. The food fairy had not arrived as she'd folded her last load of laundry.

She contemplated running to the corner market, with its treasure trove of processed goodies that could be microwaved and ready to devour in under a minute, but vetoed the idea because it required donning pants.

Tonight was a no-pants night—at least not one that possessed a zipper or buttons. With Bax out for most of the day, she vowed to stay in her cozy sweats unless there was a matter of life and death, and even then, decisions would be made on a case-by-case basis.

A heavy pounding on the front door shook the wall, stopping for a fraction of a second, only to start again, louder than before.

"Guess the neighbors came to complain about the noise in person," Olive quipped, squinting through the peephole.

Harper's green glowing eye, less than an inch away, stared at her from the other side. "Bwitch! You have five seconds to open this door or we're taking our takeout, brownies, and booze, and finding someone more appreciative of what we've endured to acquire and transport such goods."

"You had me at takeout and brownies. Hold on." She threw the lock and only barely managed to step back before the door swung open.

Harper, carrying two hefty takeout bags, stepped into the apartment, immediately followed by Rose and a piled-high plate of gooey-looking brownies. Vi brought up the rear, cradling a nondescript paper bag in one arm and a half gallon of orange juice in the other.

"You brought breakfast?" Her three favorite people invaded the kitchen.

"Not breakfast. Sex on the Beach," Vi corrected, pulling the contents from the brown bag and lining them up on the counter before searching the cabinets for glasses.

Olive beat her to it, finding Bax's stash of German beer mugs. "Not that I don't love you all—and the takeout you brought—but why?"

"Why not?" Rose set up the array of containers on the coffee table. "It's been a while since we've had a Girls' Night In, divulging our deepest and darkest secrets that may or may not be written in a five-by-eight leather-bound notebook that's decorated with a glittery unicorn."

Olive threw Harper an accusing look.

The succubus glanced up from her seat in Bax's leather reclining chair, a heaping helping of pad Thai already on her fork. "What?"

She performed the Guardian's signature move and cocked up a single eyebrow.

"I know what you're thinking, but I didn't tell them," Harper claimed.

She lifted her eyebrow higher.

"Okay, so yes. *Technically* the words came from my mouth. But I didn't offer up the information all word vomit like you're probably thinking." She switched tactics, adding, "But if someone's at fault in this scenario, look in the mirror, babe. You didn't say your little experiment was a secret, so technically, there was no breach of a friend contract. No breach, no freaky eyebrow thing, so put it away."

Rose handed Olive a container of rice. "And even if it was a secret, the real question is, why did you keep it from your wombmates?"

All eyes landed on her, her sisters' holding a speck of hurt.

She sat with a sigh, holding her food. "Because I wasn't sure I'd have the guts to actually go through with any of it. Why blab if I was probably going to chicken out and stay in my little bubble? It wouldn't be like it was the first time I got cold feet about something. It was easier keeping it to myself and seeing how things went."

"You know we'd do this with you if you wanted," Rose offered.

Vi piped up, "Unless it's something ridiculous like going on a coffee ban. You'd be on your own for that. Red Bull and Linc-gifted orgasms are basically how I'm surviving right now."

Harper cheered enthusiastically. "Now those are the kind of survival instincts of which I approve."

"No caffeine ban." Olive chuckled. "And while I know you're all willing to be my wing-witches, you're also all extremely busy doing your own things." Rose opened her mouth to protest, but Olive cut her off, adding, "As well you should be. While I don't agree with Gran's execution, she was right with that whole baby-bird thing. I'll always feel most secure doing things with you three at my side, but I need to have that same comfort when experiencing things solo—or with different copilots."

Leave it to the succubus to read between the words. "Someone's already doing your Docket thing with you?"

She focused a little too hard on her bowl of rice. "Bax saw my list and offered to help me with it."

Silence fell over the apartment, feeling ten times louder than her earlier unhappy stomach.

"What?" She glanced from person to person, her defensiveness rising.

"Nothing." Rose hid a smirk behind a small cough.

"I'm thinking a few somethings, but I'll get in trouble if I say them aloud," Vi admitted.

Harper's grin widened. "Well, I don't give a shit about a spot of trouble . . . so I'll just come right out and ask if, after the gala thing, he helped you check off items seven and/or eight?"

Olive choked on her rice, and Rose, sitting next to her, pounded on her back until she could breathe.

Vi froze with her drink on her lips. "Gala? What gala? Shit. Did I miss a thing? Am I fucking up this Primaship before the actual Exchange Ceremony?"

"You didn't miss anything. It was the NYU Alumni Gala." Olive drilled Harper with a look, noting the mischief glinting from her green eyes. "And no. Seven and eight remain unchecked."

The demon huffed. "That's a lost opportunity, Olly. A true travesty."

Honestly, she'd been a little bummed, too. During the gala, there'd been a minute or two—while dancing—when she'd almost let herself believe they'd been on a *date* date. Her nerves had eased, dropping her walls and allowing her to snuggle into his arms. He'd cuddled right back, or so she'd thought.

And then that man from the balcony had referred to her as Bax's *roommate.*

For him to know, that's how Bax must have identified her. Not a date. Not an *it's up in the air right now.* Hell, not even a friend.

A *roommate.*

Wallowing in her disappointment for the last forty-eight hours, she bounced her focus from work to pretending to work, avoiding the Guardian Angel as much as their two-bedroom apartment allowed.

She wasn't proud of her avoidance tactics, but sometimes a witch needed to go low to keep her head held high.

Because karma occasionally liked to fuck with her, the front door opened and Bax stopped short, glancing from the food to the drink containers to the three additional people spread out in their living room. "Is this an invasion?"

Vi smirked, giggling. "Were your ears burning, angel cakes?"

Olive shot her sister a warning glare. "Sorry about the takeover. They brought food, and it smelled too good to deny them entry. There's plenty here if you want to join us, or we can go to my room and get out of your hair."

"Nah. It's been a long day, so I'm heading to bed early. You all have fun." He seemed a little preoccupied as he grabbed a water bottle and disappeared into his room, closing the door behind him.

Olive's gaze wasn't the only one following him.

Vi's earlier smile tipped down. "Not that Bax has ever been Mr. Social, but that was off even for him. Or is my brooding-angel meter on the fritz?"

"It's definitely not on the fritz," Olive answered.

She'd read him the same way and had since the gala or, to narrow the timing even further, since she'd interrupted his talk with Balcony Guy, who she was 90 percent certain was his father. The thick tension had nearly choked her even in the open air, and when she dared bring it up—once—Bax had shut the topic down quick.

Message received. She hadn't brought up the gala—or the guy—since.

"Do you think the GAA placed him in the naughty corner again?" Vi whispered, her tone concerned. "You said he offered to do your list with you, and the Bax we all know and love usually operates by an *all work and no play* motto. He doesn't leave much time to experience *fun*."

"I actually had the same thought, but he's always so tight-lipped about the GAA," Olive admitted.

"Maybe someone should make sure he's okay." Vi shifted her gaze around the room, looking for volunteers.

"Don't look at me." Harper lifted her hands in a *not it* gesture.

"If I attempt a heart-to-heart with him, he'll think I have ulterior motives. It's unfortunate, I know, but justified."

"And I think I've lost my skill for tactfulness somewhere amid all the Hunting. Probably in the sewers," Rose added glumly.

Vi shot a pointed look at Olive.

"Me?" she squeaked. "Why me? Why not you?"

"Because if *I* ask, he'll just accuse me of being nosy."

"You *are* nosy . . . and it's not like it's different coming from me."

"But it is . . . because you can approach it with a dose of roommately concern."

"Fine." She grudgingly set her rice on the table and stood. "But if anyone even breathes on those brownies before I get back, hexes will fly . . . and they won't be the cute-but-awkward ones."

Three sets of eyes watched her approach his bedroom door, and when she paused to look back, she got three sets of thumbs-up.

"Come on in, angel," Bax invited from the other side before she even knocked.

She peeked in hesitantly to find him in bed shirtless, his sketchbook on his lap and his pencil in hand. He paused drawing as she came into his room.

"How did you know I was there? Or that it was me?" She struggled not to ogle his bare chest.

"The floor squeaked, so I knew someone was lingering, and both Harper and Vi would've just barged their way in, and Rose is more of a pound-on-the-door witch." His lips twisted into a coy grin that didn't quite reach his eyes. "Did you three need something from a high shelf?"

She shot him a glare, making him chuckle before she nudged a chin toward his sketchbook. "Are you working on my tattoo?"

"*Maybe.*"

"Can I see it?" She stepped deeper into the room.

"Nope."

"I can't see *my* tattoo?" She folded her arms over her chest.

"Nope . . . but good news. It's not a rabid raccoon, but an opossum isn't out of the realm of possibility. Maybe an armadillo." He snapped the sketchbook closed. "So what really brought you here? Because it wasn't to check on my progress with your piece."

She worried her bottom lip between her teeth, hesitant to meet his gaze. "You've just seemed . . . off . . . the last few days. Since the gala. And I wanted to make sure you were okay."

He wiped all traces of emotion off his face, his lips thinning. "Everything's fine."

"Because if I did something to make you feel uncomfortable or—"

"Angel," Bax interrupted, his intense gaze fixed hard on hers. "You didn't do a damn thing. Honest. There's nothing to talk about."

There was a finality in his tone, and she almost turned around and let him be. She probably should have. Instead, she embraced the knot that had been in her stomach since they drove home that night and untied it.

"You can tell me to mind my own business," she began. "Goddess knows I hate people butting into mine, but that older man on the balcony was your dad, wasn't he?"

The muscle in his jaw ticked away as he tensed. "A more apt description would be *sperm donor.* Mikael Donovan hasn't been my dad since I failed at adding myself to the long line of Donovan Warriors."

"Bax . . ." Her heart practically wept right then.

He forced a grin. "Sorry I nearly got you mixed up in family shit. I usually leave the heavy stuff for the third date."

Her cheeks instantly heated. "I never thought that was a *real* date."

Bax climbed off the bed and somehow stopped within an inch of her without her realizing, tugging her chin up. "You're right. It wasn't. When I take you out for real, you'll know it because it'll end in an immensely more pleasurable way than it did the other night."

She subconsciously wetted her bottom lip and his gaze dropped to watch, his multicolored eyes darkening the longer he stared. She'd never before understood what *waited with bated breath* meant until that very moment, because the longer she held hers, the more intense the ache in her chest grew.

"Everyone got clothes on in here?" The bedroom door swung open, startling her into a step back. Harper stood in the hallway, smirking knowingly. "Oops. Sorry. Am I interrupting your *chat*? We're cracking open Cards Against Humanity, and I refuse to be the only one receiving horrified looks because I tell the truth. But please, finish up. I'll wait."

"We're done." Olive flickered a questioning glance to Bax. "Right?"

"For now." He winked and, on way to the door, brushed his arm against hers. The small electrical zap elicited the smallest of shivers. "We should make this interesting and play teams."

The demon's eyes lit up. "Teams with shots! I'll get the bottles!"

Olive swallowed a groan. The last time they'd played a game with shots, someone ended dancing in the middle of the street in only their underwear.

12

Alanis Morissette

Nerves kicked Olive's heart rate up another few beats per minute, but this time, in a good way. The day had come to let her inner circus performer shine. She and Bax waited in Cirque du Surnaturel's front lobby, waivers signed and more than eager to cross another item off her list.

Well, *she* was ready. Bax's preparedness was still questionable.

The tense ticking of his jaw muscle ceased fifteen minutes ago, but his posture hadn't relaxed, despite kicking his leg out into a long stretch. He looked prepped to bolt.

She gently bumped into his shoulder to gain his attention. "This is on my Docket, not yours. I'm perfectly capable of doing this on my own if you're not up for it."

"I told you I'd do it with you, and I will. Besides, it's time I try new things."

"Your new thing could be filling the dishwasher with dirty dishes instead of piling them in the sink," she teased, grinning.

He shot her a look, but his lips twitched. "Someone put her sassy pants on this morning."

"Just saying it's an option, and one it appears that you've yet to experience."

"Olive? Bax?" A tall, broad-shouldered guy wearing tight leggings and an exercise tank stepped into the waiting room. He smiled, reaching out to shake each of their hands. "This is your first time here at Cirque du Surnaturel, yes?"

"Yep." She nodded, standing quicker than Bax. "We're Cirque du Surnaturel virgins."

The man laughed, amusement crinkling the faint lines cornering his eyes. "I'm Rory, lion shifter and one of the aerial instructors here at the school. Follow me, and I'll set you up with training outfits and show you to the locker room so you can change."

Bax glanced at his shorts and T-shirt. "We can't wear our own things?"

"Loose clothes can impede safe holds, and with the nature of the acts, safety is our top priority. Don't worry. We'll find you something that's both comfortable and safe."

If loose clothes impeded safety protocols, she officially declared herself extremely safe ten minutes later after she'd changed into the Cirque's training gear. Both the tank and the leggings left little to the imagination as she stepped out from the locker room and into the class.

A dozen ribbon hammocks hung from heavy-duty rings bolted to the ceiling, and beneath them, someone had tucked thick blue safety mats on the floor. A handful of people talked excitedly in the front of the room, but Bax wasn't one of them.

Heat tickled the back of her neck. She followed the sensation, not one bit surprised to find him leaning against the wall, his gaze lasered in on her. He wore an almost identical outfit to hers, but it hit home in an entirely different way. The sleeveless tank showcased his full-sleeve tattoos, and the snug fabric emphasized the tell-tale ridges from his nipple piercings.

And the leggings.

She now understood why Vi kept begging Linc to dress up as Robin Hood for Halloween, because sweet Mother Goddess and baby vampire kittens. Michelangelo's *David* paled in comparison to the man slowly making his way toward her.

He scanned her body as she stood in place, soaking up his attention while her stomach butterflies turned into overly caffeinated pterodactyls.

"Alright, future performers," Rory called out, directing everyone's attention to the front of the room. Two others stood with him, a petite dark-haired woman and a muscle-bound man who could've easily been an NFL linebacker. "These are my co-instructors for this series, Ravnoor and Neil. You'll notice there's only six of you in this class. It's designed that way so we can give you our undivided attention as well as the best chance for success. By the time you leave today, you'll feel as though you've sprouted wings."

Rory winked at Bax, either pegging him as an angel or reading his lack of enthusiasm as Ravnoor instructed everyone to pick their aerial stations.

"Only one person per hammock, big guy," Rory called out when Bax followed Olive to a pastel green hammock in the far-left row. "We're not quite ready for couples' silks. Why don't you take the one right behind your girl and we'll see where the night takes us, hmm?"

Bax drilled the lion shifter with a hard look as he claimed the spot behind her, but Rory didn't bat an eye, leading the class in a series of stretches designed to loosen and limber the body.

Ravnoor stood in the front of the room with her own hammock, commanding everyone's attention while Rory and Neil circled the group. "In this class, we'll be learning the aerial hammock, which you'll see hanging in front of you . . . but don't let the name fool you because there will be no napping."

Everyone chuckled and Olive snuck a look at Bax, who was looking at his dangling silk as if it were a snake prepped to bite.

She giggled. "I just want it on record that I gave you multiple opportunities to bail."

He shot her a look that made her chuckle harder. "Turn around and listen to the directions, angel. Safety first."

"Right now, you'll notice your silks are only a few feet off the ground," Ravnoor pointed out. "That's obviously on purpose as you are all novices."

One of the women from the front row raised her hand. "Can we get our hammock raised if we show that we've mastered the skills?"

"*Mastering* skills will take more than just tonight's class, but if anyone shows any natural talent, we might lift the hammock another foot or two. So let's start with a simple inversion."

Ravnoor stood in front of her silks and, gripping the sides, leaned backward until the fabric cradled her lower back, and then went further, spreading her knees until they frogged out. The second the hammock hit her thighs, she released her hold and extended her legs, hanging upside down in a split formation.

"Wow," Olive said in awe at the same time Bax muttered, "Fuck."

She bit the inside of her cheek to keep from laughing and watched Ravnoor perform the trick twice more before trying it herself. It took a few attempts, but on the third, she got into the frog position and hung upside down.

Blood rushed to her head as she watched Bax struggling to ease into a backbend, looking stiff as a board. "This is impossible."

"Maybe you didn't stretch enough?" she teased.

He shot her a look, eyes widening as she hung bat-like, her hands extended to the floor in a long stretch that felt good on her muscles. "Shouldn't you be holding on or something?"

"I'm doing *or something*. Seriously, Bax. Just lean back and let gravity do the rest."

"Gravity is exactly what I'm afraid of," he grumbled, attempting the lean one more time.

Rory stopped by her side, his smile wide. "You're doing incredible, Olive! Great job!"

"I'm a little nervous about extending my legs," she admitted.

"Totally understandable." Rory patted her knee. "How's your flexibility?"

"I'm definitely not on an Olympic-gymnast level, but I do okay."

He nodded, understanding. "Do you mind if I help you out? I'll guide your legs outward, and you let me know when you've hit your comfort level. Deal?"

"Sure."

"Slow and easy." Placing one hand on her knee and one on her ankle, he guided her right leg up and out while she mirrored the movement with her left. "That's good. Now a little more, shifting your hips to keep the silks in place. Good, good."

A slight burn crept into her inner thighs and knees, but she held the straddle, staying in her upside-down bat-girl position. "I did it!"

"Hell yeah, you did!" Rory cheered, as did a few of the other students and Ravnoor. "Let's ease you back into the starting position and see if you can do it again in one slow movement, and this time, I'll spot you."

She nodded and resumed the sitting position in front of her hammock. She leaned until the silks cocooned her lower back, and then Rory's hands braced her hips and easily guided her body as she shifted from the upside-down frog to the straddle.

"You've got a natural talent, Olive," Rory boasted. "Isn't she incredible, Baxter?"

"It's Bax," Bax practically growled, watching their interaction, his silks clenched in his hands, "and she's always incredible."

Hanging upside down, Olive glowered at his tone, but the ferocity of it diminished with the blood rushing to her head. Soon enough, Ravnoor moved them from the simple inversion to the proper way to fully sit, flip, and stand on the fabric. When Rory deemed her proficient enough to attempt her first mini-drop, she was more than ready . . . and didn't want the night to end.

✦ ✦ ✦

With no end in sight, Bax resigned himself to the fact he'd die with his body tangled up in this damn silk hammock. It didn't matter which trick it was, how many times he attempted it, or if the instructors helped or not.

His future didn't lie in aerial performance.

Eventually, he stopped the pretense of trying and focused on Olive's swinging figure and the lion shifter who never seemed to move more than three feet away from her.

He didn't fault Rory for the interest glinting from his eyes, but he did judge him for not making an attempt to disguise it. He and Olive had arrived together and, for all the guy knew, were *together* together. He just didn't seem to give a damn.

"Absolutely gorgeous lines, Olive." The shifter clapped, his eyes fastened on her ass as she performed an intricate wrap-hold involving a small, unraveling drop that nearly stopped Bax's heart. "I have a natural on my hands over here, Neil! Let's try a different drop with one slight difference, and this time I'll spot you. Or, if you think you're up for it, there are some pretty cool two-person silk tricks that I think we'd be able to do without any problem."

Bax growled. Enough was enough.

He twisted, kicking away his silk wraps, but instead of freeing him, they ensnared his ankle and his upper body plummeted ungracefully to the mat with a loud thud.

He missed breaking his nose by a damn millimeter.

Ignoring the close call, Bax hopped to his feet, his eyes narrowed on where the other guy's hands rested on Olive's hips. "I'll spot her, Romeo. You have other students who could probably use your help."

The instructor smiled easily, glancing around the room. "I don't mind. And it looks like Ravnoor and Neil have everything pretty well under control."

Bax kept his gaze drilled on the shifter, unwilling to blink and back down first. Not now, and definitely not when it involved Olive. He told himself it was because the guy was an unknown Supernatural, but that didn't make it true.

The lion's eyes flashed gold as his inner animal peeked to the surface. Rory cleared his throat, finally relenting with a small, vague nod. "Maybe I'll make a quick round through the room after all, see if I can give anyone any pointers."

"Maybe you should."

He glared at Rory's back as he walked away, only relaxing when the instructor began helping another circus hopeful a few spots over. His respite was temporary as he turned and faced off with a five-foot-two-inch witch with fire flickering in her dark blue eyes.

Her hands on her hips, Olive glared at him so hard he nearly lost his footing. "What in Goddess's name was that?"

"What?" He feigned innocence.

Her lips tightened. "You know damn well *what*. That peacock posturing that I just witnessed. I'm not sure how, when, or why you felt required to add to the toxic testosterone club, but you better snuff it out quick, and if you can't, you can sit in the waiting room until I'm finished with my class."

"Bet the asshole would have a field day then," he muttered under his breath. A little louder, he added, "His eyes have been glued to your ass all night, sometimes at the same time as his hands."

"He's an instructor. His job is ensuring we're doing things correctly. Or did you forget about safety being their top priority?"

"Right. Safety *for everyone in the entire class*. He needed a reminder that there are five other people who could benefit from extra attention, and I was more than happy to give it to him. No posturing. No peacocking."

Neil's barking demand to return to his mat put their conversation on hold, but not his internal thoughts. Bax went to his hammock, even more distracted by Olive's fluidly swinging movements than before, but this time, Rory maintained his distance and the rest of the class passed without him falling on his ass or acting like one.

One thing made very clear by the time they said their goodbyes to everyone at Cirque? His future definitely didn't lie in the performance arts. Another thing? Olive, not surprisingly a natural at the silks, didn't stop smiling their entire commute home.

Her excitement elevated his grumpy mood so much that by the time they stepped into the apartment, he'd nearly forgotten there was still one more class to go, and that according to Ravnoor, it was partners' night.

But hey, they'd made it through the evening without any broken appendages, and now he knew what to expect. That was a mini-win in his book.

Dropping his keys on the foyer table, he watched Olive practically float into the living room. "One more thing done off the Dare I Docket—or almost. That must feel pretty damn good."

"It feels incredible." Pride twinkled from her eyes. "And I loved it so much more than I thought I would. I may sign up for weekly classes and start the process for joining their amateur aerial team."

He froze, hands stilling. "Say what now?"

She set her things on the kitchen table, oblivious to his near panic, and headed to the kitchen. Grabbing two bottles of water, she tossed him one. "Rory handed me information about the Angelic Aerialists, and I'm thinking about it. You compete and get judged based on skill level, so it's not like I'll be flying through the air like Ravnoor anytime soon. I don't know. We'll see. At least it's something to consider."

"That's . . . great." He forced an encouraging smile.

"*And* I added a few more items to my Docket, although I'm not completely sold on them yet. They're good enough for placeholders though."

He leaned casually on the doorframe to the kitchen, fighting to rein in his obvious curiosity. "Oh yeah? So what will we be doing in the next couple weeks? Cage diving with the sharks? Slacklining?"

Fuck. Please don't let it be slacklining. Why did I throw that idea into the world?

"It is *way* too cold for cage diving." She shivered. "If it was the middle of August, *maybe*. And I looked into slacklining, but the nearest licensed company that takes out groups is a bit of a hike."

He released a relieved breath.

She gifted him a knowing smile. "You really don't have to do the list with me, Bax. There must be better ways to pass your time."

Crossing his arms over her chest, he teased, "Don't want me trailing you around the city, angel? Afraid I'll cramp your style or something?"

"I don't mean it like that. I just know you didn't really enjoy yourself tonight and—"

"I enjoyed tonight."

She cocked up a disbelieving eyebrow. "Even when you face-planted into the mat? Because I may have been hanging upside down like a bat, but I saw your pain-filled expression and it didn't scream *fun* to me. And what about work? They can't like all this extra time off."

"Seeing your enjoyment at impersonating a flying mammal is all the fun I need." He tucked a strand of hair behind her ear. "And work's not an issue. I've shifted my hours around a bit."

"Like you're working third shift or something?"

"Or something." He hated dancing around the truth but didn't see another option. His choices were to either do the Electric Slide or muck things up even more than they already were. "That means I'll be around a bit more than usual. I hope that's okay."

Her gaze flickered to his mouth. It lasted a fraction of a second, but long enough for him to get lost in a mental image of her mouth on his.

Would she taste like sweet vanilla? Or possess a heated hint of cinnamon and spice?

Staring up at him, she nibbled the bottom corner of her lip and released the softest, sexiest little sigh . . . and it obliterated all his good sense.

Hijacked his control.

It obscured every reason why this shouldn't happen until the only thing he could think about were the reasons why it should.

Giving her time to back away or, hell, run in the other direction, he slowly closed the gap between them, stopping when his feet bumped into hers. "You should probably sprint to your room and close the door behind you. Maybe lock it for good measure."

Her big blue eyes blinked up at him, her voice a sexy rasp as she asked, "Why?"

"Because unless you do, I'm three seconds away from kissing the hell out of you."

Her chest rose and fell with each breath as she watched him, her gaze sliding over every inch of his face as if struggling to decipher his sincerity. A second turned to three, then five, neither of them moving until her pink tongue slipped out and wet her bottom lip.

He groaned. "Fuck. You're killing me, angel. What do you want to happen here? What's going through your head right now?"

"Right now I'm thinking I should really wear my watch more routinely because three seconds surely must have come and gone by now." She sent a heated look back down to his mouth.

The second her meaning sank in, it was game over.

She moved a split second before he did, sliding her hands up his chest and around his neck. Bax dragged her body flush against his and captured her mouth with his.

This wasn't a kiss.

It was a complete body-and-soul experience. Cradling her head in his hands, he eagerly participated in a hot give-and-take that left him wanting more.

Of her. Of this. Of everything she wanted to offer him.

He might have instigated the moment, but this was her show to run how she pleased.

With their tongues tangling, their feet automatically moved until Olive's back hit the wall, the unexpected jolt ripping their mouths apart. She peered up at him with desire-filled eyes, her lips red and swollen as she worked to catch her breath.

Damned if he couldn't catch his either, each breath quick and shallow and making him a bit dizzy. His thoughts swirled like a carousel, too quickly for him to latch on to any specific one.

Except . . .

This couldn't lead anywhere except to someone getting hurt.

He forced his hands to drop and stepped back. "That shouldn't have happened, angel. I'm . . . I'm sorry."

Her disappointed look gnawed his stomach to shreds.

"It shouldn't have happened . . . ?" Her voice trailed off softly.

"Guess that aerial class came with more of an adrenaline rush than I thought." He cursed himself with every word out of his mouth.

Olive fixed the clothes that he'd disheveled while kissing the hell out of her, her swollen lips pressed into a tight line. "An adrenaline rush. Right. I don't know what I was thinking."

At her clipped tone, he sighed. "That's not what I meant."

"It's what you said."

"But I didn't mean it like that." He dragged a frustrated hand through his hair. "Hell, I don't know how I meant it."

"I do." Her hands emitted a soft green-and-gold glow as her Magic crackled in the air, charging their already explosive surroundings. "And you have nothing to fear because it won't happen again. I'll make sure I wear my watch from now on."

She spun toward her room, her golden hair whipping around her as she made her exit.

He hated that he'd ruined the best thing to happen to him in months, and he poised to follow her. "Olive! Please! Wait up a sec . . ."

"Don't worry about it, Baxter. It's already forgotten. Good night . . . and have fun with all your extra adrenaline." Her door slammed, the sound echoing through their apartment like a cannon.

"Fuck." Bax cursed himself ten different ways, and in every single version, he was an asshole.

And when Alanis Morissette began shaking the walls of Olive's room, he realized he was a *stupid* fucking asshole.

13

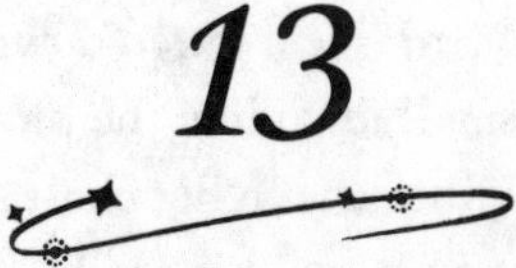

Night of Orgasms

Olive's Dare I Docket

1. ~~Run away to join the circus~~
2. ~~Do something spontaneous: Hot tub skinny-dipping~~
3. ~~Do something socially frightening: Attend the Gala~~
4. Get a tattoo
5. Enter a dance competition
6. Sing karaoke
7. Have hot, multiorgasmic sex
8. Go on a date that ENDS in hot, multiorgasmic sex
9. End up in a romance novel
10. Survive a heartbreak???

Sitting at the end of the Potion's Up bar, Olive stared at her sad excuse for a Dare I Docket. She'd read it ten times and nearly bored herself to tears. A dance competition? She did okay with the Sprinkler and on occasion, when wearing good shoes, the Running Man, but an honest-to-Goddess contest with battle rounds and freestyle?

Nope. The last time she'd attempted organized dancing had been in elementary school, a time when even the biggest goof-ups were adorable to the adults in the room.

Now, she *was* the adult in the room, and goof-ups resulted in heckling and tossed rotten vegetables . . . and yet she'd still placed it at number five, right above karaoke.

And items nine and ten? She'd jotted down nine while wishing she could escape to a small town like the protagonist in her commuting book, and ten? The ache in her chest since Bax apologized for kissing the life out of her told her she had as much of a chance as any of the others in completing it. So why the hell not?

Harper slipped her a refill on her water, her concerned eyes watching her closely. "If you stare at that list any longer, it'll spontaneously combust. Not that I don't enjoy the company, but why have you been warming my bar stool for the last two hours when you could be snuggled safe and warm at home?"

"It's only"—Olive glanced at her watch—"eight o'clock! Do you seriously think I'm that boring that I'd be in bed before nine o'clock on a weeknight?"

The succubus's hands flew up in surrender. "Whoa, bwitch. No one said the B word except you. It's colder than a witch's tit out there, and if you believe the weather people, we're in for a doozy of a storm front. I know you're not exactly winter's biggest fan."

That put a mild spin on her dislike of anything requiring thermals. Oh, she enjoyed a picturesque winter scene as much as the next person. Images of a snowy Central Park were beyond beautiful and even made it onto her screen saver a time or two . . . but that enjoyment came from the warm, dry confines of a Ryde or an apartment. When she was commuting through the elements, the scenic view became less heaven and more hellscape.

Untouched Central Park snow was a sight to behold.

Black, sludgy Thirty-Seventh Street snow with a distinctive odor was a sight to avoid at all costs.

And Harper had it right. With a cold, snowy forecast, tonight was the kind of night where she avoided travel at all costs, but after her afternoon classes and a few meetings with students, she wasn't ready to head home.

More accurately, she wasn't ready to see Bax—the angel who'd kissed the hell out of her, and then called her a mistake. Well, called the kiss a mistake and one fueled by adrenaline, but it was basically the same damn thing.

"Okay, what's that look on your face?" Harper's eyes narrowed.

"Nothing," she lied.

"Liar, liar, thongs on fire. I know that look, and it's definitely something."

"A something that is nothing." The sex demon opened her mouth to speak, but she beat her to it. "Do not say it's from lack of sex."

"I wasn't about to."

Olive cocked up a disbelieving eyebrow. "Really?"

"No. I was about to say lack of orgasms." Harper leaned over the bar top and, reading Olive's snooze-worthy list, pointed to her untouched additions. "See. They're right there and not crossed off. Thank you, Your Honor, I rest my case."

"Why is everything sex and orgasms with you?"

Harper blinked before sticking out a hand. "Excuse me, have we met? Harper Jacobs. Succubus, sexual therapist, and host of the radio talk show *Sexy Talk with Savannah*."

Olive smothered a laugh behind a groan, dropping her head onto her hands. Maybe her friend was on to something, at least way, way adjacently.

It had been an embarrassingly long time since she'd "connected" with someone on a physical level, her last with a boyfriend a few years back. Whatever could've happened with Mason had fizzled before it began because he was an opportunistic jerk-waffle. And then there'd been her kiss with a certain sexy angel that sent her stomach—and all her other witchy bits—aflutter days later.

Olive glanced at her list, her gaze lingering on one in particular. It was the last one she'd ever thought she'd seriously consider. Numbers seven and eight.

Harper, following her line of sight, squealed. "Yes! Yes! Yes!" She clapped her hands, getting giddier by the second. "I approve! And yes!"

"It's not as easy as you make it sound, Harper, and it's definitely not what you're thinking," she warned. "A witch can't just walk into a bar and up to the first random stranger she sees and invite them back to their place."

"Uh, that's exactly what a witch can do . . . but not before making sure they're not a serial killer vampire or something first."

"Then let me clarify . . . it's not something *this* witch can do. A date is one thing, but your secondary addition?" She shook her head. "Not happening. I watch way too much *Dateline*."

"Okay. Fine. It's not as fun, but I can work with that." Harper tapped her fingers on the bar top, face scrunched up in Deep-Thought Mode.

A few seconds in, she released an excited yip and dug her cell out from her cleavage. Her fingers flew over the screen before shoving it in Olive's face. "It's fucking kismet! Voilà! Multiorgasmic sex, here Olive comes . . ."

Olly shot the succubus a warning look.

Harper rolled her eyes. "Fine. No orgasmic sex. But this would technically still count as a date. Hell, you could give yourself bonus check-offs."

Taking the phone from her friend's hand, she blinked the screen into focus. "This is a Supernatural Singles Speed-Dating event. *Tonight.*"

"Perfect timing, right? And if you happen to find someone that you'd be interested in letting give you a Night of Os, I'll be your wing-person and make sure the guy doesn't eat you before he *eats* you. I'm a great judge of character . . . and rap sheets. I only fucked up that one time, but all things considered, it was a minor felony."

She glanced down at the blazer, vintage band T-shirt, and pencil skirt she'd worn to school that day. "This isn't something I'd typically wear on a date."

Harper scanned her slowly from head to toe. "How do you feel about taking scissors to that shirt and turning it into a crop? The skirt could be a bit higher, too, but making a slit up to the panty line could do the trick in a pinch."

"No to the panty slit, and you're not touching this T-shirt. It's an authentic Bon Jovi shirt from the *Slippery When Wet* Tour. *If* I agree to do this speed-date thing, it's just to check off the date aspect on the list, Harp."

The other woman sighed with a pained groan. "Fine. Ruin my fun. Just tell me you're not wearing your hideous tan period panties."

"They were the only clean ones that wouldn't give me a panty line in my skirt," she muttered defensively and pushed the phone back across the counter. "But I don't think any of it will matter. It says you need to register for the event. It's probably too late to sign up."

Harper picked up the phone and typed away before mic-dropping it on the table. "All done. You're registered and legit."

Her mouth dried. "For Supernatural Singles Speed-Dating?"

"No, to attend the Met Gala. Yes, the speed-dating, but don't worry, I promised to weed out the serial killers. I registered myself, too. Now we just have to do something about your getup, and I have just the thing in my locker." Harper dragged her off her stool and toward the employee break room.

Gage exited the back room, shooting the demon a dour look. "Where are you going? Your shift isn't over for another hour."

She waved him off. "It's deader than a zombie's sex life out there. The employees officially outnumber the patrons. I'm turning my bwitch's frown upside down with a series of raging orgasms."

"*Harper*," Olive groaned. Gage glanced at her, and her cheeks immediately heated. "There will be no orgasms."

"Manifesting things into reality with positive thinking is a real thing, and I, my sweet little witch, am manifesting an entire night of raging orgasms for you." Harper drilled a hard glare at her boss. "Don't be an orgasm-blocker, Gage."

The vampire's eye twitched. "Fine. Go. But you're working an extra hour on your next shift."

"We'll see!" Harper bumped him aside and dragged Olive into the lounge before gesturing to her shirt. "Strip that thing off. It's time for Harper to produce some succubus sorcery."

She grimaced but obeyed. "Please don't make me regret this."

"Babe, when everything is said and done, you'll be thanking me with two dozen red roses and a lifetime pass to Pleasure Palace." Harper pulled a soft, wide-necked sweater from her locker. "Now prop up the girls and put this on. We haven't got even a minute to waste."

Once Olive tugged on the sweater and slid into the leggings Harper handed her, the succubus removed her hair claw, fluffed her hair over her shoulder, and nodded. "Yep. Totally fuckable. Night of the Orgasms, here you come."

✦ ✦ ✦

Olive glanced around the posh Manhattan bar holding the Supernatural Singles Speed-Dating event, a mix of excitement and nerves twisting her insides into a pretzel.

Mostly nerves.

What had seemed a good idea an hour ago she'd second-guessed within a minute after she and Harper received their first table assignment. The redhead's heels looked about three inches high. Olive could probably make a break for the exit with a decent chance of getting away.

"One Moscato." Harper handed her a wineglass and kept one for herself as she gazed over the gathering crowd. "Look at all these possible orgasmic partners—I mean *dates*. Put it on record that I have the best ideas ever, and that record better be etched in stone. Or better yet, a permanent tattoo. Ooh, if you do that, then there's another item checked off your Docket list."

"Tattoos, by design, are permanent."

"Not the ones that come in those cute little machines outside the grocery store."

Olive shook her head, chuckling. "I'll hold off on getting that tattoo until we see if I make it through the night."

A handsome, dark-haired vampire released a piercing whistle that brought the whole crowd to a stop. "Hello and welcome! I'm Royce, and thank you, everyone, for braving the weather to be here at the Supernatural Singles Speed-Dating event! Myself and my co-host, Shavonne, have just a few housekeeping things to go over before you all potentially meet your someone special."

Harper snortled softly and muttered, "Who cares if they're special as long as they know their way around a—"

"Harper," Olive hissed quietly.

She mouthed *sorry*, pretending to pay attention.

"Just a reminder," Shavonne continued, "that our goal is to make sure you find your best matches, and so using the information you provided on registration, we've divided our event into simultaneous smaller events throughout the building. If you're in Group A, you'll be in the Lucas Room around the corner. Group B is in the Spielberg on the right. C and D in the Lee and Howard Rooms. And Group E will be right here."

"The rules are the same for each room," the vampire added. "Your ticket indicates if you're a Shaker or a Mover, with Shaker meaning you'll be the stationary guest, sitting at the table indicated on your ticket."

"And the Mover is obviously the attendee who moves from table to table," Shavonne added. "You'll have three minutes with each guest, and at the sound of the bell, the partners change. We ask you to please follow this rule. If you meet someone with whom you'd like to speak more, have them scan your personalized QR code—also on your event ticket—and you can make plans to meet up later."

"And that's pretty much it. Be respectful. Be charming. And be ready to meet your match." Royce clapped his hands excitedly and winked. "Everyone go ahead and find your seats."

Harper slipped her arm through Olive's and steered the way to their neighboring tables. She had no sooner sat than the seat across from her was pulled out.

A man, somewhere in his thirties, sat with a nervous smile. "Hi! Wow. I can't believe I'm doing this, but here we are. I'm Thomas, and—"

"Please wait until the bell chimes before beginning," Shavonne spoke from the front of the room.

A few seconds later, a chime rang and the murmur of voices filled the open space. Thomas recited what sounded like a rehearsed speech about himself and his interests, and when he finally took a breath, he looked at her expectantly. The bell went off before she even got out her name, and then it was time to switch.

Six partner swaps later, her gaze slid to the emergency exit for the tenth time. Harper caught the longing look and drilled her with a hard glare that reminded her to focus on her newest table-mate.

They weren't all horrible. Some were nervous. Some way too outgoing for her. Her Docket list might involve stepping out of her comfort zone, but she sure as hell wasn't about to step out of a plane, which was what accountant Petro stated was his go-to first *real* date. He looked absolutely horrified when she told him hers was a coffee shop.

Somewhere after the tenth swap, her next date stepped up to the table, a wide, perfect smile aimed directly at her.

He opened his suit jacket and took a seat, his green eyes twinkling as he reached out to shake her hand. "I'm Ethan . . . and I'm suddenly so glad my roommate talked me into this event. Something tells me I'll owe him a bottle of his favorite whiskey after this."

First impression: suave, charming, and handsome.

"Olive . . . and I also got talked into this event by a friend, but whether I owe her for it or not remains to be seen," she joked.

He laughed, and damn, he had a nice laugh. It didn't sound fake or strained. For the first time all night, she didn't glance at the fire exit. A brief glance at Harper revealed the sex demon giving her a not-so-hidden thumbs-up.

"I totally get it," Ethan commiserated. "I actually had to be bribed into coming."

"What do you get?" she teased.

"He has season tickets for the Yankees, so the next two games are all mine. What do you say? Want to go?" Ethan grinned.

"Guess we'll see how our next two minutes go, won't we?"

Nice, gorgeous, and with a gaze that hadn't once strayed to the cleavage that Harper had ensured would be revealed in the one-shouldered sweater, Ethan should have piqued her interest. He loved sports but preferred musical concerts. An elementary school guidance counselor by day, he volunteered evenings at the senior center.

The man was practically the perfect package.

And she didn't want to unwrap it in the least.

✦ ✦ ✦

Bax walked the city streets, his mood having darkened the longer it became obvious Olive intended on avoiding him. He tried convincing himself it bothered him because it made his job as her Guardian more difficult, but even he wasn't that delusional.

He'd fucked up. First by kissing her. Then by stopping. Then it all went to hell when he'd called it a mistake and blamed it on adrenaline.

The look on her face when those words slipped from his mouth still felt like a hot spear to the gut. He'd wanted to take them back the instant he'd said them, but her guard had already risen, and she'd visibly shut down and shut herself away.

Literally in her room.

Should he have kissed her? His superiors at the GAA would say *definitely not*.

Did Bax *regret* kissing her?

He couldn't be sorry for something that felt so damn good. Not only had he lost all sense of space and time, but the fierce rightness of it had only increased the longer she stayed in his arms, and it hadn't been his imagination. The second she slipped away, that rightness disappeared and left an aching, empty hole in his chest and it still hadn't returned.

Being a scholar wasn't necessary to know that the reason was because he'd yet to lay eyes on the witch since it happened. He'd heard her in the bathroom that morning, readying for work, but when he'd finally talked himself into a face-to-face, he'd stepped into an empty living room, the front door already closing at her back.

He spent the rest of the day stalking NYU, his picture now probably posted on campus security bulletin boards as a suspicious person. She might be rightfully pissed at him, but she'd been put on the GAA's radar for a reason. First and foremost, he needed to stay focused on the job. Winning his spot back in his friend's good graces needed to be tucked into the far-back-corner burner.

At least that's what he told himself.

Friend. People didn't devour their friends' mouths the way he had hers, and vice versa, yet it had physically pained him to pull away from her and break that connection. He might not know exactly *what* was happening between him and Olive Maxwell, but he knew it sure as hell didn't fall under friendship.

He came to a flickering red pedestrian light, his attention drawn to the bar on his right. Muted laughter filtered out from Indigo. He'd only been to the retro bar once or twice, but remembered both times it being crowded and filled to the brim with humans and Supernaturals.

That night was no different.

The pedestrian light changed, and just as he stepped off the curb, a familiar laugh froze him to the spot. A few people grumbled and stepped around him, but he didn't care. Stepping closer to the wall of windows, he spotted a familiar redheaded succubus, her head tilted back in laughter, but it wasn't Harper who sent his gut into a hard roll.

At a nearby table, Olive's face damn near glowed as she laughed, reacting to the broad-shouldered man sitting directly across from her. The stranger could've jumped straight off the cover of *Sexiest Supernatural Alive*, and his gaze never strayed from Olive's as he propped his elbows on their table and said something that made her laugh.

Again.

Something fierce and hot pumped through his veins as he took in the entire scene. He couldn't move. He could barely breathe.

And then the bastard winked at her.

Winked.

Bax's feet moved before he even registered the tinkling bell on the bar's front door. He scanned the room until he found where Olive sat with her new little friend toward the back.

"Hi. Are you here for the event?" A petite, dark-haired woman came up, her smile friendly. "You're a little late, but we could squeeze you into the next session."

"The event?" His gaze stumbled over to the poster perched on an easel. SUPERNATURAL SINGLES SPEED-DATING.

Oh, *fuck* no.

Harper's addition to Olive's Docket list immediately popped into his head, and that would happen over his dead body. "Yeah. I'm here for the event."

"Your name?" She glanced at the clipboard in her hands.

"I don't actually have to register. I can just slide right in and get started."

She glanced up at him knowingly. "I'm sorry, sir, but you need to be registered. If you're unable to do so this time around, we do have another event next month. I can get you set up right now if you'd like."

Olive's laughter drew his attention back over to her table. A bell rang and the entire room shifted. The Adonis flirting with her kissed the back of her hand before getting up and planting himself at another table. Another guy took his place.

"That won't be necessary, but thank you." He left the woman standing alone, her mouth agape, and swerved through the sea of filled tables, more than a few people stopping their conversations to watch him pass.

Harper was one of them, glancing up and doing a double take. "What are you—"

"I'll deal with you later," he practically growled.

The exchange pulled Olive's gaze away from her "date," and her blue eyes widened. "Bax? What are you—"

He forced his voice to soften. "We need to talk."

"Is something wrong? Did something happen to Vi or Rose? Gran?" she asked, worried.

"Nothing like that. I just . . . need to speak with you."

With her worry eased, she settled further into her seat and gave him one of her cool looks from earlier before gifting the man across her with a warm smile. "Sorry, Baxter, but I'm on a date right now, so if it's not an emergency, it'll have to wait until I get home."

The man across from her blinked. "You two live together?"

"Yes," Bax growled while Olive simultaneously answered, "Not like that."

"We're roommates," she clarified. "Please continue. You were saying something about your job?"

"Oh. Uh . . . okay. I work in sa—"

Bax sighed. "You're seriously making me wait for you?"

"I'm not making you do anything." Her dark blue eyes glittered dangerously as she shot him a glare. "You can wait—outside. Or you can wait at the apartment."

"This is a mistake."

"You mean like the one you made the other night? Maybe. Maybe not. But I won't know until I give it a try, will I?" she shot back.

The guy across from her shifted uncomfortably and started to get up from his seat. "Would you like me to leave the two of you alone?"

"Yes!" Bax ground out while Olive snapped, "Absolutely not! Sit back down."

The guy instantly sat and shot his gaze to an openly staring Harper. "What do I do?"

She shrugged, smirking. "I'd listen to the witch and sit, and then relax and enjoy the show. Do you think they serve popcorn here?"

Somewhere in the room, a bell chimed. The man quickly left his seat and another approached warily, his hand outstretched to pull the chair back.

Bax beat him to it, claiming it for himself. "Find another 'date.'"

The tall guy glowered. "But she's my next one. It says so on my app."

"Find. Another." He drilled him with a glare, and whatever the guy saw on his face had him lifting his hands and stepping away.

"You cannot do this," Olive hissed over the table. "You're being ridiculous, not to mention making a scene."

"This entire setup is ridiculous." He glowered. "Speed-dating, angel? Really? Do you know what kind of weirdos take part in these things?"

She leaned back in her chair, crossing her arms over her chest and looking as if she were prepping for battle. He caught a little spark of green Magic shooting off her hand. *Shit.* "Yeah, actually, I do. Weirdos like Harper and myself, considering that we're here."

"This is about your damn list, isn't it?"

Her eyes narrowed on him. "Don't you worry about my Dare I Docket because you're officially uninvited from participating in it with me anymore. Not that I invited you to do it with me in the first place. You kind of invited yourself."

Point for her.

"This isn't the way to do this, Olly. At least not safely. You have absolutely no idea who any of these guys really are."

"At this point, I don't know who you really are either."

"They could be fucking serial killers."

"At least they'd have a hobby," Olive snapped, glaring harder. Another greenish-gold spark of Magic flickered, and her eyes darkened.

He cocked up a brow. "That's what you're going with right now?" He hooked a thumb toward the guy whose seat he occupied, who was now giving one of the coordinators an earful, his hands flailing toward their table. "Even if he's not a serial killer, you think a guy who wears that much cologne actually knows his way around a clitoris even if given a map and a flashlight?"

"I happen to be great at giving directions."

"Olive . . ."

"Bax."

He sighed, throwing a still-watching Harper a glare. "Any help in getting through to her would really be appreciated right now."

"You're barking up the wrong demon, babe. If I had my way, I would've given her my free pass to Pleasure Palace and set her up in the Orgasm Room."

A throat-clear sounded behind Bax just as the woman from the door tapped his shoulder. "I'm sorry, sir, but since you're not registered for the event, I'll have to ask you to leave."

"I'm not leaving without her." He kept his gaze drilled defiantly on Olive.

"Then you *both* need to leave. Now. You're distracting the other guests, and with little time to make a connection as it is, distractions only make it more difficult. Please."

"I'm sorry for this," Olive apologized, standing and collecting her things. "I'll go."

Harper made as if to stand.

"No. No." The petite blonde ushered her back down. "Stay. Have fun. At least one of us should partake in orgasmic sex tonight."

"Are you sure?" Harper flickered her gaze toward Bax with a frown. "I got your cute backside if you need it."

"Stay," Olive muttered. "That way there's no witnesses when I kick his ass."

The redhead chuckled, giving her a small wave. After Olive stalked away, she turned that wave into a thumbs-up . . . to him. "Go get her, tiger."

Fast on her feet, Olive was already halfway down the block and about to climb into the back of a Ryde by the time he exited Indigo. "Olive! Wait!"

She paused at the open door, shot him a look that nearly shriveled his balls right there on the sidewalk, and blatantly ignored him as she climbed into the car.

He let her.

He'd won. He'd gotten her out of that meat market.

Now why the fuck didn't he feel any better?

14

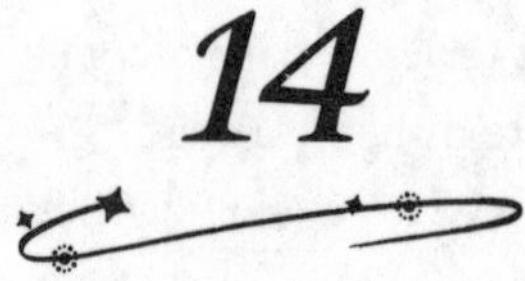

A Fuck-Ton More

Home. Shower. Curse a certain sexy angel with a raging case of angel mange. That's what Olive needed at the moment, preferably in that order, although it wasn't necessary. She was nothing if not flexible.

A thump sounded from the back of the Ryde car. She startled, turning in her seat to see a pair of multicolored eyes less than three feet away and through the rear-seat window. Bax, in all his white-and-silver-feathered glory, kept pace with the Ryde, flapping his wings mere feet from the bumper, practically riding it like Marty from *Back to the Future*. Just without the skateboard.

"Angel mange is first up then." Olive turned back in her seat and shot the driver an apologetic look. "Feel free to try and lose him. I won't mind."

Not only did they not lose him, but he dropped himself onto the trunk and lounged on the moving car like it was a freaking NYC tour bus.

Outside, the temperature dropped drastically, and the misting rain quickly turned to fat, juicy snowflakes so thick it cut visibility to within a foot all around the car. Worry about Bax freezing to death as he rode on top of the trunk slid its way through her before she could shut it down.

It had been his choice to act like a testosterone-driven Neanderthal. He'd been the one who busted out the wings and honed his inner McFly. What had he told her on a few occasions? Shifters weren't the only Supernaturals who ran hot?

Guess that statement was being put to the ultimate test.

When they eventually reached their building an hour later, she thanked her driver and scurried to the front door. Not risking a glance behind her, she quickly headed to the second floor and keyed herself into the apartment. She attempted a front-door slam, but Bax caught it, preventing it from crashing into his nose.

"Damn it. I was this close," she muttered.

Bax locked the door with a sigh as she stormed to her bedroom and threw her purse onto the nightstand. All its contents spilled, but she didn't even care.

"Can we talk *now*?" He stood in her bedroom doorway, smart enough not to step into her personal space without an invite.

Which he wouldn't be getting.

She spun, glaring at him. "At this stage, talking only increases your chances of waking up with the mange you're always so worried about, but if that's a risk you're willing to take, go for it. Talk. I hope you have your doctor on speed dial."

He dragged a hand through his hair and blew out a heavy breath. "Why are you being so damn difficult about this?"

"You did not just call me *difficult*." She propped her hands on her hips, hoping to divert the Magic prepped to spill everywhere. "*Difficult*, in condescending man-speak, means a woman isn't afraid to speak her mind when people around her are asinine jackasses. In case you're wondering, that most definitely includes you."

"It was a bad idea, Olive. You had no clue who any of those guys were," Bax pointed out needlessly.

"The entire point of speed-dating is getting *to* know them. Or it was before you got me kicked out of the event, and probably banned from every other dating event in the city."

"That wasn't my intention, but if that was the end result? Good."

Her mouth dropped as she picked up the nearest item from her fallen purse—a tampon—and threw it at him. It hit him square in the forehead and trampolined off. Because it felt good, she picked up a second one and did it again.

Super absorbency for the win.

He glanced at the fallen pink packages now lying by his feet. "Did you just throw a sanitary product at me?"

"Actually, *two*. And there's more where they came from, angel boy. I stocked up on period supplies last week. So keep letting stupid fall out of your mouth."

His jaw clenched, that sexy face muscle twitching wildly. "It's not stupid. It's concern."

"It's stupidly placed concern. Why are you so adamant that I not date? What do you have against it? Everyone in this freaking city does it! Why do you think there are a million and one online dating apps just for New York alone?"

He shifted a step closer before stopping himself. "What was happening in that bar was not dating. That was a fucking meat market and you know it. Guys who go to things like that are only in it for one thing."

She threw her hands up in the air. "And what if that's exactly what I wanted? All anyone sees me as is Olive Maxwell, the Walking Encyclopedia. The one with all the answers. The one who prefers books to people. And while that one may be pretty on the money right at this very moment, sometimes a real, breathing person is warranted . . . like for that *one thing* you mentioned. Or am I supposed to live my life wearing a chastity belt and being the weird librarian lady in the monastery?"

His face went a funny shade and he stilled. "You're saying you went there specifically to get laid?"

No. She just went to check off the freaking *date* box . . . but he didn't need to know that.

"What a concept, right?" She fake gasped. "Olive McBrainy's nether regions wanted some action that didn't come from a Lady Bic or from the Roboto-Rabbit 2000."

Silence fell over the room. Talking about her nether regions and her sex toy to Baxter Donovan hadn't been on the day's to-do list. Give her another point for spontaneity.

Embarrassment flooded her face, no doubt reddening it like a tomato until she buried that crap down deep. Instead of hiding it, she owned it, meeting his gaze head-on in a stare-down she felt straight to her core.

The air felt different. Charged. Hell, it felt *alive* . . . and so did she. Her Magic itched just below the surface of her skin, but she kept it in check, needing to see what happened next.

Bax's gaze flickered to her mouth and back. "Is that what you really want? *Action?*"

"It's what I said, isn't it?"

"And you thought you'd get it from one of those assholes at the bar?"

She shrugged a shoulder, feeling Harper's sweater drop a little more. "I'm not saying it was guaranteed *good* action, but at this point in the game, I'd be okay with an E for effort."

"You deserve a fuck-ton more than effort, angel," he murmured.

Olive couldn't move, could barely blink. All she could hear was the loud pounding of her heart, and the longer her gaze remained fastened on the Guardian Angel in front of her, the more difficult it became to breathe, too.

She attempted to say *something*, but her voice failed her. She tried again, clearing her throat. "That almost sounded . . ."

He slowly closed the distance between them, and with each step, her knees went a little soft. He stopped when their chests brushed. Not like she could breathe. *At all.* Not with the way his multicolored gaze locked on her, drowning her in their gorgeous depths.

Every second that ticked by lessened her control over her Magic until her hair whipped around her in a magical whirlwind. Bax's fingers slowly trailed over her cheek until his large hand cupped the back of her head.

"Did it sound like an offer to give you a fuck-ton more? Because that's exactly what it was, angel. Give me the go-ahead and I'll make it happen." His deep voice dropped even lower, the faint whispering rumble making her not-quite-so-dry nether regions quiver.

Hex. Me.

She found her words. "And what would that go-ahead look like? A nod? Or a thumbs-up? Or maybe I should say, 'Why the hell isn't it already happening?'"

That was the magical phrase.

His hand anchored in her hair, Bax fused their mouths together, the abrupt move startling a gasp from her, which they both used to their advantage.

Now she knew what romance authors meant when they used phrases like *a strike of a match*. Because from the first brush of lips, her body went up in the most delicious, heat-inducing flames, intensifying with each stroke of their tongues.

Standing on her tiptoes, she slid her hands behind his neck and dragged him even deeper into their kiss. The hand not fisted to the back of her hair cupped her ass in a firm grip and tugged her hard against the unmistakable bulge in his jeans.

Olive couldn't help it. She rubbed her body against it as if that alone could help her scratch her itch, but it only made her want him more, her body aching with need.

Bax emitted a low groan and ripped his mouth away, only to trail it down the column of her neck in a path of torturous nips and licks. She tilted her head to give him more access, her eyes nearly rolling back from the pleasure.

"Tell me you're sure about this, angel." He hummed his approval, his mouth meeting the curve where her neck met her shoulder. "Tell me you want me to fuck you."

"I thought me rubbing against your erection was me doing just that," she said breathlessly. "But if you want the words, too, yes, I'm sure. And yes, Bax. Fuck me. Now."

She nipped his bottom lip and he released an honest-to-Goddess growl.

Palming her ass with both hands, he guided her legs around his waist and spun, pinning her against the wall as he took a few nips of his own.

"I can't even tell you how long I've wanted to do this." His mouth found the sensitive spot just below her ear, and her eyes fluttered close.

"Do what?" She tightened her grip on his hair and refused to let him pull away.

"*This.*" Keeping her lower body pinned to the wall with his hips, he slipped his hands beneath her borrowed sweater and took his mouth off her body only long enough to yank it over her head. Then it was back, devouring a bra-covered nipple with a series of nips and sucks. "And this."

Her head plunked back against the wall, feeling his strong tugs right between her legs. She unhooked her bra and slid the straps over her arms, exposing her breasts to his hungry gaze. He cursed before diving back, kissing and pinching, and gently rolling her nipples between both his lips and his fingers.

"Fuck. I need to taste all of you," Bax groaned. "Please tell me that's what you want, too."

"Goddess, yes."

Keeping her back against the wall, he returned her feet to the floor. She opened her mouth to express her displeasure when he dropped to his knees, his hands pulling down her leggings and underwear in one firm tug and tossing them aside.

"Fucking gorgeous." He dragged his mouth up her inner thigh, making her legs wobble violently the closer he got to her already dripping sex. His breath tickled over her clit as he touched her everywhere but where she wanted him most.

"I thought you wanted to taste all of me?" She growled her complaint and rolled her hips on a chase for his mouth. "There doesn't seem to be a lot of tasting happening right now."

He gazed up at her from his spot on the floor and smirked. "Oh, there will be. Hold on, angel."

"Why do I have to—"

He widened her stance and then, pushing his massive arms between her thighs, gripped her waist . . . and stood. Olive squealed, her hands clamping onto his shoulders as he walked them the few feet to her bed, her legs dangling over his forearms.

"Brace yourself," he directed and fell backward, his broad back hitting the mattress first.

It was a strategic move that not only put her on her hands and knees, but with his smug face peering up at her from between her open legs.

"What are you doing?" she asked breathlessly.

"Getting that taste." His large hands cupped her ass, and pulled her aching sex directly down onto his eager mouth.

"Oh. My. Goddess." Lost in the pure pleasure rolling through her body, she ground her pussy harder onto his magical tongue before a fear of suffocating him had her lifting it away.

"Fuck no," he growled, his hands tightening on her hips as he guided her back to his mouth. "I want you to sit. Not hover, angel."

"But . . . asphyxiation." She panted, attempting to catch her breath.

"I'm pretty damn hard to kill." He cocked that sexy single eyebrow as if waiting for her decision. "And if it's my time? What a fucking way to go."

No way could she not accept that unspoken challenge. She lowered her body back to his mouth, and true to his word, he gave her a fuck-ton more, his tongue rolling around her clit, making her whimper before he swiped it up through her sex once, then twice, his tongue slipping deeper inside with each pass.

He alternated fucking her with his tongue and soothing her clit with gentle swipes, the two different touches quickly sending her mind and body into orbit. Orgasm unlocked and legs quaking, she fisted her bedspread and tried her best to remain upright as wave after wave of pleasure crashed through her.

"Bax," she groaned, rolling hips losing their rhythm. His firm grip held her pussy snugly to his mouth as he continued feasting, slowing gradually as she came back to earth. "That was . . . wow."

She eased off his face, fully aware she was lying there completely naked while he grinned smugly at her, still fully clothed. Uncertainty seeped its way into her headspace, but sitting up, he slid his hand into her hair and dragged her mouth to his for a hot, heavy kiss that had her tasting herself on his tongue.

His gaze remained locked on hers as he slowly eased back, keeping his mouth brushing against hers. "We aren't even close to being done here, angel. You still good with that?"

"Definitely."

"Good." He climbed off the bed and, in that sexy way men did, grabbed his T-shirt behind his neck and yanked it off.

She watched shamelessly, her gaze caressing every inch of bare skin from his colorful tattoos to the twin nipple piercings she couldn't wait to taste. As if imagining it, her tongue peeked out, wetting her bottom lip.

Bax chuckled with a low groan. "Keep looking at me like that and this will be over embarrassingly fast."

She shrugged. "That just means we can start all over from the beginning, yeah?"

"Abso-fucking-lutely." Hands reaching to his jeans, he pulled out his wallet and a condom, tossing the wrapper onto the bed and the former onto the bedside table.

Then came the buttons.

She never got the point of button flies before, but she sure did now. With every opened notch, she felt a bit closer to being gifted the holy grail of penises. As he undid his last button and pushed his jeans and boxers off his legs, she held her breath.

His engorged cock instantly sprang free.

Olive struggled to keep her mouth from hitting the ground or her eyes from plummeting from their sockets. His cock was long and thick, and not only pierced, but pierced multiple times over in a Jacob's ladder that decoratively lined up from the base of his shaft to just below the ridged head.

"Your penis is bedazzled." Her voice, breathless, dropped to a raspy purr.

His lips pulled up in a mischievous smirk as he slowly climbed onto the bed. "Never experienced one before, angel?"

"Can't say that I have. How does that all fit?"

"Oh, it'll fit." He eased her onto her back, his large hands running up her entire body until she arched her back, eagerly pushing into his touch. "It'll fit and it'll feel fucking incredible."

He took an already sensitive nipple into his mouth and gave it a firm tug before releasing it with a wet pop and doing the same with its twin.

Inch by inch, he climbed up her body and took her mouth in another scorching kiss that left her glad she was already lying down. Her legs spread to make room for him, and then, with a slow roll of his hips, Bax caressed the underside of his cock—and his piercings—along her wet folds and aching clit.

Olive hissed in startled pleasure as she glanced between them, unable to tear her gaze away from the sight until he emitted a low thrum of approval.

"You're so fucking gorgeous, angel." He studied her expressions as he slowly—and torturously—rubbed his piercings along her already quivering mound.

She smiled, unsure what to do with the compliment. "And also ready for more."

He cocked up an eyebrow. "Yeah?"

"Definitely."

Grabbing the condom, he slid the latex carefully over each and every piercing. "You tell me if it's too much, okay? No 'toughing it out.' You don't like something, you say something."

"I really don't think that will be an issue, but okay." She was already one clit rub away from coming.

Leaning over her, Bax took her mouth while he slowly slid the tip of his cock into her tight channel. She didn't feel the piercings at first, but then, with another inch, she felt every ridge.

Every ball.

Every little rub and bump.

And all those *everythings* were about to bless her with her own personal record for fastest orgasm and officially allow her to cross off the seventh item on her Docket.

✦ ✦ ✦

The force of Olive's orgasm dragged a low groan from Bax's throat. Wanting to make sure it was a good one for her, he pumped his hips gently, slowly rubbing his ladder over her G-spot over and over and allowing her to get acclimated to the sensation.

Fuck. He didn't want to come. Not yet. There were still a million and one things he wanted her to experience, but as her body pulsed around him, he wasn't sure he'd have much of a choice.

He savored the bite of her fingers digging into his ass and devoured her mouth, relinquishing his ownership of her lips as the last few quivers of her body rolled through her.

He pulled out with a groan.

She peered up at him, confused. "What are you—?"

"On your hands and knees, angel." Gripping her hips, he flipped her position, enjoying her audible gasp as he trailed his mouth up the length of her spine. He reached the back of her neck and coaxed her body upright until they both stood on their knees, his chest to her back, and his throbbing cock begging for more of her.

"Hex me," she whisper-cursed, realizing his plans. "*Yes.* Before you ask. All the yes."

He chuckled against the curve of her neck . . . because he *had* been about to ask, needing to make sure she was in this—and enjoying this—every step of the way.

Nipping the back of her neck, he brushed his cock through her folds once again, enjoying the shiver that trailed through her body. She pushed her ass back against him, silently seeking more. He was more than willing to give it to her.

He pushed inside her in one knee-quaking thrust, and withdrew and did it again, each time hitting deeper. Going farther. Her hand cupped the back of his thigh as she tried urging him into a faster rhythm, and damn if he didn't like that idea.

He kept them upright for a few more thrusts. "On your hands."

She dropped eagerly, instinctively pressing her upper chest against the mattress and giving him a gorgeous view of her curvy ass in the air. He groaned and thrust deeper . . . then slower, then hard and quick. He alternated, encouraged by her soft breathy moans for more before she began meeting his thrusts with ones of her own.

The sound of their labored breathing and meeting bodies became music to his ears as they danced themselves into a sweaty frenzy.

"Come with me, angel." Feeling the heavy sign of his impending release and not daring to break their momentum, he slid one hand to her clit. "Fuck. I want you to come around me again."

She released a soft string of curses as she pushed her body harder against his touch. Three more thrusts and just as many clit rubs and she detonated again, this time bringing him along for the ride.

Every squeeze of her body flooded him with another wave of

pleasure, and with every wave, he drowned a bit more in the heaven that was Olive Maxwell.

Wrung out and boneless, they fell in a heap to the bed, Bax carefully falling to her side so as not to crush her.

He tucked her against his body and kissed the delicate curve of her neck. "Was that a sufficient amount of fuck-ton more, angel?"

She giggled breathlessly, the sound sending a magical flutter through his chest. "That was *so much* more I think I'm now covered for the rest of my life."

He sure as hell hoped not . . . because he wanted to do it again.

And again.

Something told him that this wouldn't just leave him with another mark on his record. It would black the whole damn thing out.

And he couldn't force himself to care.

15

Minions & Snow Angels

Olive swiveled her hips side to side, keeping the rhythm with Rihanna's "If It's Lovin' That You Want" while brewing the largest—and strongest—pot of coffee she could manage. She'd woken up that morning with Bax's thick arm draped around her waist, his naked chest pressed against her back, and her memories mentally playing the night's events on repeat.

If it weren't for her pleasurably sore muscles—and the unclothed man in her bed—she would've thought it all a delicious dream. Not only had it *not* been a figment of her overactive imagination, but it also hadn't been a onetime occurrence. After a brief hiatus and a thirty-minute nap, they'd woken and done it all over again, Bax giving her that "fuck-ton more" a fuck-ton more.

Hence the need for super-caffeination. Without, she'd be dragging her ass before her first lecture class even began, making it the Mondayest Monday ever on record.

Getting lost in Rihanna's sultry tone, she didn't realize she was no longer alone until two familiar arms wrapped around her waist from behind. Bax's stubble tickled her neck as he trailed a line of kisses along the curve of her shoulder.

"Good morning." She grinned, resting her hands over his.

"Nah. It's a fucking fantastic morning."

"Eh. Fantastic would be if a miracle happened and I didn't have to go to work." She sighed, leaning her head back to look at him upside down. "You're an angel. Do you have any miracles up those tattoos?"

"I wish I could take credit for this, but . . ." Linking his fingers with hers, he steered her to the oversized window in the living room, where he tugged the blinds open. "Your miracle, my lady."

She gasped, her eyes widening as she practically pushed her face against the glass. "Holy hexes!"

Snow covered everything from the narrow two-lane road to the line of cars that now resembled white fluffy mounds instead of automobiles. Trees lining the street drooped with the weight of their wintery blanket. There was nothing that wasn't covered.

"It's gorgeous." Her gaze drifted onto an older man struggling to navigate a near waist-high snow drift while walking a Chihuahua. She giggled. "I can't believe all this happened overnight."

Bax brushed his mouth over the sensitive spot just below her ear, and she nearly melted on the spot. "And it also caused the city to declare a snow emergency. No running buses, and only underground trains will be kept open. For now."

She shot her gaze to his, finally understanding his meaning. She hightailed it to her cell phone and pumped her fist in the air when she saw the text from the college. "I have a snow day!"

He chuckled at her excitement. "So what do you want to do with it?"

"Is that a trick question?" She shot him a confused look.

"It wasn't supposed to be."

"Snow days mean staying inside and drinking hot chocolate." Her gaze reflexively drifted back to her room. "Or other things."

Smirking, he tugged her body toward his. "Not that I don't really like the sound of these *other* things, but I have a few alternate ideas that I'd like for you to consider."

"Such as?"

"What would you say to a wintery wonderland adventure?"

She narrowed her eyes warily while slowly trailing her hands up his bare chest, making sure not to miss her favorite nipple rings. "I'd say that's awfully vague, and I'd need more details before accepting an offer. Are we talking hot chocolate under a pillow fort? Or are we talking—"

"Central Park in the snow."

She paused her chest exploration and wrinkled her nose at him. "You mean Central *Park* Central Park? The one outside?"

He chuckled. "There is only one, and parks are pretty well-known for being outdoors."

"We'd leave our warm and cozy apartment to commute through the slush and muck to do what?"

"To have an adventure."

"But what does that *mean*?"

"Whatever the hell we want it to."

The gleam in his eyes glinted with determination. "How are we getting there if the roads are closed and most trains aren't running?"

No doubt seeing her thinking wheels working overtime, his lips twitched. "Guess you get to ride Angel Air one more time, and since you're one of our VIP customers, there's a complimentary hot chocolate in it for you upon arrival at our destination. The kind with real milk and chocolate. Not added water."

"That's playing dirty, Baxter Donovan."

He shrugged unapologetically. "I'd pretty much try any tactic to get you to go on a date with me, angel."

Her heart tripped over itself. "A date?"

He brushed a trail of soft, sweeping kisses over her cheeks until tenderly commandeering her lips. "You were right about the gala not being a *date* date. A real date should involve just the two of us. No work. No party crashers. Just you and me."

"And thousands of other people who probably have the same ideas as you," Olive quipped coyly.

"But at least they're there to experience some fun. What do you say? Come to the park and make snowpeople with me?" He brushed his mouth over hers once, then twice more, each time melting away her resistance until she became a melted pile of goo in his arms.

"Throw in some snow angels and you've got yourself a deal."

"It's a date. Now go pile on the layers." Grinning, he spun her toward her room and swatted her on the ass. "Your flight leaves in fifteen minutes."

They took off in ten, Bax a significant degree more comfortable in the air than he'd been the night of Vi's All Supernaturals on Deck. And he was right. It was a short flight. Five minutes after taking off from her bedroom balcony, they touched down in the center of the Bow Bridge with nary another soul in sight.

The park really did feel like a winter wonderland, the bridge blanketed in untouched snow and the serene lake twinkling as if glazed over in a single sheet of glass. She glanced around, unable to believe this usually busy part of the park was practically laid open and empty.

"Fuck, I love that smile on your face." Bax cradled her cheek, his thumb rubbing warmth into her skin. "Are you glad you agreed to leave the apartment?"

She crinkled her nose teasingly. "This is a smidge better than a pillow fort in the living room."

"Yeah?" His lips twisted into a pleased grin.

"There's only one—well, maybe two—things that could broaden the gap a little bit more."

"And what's that?"

"You said something about snowpeople, and I know I tacked on snow angels as an addendum."

"You know what? You're right. And I think I know just the perfect place for both." Taking her hand, he tugged her off the bridge and down the path to their left.

She wasn't sure what exactly he had in mind, but she suddenly couldn't wait to find out.

✦ ✦ ✦

Bax couldn't remember the last time he'd grinned this much. Hell, his cheeks almost ached, but it was a good problem to have considering when he'd woken up alone this morning, he'd been unsure how the day would pan out.

To be more precise, he'd worried Olive would regret everything they'd done the previous night—and morning. But then he'd seen her dancing her sweet ass across the kitchen, lightness in her step and a twinkle in her eye, and his panic temporarily abated.

All those fantasies he'd had about him and her since they first met suddenly didn't feel so fantastical. And they sure as hell had nothing on reality. Now that he knew how it felt to *really* have Olive Maxwell in his arms—and in his bed—there was no way he could go back to dreaming about all the what-ifs, regardless of the host of problems that created.

He'd let her guide this new direction and hoped like hell it mirrored the one he pictured.

"Oh, wow." Olive's soft gasp had him grinning even wider. She glanced around the Bethesda Fountain and the angel statues barely visible beneath the covering of snow. The only place left slightly less untouched was the terrace, and even that had swirling drifts climbing high up the long stairs. "This is gorgeous. I don't think I've ever seen anything look so beautiful."

"I have."

His words turned her toward him, and when she saw his pointedly intense gaze, she snortled, the sound so damn adorable.

"What?" Her laughter fueled his own. "I compliment you and you snort at me?"

"I have hat hair, probably a tomato-red face, and I'm ninety-eight percent sure icicles have formed on my nose."

"The hat's cute, I like tomatoes, and the icicles sparkle like diamonds."

She snortled again, this time dragging him toward the fountain, where she announced it was time to build some snow tourists. They rolled and patted and rolled again until they had nearly a dozen or more snowy out-of-towners surrounding the fountain's perimeter. Once she deemed it sufficiently crowded, she turned to the small, once-grassy clearing abutting the tree line.

Arms spread wide, she turned toward him and announced, "*Now* it's time for snow angels."

She fell backward into the plush snow with a giggle and wiggled her arms and legs.

Arms crossed, he watched her play. "And to think I practically had to bribe you with hot chocolate to get you to come outside."

"You *did* bribe me, and you bet your fine angel ass I'll be collecting, Guardian Donovan. But for now, we angel."

"That's not how you angel, angel."

She paused, frowning up at him with specks of snow dusted all over her cheeks. "No? Then how do you do it?"

"Watch and learn, babe. Watch and learn." He draped his leather jacket on what he thought was a snow-covered bench and ejected his wings.

She gasped, her eyes going wide as saucers behind her glasses. "No fucking way."

"Incoming." Grinning, he turned away from her and fell backward so his angel lay right next to hers. His body sank into the snow, and once it settled, he pushed his wings down farther toward the ground so they'd imprint better.

He turned to where Olive lay and got a faceful of snow.

He spluttered, chuckling. "What was that for?"

"That's cheating!" She tried hiding her laugh behind a low, sexy growl. "I call foul play."

"Nah. It's just using your assets, babe." He laughed and sprang to his feet, careful not to ruin his impression. He took her hands and helped her up as well, and then they both turned to look at their handiwork.

Bax slid his arm around her waist and held her close as she shivered. "What do you think?"

"Damn it. Yours looks incredible." She scanned over the nearly perfect mold of his wings before looking at hers. "Mine looks like a Minion that got caught in a snowstorm."

"But it's a cute Minion."

She rolled her eyes, but there was no disguising her smile as she wrapped her arms around his waist in a tight hug. "Thank you for this date, Bax. This is so much better than the horror fest that was the gala."

"It's my pleasure, angel." His arms followed, holding her cold cheek against his chest. "I'm at your service, forever and always."

She propped her chin on him and peered up at him through her thick lashes. "Is it time to service me some hot chocolate? Because I'm losing the feeling in most—if not all—of my appendages. Including my ass."

He slid his hands down to cup the ass in question and guided her legs back around her waist. "Grab my jacket and I'll service the hell out of you."

Her eyes darkened as she looped an arm behind his neck and held on to him tightly. "Did you mean for that to sound so dirty? Because I'm not-so-secretly hoping that you did."

"Of course I did. Hot chocolate first, as promised, so we can warm up your insides . . . and then we're heading home so I can help warm up your everything else. Sound good to you, angel?"

She brushed her mouth against his ear as he pushed off from the ground. "Sounds like a date."

16

Romance Novel (in Progress)

Olive's Dare I Docket

1. ~~Run away to join the circus~~
2. ~~Do something spontaneous: Hot tub skinny-dipping~~
3. ~~Do something socially frightening: Attend the Gala~~
4. Get a tattoo
5. Enter a dance competition
6. Sing karaoke
7. ~~Have hot, multiorgasmic sex~~
8. ~~Go on a date that ENDS in hot, multiorgasmic sex~~
9. End up in a romance novel (*in progress?*)
10. Survive a heartbreak???

Nothing could wipe the smile from Olive's face—not her cranky students, who'd obviously partied a little too hearty over the weekend and now regretted it; not a ridiculous puppy-eyed Mason popping up at her office yet again; not even her midday commute from NYU to Supernatural Council headquarters.

Actually, the latter almost transformed her grin to a grimace when a moving truck—driven by someone with no spatial awareness—kicked up a spray of city slush and sludge that ended up soaking her from the knees down. New York dug its way out from the winter weekend too fast, axing her plans with Bax to build a pillow fort in the living room and only emerge for hydration and sex-fortifying snacks.

Now it was back to reality, back to work, and back to dodging taxis while attempting to lunch with her sisters and Harper.

With Vi in all-day meetings with the Council due to Edie's absence, they decided to meet at headquarters before walking to the Italian bistro around the corner.

Crowded with both Norms and Supernaturals, the headquarters rotunda thrummed with voices, almost too loud for her ears. She made her way through the magical security detector and was picking her purse up from the conveyor belt when she caught sight of Rose and Harper waving from across the room.

She made it about six feet before nearly barreling into an unsuspecting bystander, sidestepping left a split second before collision. "Sorry. Excuse me."

The other person shifted left, too, blocking her path. "We meet again, Miss Maxwell."

She glanced up at the familiar voice. The man from the NYU gala, whose conversation with Bax she'd interrupted, stared down at her from a foot and a half additional height. From this close, there was no denying a familial resemblance.

He was tall and broad-shouldered, and his solid stance hinted that he wasn't one to challenge in a fight. Gray hair intermixed with the dirty blond, showing more in the immaculately trimmed beard that hid the same square-shaped jaw.

"Although we really didn't have a chance for introductions with how my son whisked you away the other night." He smiled, holding out his hand. "Mikael Donovan."

She tentatively accepted it and pulled away as quickly as possible. "Olive Maxwell. But it appears you already know that."

Unlike his son's, the older Donovan's gray eyes possessed a gleaming calculation, hardening to steel the longer they remained fixed on her. It made her want to fidget, but she remained still, her chin held high as she refused to look away. He was obviously the type who enjoyed making others uncomfortable and she wouldn't give him the satisfaction.

His faux smile broadened. "I know a great many things about you, one of which is that you and my son are living under the same roof."

Internal alarm bells fired off in her head.

"You see, Miss Maxwell, after multiple botched Assignments, my son is now in a precarious position with the GAA. To say his career is being held together by a strand of thread isn't far from the truth. Any outside distractions, or meaningless diversions, could result in clipped wings."

She pushed her glasses higher onto her nose and tried to decide which of Mikael's insinuations to address first: the suggestion that any relationship between her and Bax would be meaningless, or that it would result in something that sounded particularly painful.

She picked one and firmed her voice, hoping it didn't betray her uneasiness. "Clipped wings sounds a little barbaric, don't you think?"

"Oh, it's not literal clippage. Although, now that you mention it, it may as well be for an angel. I'm sure an intelligent woman such as yourself is well versed in angel hierarchy. The fact that my son—a Donovan—had been relegated to the Guardian Angel Affairs was enough of a blow to the family name, but for him to throw away even that title for a little playtime? It's unfathomable, and it's the absolute worst thing he could do for his future."

"I feel like the worst thing would be pursuing a future that would make him unhappy," she tossed back casually, keeping her own faux smile on her face.

Mikael Donovan's fake smile melted. "If you care for my son at all, Miss Maxwell, you'll do well to keep those feelings—and any others you may have toward him—to yourself. I'm not sure you'd like the fallout otherwise."

The blood chilled in her veins as she summoned a Maxwell glare of which Grandma Edie would be proud. "Was that supposed to be a threat of some kind?"

"Sweetheart, a Donovan does not threaten. We promise. You'd do well to remember that." With a final parting glare, he stormed from the headquarters rotunda, nearly mowing down Vi—who'd just joined Rose and Harper.

Vi shot visual daggers at his back. "What and who the hell was *that*?"

"Bax's father," Olive admitted grudgingly.

Three sets of eyes swung toward her, but Harper spoke first. "That was his dad? Shit. And I thought my mom was scary."

Rose's mouth spluttered. "*Our* Bax?"

"Did someone piss in his Cheerios this morning, or does he have an ingrown feather or something?" Vi asked.

"Something tells me that's his normal demeanor, sans pissing and feather ailments." She tried her best to shake off the encounter, but her hands still shook a bit. She needed a subject change while she pulled herself together, and pronto. "If I don't get a breadstick in my stomach in the next ten minutes, you'll all be left to deal with Hangry Olive."

Vi threw an arm over her shoulder. "We can't let that happen again."

They headed the two blocks to their favorite Italian bistro. As soon as the owner, Sofia, saw them step through the door, she whisked them to a corner booth, close enough to people-watch, but far enough around the corner for privacy. The older woman placed two breadstick baskets in the center of their table, took their orders, and disappeared into the back to give them to her chef husband, Antonio.

Olive glanced toward Vi as her sister ripped the head off a garlic stick and chewed aggressively. "That good of a day, huh?"

Her triplet growled, doing a great impersonation of her True

Mate. "Twice last night, my sleep was interrupted to triage 'important' calls that were the equivalent of a clogged toilet. This morning, I came into the office to more of the same but followed it up with *hours* of sitting on my ass, only getting up when refereeing Xavier and Rose's brother-in-law before they whipped out fangs and claws and destroyed the entire room."

Olive smirked. "So a *great* day. Got it."

Rose interjected, "Julius is *not* my brother-in-law. He's Damian's brother. And to play demon's advocate, Xavier grates on everyone's nerves. I can't count how many times Gran threatened to cap his fangs if he flashed them one more time and didn't start playing nice."

"Instead of preparing to become Prima, I feel like I'm a preschool teacher." Vi dropped her head to the table with a loud *thunk*. "Stake me, bake me, and throw silver in my eyes. How did Gran do this and make it seem so effortless? This is not effortless. It's the exact opposite of effortless. It's requiring *all* the effort . . . and more. It's impossible."

Olive exchanged knowing looks with Rose and Harper.

"What?" Vi picked up her head and caught it. Her head swiveled from witch to demon to witch. "Now is not the time for silence or secrets. Spill."

"It's obviously not impossible because you're doing it . . . and you've been doing it since Gran went MIA."

"Only because I haven't had a choice. It's bad enough that I'm the 'unconventional' Prima to Linc's 'unconventional' Alpha. I don't want to be the Prima who let years of forward Supernatural movement burn to the ground because she couldn't get her witch-shit together."

Vi slowly registered the reasoning behind their three smirks. "Hex me with a fucking witch wart, I'm actually doing this, aren't I? I'm prepping to become the next Prima."

"Fuck yeah, you are!" Harper held up her water glass, urging the others to do the same. "And may you shock everyone out of their stuffy suits and garters . . . and for once, I don't mean that in a succubus kind of way."

They laughed, clinking their glasses together and toasting Violet's impending ass-kickery. They joked, they commiserated, they dwelled on theories about Edie's abrupt disappearance and took bets on when she'd *poof* back into their existence. The topics shifted faster than TikTok trends, leaving Olive wide open and unsuspecting when Harper brought up her Docket list.

All eyes remained glued on her.

"What?" She hoped her wide eyes gave her a look of innocence.

"How's your list coming?" Rose asked, sipping her water. "How many have you crossed off?"

Memories of the other night, the next day, and that morning drifted into her mind, automatically flushing her cheeks. The things of which Bax—and his piercings—were capable seemed almost endless.

"A few." She took a large gulp of her water, hoping it prevented her from combusting on the spot.

"Do you think you'll finish the project in time to present your findings to the board?"

"I think I'll do as I told my students and try to complete as many items as my comfort level allows."

Harper studied her with narrowed green eyes. There was a faint twinkle, almost as if she'd called on her inner succubus. "Which have you crossed off? We can brainstorm ways to help you check off the rest."

"That's not necessary. I have everything under control." She shifted in her seat, wiping her mind of memories of her and Bax's weekend sex-fest, but damn, it was difficult . . . especially when Harper's nose literally twitched.

The redhead's lips lifted into a knowing smirk. "Sometimes two heads are better than one. Imagine what help four could be."

She shot the demon a warning look. "I'm perfectly fine with my head. I mean, my own head. But if you could convince Gage that Potion's Up needs to hold a dance competition on Saturday night, that would be great. Not sure how I'll check that one off yet."

"Gage agreeing to anything that could remotely lead to fun? Not likely." Temporarily distracted, Harper tapped her pink-painted nails on the table before a lightbulb practically lit up over her head. "But I have an idea. Actually, it's a brilliant idea."

"And that would be . . ."

"Let me see if it's as perfect a plan in reality as it is in my head and then I'll let you know."

Vi chuckled while Olive's concern grew along with her frown. "I love it when she gets all excited."

Rose snortled. "Funny, because when Harp gets that glint in her eyes, I experience the opposite. Maybe you should pull out bail money from your bank account and have it at the ready."

Harper flipped her the middle finger, laughing but not denying. "Please remember that the last time your cute asses warmed the seats of a jail's holding cell was not because of one of *my* ideas. Now, your bare bum warming the seat of a city subway car? That I take full credit for."

They all chuckled, remembering both the failed Operation Equine Freedom and the No-Pants Express subway ride. Just like that, Olive received her topic change and wiped the not-so-imaginary stress sweat from her brow.

She wasn't ashamed of what happened with Bax. They were both adults.

But she wasn't quite ready to share it—or more accurately, the memory of it—with anyone else. She enjoyed having something to call her own, and her multiorgasmic sex-fest with Baxter Donovan definitely qualified.

For now, she'd enjoy feeling like the protagonist in a romance novel (in progress)—aka list item number nine—and just hope that, unlike in most books, the floor didn't fall out from under her when she least expected it.

✦ ✦ ✦

Bax dragged the tip of his pencil into a series of loops and swirls, building an intricate design that now took up most of the page. He still had no idea what the series of intertwined shapes would be, only that when he got into a groove—like now—the only thing occupying his thoughts was a certain saucy, book-loving, sexy-as-hell witch.

A witch who had blown his mind again and again over the course of the last few days.

A witch who made him nervous as hell—not to mention horny.

A witch who now stepped into their apartment, a timid smile sliding onto her face as she caught sight of him sitting on the couch. "Hey. No work tonight?"

"Not tonight. Not tomorrow. Guess you could say I've been placed on light duty."

Concern slipped over her face. "Is that a good thing or a bad thing?"

"Depends on the day and how it progresses."

They stared, gazes locked. He barely refrained from dragging her onto his lap. *Follow her lead*, he told himself. But fuck, it was hard when all he wanted to do was taste that sweet spot just behind her ear.

Instead, he followed her as she headed into the kitchen, dropping his sketchbook on the couch cushion. She pulled out a yogurt from the fridge and visibly tensed when he cleared his throat.

"Alright, out with it, angel." Folding his arms over his chest, he prepped himself for whatever was about to come. He knew he should've tried convincing her to take an extra snow day. "What's wrong? Did something happen at school?"

Fuck. Did something happen and he wasn't there to intervene?

He scanned her for any sign she'd been hurt, but only came out of it with a semi-erection. "Olive . . . ?"

"This weekend was . . . great."

Double fuck. Did she regret it all? He'd considered them in the clear when they woke up after their winter wonderland weekend, but maybe it was simply a delayed reaction. Did she not have fun? Had he been too rough when they'd come back to the apartment to warm up?

Bax forced a neutral expression as he waited for her to collect and voice her feelings. He made it another beat before sighing. "Are we really doing this?"

"Doing what?" She turned and hit him with all the power of her big blue eyes.

He closed the distance between them, bracing his hands on the counter on either side of her hips. Not touching her, he hovered his lips less than an inch from her ear. She shivered from the almost-contact, and damn it, he did, too, his entire body vibrating with the need to run his hands over her soft skin.

But he held back, needing to ask, "Do you want to pretend this past weekend never happened?"

Her eyes snapped up from where they'd been watching his mouth. "What? No! Why, do you?"

"Fuck no . . . but you came home looking ten different types of skittish and I needed to make sure."

"It's nothing like that. It's just that this past weekend was so . . ."

"Fucking fantastic," he finished with a small grin.

She chuckled. ". . . *fucking fantastic.* Being back to reality today had me wondering if it all really happened, or if it was a product of my imagination. And if you tease me right now, I'd like to remind you that I have the ability to hex you and I'm a bit rusty. Things backfiring is not out of the realm of possibility."

"No teasing, angel. And I'd be lying if I didn't say I hadn't worried about the same thing." He gently brushed the tip of his nose with hers. "But I'm happy to report that our winter wonderland weekend was most definitely our reality, and one I would never in a million years regret."

Even if it costs me my wings.

Smiling softly, she tentatively ran her hands up his arms and over his shoulders, and whispered, "I don't think I could, either."

Bax hoisted her onto the counter before taking her mouth in a soul-searing kiss. Her taste. Her smell. The way her body rubbed against his, making him feel the most alive he had in a damn long time. Every last bit of Olive Maxwell consumed him, so much it took a few long moments and Olive's weary sigh to register the stylings of the Beatles' "Devil in Her Heart."

"My phone."

"Do you need to answer?" He trailed a line of kisses down her throat, really hoping she'd say no.

"Need to? No. But if I don't, Harper will blow my phone up with George, John, Paul, and Ringo all freaking night." The phone went silent and started up again two seconds later. "Case in point."

He chuckled. "I thought her ringtone was 'Let's Talk About Sex.'"

"It was. She likes to change it whenever I have the audacity to leave my phone sitting anywhere within her arm-span, and I had the courage to leave it at the table when I went to the restroom earlier. I'm sorry. I'll get her off the phone quick."

He helped her off the counter and, to ensure he kept his hands to himself, went back to the couch.

"What's up, Harper?" she answered the succubus's call.

He didn't *try* to eavesdrop, but the demon didn't have much of an inside voice. He heard mention of Olive's Docket list and played it cool, leaning his arms along the back of the couch as the petite witch walked closer, her eyes devouring him while still talking to her friend.

"Sure. Yeah. That sounds like a plan." Olive nibbled her bottom lip. "I'll be there."

She hung up, and he crooked his finger, his other hand guiding her to sit astride his lap. His cock didn't need much encouragement to go straight to full attention. "Fun excursion planned? Or since Harper's involved, should I be asking if it's a legal one?"

"Sometimes with Harp, it's best not to ask, but this one is actually about checking off the dance competition on my list. How bad could it be, right?"

He lifted a single eyebrow straight into his hairline.

She laughed. "Okay, yeah. Maybe I should've asked if it was legal."

He didn't let her see his rush of concern, busy plotting how to remain within arm's length of her without drawing suspicion. Her eyes flickered to his sketchbook and she gasped.

"Is this my tattoo?" She picked it up, her eyes feasting on the hundreds of decorative swirls.

"It turned out to be a rabid opossum. What do you think?" Keeping one hand low on her hip, he slid the pointer of his other around the page. "There's the tail. There's the snout."

She rolled her pretty eyes. "Funny. But seriously . . . what is it?"

"What do you think it is?"

"Besides gorgeous? It's perfect."

He watched her studying his artwork, and then his gaze landed on the etchings with new eyes. The patterned swirls, the mix of thin and thicker lines, some tangling together before flaring into their own directions and swirling again. An image slowly bloomed in his head, flowering until the entire piece opened up right in front of him.

Fuck. She was right. It was perfect.

"Oh." Her breathless voice pulled his attention back to her. Watching him carefully, she slowly traced her soft fingers over the lines of his mouth. "You have that look."

"What look?"

"That same look Rose gets when she gets called out on a Hunt.

The same one Vi gets when she calls on her Magic and it goes right. It's probably the same one that's on my face when I do research." Her lips pulled up into a soft smile. "You, Baxter Donovan, are in thrall of your path."

He chuckled. "My path? When did you take up fortune-telling? Are you pulling out the tarot cards for me next, angel?"

"Joke all you want, but I'm right. You love creating things."

It was his turn to shift awkwardly. "It calms my mind . . . and yeah, I like creating things from nothing. It makes me feel . . . special. One-of-a-kind."

She peered down at him through her long lashes, that soft smile of hers damn near melting his insides. "You *are* special, Bax. And definitely one-of-a-kind."

With her, he felt as though he was both.

"What are you doing right now?" he asked, taking a huge fucking leap.

"Right now? Sitting on your lap?"

"How do you feel about taking a ride?"

She shifted, the move rubbing her ass against his already throbbing cock. "I actually feel pretty good about it. You?"

Fingers digging into her hips, he groaned. "Fuck. That's not what I meant, but now that's what I wish I meant."

Her blue eyes twinkling mischievously as she giggled. "Where are we riding to?"

"I'm taking a page out of Harper's vague playbook and saying *you'll see.*"

This could backfire in a tremendous way . . . blow up right in his face and leave him a long-haired, eyebrow-less biker angel.

But hell if he didn't want to take it anyway.

17

New Age Goat-Yoga Studio

Olive couldn't fathom where Bax was taking them. Arms wrapped tightly around his waist, she glanced up to a string of brick commercial buildings as he veered them slowly off the road and fit his bike between two street-parked cars.

She used the sidewalk as a step stool and eased her leg off the motorcycle before waiting for him to shut off the engine.

He held a hand for her to take. "Ready to see my happy place, angel?"

"Depends if it's in that rather rough-looking biker bar across the street," she teased. "Because if it is, I'll admit that I'm not."

The spreading grin on his face threw her off. "Not the bar . . . although there may be a biker or two. Come on. I got you."

His smile disarmed her, and she slid her hand into his, letting him lead the way into the nearest gray brick building identified as Inklings by its aged bronze sign.

Bax pulled open the door and ushered her inside.

She wasn't sure what she'd expected, but the gorgeously framed art prints on the walls and the retro black-and-white waiting room with red accents most definitely wasn't it.

The young girl behind the counter glanced up, smile in place and broadening when she saw Bax. "Hey, Baxter! Did he know you were dropping in tonight?"

"Nah, Ruby. It was a last-minute decision." He pulled a manila envelope from his leather jacket's inside pocket. "Got a few designs done a bit early, so I figured I'd drop them off."

"Sure thing. Let me get him. He's in between clients, so it's perfect timing. But I should probably warn you, he's not gonna let it go."

Bax chuckled. "He wouldn't be Isaiah if he did, but thanks for the heads-up."

Ruby disappeared into the back, and while they waited, Olive dragged him to the walls and the framed artwork. A few of the pieces seemed familiar. Not that she'd seen them, but that the feeling they conjured within her was familiar.

The style. The details. The obvious care and love found in each one.

As they came up to the long counter, a tall, broad-shouldered man stepped out from a side door, his smile instant the second he laid eyes on Bax. He rubbed his hand over his well-kept beard, showcasing an extensive array of tattoos on his hands and arms.

But it was his megawatt smile that really caught her attention. Genuine and warm, he smiled at Bax as if they were long-lost friends. "Two times in a month? Who do I have to thank for this celestial event? Or are you commandeering my office again?"

"Isaiah." Bax shook the older man's hand. "Can't a guy come visit his favorite tattoo studio without it being a major event? And no, I won't keep you from your dating show again. At least not today."

Tattoo studio . . .

Her eyes widened as she glanced around the space with newly opened eyes. "Is this where you get your art done?"

Isaiah glanced her way, his smile broadening. "And you brought a friend with you who knows that a good tattoo is a work of art." He held out his hand for her next. "Isaiah Thomas, my dear. And you are?"

"Olive Maxwell." She took his hand.

Something close to awareness flickered in the older man's eyes as he exchanged a look with Bax, but it was there and gone too quick for her to really decipher.

"You have a gorgeous business here, Mr. Thomas."

"Isaiah, please. That's what all my friends call me, and I know if the big wingman here brought you that you're definitely friend material." He turned toward Bax. "Ruby said you brought some new designs?"

"Here you go." He handed over the envelope. "And I thought while I was here, I could get a little touch-up on the blue and purple on the back—only if you have time."

"For my favorite artist and soon-to-be business partner, you bet your angelic ass. Follow me." Isaiah turned, leading the way through the back halls.

"Soon-to-be partner?" Enjoying the feel of Bax's hand still wrapped around hers, she squeezed his fingers in question.

He shot a glare to the shop's owner, but Isaiah only chuckled. "I'm surprised it took you so long to bring it up this time. You're losing your touch."

"Nah. Thought I'd give you a break since we have company and all, but since the pretty witch is a *friend* and not actual company, break time's over."

Bax ignored the other man's chuckles and clarified, "I'm not Isaiah's partner, now or in the future. He seems to have gotten it in his head that he needs to retire or something, and that it should be me who buys him out."

"Because it should be." Isaiah led them into a meticulous room with a long, cushioned bench chair. "I didn't shed buckets of blood, sweat, and tears into this place only to sell it to someone who's gonna turn it into a fucking new age goat-yoga studio or something."

"That sounded awfully specific," she whispered to Bax.

"Yeah, it did." Bax grinned at the other man. "Get an offer to sell from some goat enthusiast?"

"Not happening," Isaiah growled. "The only person I'm selling to is you, kid. Now plant your ass on the seat."

Bax glanced at her, a little sheepish as he gestured to the second chair in the room. "I probably should've asked if you even wanted to be in here for my touch-up. I actually didn't plan on it until I turned off the bike."

"I'll be getting my own artwork pretty soon, so I would hope that needles don't bother me," she quipped.

While Bax took his seat on the bench, removing his shirt and giving the older man his back, Isaiah lifted his bushy eyebrows as he glanced her way. "Getting a piece of your own? What's a nice witch like you want to decorate her skin with?"

"Actually, I don't know. It's either a rabid raccoon or an opossum."

He paused in setting up his table. "Those are interesting choices. Very . . . bold."

"I'm designing one for her." Bax chuckled. "But until tonight, the whole piece hadn't come to me yet."

Olive perked up. "Until tonight? You know what it is now?"

"Pretty sure, and no, I'm not telling you. You're the one who wanted it to be a surprise." He tossed her a wink over his broad shoulder, and she didn't know whether to kick him or kiss him.

"Way to throw my words back in my face. You suck."

"Sometimes I do." His lips twitched into a sexily crooked smirk, and he sent her a loaded look.

She cleared her throat. "The artwork in the waiting room is all yours, isn't it?"

Isaiah chuckled. "Boy, she's got your number, doesn't she?"

"Don't I know it," Bax murmured before admitting a little louder, "Some, yeah."

"Most," Isaiah corrected. "Has your boy mentioned how popular he is around here? And I don't mean just here in the studio—

although we *do* have a waitlist as long as both my arms of people waiting to get a Donovan design—but nationally. Studios from all over have been in full recruit mode for as long as I can remember. Sometimes I feel like his damn publicist."

She gaped, unable to wrap her head around this new information. "How has no one told me this before? I feel like this is knowledge that should've been shared at some point in the nearly ten years we've known each other."

"Because I haven't told anyone." Bax shifted in his seat, getting a soft reprimand from the man behind him with that tattoo gun. "It's really not that big of a deal."

"Excuse me, but yes, it is. It's amazing!"

"And surprising?"

"Not at all. Why do you think I asked you to design me something I can permanently ink onto my skin? Your art is incredible. Everyone should know about it. Hell, everyone should *see* it."

Isaiah nodded approvingly. "I feel the same way, which is why I've been trying to convince him to become a tattooist exhibitor for me at the international tattoo conference this year because it's actually in New York. You'll probably be surprised, but he's dragging his feet."

"Hold up. Rewind. And repeat." She waited until Isaiah lifted the needle from Bax's back and smacked the angel on the shoulder. "Baxter Bartholomew Donovan! You tattoo your own designs, too?"

Isaiah laughed. Bax glowered. And Olive was more determined than ever to not only get him to design her tattoo, but have him tattoo it on her as well.

✦ ✦ ✦

If the old man didn't have a needle to his back, Bax would've turned around and shot him a *mind your own business* glare. Instead, he shot Olive a sheepish look. "I dabble."

Isaiah scoffed behind him. "That's like saying Derek Jeter dabbled in baseball."

"I don't do it full-time for obvious reasons like my *real* job," he explained, ignoring the former Warrior, "but I occasionally moonlight as one of Isaiah's guest artists. It's really just a way for a client to get tattooed by the person who did their actual design."

"And there's a long list of people waiting for that to happen," she pointed out. "Who are you tattooing for the convention?"

"No one, because I haven't signed up. Being on a stage and having people watching my every move—literally—is not my thing."

"But it would get more people to see your artwork, and your art is something you love to do. Why not go for it?"

"If I were a budding tattoo artist instead of a Guardian, then I would, but my future is already sealed, angel. No point in stepping *that* far out of my comfort zone for something that won't make much of a difference."

"But—"

"I appreciate the cheerleading support, but it's not necessary. I came to peace with art being a therapeutic side gig a long time ago. I'm good."

Clamping her mouth shut, she quietly crossed her arms over her chest as if physically holding herself back from continuing the argument.

Everything in him wanted to wipe that disappointed look off her face, but he didn't know any feasible way. What she suggested wasn't just improbable; it was impossible. No matter how much he wished otherwise.

The room quieted except for the buzz of the tattoo gun, and before long, Isaiah announced he was finished. Bax helped the older angel clean up, and a few minutes later, they stood in the front room saying their goodbyes.

"It was nice meeting you, Isaiah. I hope we'll see each other again soon." Olive gave the old angel a warm hug, which he eagerly accepted.

"Oh, I'm certain you will, sweetheart." He shot Bax a smug grin over her shoulder and hugged her back. "And I'd be honored if you'd entrust Inklings with placing that rabid-opossum artwork of yours . . . or we'd be thrilled to host the artist if he'd like to place the piece himself."

Bax narrowed his eyes at his old friend just as Olive's gaze shot to him.

"I'll wait outside."

Bax cursed, watching her until the front door closed.

The second it did, a heavy hand fell on his shoulder, followed by his old friend's amused chuckle. "You got your hands full with that one, kid. And it's about damn time."

"It's not like that." Except it was . . . maybe.

"We've known each other a long time, and you've never, not once, brought someone to see the place. Anybody less astute than I am would almost think that there was meaning behind that. Luckily, I'm a fucking genius, so I *know* it does." Isaiah crossed his arms. "She's the friend turned crush turned roommate turned Assignment."

Bax shot a look through the window to where she stood near his bike. "Will you watch the shit that comes out of your mouth?"

"Oh, relax." The older angel snorted. "She's too busy building an argument in her head to hear anything I'm saying. What you should be worried about is what will come from *her* mouth when you step outside. She may have given the appearance of letting things drop a bit ago, but something tells me she's not the let-it-drop type."

He wasn't wrong. "I better go, and apparently prepare for an impending argument."

Isaiah chuckled. "Good luck with that. And I was serious about the offer to use Inklings. When she's ready to get her piece placed, bring her here."

"I wouldn't suggest any other place to her."

"Hit me up if you change your mind about the convention. I know a guy who could get you in last minute." They shook hands, and Bax headed outside, Olive glancing his way before the door closed behind him.

Her gorgeous, light-the-world smile was nowhere in sight.

"Don't look at me like that. Look at me any other way but *that* way," he demanded pleadingly.

Her frown deepened. "What way are you talking about? Do I look cold? Hungry?"

"Let's not bullshit each other, angel."

"You don't want bullshit?"

"I'd prefer we didn't, no."

"Fine. Answer this: From which do you get more enjoyment, being a Guardian or being an artist?"

"It's not that simple." He busied himself grabbing the helmets from the back of the Harley.

"Actually, it is. Which one makes getting up each morning exciting, and going to bed each night more difficult? Which one doesn't feel like a chore, but something that helps you breathe easier?"

His non-answer was all she needed.

Her angry steam dissipated, giving way to something akin to sympathy. "Bax . . ."

"You, of all people, know it's not always easy to shirk tradition," he pointed out. "Donovans have been in angelic service since the first rogue demon threatened to break peace. Actually, until me, *all* Donovans worked on the front lines as Warriors. I'm the first deemed unfit for that role."

"I call witch-shit," she blurted.

"Go ahead and call it, but it doesn't make it any less true." He handed her the helmet, but she made no move to put it on, obviously not finished.

Fuck. Isaiah had just met her and he'd called it. She seemed unlikely to drop this anytime soon.

"People told Vi her whole life that she wasn't magically talented enough to become Prima," Olive reminded him, "and she's now weeks away from stepping into the position. Rose, who actually trained for the part, is currently interning to become a freaking Supernatural bounty hunter."

"And your point is what?"

"That while taking the clear, expected path may be a hell of a lot easier, the road doesn't necessarily mean happier, or that it's the right path for *you*."

"Then I should do what? Quit working for the GAA and take Isaiah up on his offer to buy Inklings? That would go over about as well as news that the Boozereamery is discontinuing their cake-batter vodka ice cream."

Olive gasped. "You are never to give life to *that* thought ever again. To even suggest it is almost unforgivable."

"Noted." Bax smirked.

"But seriously. If buying Inklings and creating art is what makes you happy, then that's what you should do. Be damned what hundreds of Donovans have done before you . . . or whatever meaningless diversions try steering you in another direction. You need to do *you*."

Olive turned away, studiously avoiding his gaze while tugging on her helmet.

The abrupt about-face tripped his internal alarm. "Where did you hear the term *meaningless diversion*?"

She shrugged, still not meeting his eyes. "I don't know."

"It's my turn to call witch-shit. In all my years occupying this earth, I've only heard one person use that term, and never as nicely as you used it."

"You really expect me to remember where I heard a turn of phrase? I could've read it in a book, or seen it on a show. Hell, I could've heard it while standing in line at Latte Time." When she finally glanced up, though, he saw the truth in her eyes immediately.

It hadn't been any of those options.

Bax's anger bubbled to the surface in the form of a low growl. "When did he corner you?"

He stepped closer, hating when she took a step back. The move was like a sharp knife through his gut, and it had him taking a deep breath. "Nothing that comes out of that man's mouth is for the benefit of anyone except himself, angel. Whatever he told you or threatened you with, forget it. *When* did he approach you? And where?"

"I ran into him at Council headquarters while I was meeting up with the girls," she finally admitted.

"And what else did he say?"

"Nothing that I took to heart." She tucked her glasses higher up on her nose and stepped close, resting her palms over his chest. "And if that's how a Donovan acts and behaves, count yourself lucky you're the first to not follow the Donovan path. Your father's an ass. If I inherited anything from Edie, it was my ability to detect assholery from miles away. He was only at three feet and practically oozing it from every orifice."

The hot tension in Bax's body slowly went from scalding to a low simmer.

He rested a hand low on her hip and tried mentally picturing the description. "What does assholery look like? Is there a slime factor, or maybe an odor? Rotten eggs would be pretty apropos."

She glowered at him, but her displeasure didn't hold water when her lips twitched. "So your plan is to joke your way out of the topic at hand?"

"Is it working?" He lifted his eyebrow, hoping she'd say yes.

He couldn't help himself. Moving his hands to both sides of the helmet, he tipped her face toward his and claimed her lips. Their softness welcomed him, parting on a seductive sigh.

Both forgetting they stood on the street for anyone to see, they devoured each other, hands roaming and mouths feasting. It took a catcall from down the block for him to reluctantly pull away, but one look at her lush lips, swollen from their kiss, and he dove back for another.

"Hey!" Isaiah's booming voice startled them apart. The angel stood at Inklings' door, a stern scowl on his face, but laughter in his eyes. "The two of you are scaring my customers away. Go suck face in front of someone else's storefront. The comic store four doors down is a good option. Bastard owner deserves a little diminishing traffic flow after all but commandeering the dumpster out back for himself."

Bax and Olive chuckled, and the petite witch apologized profusely. Bax's mentor waved it off and disappeared back into the tattoo shop, leaving Bax alone with a pink-cheeked, giggling Olive, whom he couldn't wait to get back onto their couch and into his lap.

18

The Time of Our Lives

Olive now knew what it felt like playing the live-action—human—version of Frogger, and it was an experience that she didn't want to experience again. Horns blared, and a cabbie practically sideswiped the limo next to him in order to miss a determined Harper.

The succubus waved in response to the taxi driver's spewed obscenities, not letting it deter her from her goal. "Thank you for being so patient!"

Bax hustled onto the curb and pulled Olive with him only seconds before traffic resumed roaring past.

"Thanks," she huffed. "That was a little too close for comfort."

Bax grumbled. "The last hour was too close for comfort."

"Suck it up, angel cakes." Harper rolled her eyes, leading the way up Thirty-Fourth Street, her arm tucked through Rose's. "Need I remind you that it was your choice to tag along. You could've stayed home, or found some angelic things to do."

"Figured being on hand would speed up the body identification when you all got hit by a tour bus or something."

Olive choked on a laugh because the second they'd left the Hudson Yards station, that's almost what happened. It had been heart-pumping then, but funny now thanks to Rose's quick reflexes and the fact she'd been less than a foot from the demon's backside. All that Hunt training prevented Harp from becoming a casualty of New York City tourism.

"Do something about your angelic guard dog, Olly. He's killing my mojo," Harper warned, hoisting the large duffel higher over her shoulder. "And I vowed nothing would dampen my good mood because this will be an epic tale among epic tales. No amount of surliness or alpha posturing will diminish that, and if it does, Hades help the one who caused it."

"You know what else will diminish an epic tale?" Bax goaded. "Being flattened by a tour bus."

"Not that I don't trust you implicitly, Harp," Olive refereed, "but we're almost a block away from swimming in the Hudson . . . so unless there's some kind of dance competition on the ferry, I'm not sure this is happening."

"Oh, it's happening," she said adamantly. "And it's happening right here."

The bright lights of the Javits Center lit up the block, people milling about the sidewalk and surrounding walkways. Banners waved in the breeze, indicating an ongoing event, which wasn't an uncommon occurrence. Home to many conferences and fairs throughout the year, some that people traveled to attend from all over the world, the large space could hold thousands of people without appearing crowded.

"Why are we at the Ja— Oh, fuck." Rose cursed as a scantily clad couple walked in front of them, heading toward the main doors. "Some of these people are wearing less than the painted ladies in Times Square."

"Harp . . . do you want to throw out an explanation here?" Olive shot her friend an inquisitive look as the four of them walked up the center walkway. "Maybe start with why there are a lot of people in various stages of nakedness?"

"Ta-da!" Harper posed in front of the stickered signage on the tall floor-to-ceiling windows. "It's the Steamy Feet Amateur Dancing Competition!"

Behind her, Bax cursed. "You brought Olive to dance at an amateur strip dancing competition?"

"No! No, no," Harper denied. "Well, actually . . . no. Yes, there is a risqué category that may include the shedding of clothes, but there's tons of different categories. There's country, hip-hop, classic ballroom, and freestyle. You'll even find cute little ballerinas through those doors, so you can wipe the scowl off your face, Baxter Donovan. Have a little faith in me, please."

A "ballerina" walked past them, entering the building while wearing a costume that revealed her two very naked butt cheeks and the string of floss between them.

Olive cocked up an eyebrow and shot a look toward her sister, who shrugged. "Maybe the cute little ballerinas compete in the morning hours?"

"Okay," Harper sighed, "there may be more risqué categories than normal ones, but my inside person assures me there are plenty of categories where clothes are not shed." She held up her bulging duffel. "And I even brought costumes. So what do you say? Are you, Olive Maxwell, ready to release your inner dancing queen?"

Olive suddenly shared Bax's apprehension as a pair of thonged, feather-crowned dancers walked by them, entering the building.

"Just tell me that my costume doesn't have feathers." She mentally crossed her fingers. "Or thongs."

Harper grinned wide. "Oh, you just wait, witch. You just wait."

And she did wait. They entered the event center building, Harper tracking down her inside person, who took them to registration.

The man behind the counter glanced at their group. "Names?"

Harper beamed proudly, linking her arms with Rose and Olive. "Harper Jacobs, Olive Maxwell, and Rose Maxwell."

He fiddled on a tablet before making an affirmative grunt. "I see Harper and Rose listed as a dance team, but I don't have a partner listed for Olive."

"We're all three a team."

"A *couples* competition—by definition—means a team of two. Jacobs and R. Maxwell are listed as a pair, but there's no one listed as a second for O. Maxwell."

Rose eagerly offered, "Then I'll back out and let Harper and Olive compete. I was only doing it for moral support anyway."

The registrar sighed in annoyance. "Team swapping is not allowed."

Disappointment weighted Olive's stomach. "That's okay. I don't have to dance. I'm sure I'll get another chance somewhere else."

With time ticking away on the Dare I Docket and the SupeEx Project, she'd force their group into a dance-off Wii tournament if she had to. At least in that scenario, she could ensure she didn't look like a decorative peacock.

Bax's arm brushed against her arm as he stepped up alongside her and addressed the attendant. "You said no swapping partners, but Olive never identified a partner on sign-up."

The registrar nodded, giving Bax a head-to-toe appraisal. "That's correct. It must have been an oversight and should've been caught when finalizing the list."

"Well, since there was a mix-up on your end, can she name a partner now?"

She leaned close enough to whisper. "What are you doing?"

"Do you want to check off that box?" Determination glinted from his eyes as he locked his gaze on hers.

"Yeah, but—"

"Do you trust me?"

More than she'd ever thought possible. "I do."

He turned back to the waiting registrar. "Can she?"

"She can."

"Then I'll be her partner. Bax Donovan."

"And you're not a professional dancer, correct?"

He snorted. "That would be a big no."

The man nodded, typing away on his tablet before printing out four sets of badges and their individual identification numbers.

"Are you sure about this?" she asked him warily.

"Not even a little bit, but I guess your Docket thing is rubbing off on me because this is definitely not anywhere near my comfort zone." He chuckled, giving her hand a gentle squeeze. "We got this. How long is a dance anyway? Thirty seconds? Forty-five?"

"Most songs are at least a minute and a half to two and a half minutes," Harper supplied.

Olive felt all the color drain from her face. "Oh my Goddess. What are we going to dance to?"

"Here you go." The registrar finished checking them in and handed them directions. "Your dressing rooms are labeled on the map. Make sure you give your prerecorded music to the stage manager no less than an hour before your scheduled stage time. One minute late, and you forfeit your spot in the rotation with no guarantee that you'll be squeezed in at a later time."

Feeling a bit faint, Olive reflexively accepted the paperwork.

"It's fine," Harper said as she led them down the back hallway. "It's totally fine. I have the leotards and leg warmers. There's no reason why there can't be more than one group doing *Flashdance*'s 'Maniac.' It's an iconic dance. There can never be too many wet buckets thrown around."

Flashdance . . .

Harper was right: she knew that dance well. They'd all watched that movie a million times through the years. She breathed a little easier until her attention slid to a grim-faced Bax.

He grimaced apologetically. "I have no fucking clue what or who a *Flashdance* is . . . but give me twenty minutes."

"We should just pull out of the competition," she heard herself say. "Seriously. This is New York. There have to be other dance competitions around."

Gently cupping her chin, he turned her focus to him. "Give me twenty minutes."

"Twenty minutes and then what? As much as I'm kind of glad not to wear a micro-leotard and leg warmers, I've seen *Flashdance* so many times I could do it with my eyes closed."

"*Fifteen* minutes and I'll meet you in our assigned dressing room. You trust me?"

"It's not like I have much of an option," she muttered.

He nodded, smirking. "I'll take it. Clock me."

"Where are you going?" she called after him.

"To find my dancing queen some dancing shoes."

✦ ✦ ✦

Maybe Bax had some witch somewhere in his ancestry because the feat he'd just pulled out of his ass suggested some degree of magical intervention, and with two minutes to spare until his fifteen-minute deadline.

He'd tracked down not only costumes but music, *and* already hand-delivered it to the stage manager. The only thing left was to find Olive, change, and try not to throw the fuck up because shifting his feet side to side on the Potion's Up dance floor was a far cry from what was about to happen.

Following the texted directions from Olive, he turned the corner and paused in front of the first door on the left. It opened before he knocked, and a stressed Olive stood in front of him, her gaze dropping to the garment bag in his hand.

"I'm backing out." She let him into the small room. "This is a sign that I'm not meant to cross this off my list, and I always follow signs. Traffic signs. Emergency signs. Following signs is always a good thing. They're there for a reason."

"We're not backing out." He infused his tone with more confidence than he felt and hung the garment bag on the corner coatrack. Turning toward her, he captured her hands and gently hauled her close. "We're walking out on that stage together, and we'll dance our asses off. Together."

She nibbled the corner of her lip, shaking her head. "I appreciate the sentiment and the fact you're so willing to risk embarrassment on a massive scale, but this isn't a good idea. It's more likely that we'll fall on our asses together."

"I will deny it if you ever say this to Harper, but this is one of the best ideas she's ever had. The execution was a bit shaky, but the idea? It's not good. It's great." He gently led her over to the garment bag. "What's the movie that you and your sisters could very literally recite from memory from beginning credit to end?"

"*Pride and Prejudice* . . . the Keira Knightley version?"

"Other than that one."

"*Hocus Pocus*."

He shot her an amused smirk. "Evidently there's a lot of movies that you three can recite verbatim, but this one has a great soundtrack, watermelons, and, ironically enough, a dance competition."

She thought about it a few seconds before he hummed one of the most memorable songs, and her eyes widened in recognition. "*Dirty Dancing*!"

"Bingo."

Briefly letting go of her hands, he unzipped the garment bag and opened the flaps, revealing the pastel pink dress with the full skirt. He'd even bought another dancer's spare black button-down shirt, which, when paired with his own jeans, somewhat resembled Swayze's outfit from *Dirty Dancing*'s closing scene.

Her face full of awe, Olive touched the dress. "Where did you find these?"

"Evidently people who do these contests all the time bring more outfits than they need *just in case*. The owners of these two were more than happy to part with them for a little incentive."

"Bax, I can't—"

"You can and you will, angel. It was meant to be. You know that last dance sequence like the back of your hand, and because you and our brew crew made me watch that movie with you a million times over, so do I."

"You expect me to dance to '(I've Had) The Time of My Life'? I've only ever danced to it in my living room, and the times Vi and I messed around with the lift were in the swimming pool at the Y. When we were twelve."

"Then it's a night of firsts." Grinning, he pulled the pink dress from its hanger and held it out to her. "But first, you need to slip into this. Nobody puts Olive in the corner."

She did a laughing sob but took the outfit. "When we both fall flat on our faces and the ambulance is called, I'll be reminding you that this was all your idea."

"No one's falling flat on their faces." Gripping her hips, he gently tugged her against him, and on contact, her body melted against his. "You got this . . . and I got you."

With a small curve of her lips, she palmed his neck and dragged his mouth to hers for a kiss he felt straight to his bones. Her tongue swiped against his lips, seeking admission, and the second he eagerly gave it, he never wanted her to leave.

They kissed and touched until the flowing fabric of the dress's skirt got in their way. They pulled apart chuckling, and laughed more as she tried wrestling the garment into compliance.

"I guess we should probably get dressed. I want to be ready early enough to cheer on Ro and Harper when they take the stage."

"So we're really doing this?"

"We're really doing this." She grinned. "Let's hurry up and get dirty, Baxter Donovan."

He laughed. "Those words sound fucking amazing coming from

your lips, angel, and the second we're alone with a sufficient amount of time, I'll more than happily help you get dirty."

Her cheeks pinked as she sent him a flirty smirk. "Now there's something to look forward to. I love a good after-party."

Bax groaned, his cock going semi-hard in an instant. She laughed as she left him to duck behind a privacy screen, but he glanced at the obvious bulge in his pants that would definitely hinder him honing his Swayze.

An hour later, they were dressed and backstage, watching from the side as Rose and Harper leaned back in their side-by-side chairs, a dripping waterfall falling on them from above and drenching them Jennifer Beals style. The crowd roared, many jumping to their feet.

Rose and Harper exited left, smiles on their faces as they ran up to them.

"I'd hug you, but this is a dance contest, not a wet T-shirt contest." Olive gestured to their soggy status and the twin puddles forming beneath their feet. She handed them each towels they'd gotten from one of the stagehands.

"So did you two figure out what to do?" Harper glanced over their outfits.

"Actually, Bax saved the day." She turned a megawatt smile his way that made his heart skip a beat. "We're channeling our inner Baby and Johnny and hoping it doesn't lead to broken noses or broken anything else."

"*Dirty Dancing* is absolutely perfect," Rose said supportively.

A knowing glint twinkled in the demon's eyes. "It does seem like it fits you both perfectly."

Something shifted Bax's gut instincts. "Harper, did you—"

"Maxwell and Donovan," one of the stagehands bellowed. "You're up next!"

Olive turned a little green. "Maybe this wasn't such a good idea."

"As I said, it's not. It's a great idea." He entwined his fingers with hers and, bringing their hands up to his mouth, kissed the back of her knuckles. "Let's show them how it's done, Baby."

Olive gifted him a small smile. "Alright, Johnny. Let's do it."

They walked onto the stage hand in hand, stopping at the *X* that marked the spot. With dimmed lights, they took their positions, Bax behind Olive, his hand on her waist and his face tucked intimately into her neck.

Seconds before the music started, he dropped a soft kiss just under her ear and immediately felt the tension in her body evaporate as she leaned against him trustingly. With her in his arms, his did, too.

The center of his chest warmed, preceding a rush of emotions too numerous and too fast-moving for him to latch on to any specific one. Except the one telling him that this sense of rightness should've scared the shit out of him.

Instead, it solidified his determination not only to hold on to it all, but to not let go.

Professor Maxwell

Olive's Dare I Docket

1. ~~Run away to join the circus~~
2. ~~Do something spontaneous: Hot tub skinny-dipping~~
3. ~~Do something socially frightening: Attend the Gala~~
4. Get a tattoo (in progress)
5. ~~Enter a dance competition~~
6. Sing karaoke
7. ~~Have hot, multiorgasmic sex~~
8. ~~Go on a date that ENDS in hot, multiorgasmic sex~~
9. End up in a romance novel (in more progress)
10. Do NOT get heartbroken

Olive couldn't remember the last time she'd had this much pep in her step at the end of a workday, and it wasn't even chemically altered by gallons of Red Bull, which Vi had been consuming over the last few days.

Her energy boost wasn't even from crossing another item off her Docket, although that didn't suck. The melting pot of reasons were all linked to a certain sexy angel with tattoos she wanted to spend an entire night licking.

No way could she have imagined Bax getting his Swayze on and offering to dance on a stage in front of a huge crowd. They hadn't won, but they'd gotten third place in the Nostalgic Dance category, directly behind *Footloose's* final dance scene and *Chicago*'s "Cell Block Tango" reenactments.

But she didn't need the trophy. She'd won the second she stepped onto the stage and couldn't wipe the smile off her face no matter how hard she tried. A brief run-in that morning with Mason made it waver a bit, especially after he felt he "owed it" to her to disclose that he would also be applying for the upcoming grant money.

Asswipe—to quote Bax.

After wishing him the best of luck and hexing him with a hearty pimple on the tip of his nose, she amped the smile back to full throttle and was determined to keep it there for the rest of the day. So far she'd done just that, and the day was almost over.

She tidied her desk and tucked what paperwork needed to go home with her into her satchel briefcase.

A knock on her open door pulled her gaze to the hesitant student standing in the hall. "Hey, Iliana."

"I'm sorry I don't have an appointment, Professor Maxwell." She nibbled her bottom lip, noting the packed briefcase. "If you're leaving, I could come back and see you tomorrow."

"Nonsense, you're here seeing me now." She cleaned off a chair for her student to sit and waved her in. "There you go. What's wrong?"

"What makes you think something is wrong?" Iliana asked, her eyes like a deer in the headlights.

"Because students don't usually seek out a teacher just to say hi. I know I sure as hell didn't."

Iliana settled into the chair as she nervously bit her lower lip. "It's about the Dare I Docket project."

She read the stress in the young woman's features. "About your list?"

Iliana nodded. "I'm just not so sure I can come up with ten items, much less do them."

"That's perfectly alright," she assured her. "This project's only goal is to make you *aware* of yourself and your comfort zones. In no way do I want it bringing anxiety or stress into your life, and if it is, then we need to reevaluate it. What aspect of it is most worrisome to you?"

"I guess the list itself. I've seen my friends' Dockets, and some of them are definitely embracing the challenge. My roommate even added walking through Times Square by herself, and the *thought* of that . . . ?" Iliana shivered, a grim smile on her face.

Olive chuckled. "That is pretty nightmare-worthy."

"I'm already bumping against my limits just by taking the subway to get to class every day," she admitted. "I don't do well with large groups of people, especially in close confines."

"It's already stretching your comfort zone."

The young woman nodded. "Exactly. Omar promising to stick to my side like glue at the gala is the only reason why I made it through *that* experience."

"Then use it for your list—all of it."

She blinked, looking unsure. "But I'm already doing it . . . and the gala is over. When I compare that to the items on my friends' lists, it just feels . . . inadequate."

"You want to hear a secret?"

"Sure."

Olive leaned over, whispering not so softly, "I used the gala as an item on my own list, too."

The student's eyes widened. "You're making a Docket?"

"I am. And you want to know what else?"

"What?"

"Your friends are your friends, and *you* are you. Their boundaries are not yours, and vice versa. How do you feel when you make it to class after taking the subway?"

Iliana looked deep in thought. "Proud . . . and when I get a seat to myself and not next to someone eating a raw onion, ecstatic."

"Then it's the perfect item to put on your list." Iliana opened her mouth to argue, but Olive beat her to it. "Your friends may be living in their comfort zone on a daily basis, and by visiting Times Square, they'd finally be breaching it. But you're leaving your comfort zone each and every time you descend those stairs to get on the train to get to school. And something tells me that if you think about it, there are probably at least a couple more things that fit that same criteria."

"I guess attending family dinner at my dad's place each week would fit, too. Goddess knows I have to psych myself up for it every Sunday."

Olive chuckled. "Then it looks like you found another. I don't want you stressing over this, Iliana. You do what—and how many—you can do, and that's it. No one will be graded on the number of items on your Docket, or 'how far' they go."

Iliana's small smile bloomed into a full one as she stood, clutching her backpack to her chest. "Thank you, Professor Maxwell. I'm really glad I came to talk with you."

"I am, too." She followed her to the door. "And if you know of any other of your classmates who are struggling with this same thing, pass them the info . . . or send them my way so I can put their minds at ease, too, okay?"

Iliana nodded and pulled open the door, only to nearly collide with the large form that had been just about to knock.

"Sorry," Bax apologized immediately. "Didn't mean to frighten anyone. Iliana, right?"

"Uh, yeah." The petite student glanced up and up, hugging her bag tighter. "No. You didn't. I'm just . . . hi, Mr. Donovan."

"Just Bax."

"Okay." She gulped, frozen in position.

"Uh, Bax?" Olive smirked.

"Yeah, angel?" His gaze slid to her.

"Could you maybe move aside and let Iliana get on her way?"

"Oh. Shit." He moved to the side quickly. "Sorry about that."

"Thank you," Iliana mumbled, quickly bypassing him. "And thank you again, Professor."

Olive and Bax both watched the college student hustle down the hall before Olive glanced back to a smirking Guardian Angel. "What?"

"I'm kind of torn about what to call you now." He stepped into the office, closing the door behind them.

"You mean other than my name?" She fiddled with the already organized things on her desk.

"Calling you *angel* has always felt right to me, but *Professor*?" He slowly closed the distance, sliding in behind her to lean his hands on her desk. The move pushed his chest against her back and brought his mouth close to her ear. "*Professor* would have a nice ring to it when you're naked and underneath me. Or above. Actually, I'm sure it works in a varying array of positions."

A wave of desire skated over her body, making each breath a bit labored until it sounded as if she'd just finished a marathon. "That does sound nice."

He brushed his lips over the sensitive spot beneath her ear. "Really damn nice."

"Maybe we should see if it sounds nice in reality." She wasn't sure if this would cross anything off her Docket, but she didn't care.

She just wanted him to make good on the image he'd painted inside her head.

"Don't move," he ordered gently before crossing the office and flipping the door lock. When he turned back to her, his hot gaze nearly melted her on the spot. "Hands on the desk, and no moving them."

"But how will I—"

"No. Moving. Professor."

Did she just shiver? Yeah, she did, but how, she didn't know, considering a raging inferno practically burned her from the inside, originating in all her tingly bits and fanning out until a cool sweat broke out across her forehead.

She did as he said, keeping her palms flat on her desk as she watched him make his way around the room until he resumed his spot behind her. His large hands coasted over her silk shirt and palmed her breasts, taking the time to pinch her already aching nipples through the fabrics of her top and bra.

She sucked down a small, needy moan.

Bax gently nipped the spot where her neck met her shoulder. "Unless these walls are soundproof, which I highly doubt, you'll probably want to keep the moaning down to a minimum."

"Yeah, I'm not sure I can do that because when you do *that* . . . the sounds come automatically."

"Does that mean you want me to stop?" he teased.

"Fuck no. Just . . . give me a second." She closed her eyes and tried focusing on the draw of her Magic and not Bax's deft fingers unbuttoning her blouse.

It took a few tries, her concentration short-circuiting, but by the time her shirt hung entirely open and her breasts spilled free into his hands, her Magic did, too. She filled it with her intention, and a silencing spell rained over the room.

"There." She poorly stifled another groan as he plucked her aching nipple. "Cloaking spell. Now you can keep doing *that* and no one will hear a damn thing."

"Isn't that a pretty handy spell? What do you say we put it to the test?"

"I say that's a really, really good idea." She grinned as his hands slid under her simple pencil skirt, knowing what he'd find.

"Well, well, well. What do we have here?" His voice, a low purr, dropped even lower in pitch.

She failed suppressing a small chuckle. "A garter belt. Do you like it?"

"It's hidden beneath this rather prim and proper skirt. I can't say for sure."

"Then maybe you should *un*-hide it and let me know what you think."

"Stay in this position, angel." He leaned back, using his fingers to slowly inch up the hem of her skirt until it sat snugly over her hips.

He sucked in a quick breath the second he laid eyes on the black lace belt and matching panties she'd slipped into that morning. She still didn't know what had possessed her to tug the things from the back of her weekend panty drawer, but she had, and considering his reaction, she was thrilled she did.

With more patience than she could have ever conjured herself, he took his time unclipping each and every thin clasp, and after undoing the last one, he slowly guided her panties down her legs.

She turned her head to peer at him where he remained on his knees behind her. "What are you—"

"Ah-ah-ah, Professor. Hands on the table." He reprimanded with a gentle nip of her left butt cheek.

She pushed her palms flat onto the desk, not realizing that she'd picked them up, and then he answered her question by guiding her legs farther apart and trailing one hand through the blatant evidence of her arousal.

"You're so damn wet." His finger lightly brushed against her sensitive clit, sending her into a pleasure-filled cry. "And about to be so much wetter."

"Goddess, yes." She tilted her hips, the only thing she could do without moving her hands.

Bax ran his tongue up the length of her slit, using both his mouth and hands to make her *so much wetter.* He alternated between quick flicks and caressing touches. Her hips moved in sync with him, each swivel silently pleading for more.

They worked in tandem until she was a mass of quivering need and ready to burst. "I want you inside me when I come. Now."

He stood, fumbling with his wallet. "Fuck. I don't have a condom. I didn't exactly come here with this in mind."

She wasn't sure whether to be happy or disappointed by that fact. "I renewed my MEBC last week, so I'm good if you are."

MEBC—magically enhanced birth control. One spell a month kept the positive sign away. Praise be magical marvels.

Bax eased her chin toward him, locking her gaze with his. "Are you sure?"

She lifted one hand from the desk and dragged his mouth to hers, tasting herself on his tongue. "I wouldn't have brought it up if I wasn't. And remember, while I'm spread open and leaning over my desk, it's *Professor.*"

✦ ✦ ✦

Bax chuckled. "Yes, *Professor.*"

He leaned back far enough to soak in the sight of her near-naked body, and nearly swallowed his tongue. He really hadn't come here for this, but now that it was happening, no way would he turn it down. He'd enjoy the hell out of it, and that meant taking it a bit slower or it would be over far sooner than either of them wanted.

Arching her back, Olive brushed her ass against the bulge in his jeans where his erection already pushed painfully against the zipper. "No more teasing."

No way could he ignore the lady.

He attacked his zipper, and his cock sprang free, obviously more than ready to fulfill her wishes, too. He gently eased her legs farther apart and slid his throbbing length through her wetness. They both groaned on contact, and he did it again, this time pushing into her a bit farther.

With every glide through her slit, he slid deeper and deeper until, with one hard thrust, he fully seated himself into her heat, his lower abdomen snug against her ass.

He clamped his hands on her hips and leaned forward, dropping a trail of kisses along her exposed shoulder and neck as he gently pushed her into the desk. "You should probably hold on to something, Professor."

"Just don't knock over my books," she said, bracing herself against her desk.

His chuckle disappeared with the first hard thrust, and on his second, he cursed as her body wrapped tight around him. With every move of his hips, she pushed back, impaling herself on his length and setting a brutal pace that had them both panting in no time.

She straightened her arms, the move changing the angle and lifting her upper body closer to his. With the heaviness of impending release, he reached one hand between her legs and brushed his fingers along her clit.

"Don't stop." Olive gasped as they both chased their releases. "Holy hexes, Bax."

She erupted around his length, the force of her body clamping around his tugging forward his own pleasure. They came together in a rush of sensations, each slightly losing their rhythm as their bodies quaked through wave after wave of heated pleasure.

With a heavy sigh, she dropped her forehead to the desk. "That was . . . wow."

He missed the skin-on-skin contact the second he slid from her pliant body. "That was *wow* and a whole host of other adjectives."

She turned toward him with a sheepish smile, giving him a peek at her bare breasts before slowly restraining them back into her bra. "Not that I'm at all complaining about you being here because *wow* . . . but why *are* you here?"

He smirked and straightened out his own clothes, pocketing her panties before she could bend to put them on again. She rolled her eyes at him as she fixed her skirt back into place.

"I was in the area, saw the time, and figured I'd offer my favorite professor a ride home." With all his bits tucked away, he drew her into his arms and savored the feel of her hands running up his chest and into his hair. "Unless you want to ride in an overcrowded train for forty-five minutes. If you do, I'll leave you to it and just meet you at home."

She grinned mischievously. "I'll take that ride, but I'll need my panties for the commute."

He shrugged coyly. "I think I'll hold on to them for now."

It was a challenge she met as she slipped from his hold and hooked her work bag over her shoulder. Tucking her glasses higher up on her nose, she lifted a single eyebrow. "Well? You ready? Because I'm really hoping with me skipping the train that we'll have a chance to *wow* again before getting ready for Vi's party tonight."

He met her at the door, and wrapping his hand around her nape, dragged her toward him for a slow, sensual kiss that left his knees a bit weak. "We'll definitely be wowing again, *Professor.*"

Right now, Bax couldn't think of a single reason why that would be considered a bad thing.

20

An Angel's Wingspan Doesn't Matter

Avoiding Harper and her pheromone-smelling super-nose had turned into an Olympic sport, and the longer that Friends' Night went on, the less likely Olive was to become a gold medalist. The thoughtful look currently on the succubus's face indicated that even her chance at silver had come and gone.

Gone a long, long time ago.

"Here you go. Two pitchers of golden ale, and two magical mango margaritas." Gage slid the four large pitchers toward her. "Guess it's a night for celebration, huh? The big day is in what? Two days?"

She still couldn't believe that in less than forty-eight hours, Violet would be Prima. "Two days."

"How's Vi holding up?" The vampire glanced across Potion's Up to where their group had commandeered the entire back half of the bar.

Sitting on Lincoln's lap, Vi laughed at something Julius, the demon council representative—and Damian's brother—said. On the outside her sister was calm, cool, and collected, even winning the dart competition they'd held. But it was all an act.

They were all a bit on edge—Vi more than anyone else. Edie had yet to return to town, sending out only the vaguest of vague texts to the three sisters.

"She's keeping it together," she assured the vampire. "At least enough that she won't blow up your bar again."

Gage chuckled. "Good. Because my insurance went through the roof after the last implosion. If they hike it up again, I'll be forced to shut the place down."

"You've been significantly less growly lately, boss." Harper bounded up to the bar, picking up two of the four pitchers. "Keep it up and you'll soon have me thinking that you've been taken over by a pod person . . . or that I had you pegged wrong all along. But the first option is probably more likely."

He shook his head, but the smile was still there, albeit a little more resigned. "Keep it up, Jacobs, and next time you ask for a night off, I won't let you have it. I'll actually make you work a double."

"All posturing." Harper waved him off. "Because my best friend is about to become the Head Bwitch in Charge, and when she says it's margarita night, it's margarita night. Don't make me sic her on you, Gage. We both know how that will end."

He waved her off, heading toward the other end of the bar to fill additional orders. The succubus handed Olive the margarita pitchers before grabbing the beer and leading the way to their claimed area of the bar.

"It was a very decent attempt, Maxwell, and I admit, you almost had me fooled." Harper wiggled her eyebrows.

"What?" She didn't have to manufacture confusion this time. "I don't know what you're talking about."

"Please. There's no missing it with a nose of my caliber. You have gotten laid . . . well and recently. And I mean *recently*. Instead of pre-party drink, you had a pre-party fu—"

"Harper!"

"What?" The sex demon looked way too innocent. "I was about to congratulate you! Or maybe I should congratulate a certain sexy Guardian Angel for a job well done."

"Who said Bax was involved?" she asked curiously. They'd never really said whether their . . . whatever they had . . . was to be kept between them only.

"You know how Linc's and Adrian's shifter sniffers can detect smells and the lunch you had last week? Well, there's a distinct familiarity between pheromones when people have been bumping the not-so-uglies. You and Bax have smelled like each other for weeks now."

"Going around sniffing people again, Harp?" Bax asked, taking the pitchers from Olive and setting them on their table. "We've talked about this before. It'll eventually get you tossed in a jail cell . . . again."

Harper stuck her tongue out at him in response, making Olive chuckle.

With the new round of drinks, the horde descended. Everyone had shown up for the informal celebration. Bax took a seat at the table they'd pulled up closer to the corner booth and pushed out the chair next to him.

Olive claimed it for herself and, ignoring Harper's not-so-subtle smirk, took a small sip of her drink.

Vi glanced at her cell phone and groaned. "I swear, she's trying to kill me. Maybe that's her real endgame. Maybe she's attempting to take me out so she can be the HWIC forever."

"HWIC?" Linc asked, gazing at his mate adoringly.

"Head Witch in Charge," Olive, Rose, and Vi answered simultaneously.

"Dude," Adrian chuckled, "even I knew that much. You better brush up on your witch lingo if you're going to be the Prima's official sidepiece."

"*Don't fret. You got this, bae*," Vi read from her cell. The eldest triplet dropped her head onto Linc's shoulder. "That's seriously what Gran just texted me. Not only is she still adamant on using the term *bae*, but it's like she doesn't know me at all. *Don't fret*? The only thing I've got about Friday is a raging case of anxiety and a chin pimple of volcanic-sized proportions."

She slid a hopeful look Olive's way. "Did she text you?"

"Not since the other day when she told me where to look for the ceremony specifics." Olive woke her phone and shook her head at the blank screen. "Yeah. Nothing." Her phone dinged with a text. "Oh, wait. *Tell your sister to stop fretting . . . and that I'll continue to use bae whenever the hell I want.*"

"What the actual fuck? How does she do that?" Vi gaped open-mouthed, searching the bar as if Edie hid beneath the table. "I'll never achieve that level of fuckery. That is some serious epic-level shit."

"It makes you wonder if Gran thought the same thing when she was in your shoes."

Bax chuckled. "A young Edie taking on the world and all the world's Supernaturals. Now wouldn't that be a good documentary."

As Olive sipped her drink, his hand settled just above her knee, fingers gently tickling the inside of her thigh. She fought to keep her face impassive as warmth originated from the point of contact and zip-lined straight between her legs.

She shifted casually in her seat in an attempt not to draw attention and saw the damn sexy angel smirk knowingly.

Harper hadn't been wrong when she said Olive must have been laid well and recently because while she'd showered in preparation for tonight, Bax had surreptitiously hidden her outfit, leaving her to stalk through the apartment half naked looking for it.

He'd hidden the dress beneath his pillow, and so naturally, one thing led to another and they'd been a little late—and a little disheveled—to tonight's meetup.

Bax's hand slid higher up on her thigh, and she spread her legs a bit more, welcoming the touch. Sitting close, every inch of her body was already hypersensitized, but as his fingers flirted with the edge of her quickly dampening panties, she felt like a live wire prepped to ignite.

Her Magic agreed, crackling just beneath her skin's surface until she practically had to Lamaze breathe right there at the table.

As if sensing her limit, he moved his hand and relocated it along the back of her chair. He leaned close, whispering, "You okay over there, Professor?"

She cleared her throat, feigning an inner calm. "Never been better."

"You sure about that?" He chuckled when she lifted an elbow, not-so-gently digging it into his side. His gaze slid over to the makeshift stage next to the jukebox. "Looks like Gage got himself one of those karaoke machines."

Her attention snapped to where the vampire was definitely setting up a portable karaoke machine right next to the slightly raised platform used by guest singers. "When did he get one of those? Vi's been after him forever to get one and he's always refused."

He shrugged. "Guess he finally ran out of reasons to say no."

She studied him carefully.

Reading his thoughts, much less his emotions, was damn near impossible thanks to all that damn Guardian training, but her gut instinct screamed that the broody vampire wouldn't have done a 180 without some kind of outside influence.

"You did this." They locked gazes in an epic stare-down.

"I don't know what you're talking about." He remained straight-faced for all of two seconds before she caught the slight left-side twitch of his top lip.

"You, Baxter Donovan, are a world-class liar." She laughed, but she laughed alone, all humor on the angel's face slowly melting away.

It was like someone had flipped a switch, making him go instantly from light angel to dark without a stop in between.

She squeezed his hand, showing her concern as she tried throwing more questions at him through her eyes alone. "Are you okay?"

"Oh my Goddess!" Vi squealed, seeing Potion's new addition, and yanked up her mate. "First dibs!"

Harper already rubbed her temples as she shot Bax an accusing glare. "If you don't save us all from listening to Vi's singing, then you, sir, are no Guardian Angel. At least not a good one."

He shrugged. "Who said I was any good in the first place? Because I'd like to clear them of that notion."

"If no one stops her, she'll cue the next ten songs . . . at least. May I remind you of the bleeding-eardrum urgent care visit of five years ago? And that was only after two songs."

Flipping through the computerized song list, the soon-to-be Prima jumped excitedly. "Ooh! They have all of T-Swift on here! I'll start with the first record and work my way through to the newer stuff."

Harper shot the two of them a severe look. "If she gets to the *Fearless* album, the two of you are dead to me. You get me? D-E-A-D."

Olive stood, pushing a grin onto her face, and held her hand out to the sexy angel. "I'm rather fond of living, so let's go. If we can Baby and Johnny in front of a crowd of hundreds, we can sure as hell do this. Maybe they'll have '(I've Had) The Time of My Life' as a song choice."

She almost expected him to say no. The dark glint still loitered in his usually twinkling eyes, and his jaw looked tense enough to crack as his gaze shot from her outstretched hand to her face.

Seconds before she thought she'd be singing a solo, his fingers wrapped tightly around hers and that small, sexily coy smile that never ceased to threaten the state of her panties was back. She let out a relieved breath . . . but she couldn't help being curious about what exactly had held it hostage to begin with.

✦ ✦ ✦

After the karaoke machine's arrival, it didn't take long for a competitive wave to sweep over their entire group. They paired into teams, Harper even reluctantly accepting Adrian as her partner, and tried one-upping one another with Gage playing the part of the audience-applause-o-meter.

Bax laughed more that night than he had in a long time.

Friends' Nights were nothing unusual. They had them all the time. The difference was that he was around, not tied up with the GAA or chasing after some ridiculous Assignment whose only goal was to test how many risky behaviors it took until their luck ran out.

And that was the problem. Technically he *was* currently tied up with a GAA Assignment, and that tie had so many fucking knots not even a Scout could free him. The damn things were knotted and painted with Gorilla Glue and then knotted again.

When Olive had called him a liar—albeit innocently and in jest—he'd felt sucker punched in the gut. Not because it wasn't true.

Because it was.

He'd been lying to her for weeks every time she commented on the GAA or his sudden shift from being nowhere to everywhere. More than once he'd attempted steering the conversation toward avoidance and away from blatant mistruths, but fuck.

It was hard . . . and it did things to his insides he wasn't so sure he'd ever be able to correct.

Olive, his *Assignment*, sat next to him minutes after they'd belted out "(I've Had) The Time of My Life," blessedly ignorant to the fact that even when enjoying the hell out of his time with her, he was technically on the damn clock. It just didn't feel that way.

And that was one of many signs indicating he needed to tread carefully.

As Vi and a reluctant Linc belted out Sonny and Cher's "I Got You Babe," Bax's phone vibrated against his ass. He ignored it until it eventually stopped, only for it to start up again three seconds later.

"Something wrong? Do you have to go in to work?" Olive asked, her tone concerned, as he pulled the cell from his pocket and read the caller ID. *The GAA.* "It's okay if you do. I'll get home fine."

"Nah. It can wait." He shoved the phone back in his pocket and draped his arm over her chair, making sure to run his fingers over the back of her neck in the process.

She shivered, and he did it again, fighting the urge to drag her onto his lap. They hadn't discussed naming whatever was happening between them, and until they did, he refused to announce it to the world and risk pushing her into a corner she didn't want.

Maybe by the time that happened—if it did—he'd have figured it out himself.

The only two things he did know was that he was quickly becoming addicted to her presence, and he was in no way ready to hear her call this between them *all good fun and stress relief.*

With Olive distracted and cheering on Vi and Linc on the makeshift stage, he soaked in the sight of her. Her smile, big enough to be a beacon for lighthouses everywhere, made her entire face glow despite Potion's dim bar lighting. And her eyes damn near sparkled, happiness peeking from those gorgeous blue eyes like stars on a clear, dark night.

But that was what was visible to the naked eye. What really took his breath away was her beauty on the inside.

Some people pretended at sweetness and generosity by dishing out fake platitudes and half-ass magnanimous actions, but Olive embodied them both in everything she did, as well as strength and resilience and a heaping dose of brilliance.

The longer he watched her, the longer she unknowingly held him hostage.

She caught him staring and smiled nervously. "What?"

"Nothing. You're just . . ." Movement from the other side of the room caught his eye. He stiffened. "Fuck."

Her eyes widened. "I'm just *fuck*?"

"What? No. Shit." He reset, struggling to swallow his sudden annoyance with a chuckle. "I got to hit the bathroom. You need anything?"

"Do I need anything from the bathroom?" she teased coyly. "Nah. I'm good, but thanks for checking."

He laughed for real. "Fine. No supersoft toilet paper for you."

"Like Gage pays for the supersoft. The stuff he gets could give a person paper cuts in very unfortunate places."

"Noted. Next time, bring some from home." He barely caught himself from leaning over and kissing her. "I'll be right back."

He headed toward the other side of the room, drilling the unexpected arrival with a dark look before nudging his chin toward the back hall. He got a faint nod in return, and ten seconds later, he spun around.

"Trust me, this wasn't my idea," Patrick, the Commissioner's assistant, immediately preempted his line of questions. "But you can't ignore the Commissioner and expect her to just throw her hands up and be like *Oh well*. You've met her."

"I ignored two phone calls, and one was literally like ten minutes ago," he lied.

Patrick's disbelieving look called him out on his bullshit. "You ignored two phone calls today, and both the call *and* text yesterday. How long did you think she'd let it go before she sent someone to track your behind? Just be thankful she sent me and not a Supernatural Hunter. I hear your Assignment's sister is making a pretty decent name for herself in that arena."

He snorted. Wouldn't it be something if Rose had been sent to track his ass down?

"Glad you're taking this seriously, GA Donovan." Patrick frowned at his grin, folding his arm across his chest. "I don't think you're aware exactly how rickety your standing is within the GAA."

That smothered all previous humor. "Oh, I'm plenty aware, Patty. Trust me."

"Your father can't rescue you from another screwup."

"I never asked that man to do a damn thing," Bax growled, his anger surging. "And let's get one thing clear right now. Anything that he may have done, any string he may have pulled in the past, was definitely not for *me*. It was to save what little reputation the Donovan name still has."

"I just thought you should know the severity of the situation. This *will* be your last chance to keep your wings in active duty." A healthy dose of understanding emanated from the other angel as he slid a pointed look across the room.

His gaze followed Patrick's attention to where Olive watched them, her eyes narrowed. He forced a reassuring smile onto his face, knowing it probably looked as if he were constipated, and turned back to the other man. "I'm aware, but thank you for reaffirming it."

Patrick nodded, prepping to turn away, and stopped. "Can I give you a little unsolicited advice?"

"Isn't all your advice unsolicited?"

The angel admin rolled his eyes. "Not all angels' wings are made from the same feathers."

He cocked up an eyebrow. "Wow. Enlightening. Thank you."

"I mean to say that an angel's wingspan doesn't matter, it's—"

"My *wingspan* is just fine." Bax's tease got a tired sigh from the other man. "I get what you're trying to say, and I know."

"You do?"

He nodded. "It's okay to steer away from the path that others have set for you . . . Just make sure you have good off-roading tires for the trip." Which was basically the same thing a certain smart, sexy witch had told him a few times.

Patrick opened and closed his mouth a few times. "Yeah, I guess that sums up what I was trying to say. Now that I've said it, and have delivered the Commissioner's message that your last two field reports are now 'startlingly overdue,' I'm heading back to my pinochle tournament. Sam is holding my spot, and I don't trust him not to mess with my standings."

"Thanks for the heads-up, Pat," Bax said sincerely.

Patrick nodded and took off, leaving Bax to head back to the table and reclaim his seat. Vi and Linc had been ousted off the stage, and Rose and Damian had taken their place, the demon veterinarian looking like he'd rather be standing in hell than holding a microphone.

"Did I miss anything good?" His arm brushed against Olive's as he sat, the faint contact sending little zaps of heat through his body.

"Just Damian looking as if he'd rather be having a root canal without anesthesia," Olive quipped, grinning. "Everything okay? It didn't look like you actually got to use the bathroom."

He not-so-casually dragged his fingers across the back of her neck until he propped his arm along her shoulders. "Keeping tabs on me, angel?"

"Just striving to be more aware of my surroundings, and everything in general. I can't help wondering if Edie gave warnings before she went MIA and we were too self-involved to see it." She tucked her glasses higher onto her nose, a strand of hair getting caught in the frame in the process.

He gently freed it before cupping her jaw. "Everything's okay. I won't be pulling an MIA anytime soon. Guardian's Promise. And Edie will be here when she needs to be here. Knowing her, it'll be with a grand entrance, margarita in hand."

"You're not wrong there." She snortled, looking a few degrees less on edge, and he counted that as a win. "Looks like we're up again."

"Then let's go and knock some socks off." He took her hand and led the way, already knowing which song he hoped was on that list . . . and it was Florida Georgia Line's "Stay."

21

Bend Me, Twist Me, Stretch Me

This was either the best idea Olive ever had, or one that would go down in infamy as the worst. Bax's reaction would be the judge once she took off his blindfold and he saw where they were and what they were about to do.

Was it a risk? Yes.

Was it worth it? Hopefully.

But they'd spent weeks beefing up her Docket list, checking off items she'd never imagined possible, and he'd been there with her through it all. Her own personal tattooed cheerleading section. He claimed he didn't need a list of his own, or anything in return, but he needed *this*.

And if he put up a fuss, it was technically for her, too.

She navigated around the crowd so neither she nor the broody angel at her side ran into anyone, and to say her copilot didn't like not being in control was a vast understatement. Eyes covered with her favorite unicorn sleep mask, he had grumbled the entire cab ride while she assured the driver that she was not committing a felony.

Surprisingly enough, it hadn't taken a whole lot of convincing, which, in hindsight, might be a little on the scary side.

Bax stumbled again, this time on air, and muttered his displeasure. "How much longer until this damn thing can come off?"

"Soon." Grinning, she held tightly onto his arm. "Honestly. No one has ever kidnapped you by cab before and it shows."

"Funny. But seriously . . . it sounds like there are tons of people around, and maybe it's the Guardian in me, but I don't like being unable to canvass the area for threats."

"There's no threats anywhere near here."

"Are we in the city?"

"Yeah."

"In public?"

"Obviously."

"Then there are threats. You're just not trained to see them."

She rolled her eyes, knowing he couldn't see her. "Trained or not, you'll just have to deal with the blindfold a few more minutes."

He frowned, his ears practically straining as he attempted to decipher where in the city they were. Maybe she should've gotten earplugs to go along with the eye mask.

"We better not be in Times Square or—"

"Oh, for the love of Goddess, we're not in Times Square!" She chuckled because although the National Tattoo Convention didn't draw the same crowd as New Year's Rockin' Eve, it sure as hell looked like it.

She'd never seen so many tattoos and piercings in one location. It was a visual feast for the eyes, and she couldn't wait to get to where they were going so she could look her fill.

Her phone dinged with a text, and keeping one hand on Bax's arm, she pulled it from her pants pocket.

Isaiah: The stage is about to go hot! ETA?

Almost there, she typed one-handed.

Shoving the phone back in the hidden pocket in her yoga pants, she hustled faster. Two turns and a short slalom sprint later, they stepped into Exhibit Hall, a monstrously open room filled with tattoo artists who'd traveled far and wide to showcase their art. Some sat in chairs getting inked, and others meandered from setup to setup, watching the process.

She scanned the room for Inklings' brightly displayed banner and found Isaiah and Ruby instantly, the young woman waving her hands to get her attention.

She put her finger to her lips as they approached, and Isaiah, seeing Bax's blindfold, fought laughter so hard tears sprang to his eyes. The older man doubled over in a fight to contain it.

Ruby leaned closer and whispered, "I have his workstation set up exactly how he likes it. The demo starts in ten minutes."

Olive nodded, trying not to look at the quickly growing crowd in front of their station. "Are these people all . . ."

"Waiting to see him in action." Ruby nodded enthusiastically. "He doesn't realize how sought-after he's become. The setup is behind the privacy screen, so once you're both ready to go, I'll take it down and we'll start."

"Thanks, Rubes."

"Rubes?" Bax's head tilted, reminding her of an adorable puppy attempting to figure something out. "Tell me where we are, angel. Besides, this mask is chafing my delicate skin."

With a roll of her eyes, she led him behind the privacy screen and, with a flick of her fingers and spark of her Magic, *poof*'d away the sleep mask.

He rubbed his eyes and squinted at the bright lights of the convention center. With a wall at their back, there wasn't much for him to see, but he peeked around the screen and sucked in a breath.

"Where the fuck are we?" He shot her a dark look.

"First, please remember we're in public. You can't kill me. Also, if you do, not only would it probably be against some Guardian Angel code of conduct rule or something, but I have two sisters and a Harper who would literally—and very capably—hunt you to the ends of the earth and make you suffer for all eternity."

"Angel . . ."

She captured his face between her hands and tugged his attention to her. "A skill like yours should be shared with the world, Bax. You're not doing yourself, or any of your adoring fans, any favors by sticking your head in the sand."

He scoffed. "Adoring fans?"

"If that growing crowd out there is any indication of your fandom, then yes. Adoring fans. I can't guarantee no one in the crowd won't throw rotten tomatoes at you, but considering they're not really in season right now, the risk of that is pretty low."

"You signed me up for the tattoo convention." He released a small sigh.

But he didn't throw his hands up and rant. He didn't say *fuck this* and walk out. She counted that as a win.

"Technically," she added, "Isaiah signed up Inklings, and as a participating booth, he was allowed to submit someone for a demo."

"And he subbed my name?" Bax guessed correctly.

"Actually," Isaiah's voice shouted from over the privacy screen, "your woman strong-armed me into it with her hocus-pocus. Scary witch, that girl. Make sure you never get on her bad side because she can make sparks fly. Literally."

"Yeah, I'm sure it took a lot of magical strong-arming. You've been begging me to do this show for a year."

Isaiah chuckled, not denying the accusation.

"But it was my idea," she admitted, taking responsibility for his annoyance.

Looking at her, his expression softened, and the fight drained from his body. "Did this brilliant idea of yours include a design, or a client on which I'm supposed to place it? You know I don't put random dolphins on strangers' skin. There needs to be a connection. Both with the person and the artwork, and the artwork and me."

"Got it covered." She dropped her backpack onto the table and pulled out the familiar sketchbook. "Here."

Still looking confused, he took his sketchbook. "And what am I supposed to do with this?"

"You said you were almost done with my design."

Realization shone from his eyes as his mouth dropped. "You think I'm tattooing you here and now?"

"No time like the present, right?"

"Actually, I said it was *almost* finished, not that it was done. And you haven't seen it in days! What if you end up hating it and I have to start all over again?"

"I won't hate it. It's not possible."

"Do you like everything you see? Because I should probably remind you of the time you threatened to gouge your eyes out with a spoon if you saw one more person wearing socks with sandals."

She rolled her eyes. "You can't blame me for that. It's unnatural. And I know I'll love the tattoo because you designed it."

"This isn't a wardrobe decision, angel. It's permanent. This is enchanted ink, made to ensure it sticks around even on Supernaturals."

It was time to play dirty.

Propping her hands on her hips, she shot him a stern glare worthy of an Edie Award. "Baxter Donovan, you told me that you'd stand by my side as I completed my Docket list, and now it's time to put your hands where your mouth is . . . or whatever. You know where I want this design, so bend me, twist me, stretch me until it hurts oh so good, but damn it, you're putting your artwork on me right the hell now, and I don't want to hear another excuse. Do I make myself clear?"

Her Magic crackled, lifting her hair off her shoulders.

Isaiah's low chuckle came from the other side of the partition. "What did I say about not pissing off the witch?"

"Shut the fuck up, man," Bax grumbled at his friend, only making him laugh harder.

Olive refused to show even a smidge of the nerves now attacking her stomach like overly caffeinated butterflies. Whatever he saw on her face must have finally convinced him there was no changing her mind.

He sighed, running his palm over his face.

"Is that you waving the white flag of surrender?" She grinned triumphantly.

"Far be it from me to tell a witch what she wants." Caving, he dragged her body flush against his and took her mouth in a slow, heavy kiss that had their tongues pillaging and plundering like horny pirates.

She threaded her fingers through his hair and enjoyed the ride as her body very nearly literally lit up.

The privacy curtain hesitantly parted and Isaiah's amused face poked through. "Not to rush you or anything, but we've developed quite a crowd out here, and they're looking a bit eager to see some ink on skin. Not skin on skin . . . although I could be reading the room wrong."

A handful of chuckles sounded from a few feet away.

Bax's eyes lasered in on her. "You're absolutely sure about this?"

"Never been surer in my life," she stated truthfully.

"I may have finished the bulk of the piece, but I haven't finished the shading or color scheme or—"

She silenced his rambling with her lips against his. "I trust you, wingman. Do whatever feels right and it'll be amazing."

"Then I guess we're doing this." He helped her onto the tattoo bench and made sure she was comfortable. "While Ruby helps get you draped so you're not flashing any bits you don't want flashed,

I'll turn your piece into a placement stencil . . . and then we'll get started."

"I can't wait."

And she couldn't. Every cell in her body vibrated with excitement, and her Magic totally agreed. Docket item number four, get ready to be crossed off!

✦ ✦ ✦

Sufficiently sprawled, bald, and stenciled, Olive waited patiently while Bax got his shit together, and it took more time than he anticipated. This wasn't his first time behind the gun. He'd tattooed tons of clients. More than he could honestly count.

He just hadn't tattooed anything as meaningful—on *someone* meaningful—until now, and he did not want to fuck it up. Yeah, he had the image in his head, the exact shades and delicate wisps of colors, but that didn't mean she'd like it, much less love it, and a lifetime was a damn long time to have something on your skin you hated.

"Will you stop second-guessing yourself?" Olive admonished him, peering up at him through her thick lashes.

"Reading my mind now, angel?" A grin pulled at his lips.

Lying on her side, her right arm draped above her head to lengthen her torso, she looked too sexy for his own good. The outlined stencil went from the bottom swell of her breast to her lower hip.

Along the way, they'd prop her forward and lean her back to ensure the vines swirled with her body's curves, but this was where they'd start.

"This is a beast of a piece. You sure you don't want it shrunk and fitted to the back of your shoulder or something?" he asked hopefully.

"And lose even a millimeter of detail? Not a chance. Stem to stern, Mr. Donovan. Hop to it. Isaiah sufficiently numbed me up, so I'll be fine."

"That cream doesn't last forever. If the pain gets to be too much—"

"I'll just hex you." The look on his face made her chuckle. "I mean I'll tell you."

He shot her a warning look.

"I *promise*. Cross my heart."

"Sometimes I get a little in the zone when I tattoo, so a crowbar to my head may be needed to get my attention."

"Crowbar is already in my purse."

"And you're taking a break every hour regardless of whether you think you need it. Isaiah already set the timer."

"Then it's about to go off any second because you've been yammering at me for what feels like an hour." Taking a page from his own book, she lifted a single delicate eyebrow.

Those in the crowd closest to them chuckled, and so did he.

"Point made, angel." He pulled his chair closer and got into position, starting at the northernmost tip of the tattoo. "Breathe, meditate, and Ruby has music and headphones at the ready should you need them as a distraction."

The first touch to skin was always the most nerve-racking, but as he settled into a groove and let his familiarity with the canvas guide him, it was like the tattoo gun moved on its own.

Olive didn't flinch or twitch, much less grimace, and her stoicism had him checking in with her all the more. As he worked his way down her torso, outlining the entire piece first, the watching crowd grew larger until the event staff was forced to create a secondary foot-traffic route around the rest of the room.

They took hourly breaks, Olive grumbling through them but drinking and eating her snacks under his watchful eye, and then they got back to it. Large pieces tended to take a few sitting sessions, both for the artists and the client, but it soon became apparent that neither he nor Olive wanted—or needed—to prolong it.

His fingers had never been so nimble, and Olive, determined to have a finished piece by day's end, shifted and rolled when he asked, even holding her breath a few times. He didn't realize how much time had passed until the crowd slowly thinned and a few nearby booths packed up their tables.

"I think it's almost done," he murmured, using a slightly darker shade of pink to deepen a few shadowed areas. "Just a little touch here and . . ."

Isaiah approached from behind and looked over his shoulder. "Holy shit, man. That's . . ."

"Yeah." He leaned back in his chair and rolled his neck, realizing he hadn't moved in quite a while when it cracked loudly. "It turned out great."

"It did?" Eagerness lit up Olive's eyes.

Isaiah snorted. "Sweetheart, he's being ridiculously modest. It's fucking incredible. I don't know that I've ever seen a piece both so fucking realistic and artistic at the same time."

"I want to see," she said immediately. "Like *now*."

Bax smiled as he helped her sit up. By the time she got to her feet, Isaiah had handed him the full-length mirror, and he leaned it against the nearby table.

"If you don't like something, we can alter it," he tried reassuring her.

"Why are you so convinced I won't like it?" She squeezed his hand. "Move over and let me look in the mirror."

He forced himself to move behind her, letting her have an unobstructed view.

She gasped, her eyes nearly widening to the size of her glasses. Stepping closer to the mirror, she studied every inch, even reaching out to touch the reflection. "Oh my Goddess, Bax. It's gorgeous!"

Studying her for any sign of a lie, he fidgeted on his feet, nervous. "You like it?"

"Like it? I fucking love it!" She locked gazes with him in the mirror. "And it's definitely not a rabid raccoon."

He chuckled, stepping closer and gently running his fingers near—but not touching—the pinked skin. "Cherry blossoms symbolize different things to different cultures, but the most common theme is beauty, strength, and sexuality. And the tree represents added strength and resilience. So in a biological sense, the entire package is you."

He followed her gaze as she took it all in, every swirl of brown and cream to the deep rich pinks of the dancing blossoms. The cherry blossom tree swerved with her curves, making the entire thing come to life.

He glanced up to see her wiping tears off her cheeks.

"Hey." He gently turned her toward him, and she immediately flung her arms around his waist, hissing as she did so. "You'll be a bit sore for a few days, but it should heal up nicely once we get it covered with a Saniderm."

"I don't know how to thank you." Her words were muffled against his chest.

"You just did, angel." He held her a bit longer before regretfully easing back. "You thanked me by trusting me with something like this."

"Like I wouldn't." She brushed her hands over the damp spots. "I made your shirt all wet."

"You can dampen my shirt any day."

She chuckled as Ruby approached, a camera in hand. "Do you mind if we get some shots of the final product?"

Olive shook her head, drying more tears off her face. "Tell me where you want me."

The two of them found a perfect spot before Ruby guided her

into pose after pose, searching for the perfect positions to bring out every detail of the cherry blossom tree.

Isaiah came up next to him and bumped his shoulder as they watched. "She's something special, isn't she?"

"Are you talking about the piece or the woman?" he asked.

"What do you think? Finding someone with the ability to trust that deeply is a bit like finding a unicorn in the city. It's definitely something to treasure."

Something akin to guilt turned Bax's stomach. "Yeah. It is."

"Don't muck it up, kid." With a faint nod, the older man went to finish packing up Inklings' table, saying so damn much with just those five words.

He glanced back to where Ruby and Olive laughed together looking at the pictures, and that unsettled sensation in his stomach turned to a fucking boulder. She'd trusted him, not only to create something beautiful just for her, but to put it on her skin, sight unseen. She'd trusted his skill, his imagination, and his knowledge of what she'd like.

He coveted that level of trust . . . but he also knew he didn't deserve it.

Not even an ounce of it.

But hell if he didn't want to.

22

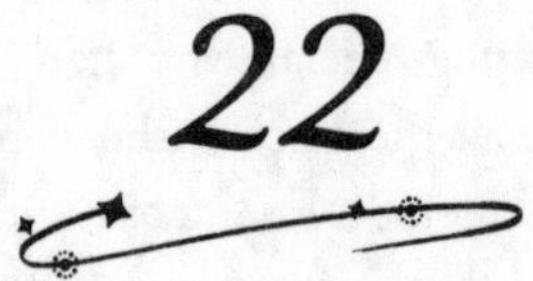

Flying Pigs & Getaway Cars

In gorgeous hues of pink and orange, the daylight's last remnants hung in the sky, an enchanting backdrop made even more magical with the slowly rising moon.

Day and night.

An end and a beginning.

An Exchange Ceremony, passing the magical torch from one Prima to the next. Since there hadn't been two simultaneously living Primas in close to 150 years, no one alive had ever been to an Exchange. For Olive, that meant using Edie's vague text suggestions and diving into historical magical texts and tomes, researching the intricacies of the ceremony right down to the date, time, and vows.

Research: Olive Maxwell's happy place.

With everything set and a crowd of spectators taking their seats beneath the oversized awning that had been erected on Edie's property, the countdown began. All they needed now were the Prima and the Prima Apparent.

Plastering a smile to her face and giving polite nods to everyone who tried stopping her, Olive hustled up the stone path to Edie's cottage for the tenth time in as many minutes.

The second she opened the front door she was assaulted by a

flying pink object. The stuffed pig bounced off her forehead and dropped to the ground with a squeak.

"Pigs are flying now, huh? It must be the apocalypse," she joked dryly.

"Look who's joking." Vi, her voice higher pitched than normal, paced the small living room. "She's *filled* with jokes. If our serious sister busting out with a comedy routine isn't a sign that this shouldn't be happening, I don't know what is. We can postpone this stupid thing, right?"

"Sure." Olive stepped into the cabin to see Rose playing the part of lion tamer, and Vi, the skittish lion.

"Yeah?" Vi looked hopeful. "Great! Then let's call today a wash and reschedule it for . . . when do the charts say there can be another Exchange?"

"That would be in"—she glanced at the nonexistent watch on her wrist—"five years."

"Okay. I can—" Vi paused her meltdown to shoot her a look. "*Five* years?"

"Give or take a week or two."

Her sister gulped and, lifting the hem of her bead-trimmed lavender dress to reveal her favorite dark purple Converse, resumed pacing. "It's not ideal, but it'll do. Especially considering we're missing a very key ingredient—er, person—required for this magical shindig."

Rose smirked. "Is it considered a shindig, or is it more of a ritual? The after-party could definitely be called a shindig . . . or a soiree."

Olive wrinkled her nose. "*Soiree* sounds too formal. I'd go with *hootenanny*."

"Ooh, I like that."

Vi closed her eyes on a heavy sigh and softly muttered what sounded like a prayer to Goddess for strength and patience . . . and new sisters.

"I won't tell you to calm down," Olive interjected calmly, approaching the eldest triplet as if she were a startled horse.

"Good. Because we both know that's the worst thing to say to someone freaking out." Vi finally opened her eyes, looking only slightly less stressed. "I wasn't even this worked up over my Bonding Ceremony with Linc! And that is for *literal ever*!"

"It's normal to be nervous, Vi. I'd be worried if you weren't."

"Then you shouldn't be worried at all," her sister quipped dryly. "But seriously, how can we have an Exchange Ceremony when the person with whom I'm supposed to exchange hasn't graced us with her presence?"

"Gran *will* be here," Rose stated firmly.

"Yeah? When? Because it looks like the sun is close to a full set, and the only people I see are my two womb-mates and—"

A glimmering flash of light silenced them all. Once the piercing pain diminished, Olive coaxed her eyes open again to realize they were no longer the only people in the room.

Edie, decked out in a gorgeous, midnight blue gown, her silver hair piled high on her head in elaborate curls, glanced around the room. Her gaze bounced from triplet to triplet. "What's everyone standing around for? Let's get this show on the road."

All three sisters talked at once, fighting to be heard over the others as they demanded answers to their spewed questions. With a wave of the older witch's hands, the questions ceased.

"Ah. Much better. Now where were we? Ah, yes. The ceremony." She glanced from granddaughter to granddaughter. "You three look magnificent."

"Gran," Olive broke the silence.

"Yes, bae?" Edie's silver eyes drifted her way.

"You're seriously not explaining where you've been for the last few *weeks*?"

Rose added, "And why?"

"I told you all why." Edie looked confused.

"You mean in your vague letters?" Olive asked. "Or in your oh so many other correspondences? And by *oh so many*, I mean none."

"I texted."

"*Twice*, Gran. And once was just to ensure I told Vi to stop freaking out. That's not exactly a detailed explanation of why you left without a word to anyone."

"I suppose you're right, and we'll get to explanations later. I'm fairly certain there's someplace we need to be in a few minutes, and it'll take me an extra bit to walk the path. My hips got quite the workout these last few weeks and are a bit sore."

Olive grimaced. "That's one explanation I beg you to keep to yourself."

"Same," Rose seconded immediately.

"Hear, hear." Vi nodded enthusiastically.

Edie smiled mischievously, her eyes glazing over as if she were reliving a good memory. "Oh, but it's a good one. On my booze cruise, there was this gorgeous young gentleman who—"

"Gran," the triplets cried out simultaneously.

"No fun." Edie smirked.

"I'm heading outside to light the candles. But first . . ." Olive pulled a nervous Vi into her arms for a massive hug, and Rose joined them in a triplet embrace. "You're about to do magical things, sis. Don't forget that."

"Yep. You got this," Rose agreed.

"Go. Both of you." Her voice heavy with emotion, Vi shooed them away and quickly blotted tears from under her eyes. "Make sure the getaway car is idling."

"You won't need it." Olive flipped a thumbs-up on her way out the door, Rose close on her heels.

The second the door closed behind them, they each let out a nervous breath.

"Am I a horrible sister for thanking the Goddess that it's not me about to walk that aisle?" Rose's guilt had her chewing on her thumbnail, a new habit she seemed to have picked up as a Hunter.

"If it does, then we'll be horrible sisters together."

Chuckling, they hustled to the riverside Magic circle and divided and conquered. Rose, eliciting the help of Linc and the guys, wrangled wayward guests back beneath the tent while Olive bypassed the bulk of the crowd and headed to the altar.

With a quick call on her Magic, she fired up the first candle, and then the second. As she turned toward a third, a large shadow drifted into her way. Startled by the unexpected barrier, she barely stopped the spell before it scorched the innocent bystander.

"Miss Maxwell. We meet again," the familiar voice droned.

Not-so-innocent bystander, she internally corrected herself, cursing her quick reflexes.

"I didn't realize you'd be in attendance, Mr. Donovan"—*aka who the hex invited you?*

A grin slithered onto his face as if reading her mind. "Representative Ramón was kind enough to invite me along as head of his security detail. After all, who's to know when there will next be an Exchange Ceremony? It's history in the making."

"Definitely is. Now if you'll excuse me, I have candles to light." She sidestepped him, heading to the next taper. His presence remained irritatingly close. "You may want to find a seat before you end up sitting in the last row . . . or on the prickly bush in the back."

He chuckled. "You're very humorous. I can see why my son is so taken with you."

She sighed and turned to him, her hands on her hips. "Is there something else I can do for you, other than showing you back to your car . . . or portal."

"From what I was told by the GAA Commissioner, you're already doing it. And since Commissioner Wright isn't here, I'd like to issue a thank-you on behalf of us both."

"A thank-you for what?" Something told her she'd just played into this man's agenda, whatever that might be.

"I'm sure you've heard of the Guardian Angel shortage, and now that the GAA has downgraded your Risk Assessment to low, your GA is free to put his focus elsewhere. It's always a win when an angel successfully sees their Assignment through a rough patch. It reflects well not only on the company, but on the Guardian."

He stood in front of her, relaxed, without a care in the world, and wearing that eel-like smile as she slowly digested his words.

It finally clicked.

"You're saying I have a Guardian Angel?" She dwelled on the possibility, nixing the idea and then considering it a few times over.

"You *did*, for the last few weeks, but I believe his Assignment ceased—officially—as of early this morning. Perhaps with a successful conclusion under his belt, Bax can focus on his Guardian duties and less on all previous distractions." Mikael Donovan smiled as her heart stalled in her chest. "Thank you for being a perfect Assignment, Miss Maxwell. I'll let you get back to your task."

He damn near glided toward the back row, and with each step he took he trampled on her heart again and again until there was no doubt there'd be imprints of the soles of his shoes.

The older Donovan didn't exactly declare Bax her Guardian, but the insinuation was heavier than an entire fleet of tanker trucks. Was it true? What would be the point of lying? Especially about something that could be verified easily enough?

She mentally rewound time, realizing it had been weeks since she'd moved into the apartment, and it had been not long after that when Bax suddenly began appearing at every Friends' Night and offered his assistance with her Docket list.

And for the last few weeks, at night, she'd been easily occupied either in her bed . . . or in his.

Nausea rolled her stomach as the coincidences added up one after another, way too many for her to immediately dismiss no matter how much she wanted to.

As if sensing his exact location, her gaze turned toward the last row.

Sitting between Adrian and Damian, with Harper on an end seat, Bax stared right at her, his face void of emotion. A blank slate. Not a grin or facial twitch. Not a damn flicker or a hint of his thoughts.

Nothing.

Not until he turned toward where Mikael was taking his seat on the far side of Representative Ramón. Laying his eyes on his father, Bax's face darkened, heavy with what looked like anger.

That was all the confirmation she needed that what the older angel said was glaringly true. She turned her focus back onto the remaining candles.

"Hey. You okay?" Rose took over lighting the last candle when Olive couldn't direct her Magic to do so after three attempts. "You look a little pale."

"I'm fine." *For someone one Bax-thought away from throwing up.*

Rose looked at her disbelievingly but nodded before leading the way to their front-row seats. As Vi's womb-mates and the complete Triad, their small ceremonial role was to bless the Exchange with their Magic.

Olive's knees buckled, making it a good thing they sat when they did.

The man who'd been spending a lot of time with her—much of it, lately, naked—had been very literally paid to do so.

✦ ✦ ✦

Bax didn't need his Guardian senses to know something had shifted in the air; the atmosphere was heavily charged, and with a lot more than Magic.

He'd spent the better part of the morning striving to get Olive alone, to rid himself of the weight lying heavy in the center of his chest. To tell her about his Assignment and the GAA. Hell, even his father's involvement in all of it. Because the longer he stayed quiet, the more the lie pressed on him until he could barely breathe.

He couldn't count the times she'd questioned his increased presence over the last few weeks. Even Harper noticed, and she didn't often notice things that didn't involve sex and/or orgasms. But the threat of another broken GA rule had kept him silent.

One more strike and he was out.

No Guardian Angel Affairs. No steady income.

But also less stress, fewer expectations, and the ultimate bonus of boiling his father's blood.

But this wasn't something you just blurted. You couldn't bust out with a "By the way, the reason I've been around so much lately is because I'm your Guardian Angel" and go about your day. He'd tried talking to her about it last night, but Vi had stopped by in a panic because no one had yet heard from or seen Edie.

Tonight, after the Exchange Ceremony, he'd come clean. He'd booked a room at the after-party hotel, and when it was just the two of them and no distractions, he'd tell her *everything*.

Every last conversation. Every expectation. Every damn thing, regardless of the rules broken.

But the more he watched Olive during the Exchange Ceremony, the more certain he became that he was too late. She hadn't looked his way even once. Not a flicker, a glance, or . . . fuck, he'd even take a seething scowl at this point.

Everyone clapped as Vi and Edie, standing in the center of the magical circle, hugged. Vi embraced her sisters next, quickly followed by Linc and her beaming parents. The Exchange finished, a new Prima reigned, and he knew his friend would make an incredible one.

As the granddaughter-and-grandmother duo walked side by

side down the nature-laden aisle, the witnesses lined up to express their congratulations.

Adrian glanced over at the white-knuckled fists in his lap. "You okay, man? You look like you're ready to blow a fuse or something."

"Or something . . ."

Adrian waited for an explanation, which he didn't give.

"I'll meet you at the hotel. There's something I have to do."

"You need backup?" the lion shifter offered.

"Nah. I got this. Grab me a beer from the bar when you get to the hotel."

Adrian looked at him funny, but followed Harper and Damian as they headed toward the portal. He stayed behind, waiting until the crowd thinned to easily find the person with whom he needed a few words.

"Mikael!" Bax barked, earning his father's attention.

The angel turned and waited, his hands casually resting in his suit pockets. "There's my prodigal son. Commissioner Wright tells me you finally turned in your last two field reports. I hope you'll treat your next Assignment with a bit more professionalism."

"What did you say to her?" His tone earned him a few glances as people headed past them to the portal, but he didn't care. "Don't do either of us the disservice of pretending you don't know who I'm talking about. Olive was fine all day . . . until you spoke with her."

Mikael grinned like the bastard he was. "Now that you mention it, I did notice her enthusiasm for our conversation waned the longer it went on. Do you think I should take offense?"

He balled his fists at his side and stepped closer. "*What* did you say to her?"

"Nothing that warrants the scowl on your face or the tone in your voice." Mikael dragged the seconds out, playing his usual games. "I told her that I was relieved her Risk Assessment had diminished, and that you were once again put on rotation."

That heavy weight hanging on his chest pressed harder. "You told her I was her Guardian."

"I very definitely did *not* say that. That would be breaking the GAA Code." Mikael smirked mischievously.

"You may not have spoken the words verbatim, but you knew exactly what you were alluding to. What the hell is your endgame? What the fuck do you want out of this?"

"I've done you a favor, and you're acting as though I've done you some great injury," the Warrior Angel snapped.

"A favor."

"Do you think me so unobservant as to not see what the witch means to you?" Spittle flew in all directions as Mikael hissed. "Continue down that road and it will lead you to nowhere, your reputation as a Guardian dragged through the mud and muck, unable to be cleaned again."

"You mean nowhere *you* want it to go. I don't give a shit about my *reputation*."

"Which means it's up to me as your father to care *for* you."

Bax scoffed. "That's rich coming from you. You haven't been a father since I left the Warrior Academy. Just do us both a favor—denounce me as a member of your family, and leave me to my own devices. Hell, my own life."

"I would have if I could." Mikael's temper flared. "That only works for angels who don't have my standing. As a Warrior, it's already assumed that my entire bloodline will follow in my footsteps. There is no denouncing."

"Then I guess that really sucks for you, but I'm done giving a shit about how my choices affect you." He stood up to his father. "Actually, I'm done giving a shit about anything and everything that doesn't make me happy. That means you better prepare yourself, old man."

"Do not threaten me. I am a leader of the Angelic Army."

"I'm not threatening you. I'm extending you the courtesy of telling you how things will be playing out over the next few days. You may want to brace yourself because I can assure you that it won't follow the road you're hoping for."

Bax left the bastard standing alone on the stone path and stepped through the portal, his stomach immediately dropping as Magic swept him up and spit him out in the hotel foyer.

People filled the large rotunda, all eager to celebrate the ushering in of a new Prima, and to hopefully get a glimpse of the witches themselves.

There was only one witch he wanted to lay eyes on, and as much as he adored Vi, it wasn't her.

With a determination he'd never felt before, he set off to find himself a doe-eyed and book-loving college professor and hoped himself magically capable of undoing all the mistakes he'd racked up in the last few weeks.

23

No Poofing for You

Being a Maxwell came with a lot of expectations and people waiting for you to come up short. Olive had smiled more in the last twelve hours than she had in the last ten years of her life, putting her at serious risk of her lips being frozen in that position permanently.

Like the Joker.

On the bright side, pretending her heart wasn't breaking more with every passing minute wouldn't require much effort.

Tonight's goals: keep busy, avoid a certain tattooed angel, and pull an all-nighter gathering data for her final SupeEx Project presentation to the board.

Easy-peasy cauldron-breezy.

"Remind me why I can't climb into my jeans." Vi glanced longingly at the duffel bag on the bed, her favorite threadbare jeans and hoodie peeking out from the open zipper. "I hear comfort is key to being a leader. Forcing someone into wearing rib-cracking corsets and then telling them to make life-altering decisions doesn't seem the best life choice. They'd be apt to say anything just so long as it meant getting out of the contraption faster."

Smirking, Olive helped her sister step out of her Exchange Ceremony gown and into a stylish yet simpler cocktail dress with gorgeous hues of blue and purple. "You just need to endure three loops around the room. You can manage that even in a corset . . . which you're not wearing."

"Three? Why not four? Or six? Why three?"

She cocked up an eyebrow. "You want to stick around for six?"

"Fuck no. Just curious why the odd number. Three it is. These might be the fastest laps I've run anywhere *ever*. Okay, spill, Olly."

She carefully hung the ceremonial gown back on the hanger, avoiding eye contact. "I'm sure I'll spill something tonight. You know me. If I don't drop something on the boobs, I'm not eating or drinking."

"That's how you're playing it?"

"What are we playing?" Rose entered the bedroom with Harper on her heels. "If it's hide-and-seek, I'll hide first . . . upstairs and away from the crowd waiting downstairs."

Vi groaned. "There's a crowd already?"

"People want to congratulate the new Prima. Of course there's a crowd."

"Or they want to be able to say they were there when the new Prima literally fell on her face or magically burned off her eyebrows," Vi muttered before turning to throw a stern look Olive's way. "But I was talking to our baby sister. Something's up in Olive Land and she's not sharing."

Rose turned her way. "Not sharing isn't allowed."

"It's not important," she said defensively.

"You have been quiet and more introverted today," Rose said thoughtfully.

"It's been a big day. Lots of people. Tons of responsibility."

Vi was already shaking her head. "I'm not buying it."

"You're leaving something out," Rose added. "Something big. I can feel it in my bones."

"You've been spending a lot of time in sewers lately. Maybe that's a lack of vitamin D. You should increase your yogurt intake."

At her sisters' unamused looks, she flickered her gaze to a silent Harper. The succubus gifted her a supportive nod.

She'd mentally rehearsed this reveal no less than a dozen times over the last few days, but it never sounded good enough. "So . . . I've been kinda seeing someone for the last few weeks."

Whoever said silence wasn't loud obviously wasn't standing in that hotel room. But after a few earsplitting seconds of it came the questions.

Who? How? What was the sex like? That last one was from Harper, who shot her an unconcerned shrug when she flung an exasperated look her way.

She held up her hand to quiet everyone. "It wasn't a big deal, which is why I didn't say anything. And I'm pretty sure it's already over, so I'm kind of glad that I didn't clue you all in. No point getting attached to something that's only temporary, right?"

Vi and Rose both shared looks before busting out laughing.

"What? What's so funny?" She folded her arms, slightly affronted.

"Oh, my dear, sweet Olive-bug." Vi draped an arm over her shoulder and steered her to sit on the bed. "Are you forgetting who you're talking to? Me, Miss Fake-Dating-My-Childhood-Nemesis, and Ro, Miss I-Can-Have-Earth-Shattering-Sex-with-a-Gorgeous-Demon-Animal-Lover-and-Not-Catch-Feelings. We're walking proof that saying something isn't a big deal—and only temporary—doesn't make it so."

"It's temporary when I'm pretty sure it only happened because he was forced to stick to me like Rose on *Supernatural* binge watches."

"That's pretty close," Rose admitted.

"Why was he *forced* to stick to you?" Vi asked.

"Have you talked to him about it?" Harper asked, her voice uncommonly quiet. Because of course she'd known for Goddess knew how long. "Maybe it's best if you talk and clear up any assumptions . . . or miscommunication."

Olive swallowed the lump forming in her throat. "I don't think I can just yet. I'm not sure I'm emotionally ready to handle what he might say. What if it wasn't real? What if the only reason it happened wasn't because of actual feelings, but because of forced proximity? The coincidental timing alone makes me question everything."

"Oh, babe." Vi dropped onto the mattress next to her, making it dip. "Then take time to prepare yourself, but don't take too long. The longer you wait, the more all those doubts and unknowns eat away at your stomach lining."

Rose agreed. "She's right. Unless you have the ability to read someone's mind or feelings, you really don't know for sure. The only way you can know is to ask."

"What she said"—Vi pointed to their triplet—"and way better than me."

Nibbling her bottom lip, Olive hesitantly met each sympathetic gaze. "Sometimes ignorance really is bliss."

"Is that what bliss looks like?" Vi wagged a finger in front of her frowning face. "Because if it is, then I've been doing it all wrong and I'm kinda relieved about it."

A knock on the door sent Harper to answer it, and Olive couldn't help but stiffen until Linc appeared in the doorway. Perhaps it hadn't been the most mature course of action, but she'd been avoiding all potential run-ins with a certain tattooed angel until she managed to get her head—and her heart—on a little straighter.

Too bad they were both still tipped on their sides.

Linc swept Vi into an embrace, kissing her until they both needed the oxygen. "I've come to collect the Prima. Her adoring fans are waiting."

She groaned dramatically. "Not you, too. You're damn lucky you're the only person who's perfectly compatible with my soul, wolf-man, or else your ass would be mine."

He kissed her on the nose. "My ass is already yours, princess. As is the rest of me."

Harper faux gagged—or maybe it wasn't fake because she looked a little green. "Don't get me wrong, I love that you and Rose have found a steady stream of what I can only imagine is phenomenal soul mate sex, but can you keep all that other stuff for the bedroom?"

They laughed, but Rose asked, "What? You mean *love*?"

Harper gagged again. "Stop it. Stop saying that word! Right now!"

"What word? *Love*?"

Harper clapped her hands over her ears and hustled from the room, and Rose followed, chanting *love* over and over again, leaving Olive alone with the mated couple.

"I'll let Gran know you're on your way downstairs." She tried escaping before Vi remembered what they'd been talking about.

"Olly," Vi called as she reached the door.

"Yeah?"

"If that guy really was only in it because of the convenience, then he doesn't deserve you. You know that, right? You deserve so much more. You're *worth* so much more. You're worth—and you deserve—*everything*."

She smiled wanly, blinking tears away. "Thanks, sis."

Vi nodded, adding, "What he *does* deserve is a meetup in a dark, isolated alley with a newly anointed Prima who's just getting used to all this extra juice. If you set up the date and time, I'll make sure I'm there."

She chuckled. "Noted, but it won't come to that."

Because she hoped to keep her sisters out of this at all costs.

Bax had been part of their friend group forever and to out him would put all those relationships at risk. This wasn't an issue between Bax and Vi. Or Rose. Or Harper.

This was between Bax and Olive.

Two lovers who shared phenomenal sex and copious orgasms.

Two friends who encouraged each other through scary, out-of-the-comfort-zone experiences.

Two roommates who—*shit*.

Roommates.

They were two Supernaturals who lived under the same roof and ate on the same plates and got naked in the same shower—sometimes at the same time.

Keeping a spare set of clothes and PJs in her office suddenly became her most genius idea ever. *Great job, Past Olive!* She'd eventually have that clear-the-air moment with her Guardian Angel, but she needed to weed through all the other stressors in her life first.

✦ ✦ ✦

After her fifth disappearance, it became clear to Bax that Olive was hell-bent on avoiding him at all costs. One minute she'd be standing less than three feet away, and in the next, thanks to Edie's *poof* spell, by the exit clear across the room. Breathless and sweaty, he didn't know how much longer he could keep up.

Which was probably her idea . . . wear him down until he face-planted in the champagne fountain.

But this time, her luck officially ran out. He'd glimpsed her emerald dress disappearing into the bathroom, and like any self-respecting individual prepping to switch into full grovel mode, he camped outside the door and waited for her in the hall.

Did he get a few curious looks?

Yes.

Did he give a damn?

Not in the least.

He waited, and ten minutes later still stood in the same spot, but he did so while keeping track of the time. With only a few seconds until he said *fuck it* and entered with a called-out warning, she stepped into the hall and came to an abrupt stop.

Her signature green Magic immediately sprang onto her fingertips, and he leapt forward, grasping her hand. "Yeah, I don't think so, angel. You're not *poof*-ing this time."

"I have things to do, Baxter."

"Since when do you call me Baxter?" His brow furrowed, and he knew without a doubt. She knew everything. "I know it's a busy night, but we really should talk. We *need* to talk. About a lot."

She let out a sound that sounded like a cross between a laugh and a sob, but she kept her chin up and her eyes guarded. "Yeah, we do, but I really can't right now."

She pulled away and hustled down the hall as if the hem of her dress were on fire. His chest ached as if she had taken a piece of himself with her.

Fuck. He'd known this would blow up in his face. "I wanted to tell you so damn bad, angel! Please, just . . . wait."

She froze, her shoulders lifting and dropping a few times before she turned. The pained look on her face nearly did him in, and as bad as he wanted to close the distance and pull her into his arms, he remained rooted to the ground.

"I wanted to tell you that I was assigned as your Guardian the second it happened, and then a million times more after," he admitted truthfully. "But it's—"

"A rule. I figured." She took a shuddering breath. "I'm still trying to figure out how or why the GAA considered me high-risk enough to be assigned a Guardian."

He could practically see the walls she'd built around herself. He gave her a pained, wary smile. "I'm still trying to figure that out myself."

"I assume it had something to do with the Dare I Docket?"

Bax felt a small tinge of relief when he realized he wasn't getting the pure anger he'd expected. "That would be my best bet."

"So you weren't assigned as my Guardian when you asked me to move in with you?" Her voice slowly diminished toward the end of her question, and he saw it had taken a lot for her to ask.

"No, angel. I asked you to move into the apartment well before the GAA handed me your file. I—"

She held up her hand to stop him and he couldn't help but obey. "I know there's a lot we should hash out right now, but I just . . . can't. I need a little time to wrap my head around everything and I need you to give that time to me. Please."

He nodded. "Of course."

"I'm not angry that you didn't tell me about being my Guardian. I mean, I'm disappointed that you couldn't tell me, and I may not like that you didn't, but I understand why. It's just . . . everything else."

Fuck. Bax didn't know whether to be relieved now or even more worried. "Okay. Anything you need, angel, it's yours."

She turned to leave but paused, her dark blue eyes swimming with so many different emotions. She looked to be fighting with herself before she asked, "I do just want to know one thing right now. And all I need is a simple yes or no answer."

"Hit me."

She took a beat. "Did you offer to do the Docket with me because it would keep you close in case anything happened?"

"It's not as si—"

"Yes or no, Bax. Did you do the list with me because you were assigned as my Guardian Angel?"

A lump formed in the center of his throat, growing with each passing second. "Yes."

Olive's lips trembled. She nodded and turned, but not before he saw the sheen of tears in her eyes. He called out to her, but she only hurried faster until, with a wave of green Magic, she *poof*'d.

Disappeared.

And left behind what felt like an aching hole in his chest.

With a heavy groan, he leaned against the wall. He was used to fucking things up, but this one hurt the worst. This time it hadn't only affected him but someone he cared about.

Someone he cared about *a lot*.

"*You're* the one?" Vi stepped from around the corner, a wary Rose standing on her left. "Okay. Wow. I admit I didn't see that coming. I mean, I'd always hoped that you two kids would get out of each other's way to see the possibilities there, but I didn't have *Bax lying to get into my sister's pants* on my bingo card for this year."

"That is *not* what happened," he denied forcefully, pushing off the wall.

"Then let me rephrase. You didn't lie to get *into* her bed, but you got there under false pretenses. Does that sound about right, or should I try and rephrase it again?"

"You don't have the whole story . . . or even a fraction of it."

"And whose fault is that?"

That barb stung, but he stood firm. "I love you, Vi. I love you both." He shot a look to Rose. "And I love how much you love your sister, but I'm asking you—lovingly—to back off. This is between me and Olive. No one else."

She snortled. "You know better than anyone that if someone fucks with one Maxwell sister, you fuck with them all."

"Vi . . ."

He stepped closer and was instantly hit with a wave of Magic. It lifted him like he weighed nothing and pinned him to the wall. But it didn't come from the new Prima.

It came from Rose.

Her magical pink signature flickered in the air. "It's probably in your best interest that you keep your distance. Vi's Magic has grown since the Exchange Ceremony. She could probably blow a hole right through your chest without even trying."

"His chest isn't the body part I'm contemplating blowing apart," Vi added with a glare, pointedly flicking her gaze to his crotch.

"Vi. Rose." Movement behind the sisters caught his attention. "*Harper.* You know the last thing I'd ever want to do is to hurt Olive."

"It might be the last, but it's what you did," Harper stated.

That ache in his chest intensified at her words because they were true. He knew from firsthand experience that intentions didn't mean squat. Just because you never wanted one of your actions to hurt someone didn't mean it couldn't happen.

To Olive, it *did* happen.

She'd given him so much over the last few weeks and all he'd given her were half-truths and a damn tattoo.

Rose released him from her hold and he dropped like a rock. "Just so you know, this isn't fixable with cake-batter vodka ice cream. The Boozereamery won't work this time around."

Harper and the sisters left as quietly as they'd appeared, leaving him alone in the corridor with an itch on his back that he really hoped wasn't a hexed case of angel mange.

24

Praise Be the Goddess of Orgasms

Work usually soothed Olive's soul, but she'd done as much as she could to prepare for her presentation to the board and she didn't feel very soothed. She felt the exact opposite.

Enflamed.

Like an irritating hemorrhoid that didn't abate despite gallons of steroids and witch hazel ointment.

Leaving the party—*fleeing* Vi's party—wasn't one of her finer moments, but flight overtook fight, and since redos weren't possible, she just felt enflamed. No better word existed for it.

The feeling churning inside her wasn't caused by a single thing, but by a cascade of dominos hitting one another, creating a rippling effect until everything fell ass over end. Including her.

She didn't doubt Bax's move-in offer came before she'd been his Assignment, and even though she didn't like it, she didn't even blame him for not telling her he was her Guardian. Rules were rules, and angels were big on them.

What bothered her most was that the warning signs had been right in front of her and she hadn't seen them. The most obvious? Mr. I Work Twenty-Four-Seven, Three-Sixty-Five suddenly being way too available and too eager to tag along to places that should've sent him running in the other direction.

He'd forced himself up a mountain, knowing he'd have an angelic heart attack on the way down, and he'd done it because she'd been his Assignment. And it hadn't been the only time.

Cirque du Surnaturel. The dance-off. Probably even the karaoke night at Potion's Up and all those rides to work and home.

And their winter wonderland morning in the park.

That one hurt to think about, so much that when she did, breathing became difficult. Their *date.* Their first *real* date, or so she'd thought. Now a hovering shadow clouded over what she'd remembered as a day filled with Magic and wonder and so many possibilities.

All of it was tainted because while she'd been having the time of her life, making memories she'd cherish forever, Bax had been doing his *job*, hurdling obstacles so he could write up a report for the GAA.

"Maybe I shouldn't have erased *survive a heartbreak* from spot number ten." Olive drained the remnants of her third Red Bull and tossed the empty can toward the recycling bucket to join the others.

Her office door opened, and the can, now a projectile, smacked the person stepping inside right between the eyes.

"What the actual fuck? Is this payback for the flying stuffed pig?" Vi rubbed a blossoming red spot on her forehead. "What's the punishment for assaulting the new Prima?"

"Maybe the same for breaking and entering," she grumbled.

Vi wasn't alone. Rose and Harper filed into her cramped office, still wearing their dresses from the after-party while Olive had climbed into the PJs she'd left there when she'd been in the throes of roommate woes.

The world really had come full circle.

Harper grimaced as she cleaned a layer of white cheddar Cheetos dust off the closer of two chairs. "The charges would never stick because we didn't break anything getting in here and you have a literal welcome mat outside the door."

Damn. She'd forgotten about that impulse Target buy.

She bounded to the door and, sticking her head into the hall, flicked her fingers and turned her ALL WELCOME mat into ALL UN-WELCOME. "There. Bolded, highlighted, and italicized. Surely you three have better things to do, so please, don't let me keep you from doing them."

"You are ridiculously smart, but simultaneously ridonkulously stupid if you think we're leaving you here to sulk alone." Ro perched her ass against her desk. "Sulking is best done with sisters and ice cream."

She pointedly glanced at their empty hands. "I don't see any ice cream."

"Told you we should've stopped at the boozy ice cream store," Harper muttered.

"They weren't open. It's like one in the morning."

"The owners live upstairs. A few thrown pebbles at a window and voilà. Ice cream."

"Or another night in a jail cell because of a disturbing-the-peace charge," Vi quipped with a smirk. "I'm the Prima now. I can't afford to get tossed in the slammer again."

"You've been the Prima for all of two seconds and you're already a killjoy, Maxwell. Besides, I'd like to remind you that it wasn't my idea that got you into that predicament."

The sex demon swung a pointed look to Rose, who rolled her eyes. "I have one lapse of judgment and it goes down in infamy. And it wasn't bad judgment, just bad execution."

"You can call a vibrating dildo a sex toy, Vi can call it a household appliance, but it doesn't mean it's not the same thing. A good time."

"Sometimes I wonder if you actually register the words before they come out of your mouth." Rose chuckled with a small shake of her head.

"Look," Olive interjected, heading back to her spot behind her desk, "I appreciate you three coming all the way out here, but it wasn't necessary. I'm fine. I'm totally fine. I'm better than fine."

Vi frowned. "Your voice is doing that high-pitched thing where it gets higher the longer you talk. That means you're most definitely not fine, babe."

"I didn't say I was sing-from-the-rooftops fine, but I'm . . . humming from the first floor."

Three disbelieving snorts chorused simultaneously through the room.

"Okay, I'm mentally mouthing the words from the basement. The point is that I don't have the time to be anything other than fine."

"We know it's Bax," Vi blurted.

Her eyes widened. "What? How did you—"

"We kinda overheard the two of you in the hall earlier tonight." Rose smiled wanly. "We didn't mean to eavesdrop, but—"

"She didn't, but the second I realized what the two of you were talking about, *I* did," Vi admitted.

"He couldn't tell me he was my Guardian," Olive defended him automatically.

"Yeah, we heard that part. We also heard the bit about doing the Docket with you—"

"Because it was his job to keep tabs on me." There came that damn ache in her chest. She took a deep breath and tried—and failed—to meditate it away. "Bax and I are both adults who had intense—but brief—sexual interactions. We never talked about what it was, or where it was headed. We didn't talk about why it was all happening now after knowing each other for years. We just enjoyed the moments as they came. It shouldn't bother me that it had been his job to babysit me every day. Or that all my experiences for the Dare I

Docket will forever have his memory embedded in them. It's fine. I'm fine. Everything's just *fine*."

Rose glanced nervously to the desk. "Your desk calendar won't be so fine if you don't tone down your fine-level some."

She glanced to her hands, alit with her emerald Magic, currently setting her desk calendar on fire. Vi summoned a swell of water that shot from her palms like a Super Soaker, the quick thinking immediately extinguishing the calendar flames . . . and Olive.

With a heavy, wet sigh, Olive sank into her office chair with a loud squish. "Maybe I'm not as fine as I thought."

"Gee, you think?" Harper quipped.

"It's just that Bax has always been a little standoffish, and part of me didn't want to question why it was that he was suddenly always around."

"Because you're an awesome person," Vi stated firmly. "Who wouldn't want to hang around you? There's no reason to question it."

"I second that motion," quipped another voice.

They all snapped their heads to the corner of the room, mouths open.

"When the hell did you get here?" Vi demanded of their grandmother, who sat comfortably in a cushioned chair that most definitely didn't belong in Olive's office.

"Some point around the mention of sex toys and good times." Edie shrugged. "But that doesn't really matter. What does is whatever comes next."

"I don't know what you mean, Gran," Olive admitted. "Tomorrow—or technically later today—I'll present my findings on the Dare I Docket and hope that the board sees the necessity for the SupeEx Project as much as I do. The findings are pretty clear. Sometimes stepping out of the comforting shadows is a necessary evil."

Edie nodded, studying her carefully. "Are you sure it's the act itself that's the contributing factor?"

"I sure as hell hope so, because if it's not, then the project that I assigned to my class and the list I've been killing myself to try and complete will've been for nothing."

"Nothing? Are you sure about that?"

"Well, yeah, Gran. The point of the Docket was to show that forward movement and personal growth only happen when you physically deviate from your norm in some small way," Olive pointed out. "In order to understand one another, we need to walk *beside* one another."

Edie watched her silently with her all-knowing silver eyes, and the longer she did, the more Olive fidgeted. "What are you trying to say here because I'm coming up blank?"

"Ooh! Ooh!" Vi waved her hand in the air. "Call on me! I know this one! I know!"

Olive wished she did. She tossed around her grandmother's words, knowing there wasn't anything that came from the witch's mouth that didn't have meaning. Dragging her unicorn notebook from her desk, she flipped open her Docket and stared.

What was she missing?

The botched hot tub incident, where Bax saved her from drowning in three feet of water. Classes at Cirque du Surnaturel, where the silks kept tangling in his bulky appendages. The gala he attended with her.

The couples dance competition . . .

Karaoke night.

The park.

All the multiorgasmic sex.

They were all so varied and out of her comfort level. Nothing tied it all together except . . .

Bax.

He'd been the common denominator. Every single item on this list, she'd experienced it with *him* at her side—and in the case of numbers seven and eight, in multiple positions. She even wore the tattoo he designed *for* her, and placed on her himself.

There wasn't anything on this Docket that she couldn't have done on her own, but what made the most impact on her over the last few weeks wasn't the *activities* on this list. It was the people she'd experienced it all with. It was Harper and her friends. It was Isaiah and Ruby. Even the difficult registrar at the Javits.

It was *Bax*.

"It's not the what, or when, or even the where," she heard herself murmur. "It's the who you do it with."

She glanced up at Edie to see the older woman's beaming smile. "Buy this witch an ice cream cone because I think she's got it. Now apply that to why I went AWOL and you have yourself a pretty solid epiphany."

"Gran!" Vi gasped.

"You left so that we'd all move forward on our own," guessed Rose.

"Not on your own," Edie corrected.

"Together," Olive added. "You wanted us to each step into our new roles in life by—"

"Learning to lean on those who only wish to see you succeed, and whose only goal is to support you as you make it happen *yourself*."

"And you're not that person?"

"Oh, I'm the one who wants to see you succeed the most, and everything I do is to support the three of you as you walk through life and get closer to your destinies. But I also know I'm not the only one. I won't be around forever, my dears. I need to get my wise-old-grandma teaching in while I can." She winked, letting them know she was joking without actually making a joke.

Olive shook her head. "I get that for Vi and Rose, Gran. They've found their soul mates in Linc and Damian, and there isn't anything they wouldn't do for them. Sorry to tell you, but your plan kinda backfired with me."

Edie scrunched up her nose. "Did it really?"

"If you're suggesting that Bax is the one to give me that *Jerry Maguire* moment, you are so, so wrong. We're definitely not like that."

"You're sure?"

"He literally earned a paycheck to spend time with me, Gran. That's not really indicative of a real friendship, much less true love."

"Did you ask him if he would've done it all regardless of that paycheck?" Edie asked knowingly.

"No, but—"

"And how do you feel about having shared those experiences with him? Would they have been just as meaningful if you'd done them solo? Or with someone else at your side?"

"No . . ." she admitted softly. "It wouldn't have felt the same."

"Which means what?"

Vi blew out a heavy breath, looking as if she were about to bust. "Oh my Goddess. Say it already or I will implode, and you know my track record. It's totally possible."

"I'm in love with Bax," Olive realized aloud.

"About damn time," Rose muttered.

"Praise be the Goddess of orgasms," Harper howled.

"That was painful even for me," Vi chided.

She took turns shooting them all glares. "You're saying that you all knew?"

A *hell yeah* chorus went through the room, even from Edie.

Vi added, "And I'll go one step further and say that anyone who saw the two of you together clearly realized that the only people either of you saw was one another."

Rose bumped into her shoulder. "In case you're wondering, that means your feelings are definitely not one-sided."

"But—"

"Oh, I'm not saying Baxter didn't fuck up. That angel has some serious lessoning to learn. But I'm saying that if you ask him why he did everything he did, I'd bet you'd get a different answer than 'for the paycheck.'" She shrugged. "That's just me, but what do I know? Maybe he racked up some serious bonus bucks for dealing with your shit. I mean, you did make him join the damn circus."

This time, they all chuckled and Olive hesitantly joined. Because they were right. All of them.

It wasn't *what* you did that moved you forward the most, but the people who stood by your side when you did it. It was your family—your *found* family. The ones you chose to surround yourself with because them not being part of your life wasn't a possibility you wanted to think about.

She'd spent a painstaking number of hours adding things to her list she'd erroneously believed were needed to make her the tiniest bit more comfortable in an uncomfortable situation, something she'd told her students not to do.

She sank into her chair with a heavy groan. "I really need to talk to Bax—be damned if I'm emotionally ready for it or not."

She loved him. She was *in* love with him, and she didn't give a damn what kind of things she did moving forward as long as he was right there with her when she did them. He literally *was* her wingman.

She sprang to her feet. "I really need to talk to my wingman. Or winged man."

"Your man?" Harper supplied.

"Yes!" Olive pointed at her. "And I need to do it right now."

"Uh, no, you don't." Vi blocked her path to the door.

"What? Why?" She glanced at her sweatpants and flip-flops. "If I remember correctly, you went to Linc's hearing in your duck PJs."

"I'm not talking about your outfit, Olly." She held up a familiar flash drive, the one that held her presentation about SupeEx.

The one that now put emphasis on the *wrong* thing. It didn't matter where they sent students accepted into SupeEx, but *who* they sent them to.

"I need to put a different spin on it . . . on all of it." She glanced at the tail-wagging cat clock on her wall. "And my meeting with the board is in seven hours. That's not even possible. I'll never be able to make that kind of a focused change in that amount of time."

Everyone began kicking off their shoes. Even Edie.

"What do you all think you're doing?" she asked, confused.

"Isn't it obvious?" Vi tossed the old flash drive to her, her smirk broadening. "We're doing what Maxwells—and honorary Maxwells—do when one of our own is in a bind. We're pulling up our big-witch panties, dusting off the magical fingers, and preparing to blow some minds with our keen intellect."

Rose chuckled. "She means we're sticking around to help you flesh out ideas and put it all together. We're here to help, Olly. All Witches—and honorary witches—on Deck."

✦ ✦ ✦

Nothing helped improve Bax's mood. He'd dropped into his community gym and whaled on the heavy bag until he sweated through his damn suit. When that didn't work, he contemplated heading over to Inklings for some new ink, but realized after showing up that Isaiah, fond of keeping normal hours, wasn't open at one in the morning.

With not many options available that didn't require lawbreaking, he opted for Potion's Up, and when he'd stepped into the bar, Gage had taken one look at him and shoved a vodka at him. At least it looked and smelled like vodka. He didn't drink it, opting instead for ice water, a corner booth, and openly glaring at anyone who dared break his solitude.

Only one brave soul had attempted it in the last thirty minutes, so it looked like word had finally gotten around: *Don't fuck with the pissed-off angel sitting alone in the corner.*

Potion's front door opened, the attached chime ringing to alert those present that someone had either come or gone. The charged shift in the air told Bax the incoming someone new was a Supernatural, but he didn't bother turning around in his seat. He knew exactly who'd arrived, and that there was a 99 percent chance they were there for him.

Whether it was to talk to him or kick his ass, he was a bit less certain.

Linc dropped into the seat on his left while Adrian and Damian slipped into either side of the booth, penning him in.

Linc grimaced at his tall glass. "You should've just asked Gage to give you the damn bottle."

"It's water," Bax grumbled.

"Not sure that makes it much better." Damian chuckled.

"You three are here to what? Heckle me? Kick my ass? Make me feel like more of a piece of shit, not like that's possible, but hey, why not give it a whirl?"

"You want me to kick your ass?" Linc asked. "I can do that. It may give me points with Vi if I tell her I made you bleed, or at the very least gave you a swollen eye."

"If you're doing it, then go ahead. First few punches are free, but after that I make no guarantees."

"What the hell, Bax?"

"I think that's pretty damn gracious."

"I'm not talking about the ass-kicking."

He let his head fall back as he stared at the ceiling. "I know, and there isn't an excuse, at least not a good one. I fucked up. I should've told her about everything before we crossed that line from friends to more."

Linc shot up a single eyebrow.

"Okay, I should've told Commissioner Wright where to stick Olive's file and never taken her on as an Assignment to begin with. If I'd never been appointed her Guardian, I wouldn't have had to dance around the truth, and she wouldn't be thinking that the only reason I've spent time with her over the last few weeks was because of a fucking job."

All three Supernaturals emitted varying noises.

"What?" Bax took turns glaring at each of them. "You all have something to say? Spill. Otherwise, keep your noises to yourself."

"Alright, I'll bite," Damian said first, leaning back in his seat and already looking smug. "Could you have really turned down the appointment as Olly's Guardian?"

"I could have—"

"I'm not asking if it was technically possible for you to turn it down. I'm asking if you *could* have. Could you really have turned Olive's well-being over to someone else? From what limited knowledge I have on the GAA, people don't get assigned Guardians at random. There was obviously a reason she'd been flagged."

Bax didn't think about it long. *No.* Putting Olive's life in the hands of someone else, potentially someone with black marks on their record more numerous than his, wasn't even a possibility he would've entertained.

"I would've stuck by her side whether I was officially assigned or not," he admitted.

"Then there you go. You can at least stop beating yourself up about that much. Now focus on the shit you actually can—and should—clear up."

"Like?"

"Like the fact the woman you're in love with thinks the only reason you've been spending quality time with her lately is because her name ended up on your fucking file. Unless that *is* the only reason why you did. In that case, let's round back to that ass-kicking."

That heavy weight sitting on Bax's chest expanded.

He lived in an amazing city and was fortunate enough to be part of an incredible found family. He could do or be anything, and yet he hadn't known what it was to experience life—and fully enjoy it—until the day he hauled Olive's dozen boxes of books into what used to be his bedroom.

She'd opened eyes he didn't know had been closed.

She'd warmed a heart that he didn't realize had been cold.

She'd filled a part of his life he hadn't realized had been empty . . . until he faced the real threat of her no longer being there.

He loved her . . . was *in* love with her.

The realization of it would've sent the old Bax running, screaming in denial all the way to the GAA, where he'd do his damned best—or at least 50 percent of his best—to prove he hadn't broken yet another Guardian rule.

But the Bax of today didn't run.

He sat on that damn chair, fear paralyzing him and preventing him from figuring out his next step. A step that could solve everything . . . or make it a million times worse.

"Being her Guardian may have given me an opportunity to spend these weeks together, but it sure as hell isn't the reason why I did it. I *love* Olive," Bax admitted aloud. "I'm so in love with her that I can't see or think straight. Hell, right now, even thinking about not having her in my life is making it hard to breathe."

"Pretty sure I know the answer since you're cowering in a bar, but did you tell her all that?" asked Damian.

He shifted his gaze from friend to friend. "No. She said she needed time to gather her thoughts and I didn't have a right to push her. *Fuck.* I really fucked all this up good, didn't I?"

Linc smacked him on the back. "Welcome to the club, man. Love—it's both the best thing to ever happen to you, and the fucking scariest."

Damian chuckled. "I second that . . . and there's no scarier place to be than in the doghouse. Linc knows all about that."

The shifter growled playfully. "I'm not the only one, buddy. Which one of us gave our woman signed papers that literally said *have a nice life*?"

"First, they did not say *have a nice life*. They stated she'd finished her community service hours and no longer needed to show up at the sanctuary."

"You explain, and it still sounds like a dick move."

"It was, one she already kicked my ass for many times over, but we're not here about my dickish move. Or even yours. We're here about his." Damian aimed a chin-nod in Bax's direction. "So in hindsight, you gave her the time she needed. Good on you. But now you need to make yourself clear on where exactly you stand."

"By her side. Always."

"And what's your plan to get there?"

A slow smile crept onto his face. "First, I need to notify the GAA that I broke a rule. Second, I need to see a man about a tattoo shop. And then I need to find my witch about forever."

25

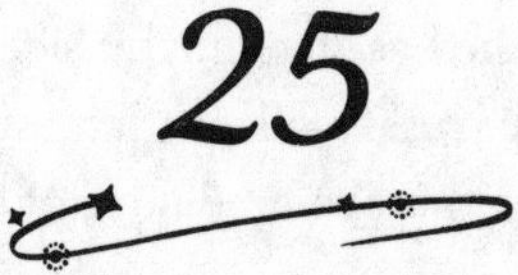

Follow Your Heart

Olive paced the corridor and, with each full circuit, wore a path in the floor a bit more. Under normal circumstances and in any other situation, she would've felt bad. In this one, she didn't. Maybe a smidge of guilt, but the second regret surfaced, the incredible desire for this to be over overpowered it.

Regardless of the outcome.

Mason and Celeste stood closest to the boardroom door as they, too, waited for the board's decision. They'd all presented their facts and data, not to mention their plans if they were awarded the grant money.

Olive and the others—even Edie—had pulled an all-nighter throwing ideas together in some way that could be considered a presentation, and she was proud of the results. Vi, in her new role as Prima, even lined up an incredible list of Supernatural mentors that almost had her wanting to take part in the program herself.

The boardroom door opened, and the secretary nodded. "They'll see you now."

The three of them headed to follow, Mason giving Olive a smug smirk. "No hard feelings, okay? There's always next time."

She forced a smile. "Good to know you won't be even more of a jerk after my department gets the award."

He frowned, looking shocked she'd spoken out. She gave herself a mental pat on the back and entered the conference room, her head held high. The secretary led them to the front, where the table of twelve members watched as they filed inside. With the exception of Mrs. Artugo—one of the college's largest donors, who flashed her a saucy wink and a thumbs-up—none of the faces held signs of emotion.

There was nothing to read, nothing to indicate which way this would go.

But after she'd given her speech and laid out the plan for the new SupeEx Mentorship Program, she'd made peace with the fact that what happened in this room didn't matter. Would it make getting SupeEx off the ground easier?

Absolutely.

But she didn't *need* it. Vi kept the Kids' Community Center open and thriving, with more kids taking advantage of the services it provided every day. With a bit of ingenuity, luck, and the backup of the people around her, she'd make SupeEx happen with or without the board's money.

A small part of her almost wished they'd turn her down, because as great as this money would be, it came with strings, reports, and constant expectations that needed to be met.

People weren't a quota, and their lives were more than data. Somewhere along the line, she'd temporarily forgotten that, and thanks to her Docket, she now remembered.

"I'd like to congratulate the three of you for bringing three extremely thought-out, provocative, and educational plans to this board, but as you know, this particular grant can only be awarded to one." The board head hesitated, dragging this on like the Academy Awards. "We in no way want this to discourage the others, and we praise each one of you on your dedication to bringing excellence and prestige to this institution. So without prolonging the inevitable . . ."

Olive braced herself for the next words . . . because once this was done, she had one last thing she needed to cross off her Docket.

One that she'd added just that morning.

Follow your heart.

✦ ✦ ✦

For the first time in longer than he could remember, tension didn't riddle Bax's shoulders—or hell, his entire body—the second he stepped into this building. He walked through the corridor of the GAA without a care in the world, his stride easy, not the least bit concerned about what lay ahead.

Fixing things with Olive was an entirely different hurdle, one he'd tackle once this wasn't hanging over his head.

He took the stairs to the top floor, exiting straight into Commissioner Wright's office lobby. Patrick glanced up from his desk, his eyes wide behind his glasses.

"Hey, Patty. She in?" Bax didn't wait for an answer as he glided toward the door.

The secretary shot up out of his seat. "You can't just go in there. She's in a meeting, and—"

"And she's about to be in a meeting with me."

Patrick sprinted in front of him, literally widening his arms the width of the door as he blocked his entrance. "Think about whatever it is you're about to do. You're not exactly on good footing right now, Baxter. You already have one toe off the cloud, so to speak."

"Only one? Damn. I should've worked a little harder to make it a whole appendage."

Patrick frowned. "I'm serious."

"So am I, and I appreciate the warning, but I know exactly what I'm doing. I don't need to think it over any further."

Patrick emitted a resounding sigh. "Fine. But she didn't want to be disturbed, so . . ."

"I'll make it look like I didn't give you much of a choice. Guardian's Promise?" He winked.

The angel secretary muttered a string of not very angelic curses as he shooed Bax back a step or two and physically braced himself to come face-to-face with the Commissioner's wrath. He lifted his hand and knocked before opening the door.

"Commissioner Wright, my apologies . . ." Patrick began.

"I told you I wasn't to be disturbed," Wright's voice snapped.

"I know, ma'am. I'm sorry, but there's a—"

"Bax Donovan to see you." Bax gently shouldered the other man aside, pushing his way through the door.

"I'm sorry, ma'am," Patrick apologized. "Should I—"

"Leave us, Patrick. I suppose now is as good a time as any to handle this little issue." The Commissioner looked at Bax coolly, but it was nothing compared to the glare from his father.

Mikael sat in one of the spare chairs, dressed in a suit and tie, a far cry from his battle armor.

"Guess rogue demons packed up shop and called the war over, huh?" he goaded. "That's the only reason I can think why you've been here at the GAA and in New York so much."

"Why your father is here is not your concern," Commissioner Wright snapped. "What you should be concerned about is your own future here at the GAA."

"I'm not concerned about that at all," he said blithely.

"You should be."

"Nah. Because the GAA is no longer part of my future." He yanked the paperwork from his back jeans pocket and tossed it onto Wright's desk. "Happy Resignation Day, Commissioner. You're no longer forced into dealing with my rule-breaking outlaw-angel ways because I quit."

She jumped up from her chair, her mouth opening and closing as she picked up his resignation. "You can't just *resign*."

"Pretty sure I just did. It says it on that paper right there. First line."

Mikael's typical frown marred his face as he stood, squaring his broad shoulders. "You're obviously not thinking clearly."

He slowly turned to his sperm donor. "On the contrary, my thoughts are clearer than they've been in . . . well, ever."

"I was here discussing your latest mishap with the Commissioner, and she's agreed to an arrangement that entails—"

"*My* mishap?" He narrowed his eyes, stepping closer to his father. "Don't you mean when *you* tried imploding my love life by divulging my work status to Olive?"

"I did no such thing," Mikael denied. "And that's a pretty heavy accusation."

"Good thing I have broad shoulders. But you know what, *Dad*? Your endgame may have been to put my life more directly under your thumb, but you ended up doing the exact opposite. You gave me a reason to step out from under it."

Commissioner Wright babbled. "Perhaps we shouldn't be too hasty. You are, after all, a great asset to the GAA, Bax. Breaking two of the three GAA rules isn't as bad as one may think. We can spin it to the higher-ups."

"Three," he clarified.

"Three what?"

"I've now broken three rules, so I'm pretty sure there's no way for you to spin that. Not that I'd want you to. I fell in love with my Assignment. I took risks with her because I wanted her to be happy, to see the smile on her face. And I'd do it all over again if given the chance." Bax glanced to his father and back. "Consider my wings clipped, Commissioner. You have a good day now. Oh, and that last report? It includes information about an angel, Warrior class, divulging classified information to an Assignment. It's probably one of my best field reports yet. Happy reading."

Bax stormed out, making it to the waiting elevator by the time Mikael caught up with him, his face red and fuming. "Who the fuck do you think you are?"

He smiled. "I'm a Donovan, and I'm late setting things in motion so that I can win back the woman I love."

The elevator opened, and he stepped inside, his grin real and growing at the sight of his father's obvious displeasure.

One item off his to-do list done. It was time to move on to the next . . . and then he was seeing a witch about a lifetime of happily-ever-after.

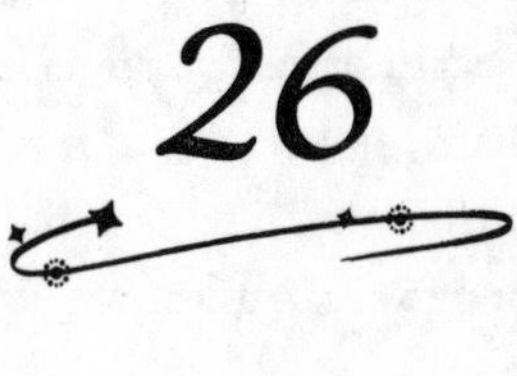

26

Poof!

Olive had hated hide-and-seek even as a kid. She'd always ended up as the person stuck seeking, and because she'd always followed the rules, she didn't often get the chance to hide. Her sucky childhood search record had followed her into adulthood because just when she thought she'd caught Bax's trail, it ended up cold.

Right now, the frozen tundra was their apartment, where he'd been recently but not currently.

"At least his clothes aren't packed," she murmured to herself, standing in her living room and attempting to revamp her plan of attack.

A lightbulb flashed and burst, and a split second later, Vi, Rose, and a slightly nauseous-looking Harper stood in front of her less than three feet away.

Harper lurched toward the kitchen garbage can and discarded all her stomach contents. "I don't care what you bwitches say, that *poof*-ing thing is not natural. Next time, warn a demon, okay? I need to clench my bits before I go magically hurtling through time and space or however the fuck that shit is possible."

"What are you three doing here?" Olive asked, confused.

Vi gave her a WTF look. "We stopped by the college to find out what happened at the board meeting and—"

"That's not important right now. I need to talk to Bax, and I can't find him anywhere, and before you ask, *yes*, I've called him. And texted. It's like he *poof*'d off the face of the earth."

"Off the face of the earth or he's at the GAA."

Olive blinked. "What?"

"Guardian Angel Affairs is like one big . . . Wait, am I the only one to know this? How can I know something that you and Rose—"

"Vi, I would very much like to be in the know, so could you please spill the info already?"

"The GAA, like a lot of Supernatural buildings, isn't fond of modern technology. But there's something about the GAA specifically that not only knocks it offline while you're in the building, but for a while outside of it. It's kind of like a technology hangover or something. I only know because my Disney Emoji Blitz wasn't working after Gran and I made an official visit and I was pissed because there was supposed to be infinite lives for an hour."

Olive, Rose, and Harper all turned to look at the oldest triplet.

"What? You all have your vices. Mine is lining up the faces of the cute little cartoon characters and watching them blow up. Don't judge."

Olive battled through her exhaustion, "Okay, so the GAA is almost clear across town. It'll take me forever to get there and—"

"What the Goddess are you talking about?" Vi asked, confused. "Gran taught us the *poof* spell for a reason. Use it."

"I've been *poof*-ing all morning and afternoon. I'm running low on magical juice right now."

And that had *never* happened to her before.

Vi ushered her closer. "Well, come on then and hop aboard the SS *Prima*. Evidently this new position came with an unfathomable well of energy because I'm not even winded."

"Are you sure?"

"Bwitch, get over here." Grinning, her sister held out her hand.

Harper picked up a small mixing bowl before latching onto Rose's arm. "At least this time I'm prepared."

"In three, two . . ." Vi *poof*'d them all, and in another half second *poof*'d again, this time into a space significantly more crowded than Olive's living room.

A trio of unsuspecting angels nearly plowed into them as they appeared.

"Sorry," Rose called out when the angels shot them dirty looks. "Or not . . . jerks."

Vi glanced around the crowded rotunda. "How are we supposed to find Bax in this zoo? There's not this many people in Times Square."

"It's not a matter of finding him in the zoo. It's about finding the correct zookeeper to point you toward the right habitat." Olive scanned the room, making sure to sweep over every corner, and then she did it a second time. On the third pass, she hit the jackpot. "Got it."

"Bax?" Vi rose to her toes in an attempt to peer over people's heads.

"No . . . but someone who knows him, and I'd pay any bit of money that he knows where he is." She crossed the room like a woman on a mission, and she was. The guy she'd seen with Bax the night of Potion's Up karaoke looked her way, his eyes widening.

Yeah, he knew exactly who she was.

"I was hoping for a word. I'm sorry, I don't know your name." She kept her voice polite and calm, calling on the Maxwell politeness. For now.

"Patrick," the man almost squeaked.

"Patrick. I'm Olive. I'm hoping you could point me in the direction of Baxter Donovan. I have reason to believe that he might be floating around here somewhere."

"He's not here."

She sighed, more than a little tired. "Can I be straight with you, if that's okay?"

"Um . . . okay."

"I'm extremely sleep-deprived, and to add onto that, I had to stand in front of snooty intellectuals and defend my labor-of-love project. It's been A Day, you know? I realized I've fallen in love with my roommate only after I told him to give me time and space, and now that I've realized my mistake, I've *poof*'d all over this city so I can tell him how I *really* feel. And I can't find him."

"Did you try his cell phone?" Patrick asked.

Her head pounded like a drumline was using it for band practice. "You seem like a decent guy, so I'm pretending you didn't just insult my intelligence by asking me that."

The awkward man shifted nervously on his feet. "I'm sorry, but I don't think I can help you."

"And I'm pretty sure you can because we both know he was here."

"He was. Came in on the breeze and left like a hurricane, but he left the GAA hours ago, and I've been dealing with the fallout ever since."

"The fallout? Is he okay?" Concern kicked her heart rate up a few dozen beats per minute, the sound echoing in her ears.

"I think the answer to that is pretty debatable."

"Do you know where he went or when he might be back?"

"He won't *be* back, thanks to you," a sharp, familiar voice snapped.

She turned to Mikael Donovan, a groan falling from her lips. "You really are the gift that keeps on giving, aren't you?"

"Three witches and a demon don't belong at the GAA. I suggest you leave before I have you forcefully removed."

Harper bristled. "Whoa, whoa, whoa. I don't like how you said *demon*. You made it sound derogatory."

"And I don't really give a fuck what you think. You shouldn't be here. None of you." He turned a hard glare on Olive. "*Especially* not you. You've done enough damage, witch."

Vi's Magic crackled, reacting to the open hostility. "I don't know who the fuck you think you are, asshole, but—"

"He's Bax's father," Olive muttered, "and I use that term very, very loosely."

Mikael growled. "Excuse me?"

"I'm not sure there is an excuse for you." She stepped closer, getting angrier by the second. "A parent should support their child above everything and everyone else. They should comfort and nurture, guide and redirect if they get lost. But you? There aren't words for what you do. So no, I won't excuse you. Because you're a grown-ass adult who should know better but doesn't. Or worse, one who knows better but just doesn't care."

"Perhaps, but I'm not the reason he's throwing away his entire future. You are!"

"What are you talking about?"

"I'm talking about the Guardian Rules of Conduct. The rules, which he's always had difficulty following, except for rule number three. It's the only reason why he's hung on to his position within the GAA. Until now. Until *you* had him breaking even that one. So you see, Miss Maxwell, I may be demanding of my son, but I do so because I see his potential. You do nothing but squander it with just being . . . you."

Pushing up her imaginary sleeves, Vi's fingers sparked. "You did not just . . . Prima or not, your ass—"

Keeping a hard glare on the older man, Olive grabbed her sisters' and Harper's hands, and used the last bit of magical oomph she had to *poof*. Thanks to her foggy head and murky thoughts, they ended up a block away from Potion's.

"Why did you just do that?" Vi demanded, angry. "I wanted to pluck every single feather off that dickhead angel's wings."

"That's why I got us out of there. He's not worth the energy, and he's definitely not worth whatever would happen if the *Prima* physically attacked an Angelic Army general."

"It would've been worth it, if you ask me," Vi mumbled grumpily.

"I love you, Vi, but I can fight my own battles when they need to be fought. The one with him didn't. Giving him the time of day just gives him more reasons to stick around." She sighed, her shoulders slumping. "But now I'm back to square one, and no Bax."

Rose hugged her tight. "I'm so sorry, Olly. He'll show up."

"Yeah." Although she didn't sound so sure even to her own ears.

"Well, we're near Potion's. Let's stop in for a drink or something."

"I think I'll just head home. You're right. He'll show up at some point. With hair like his, he'll eventually pick up his hair products, right?" she joked, making the other three chuckle.

She hugged them all, thanking them for their help, and headed down the street. She didn't even bother with the subway, wanting extra time to clear her head. She walked. And walked. And by the time she soaked in her surroundings, Inklings' neon sign blinked steadily across the street.

She almost didn't have it in her to experience one more cold trail . . .

27

The Third Rule's the Charm

Varied emotions swirled through Bax like an emotional tie-dye job. Excitement was a big one. So was fear. And a healthy dose of What the Actual Fuck summed up the three main hard-hitters.

Then there was a dash of relief.

After all this time playing the what-if game, he'd made the flying leap, and for an angel who didn't like flying—literally and metaphorically—that was a big fucking deal.

He still couldn't believe it, and yet he'd signed his name probably a dozen times if not more.

"You sure about this, kid?" Isaiah watched him closely. "You kinda look like you're about to hurl. I can rip them up, or I can hold on to them for a bit and wait for you to process it all."

He shook his head. "Nah, man. It's the right thing, and you're right. It's long overdue."

"Then I'll send these to the lawyer in the morning, and it'll be official. And speaking of gorgeous witches who a sorry ass like you definitely doesn't deserve, where is your gorgeous companion? I figured she'd be standing by your side blowing a party horn and throwing confetti or something."

"You weren't speaking of gorgeous witches. You were just talking about puke." He pointedly didn't answer the question.

"What the fuck did you do?"

"I'm fixing it . . . or I'm trying. I just needed to do some housekeeping things while I figure out how to make that happen."

Ruby stuck her head in the room. "Hey, Isaiah. I know you said you needed a few, but you've got a visitor out front."

Isaiah stood and clamped a hand on his shoulder. "You're welcome to stay if you want to clear your head, kid. Hell, you never have to leave now."

The older man laughed as he headed out, and Bax contemplated taking a damn nap in the shop. Isaiah always kept a cot and some blankets in one of the back rooms in case of late nights or early mornings.

The extra time and space might help him figure his shit out, but neither space—nor hiding in Inklings' back room—would win him back the woman he loved.

He stood with renewed determination, and a new plan. He'd check the apartment again, and he'd go from there. Hell, he'd beg her sisters to do a locating spell on her if he had to, and considering what Linc had said about Vi's threat to his manhood, that was one hell of a risk.

Isaiah ducked his head into the room, failing to withhold a smirk. "You get that shit figured out yet?"

"Pretty much, why?"

"Come out front, will ya? One of your former clients has a complaint they want to share with you about recent work."

He lifted his eyebrows. "A complaint about *my* work? What the fuck aren't they happy about? How incredible it looks?"

He shrugged. "Beats the hell out of me, but you know client expectations and shit. You coming?"

He stormed out to the front showroom, ready to give his speech about art and client matching and the reasoning behind his required consultations, when he came to an abrupt stop.

Olive leaned against the front counter, a small, tired smile on her face as she spoke with Ruby. All of her looked tired, even her hair, if that were possible, and still, she was the best and most beautiful sight he'd ever seen.

She hadn't yet noticed him, and he took his time soaking in the sight of her, realizing just how afraid he'd been that he wouldn't get the chance to do so again.

Yeah, they were still roommates. They'd have to lay eyes on one another eventually. Unless one of them moved out under the cover of night, but he didn't want to think about that. At all. Just the idea of it tightened that damn knot in his chest.

That mediocre speech he planned all afternoon went up in a plume of smoke. Words couldn't express how sorry he was, nor his regret over how everything had played out.

Ruby and Olive talked a bit more, Isaiah's assistant eventually handing over a tube of after-care ointment. She shouldn't need more yet, and concern went through him. Infection wasn't totally impossible. They were careful at exhibit shows, but things still happened when you weren't in your normal environment.

"Is your tattoo okay?" Bax asked in way of greeting.

Olive's gaze froze on Ruby's like a deer caught in the headlights. The shop assistant glanced at Isaiah, who subtly motioned her toward him before they left them alone. Silence deafened him to everything but the harsh pounding of his heart.

"It's fine." She slowly turned and laid her gorgeous blue eyes on him. "I misplaced the first tube and wanted to make sure I had one on hand when the Saniderm came off."

He nodded. *Shop talk.* He could do that . . . for now. "I can take off the derm and check it out for you. Make sure it all looks good."

She hesitated. "Okay."

He led her to one of the already-set-up back rooms. "Hop up on the table and then lie down in the position I inked you."

He grabbed another tube of after-care cream while she got comfortable, taking his time to collect his thoughts and prep his grovel. When he turned back, he caught her watching him carefully.

"Sometimes these buggers can be a real bitch to get off, so let me know if it hurts too much, okay?" He waited for her nod and got to work, gently peeling back one edge at a time.

She never took her eyes off him, not even to watch the grand reveal of her masterful tattoo. It really was his best work, but that had been because of the inspiration and the canvas. Coincidentally the same person.

With the last of the Saniderm peeled away, he cleaned the remaining patches of ink and threw all the gauze in the trash before studying his handiwork.

"Does any of this hurt?" He gently ran his fingers over the bark of the blossom tree. "No soreness or heat anywhere that you can feel?"

"Nope. It feels . . . good."

His hands froze, eyes snapping up to meet hers. A small smile flirted on her lips, and his heart lurched. "Good. That's . . . good."

"Yep. Good."

"Definitely good."

They stared at one another until the silence turned comical, both bursting into awkward laughter.

Bax asked, "How did your presentation go?" at the same time Olive admitted, "I've been looking everywhere for you."

"You've been looking everywhere for me?" His hope swelled and damn was it difficult not to get too excited.

"Maybe not everywhere." Her cheeks flushed. "Our apartment, and Potion's, and I tried a few other spots before Vi suggested the GAA . . . and then here."

"You went to the GAA? What the hell for?"

"Vi mentioned that the security measures they have in place really screw with modern technology, and since your phone wasn't connecting, I thought it was as good of a guess as any other." She tucked her glasses higher on her nose. "And I guess you were there, but were long gone by the time I showed up."

"I didn't stick around long."

"I gathered that much. Patrick seems like a nice guy . . . a bit on the nervous side, but nice."

"He's a little too enthusiastic and by the book when it comes to the GAA, but he's a decent guy. That's who told you I'd been there?"

She nodded. "And then your . . . Mikael . . . confirmed it."

He stiffened. "What did that bastard say to you?"

She smiled wanly. "Nothing much that I didn't anticipate . . . but he did allude to something that confused me a bit."

"Anything that man alluded to is not something to give much thought, angel. Trust me."

"So you didn't break Guardian Rule of Conduct number three?"

"Son of a bitch." He slammed one of the drawers harder than he meant, the sound rattling in the room. Keeping his back to her, he leaned on the counter to collect himself. That was not how he wanted her to find out how he felt. "And what did he say about the third rule?"

Behind him, she climbed off the table, her clothes ruffling. "Something about it being the only rule you hadn't broken . . . until me. Is it because we . . . did what we did?"

A wry grin on his face, he turned, making sure to keep his distance or else he'd be crossing the room and hauling her into his arms. "You mean all the sex?"

Her lips twitched. "That would be what I mean, yes."

"Rule three of the Guardian Rules of Conduct isn't about sex." His heart pounded in his chest as he watched her carefully.

She didn't know.

"I know there are things you can't talk about being with the GAA," Olive added. "And I get that you couldn't tell me about being my appointed Guardian, but—"

"You have to know that I didn't plan to hide it from you." He pushed off the table and took a step, stopping himself.

"You don't need to explain, Bax."

"Yes, actually, I do. Never in my wildest dreams . . . okay, maybe in my wildest . . . could I have ever believed any reality where there was a you-and-I. That was a fantasy that kept me warm at night," he admitted in a rush.

Her eyes widened. "You thought about it? About us?"

His throat dried, making it difficult to swallow. "All the fucking time . . . and way before I asked you to move into the apartment."

"You've never said anything. You never gave any indication . . ."

"Because the GAA makes it nearly impossible to form any kind of meaningful relationship. It's literally part of the job to be secretive, and to fly under the radar of nearly every situation. Offering you my second room was a way to selfishly get a little taste of what I was missing . . . and then you moved in and I realized I was missing a whole hell of a lot more than I ever imagined. And definitely more than I liked."

He cleared his throat and shifted awkwardly on his feet. "The reason I didn't fight being appointed as your Guardian was because I never could've allowed your life to be in the hands of someone else. Someone who didn't care about you the way I did. You asked me after the Exchange Ceremony if I offered to do your Dare I Docket with you because I was appointed as your Guardian."

"Bax, I don't—"

"No, you need to hear this, angel."

She nibbled on that bottom part of her lower lip, making him want to rescue it yet again as she nodded. "Okay . . ."

He took a deep breath and attempted to rein in his emotions. "Yes, being your Guardian gave me the *opportunity* to be close to you. It gave me the chance to dance with you and make snow angels in the park. All the things we did together that I will remember for the rest of my life. But *you're* the reason I did it."

"Really?" Tears welled in her big blue eyes, threatening to spill over.

Bax lost his ability to keep his distance. Gently cupping her cheeks, he tilted her face up toward him. "You are the reason I broke the third rule, angel. That much Mikael got right."

"What's the third rule?" she whispered.

He took a deep breath and kept his gaze locked on hers so she could see the truth in his eyes. "The third Guardian Rule of Conduct is *Don't fall in love with your Assignment*."

Olive blinked.

He fidgeted, smiling nervously. "I love you, angel. I'm *in* love with you, and if there was a way to break that third rule more than once, it would be pulverized into a fine, powdery dust because you're not just my roommate or my friend. You're my everything."

✦ ✦ ✦

Olive's heart stalled, sending her equilibrium off balance as she fell into the warmth of Baxter Donovan's dual-colored eyes.

She prayed to Goddess her knees remained locked as she tried to find her balance . . . and her voice. "You what?"

"I'm in love with you, Olive Maxwell." A small, nervous smile formed on his lips. "Rule-breaking, earth-shattering, heaven-quaking in love."

"I don't know what to say."

Fuck . . . it was too late. Disappointment blinked across his face. "I understand."

"Please don't . . ." She stumbled, grabbing at his arms when he made motions to step away.

His brow wrinkled, clearly confused. "Don't love you? Because it's a bit late for that, angel."

"Not that . . . please don't . . . *understand* about me not knowing what to say."

"Right now, I don't understand what either one of us is saying . . . or trying to." He chuckled nervously.

She grinned. "Let's rewind and let me start again. I met with the board today, and I got the grant money."

"That's fucking incredible!" He tugged her into a hard hug and picked her off the ground. "Congratulations! I'm so happy for you! Operation SupeEx has achieved liftoff."

"Well, yes and no."

After a short spin, he returned her feet to the ground, but didn't unravel his arms as he peered down at her. "What do you mean?"

It was her turn to look nervous as she cleared her throat, forcing herself to keep eye contact. "Doing the Docket list was definitely pivotal for me as far as personal growth, but it wasn't because of the circus classes or the skinny-dipping. It wasn't even because I crossed off the multiorgasmic sex. It actually wasn't because of any one item on the list, or even the sum of them."

"Then what was it?"

"It was because of the person I did it all with. *You.* If anyone else had been next to me, it wouldn't have felt the same. It wouldn't have *been* the same. It wouldn't have meant as much to me."

He waited silently, letting her find the words to continue.

"The SupeEx Project transformed from an exchange program to a mentorship one because you helped me realize that when everything is boiled down to the fundamentals, it's not about the what and the where. What's important is the *whom.*" She blew out a slow, nervous breath. "You're my *who*, Baxter Donovan. I don't care what we do or where we do it as long as we do it with each other . . . because I'm in love with you, too."

A slow, easy smile slid onto Bax's face. "Yeah?"

Taking that as a good sign, she coasted her hands up his arms and tangled her fingers through his hair. "Yeah. I mean, I did let you design a tattoo for me and permanently ink it onto my body sight unseen."

"And you're saying that you'd be okay with staying roommates?" He brushed a teasing kiss across her lips.

She smiled, nodding. "I could probably be convinced."

"And you'd be okay if your chosen *who* just spent his life's savings buying a tattoo parlor from a crotchety old curmudgeon who is currently standing in the hallway eavesdropping on everything we say?"

"Hey! I resent that remark!" Isaiah's head popped into the open doorway, but he wasn't alone.

Vi, Rose, and Harper each glanced around, various grins on their faces.

At Olive's questioning look, Vi laughed. "Oh, please. Did you think we'd really miss this?"

Rose smirked mischievously. "We've been waiting forever."

"If we waited any longer, we were prepared to take matters into our own hands," Harper added, exasperated. "Which I was kind of looking forward to, but it's good that you unmucked your way through it yourselves instead."

They all chuckled, until Olive felt as if she needed to pinch herself because of the amount of happy coursing through her.

She slowly dragged Bax's head closer until their noses touched. "Baxter Donovan, I'd be more than happy to be the witchy roommate to your broke artist, but I insist we come up with our very own couple's docket."

He cocked up a single eyebrow. "Yeah? And what all would we put on this list? Vacations? Date nights?"

She shook her head, grinning. "Only one thing."

"Only one? What?"

"To love each other openly, honestly, and completely."

Bax brushed his mouth against hers once, then twice. "That's definitely a docket item I'd be willing to put all my energy behind . . . but I have one other thing to add to it."

"What's that?"

He smirked. "Lots and lots of multiorgasmic sex—with and without dates."

She laughed. "I can get behind that addendum."

This time when they took each other's mouths in a searing kiss, the earth wasn't the only thing scorched. A gorgeous mist of green and gold surrounded them, Magic itself linking not just their hearts, but their souls.

Epilogue

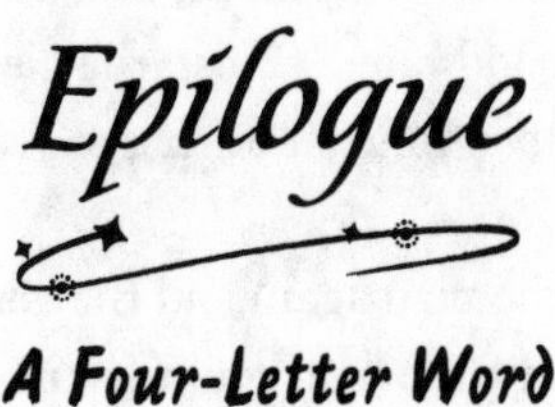

A Four-Letter Word

Everything was on the line, and although things looked grim and those standing next to her couldn't quite see the path to success, Olive did. She saw it *for* them . . . and now she just needed to convince them.

"It can't be done." Rose smacked her mittens against her snow pants to knock away the remnants of their last failed attempt. "I don't know what kind of hocus-pocus they're using, but their perimeter is practically impenetrable."

Vi nodded. "There's no way in hell we're reaching that flag without taking severe casualties . . . not unless we—"

"Use Magic?" Harper asked.

"That would be cheating, Harp," Olive reminded her friend.

"Why the hell do you think I chose to be on the team with literal witches and not Team Angels and Shifters and Demons OH MY! Flick your fingers, send a little burst of air to knock them off their feet, and voilà! Point us."

"It doesn't have to be a big gust," Vi conspired.

Olive was already shaking her head. "We already agreed on the terms of the game. No one is allowed to sprout fur or feathers, *or* flick fingers. We just need a diversion. Two people to create a distraction while the other two go for their flag."

Truthfully, they'd already tried distraction and it hadn't worked, but they were running out of both time and options. Central Park closed to the public in less than half an hour, and if she and the girls didn't clinch another win, they'd lose the entire series.

"Okay . . ." Olive glowered across the field, not seeing their opponents—aka their significant others, plus Adrian. "This is what we're going to do."

She ran through the plan again and they broke apart, each getting into position before the final countdown began. When the bell chimed, they moved simultaneously to their individual hot zones, Olive creeping forward carefully, staying to the shadows as much as possible, while Harper and Rose purposefully created a scene.

One foot at a time, she approached the guys' snow bunker, and couldn't help the tilting sensation in her gut telling her something wasn't quite right. She'd reached their home base way too easily and without a single sighting.

Pausing two feet from her prize, Olive froze and listened . . . to nothing.

Not entirely nothing because even for just after midnight, the recent snowfall had brought tons of people out to enjoy the winter night. But on their temporary battleground?

Crickets.

Nothing. Not even from her team.

"Harper?" Olive whispered, glancing around the empty bunker. "Vi? Rose?"

A faint breeze flew by her back, and she spun, nearly colliding with a six-foot wall of man muscle.

Bax grinned mischievously. "Got ya, angel."

He swooped her into a kiss, temporarily silencing her protests and evaporating her disappointment over losing to the guys yet again.

"Mm." She moaned as he slowly pulled away, her arms still wrapped tightly around his neck. "Losing isn't all that bad when it happens like that."

"I'm glad you think so."

"No! No! No!" Harper protested loudly, each emphatic *no* broken up by a slight gagging sound. "Everyone needs to put all this love shit away right now. Bury it under the snow if you have to, but *no*!"

Olive laughed as she and Bax stepped out from the guys' home bunker to lay eyes on her sisters, each one entwined in the arms of her mate, caught much like she'd been a minute ago.

"Oh, come on, Harp," Olive teased. "Maybe you should try it on for size and see how you like it."

"No," the succubus said emphatically. "Just like empire-waist dresses, I don't need to try 'love' on to know that I won't like the way it looks on me."

"It's not a four-letter word, you know." Adrian leveled the sex demon with his best sultry grin. "I guess technically it is, but not that way."

"You were right the first time. It's a four-letter word . . . and it's also in whatever food or drink you all have been consuming. From now on, I'm bringing my own stuff to Friend Nights."

Laughing and joking, they headed back toward the street, Olive grinning the entire way as she enjoyed being surrounded by the people she loved most.

"What's got that glowing look on your face, angel?" Bax's hand firmed where it hooked around her waist, holding her close to his side.

"Just happy . . . and realizing that Gran was right."

"Isn't she usually?" he teased, making her chuckle.

"Yeah, but this time she was *really* right. Everyone has a spark of Magic, and when you follow it, there really is no possibility of straying from your true path."

"I totally agree."

"You do?" she asked, glancing up at him.

"I do. Because I have my Magic right here. Because my Magic is *you*." He leaned down and kissed the tip of her nose.

She beamed at him, her cheeks practically cracking both from cold and happiness. "That was good, wingman. That was damn good."

A gag behind them had them both turning to where Harper ran toward a nearby trash can. She heaved a few more times, and once finished, shot them a glare. "Okay, seriously now, this shit isn't funny anymore. It's like I'm allergic to all the . . ."

Olive kicked up an eyebrow. *Love?* she mouthed in question.

Harper's complexion turned green and she clutched her stomach. "I hate you. All of you."

"No, you don't . . . you *love* us."

"I know . . . assholes."

Olive's Dare I Docket

1. ~~Run away to join the circus~~
2. ~~Do something spontaneous: Hot tub skinny-dipping~~
3. ~~Do something socially frightening: Attend the Gala~~
4. ~~Get a tattoo~~
5. ~~Enter a dance competition~~
6. ~~Sing karaoke~~
7. ~~Have hot, multiorgasmic sex~~
8. ~~Go on a date that ENDS in hot, multiorgasmic sex~~
9. ~~End up in a romance novel~~
10. Have a happily ever after

Acknowledgments

It takes an entire coven to get another witchy book into the world, and I'm so blessed to have the best one around. Thank you to my family for always being my biggest supporters (especially to Teens #1 and #2 for fueling my sass-pirations). And to the Hubby: you may not have a single tattoo, but I'll keep you around for hero inspiration anyway. 😉

I want to thank the entire SMP team, from Kerri and the incredible art department for getting my gorgeous, curvy girls onto the front of magical covers, to Sara LaCotti & Marissa Sangiacomo and the rest of the marketing & publicity teams for their incredible ideas and support in getting this book out there in front of the readers. And of course to my editor, Tiffany Shelton, who helps me make my words shine and the characters pop off the page . . . and who also makes sure that certain scenarios are anatomically possible & clothes don't magically disappear (unless actual *magic* was involved).

Kristin Dwyer & Molly, from LEO PR, you all are amazing, and I'm so beyond lucky to have you on this wild, witchy ride with me, keeping me on track on days that end in a *Y* (😉). You're both rock stars! And as always, my Agent Extraordinaire, Sarah E. Younger . . . this is our *tenth* book together, a milestone that never would've happened if you hadn't taken a chance on an aspiring author all those years ago (we won't give it a number b/c then we'll both feel old). A mere thank-you can never express how lucky I am to have you in my corner. Here's to ten more books and then ten more after that and so on . . .

A big shout-out to my Emotional Support Writers: my #Girls-WriteNight . . . Tif Marcelo, Jeanette Escudero, Annie Rains & Rachel Lacey. I love you four to the moon and back. And thank you to all the amazing readers, and to all my bookish friends I've met through the years. Your support, notes, posts, likes, and shares fill this witch's heart on a daily basis, and you really have all become part of my coven whether you meant for it to happen or not.

About the Author

Amie Otto

April Asher, aka April Hunt, was hooked on romantic stories from the time she first snuck a bodice-ripper romance out of her mom's bedside table. She now lives her own happily ever after with her college-sweetheart husband, their two children, and a cat who thinks she's more dog—and human—than feline. By day, April dons dark-blue nursing scrubs and drinks way too much caffeine. By night, she still consumes too much caffeine, but she does it with a laptop in hand, and from her favorite side of the couch.

From the far left cushion, April Asher pens laugh-out-loud romantic comedies with a paranormal twist, but when she's not putting her characters into embarrassing situations with supernatural entities, she also writes high-octane romantic suspense as April Hunt, her thrill-seeking alter ego.